THE SECRET SOULBOND

CALATINI TALES BOOK 3

KATHERINE DOTTERER

KatSpell Press

The Secret Soulbond

Copyright © 2023 by Katherine Dotterer

All rights reserved.

This is a work of fiction. All characters, organizations, and events portrayed in this novel are either products of the author's imagination or are used fictitiously.

No part of this book may be reproduced in any form or by any electronic or mechanical means, including information storage and retrieval systems, without written permission from the author, except for the use of brief quotations in a book review.

This work was not generated with AI (artificial intelligence.) Any use of this work to train generative AI is expressly prohibited.

Cover by 100 Covers

Edited by Susan Bischoff, Lauralynn Elliott

A KatSpell Press Book

- ISBN 978-1-955614-09-2 (ebook)
- ISBN 978-1-955614-10-8 (trade paperback)

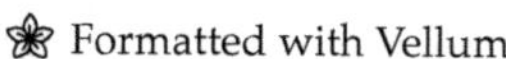 Formatted with Vellum

CONTENTS

ABOUT THE SECRET SOULBOND

In the Regency-inspired kingdom of Calatini, two powerful houses nurse a generations-old feud... while their heirs conceal their secret soulbond.

Lady Annalise Greysnowe is the most beautiful lady in Calatini but conceals her true self behind an ice-perfect mask. Her ambitious parents can't wait to marry her to the king or any wealthy lord that will improve their standing at court. Anyone except the one gentleman she truly desires—Dare, the genial Count of Ravenstone and her family's ancestral enemy.

Despite the feud, Dare only seeks peace with Annalise's family. As a nature witch, he knows that such strife simply harms everyone involved. Plus, he can't forget his intense attraction to Annalise. Something more than her otherworldly beauty calls to him—perhaps it's her love of animals, or her warm and radiant smile whenever she rides her beloved horse, or the hints of potent magic akin to his own.

For Annalise is a rare and coveted soul healer able to heal anything at the risk of forming an irrevocable soulbond. Yet when Dare is nearly killed, she must use her secret powers to heal him, forever binding herself to her family's enemy. Annalise and Dare agree to conceal their soulbond until they can convince her family to end the feud and accept their marriage. But her parents refuse to relent, and their forbidden love activates an ancient curse, so not even their powerful soulbond may be enough to keep them together...

THE SECRET SOULBOND **is a Romeo and Juliet romance that sparkles with magic and ends with a heartwarming happily-ever-after. The Calatini Tales will spellbind any reader looking for lush fantasy romance.**

CHAPTER 1

A serene smile fixed on her lips, Annalise suppressed a sigh as she sipped her sparkling wine and eyed the auras of the fashionable guests at the Duchess of Wildewall's summer ball. To the soul healers and seers who could read them, auras glowed brighter than jewels and reflected people's souls, emotions, health, and magic. Not that the motes revealing magic were common among humans. Unlike magical creatures, humans couldn't generate magical energy, so less than a quarter of humans were witches who could sense and wield magic, and only witches possessed motes inside their auras. Other humans just showed magic outside their auras when using enchanted items or already created spells.

Because of everything reflected in people's auras, watching people and reading their auras was illuminating and the most interesting part of any court event for her. Yet after six years at court, the rainbow of auras in the teeming ballroom was unremarkable. She almost sighed. If only she could return to her family's townhouse and cuddle with her angelcat Finn while listening to her two mated faebirds, Rain and Aria, sing sweet love songs to each other. But unless she was ill, Mother and Father would never let her leave a ball hosted by the head of their duchy before the dancing had started. And as a powerful soul healer, she rarely suffered illness.

Maintaining her faint smile, Annalise swallowed another sip of sparkling wine. Lady Snow—what court called her for her cool serenity as well as her pale coloring and ice-perfect beauty—mustn't appear bored or forlorn after being abandoned by her escort King Devon for state affairs once again. Not that she was forlorn. She enjoyed the king's escort because he was a kind gentleman and prevented Mother and Father from shoving her at every unwed duke or duke's heir, regardless of their age or disposition. But she didn't love the king. Thank the Goddess. With her secret powers and her family's centuries-long feud with the Ravenstones, she could never become queen.

She nearly grimaced as she twirled her flute of sparkling wine against her lips. Because their ambitions and obsession with the ridiculous Greysnowe-Ravenstone feud often blinded them, Mother and Father couldn't see how impossible it was for her to become queen, a feat no Greysnowe or Ravenstone had ever managed. Hoping for that, they'd even named her after Calatini's first queen. And when she'd blossomed into an other-worldly beauty, they'd been ecstatic and even more certain she was meant to be queen. 'Twas fortunate they'd never discovered her powers as a soul healer.

A faint chill prickling her neck, she clung to her serene smile. Soul healers were coveted because they were extremely rare, female witches who could heal nearly anything, although they formed an irrevocable soulbond the first time they healed an intelligent creature's fatal wound or ailment. As descendants of Esme the Great, Greysnowes bore soul healer daughters every few generations, but they often forced those daughters into forming soulbonds with advantageous gentlemen. 'Twas why, when she'd proudly revealed her first soul-healing to her former nursemaid Alice, Alice had warned her *never* to reveal her powers to anyone, even Mother and Father.

Annalise made herself sip her sparkling wine. Alice was

doubtless right—although Mother and Father loved both of their children, if they knew of her powers, they'd likely be tempted to force her into forming a soulbond with King Devon. That way, she'd have to become queen, and they'd finally best the "treacherous" Ravenstones. They couldn't see that her becoming queen would only inflame the feud. She almost tsked. After three centuries of strife, the two feuding families should just forgive the past and learn to live in harmony.

She sighed and drained her sparkling wine. Not that Mother and Father ever would.

His aura an irrepressible orange with ivory motes like always, Alex smirked as he strode over and handed her a fresh flute of sparkling wine. At eighteen, her younger brother had been living in Ormas for less than three months, so he still found court events diverting. "Why the sigh? The perfect Lady Snow is the most beautiful lady here tonight. According to Mother, your life should be complete at such a triumph."

Annalise allowed herself a tiny shrug. Revealing more emotion in public would attract notice, which might cause someone to realize she was a soul healer and seek to exploit her. But because 'twas Alex, she let her voice sharpen, "I'm the most beautiful lady wherever I go." Since soul healers altered their souls to heal, their transparent auras with electrum motes possessed extra energy, and that made her physical beauty irresistible. Not that her brother knew about her powers. She couldn't burden him with her secrets, and if he knew, Mother and Father might somehow discover her powers too. She quirked a wry smile. "Besides, Mother would only say my life was complete if King Devon proposed."

Alex scowled, his blue eyes darkening. "Unlikely, considering he's abandoned you yet again. He should treat you with more respect."

She hummed and glanced toward King Devon and Lord Farson debating near the refreshments table. The councilor represented the Golddell duchy where the magical, horse-like nightmara lived, so his urgent matter probably involved the king remaining unwed with the nightmara delegation arriving in two months to renew the Nightmara-Calatini Treaty. Since they were matriarchal, the nightmara would only negotiate with queens, and Calatini's legendary treaty with the nightmara was essential because it earned the trust of other magical creatures, who mostly lived north of the Walle since the catastrophic Stone Wars between humans and magical creatures.

She shook her head. "He treats me as respectfully as he would a sister, but state affairs often intrude. And even though I don't wish to marry him, I'm grateful for his escort."

Alex winced as he eyed Mother and Father, who were beaming as they spoke with the suave Duke of Oakmoor, another of the king's councilors. Although their parents' age and an infamous rakehell, the duke was still unwed, influential, and wealthy, so Mother and Father often pandered to him or those like him. "I suppose the king's escort *does* curb Father and Mother. But I wish you could find a gentleman you truly want courting you."

Her chest squeezing, Annalise managed a smile and sipped her sparkling wine. After all her seasons at court, finding that was unlikely. Court was all about appearances, so most gentlemen never noticed more than her beauty and wealthy parents. And the few who saw her as a person were already in love with another, otherwise uninterested, or an impossible choice. "Perhaps one day."

Alex tsked. "Soon, hopefully. You'll be twenty-four on Summerday next month." He waggled his brows. "Practically a crone. Goddess knows if you can even still bear children."

She almost snorted. *That* was no concern. Soul healers were incredibly fertile and bore children at least a decade longer than other ladies. No, her true concern was finding a trustworthy gentleman who could love the person she was inside and wouldn't exploit her powers. "I'm certain I could—if I ever find a gentleman worthy of being their father."

Annalise was about to continue, but then her skin tingled when powerful nature magic swept across the ballroom. *He* had arrived. Her heart fluttering like always at his presence, she swallowed and licked her lips then forced herself to turn casually toward the back where Lord Ravenstone was greeting the Duchess of Wildewall with a genial smile. Goddess, why must she always react to him?

She suppressed a shiver as her tingling burgeoned. Although the Greysnowe's ancestral enemy, Lord Ravenstone had fascinated her since they'd met in that quiet park during their first season. His lush green aura covered with bronze motes revealed his harmonious and accepting nature as well as his potent powers as a nature witch. He and the royal witch were the only ones at court whose powers rivaled hers as a soul healer. Like her, they must be Rhiannon descendants, the strongest of all witches. Yet unlike her, neither could read auras without a difficult spell, so they fortunately couldn't recognize her powers like she did theirs. Although if he did, Lord Ravenstone was too considerate to exploit her—as a nature witch, he respected all living things and always sought to build connections, and he was steady and strong like a mighty oak.

Then Lord Ravenstone finished greeting their hostess, and his amber eyes met hers across the ballroom.

Although she should look away to feign disinterest, Annalise couldn't resist returning his intense stare. His powers and kind-hearted nature weren't all that separated him from the other gentlemen at court. More active than most, he wore simple attire with his shoulder-length, black hair in a neat queue, and a short beard covered his rugged face. His movements always bursted with energy, and he was renowned as a skilled swordsman, a fearless rider, and a keen hunter. And he beamed whenever outdoors—sometimes resembling a sunbathing tygris, a massive feline who ruled the torrid grasslands far south of Calatini.

Her breath quickened. Plus, like Alex and King Devon, Lord Ravenstone saw more than her beauty. When they'd first met, he'd talked to her like a person and never ogled. Even after learning they were ancestral enemies, he'd remained respectful. Yet because of the feud, they only saw each other a few times a season, across crowded court events. However, he always noticed details about her no one else did, like Finn's fur on her bodice. And although they never spoke, her chest ached when he quit his hunt for a wife midway through the season every year and returned home to Wildewall.

Then Alex poked her arm with a frown. "Why are you staring at *Lord Ravenstone* like that? And why is the cad returning your stare?"

Her heart lurching, Annalise jerked back and almost spilled sparkling wine on her soft-white ballgown. The first time seeing Lord Ravenstone each season was always the hardest. Thankfully, Mother and Father had never noticed her initial reaction, and she could control herself better later. "He's not a cad. Ask anyone at court, other than Mother and Father, of course. They're too blinded by the ridiculous feud."

Alex glowered at Lord Ravenstone, who began greeting other guests. "Are they? Since Father identified Lord Ravenstone during a horse auction at Aherne's the first week of the season, I've seen Lord Ravenstone at events for gentlemen, but he never acknowledges me."

She shook her head and sipped her sparkling wine. Provoking reactions from people amused her brash younger brother, particularly when they attempted to ignore him. And he could always decipher the pranks or quips that would best provoke someone—especially Mother and Father. Once she'd blossomed, they'd often ignored him to focus on using her to further their ambitions. So Alex had time to develop tactics certain to provoke them, from dipping her hair in ink when he was six, to declaring politics boring when he was seventeen. But provoking a Ravenstone likewise wasn't prudent.

She arched her brows at Alex. "Were you glowering at the

count the way you are now? Given the feud, I'd ignore you too if I were him."

Alex scowled. "I was perfectly civil—mostly. I may have jested we cross swords to settle the feud a time or two. But I smiled when I did to show I didn't actually care about the feud."

Her breath freezing, Annalise almost gaped. Challenging Lord Ravenstone was far beyond Alex's usual brashness. No wonder the genial count had ignored him. "Are you *mad*? A duel between a Greysnowe and a Ravenstone is certain to end in tragedy and inflame the feud. Besides, Lord Ravenstone is one of the most skilled swordsmen in Calatini and could easily trounce you."

Alex shrugged as he finished his sparkling wine. "His skill is why I wanted to cross swords. Such a bout should be exciting, and I might learn some new swordplay."

She laid her hand on Alex's arm and leaned toward him with a beseeching smile. Somehow, she must convince him to give up that mad scheme. "Please don't challenge Lord Ravenstone again. I couldn't bear if you were wounded or wounded the count."

His eyes narrow, Alex scrutinized her for a long moment. Then he smirked and patted her hand. "I shan't be wounded."

Annalise stiffened. She'd not convinced him at all. Perhaps she should recount all the strife between the Greysnowes and Ravenstones since the failed betrothal three centuries ago had started the feud. Her stomach clenched. A failed betrothal because a soul healer had jilted her Ravenstone betrothed once she formed a soulbond with his fatally wounded cousin and best friend.

She'd opened her mouth to begin when the Duke of Oakmoor strode over. Mother and Father must have encouraged the rakehell duke to pursue her during their conversation, probably hoping a dance with him would make King Devon jealous.

The duke swept a florid bow, the white motes flickering in his charming yellow aura. He was another of the few with magic at court, although his erratic magic had only appeared last year. Unusual, considering the powers of most witches finished developing when their bodies fully matured. His overpowering sandalwood scent swamping her, the duke kissed her hand with a smoldering glance. "Dare I hope your first dance is still unclaimed, Lady Annalise?"

Her skin tightening, she tugged her hand free. Empty flirting like the duke's was why she disliked court. If only she could refuse him. Yet if she did, Mother and Father would complain about it for the next week. Swallowing a sigh, she smiled at the duke and inclined her head. "My first dance is yours if you want it."

The Duke of Oakmoor offered his arm and purred, "Shall we?"

Almost sighing again, Annalise laid her fingers on his arm, and they glided out onto the floor. At least the rakehell duke couldn't do more than flirt in the middle of a crowded ballroom.

CHAPTER 2

When the intriguing Lady Annalise began dancing with the suave Duke of Oakmoor, Dare stiffened and couldn't help watching her as he continued greeting other guests. Goddess, she was radiant, especially in that shimmering, soft-white ballgown. Despite the enmity between Ravenstones and Greysnowes for the past eleven generations, Lady Annalise drew him like a lodestone whenever they met. Not because of the otherworldly beauty which made her the most beautiful lady in Calatini, but because of the deep kindness and serene strength that imbued her every action as well as the love of nature and potent magic she'd revealed at their secret encounter during their first season.

He suppressed a sigh then greeted Lord Treyvan and his wife, the former Miss Midor he'd briefly courted when she was first presented. In the six years since meeting Lady Annalise, he'd never met another lady so likeminded and perfect for him, although Lady Treyvan had almost come close. As a powerful nature witch, having a kind and strong wife who loved nature was essential. Only such a lady would enjoy the same outdoor pursuits and understand his acceptance of all living things and his growing menagerie of horses, hellhounds, angelcats, and, one day soon, draklizards. Which Lady Annalise would.

Moving past the Treyvans, Dare allowed himself to glance at Lady Annalise twirling about the floor as graceful as an ethereal siren during a courtship flight. Despite her perfect behavior at court, she always appeared most contented outdoors—much more than other ladies, except for Mother, who was a nature witch like him. Lady Annalise beamed whenever riding, so she'd relish hours riding with her husband. And she'd a growing menagerie of her own—her massive, pale-gray stallion who most ladies wouldn't dare ride, her angelcat Finn who she'd rescued at their unforgettable secret encounter, and likely two faebirds from the sapphire and amethyst feathers she sometimes wore in her white-blonde hair.

He smiled as warmth flooded his chest. Lady Annalise's menagerie revealed her deep kindness too. Considering how her stallion responded to her, the massive horse adored her, so she must lavish him with affection. And from the few white hairs always adorning her gowns, she must cuddle Finn often like an affectionate angelcat would crave. Also keeping two fragile faebirds, who required another faebird and constant tending to thrive, revealed a steadfast devotion.

Still darting glances at Lady Annalise, Dare greeted Sir Ellis Campbell and his wife Lady Helena Campbell, friends from Lady Ducharme's fencing salon. In addition to Lady Annalise's pets, her conduct at court proved her kindness. Although a beauty like her could easily needle others without censure, she treated everyone with calm consideration. Perhaps like him, she could see how harming others would be akin to harming herself since her magical powers somehow impacted nature. Not that he knew precisely what class of witch she was.

After assuring the Campbells he'd attend Lady Ducharme's again soon, he continued about the ballroom and kept glancing at Lady Annalise. Although the blinding white glow of powerful magic had surrounded her when they'd met, her spell had been mostly hidden. She wasn't a nature witch—alike witches could recognize their own—but her spell *had* impacted nature. As powerful Rhiannon descendants, he and Mother were sensitive to those types of magic even though most other nature witches weren't. Without a probing spell to analyze active magic, he could still sense when a witch healer invoked healing sight, a sea witch calmed the waves, a werebeast shifted between forms, or other spells affecting nature.

Smoothing his beard to conceal his wry smile, Dare greeted Lord Islaye, Mother's childhood friend and the Minister of Magic who also represented Magehaven, the other northern duchy neighboring his beloved Wildewall. Although he could have performed a difficult aura spell to determine Lady Annalise's magical abilities, he never had because 'twould be an intrusion. And since they'd not truly spoken since their secret encounter before they'd known their families were ancestral enemies, Lady Annalise had never told him about her magic. Yet he knew she was a powerful witch, probably a Rhiannon descendant like him.

Dare almost sighed as he left Lord Islaye while still watching Lady Annalise. Even without knowing her class of witch, the invisible allure of her magic made his chest ache. Only another Rhiannon descendant could understand how natural using magic was for them. Since they could perform magic with will alone and usually set their spells' magical costs, they could use everyday magic without worry, unlike other witches or humans without magic. Having a wife with powers equaling or surpassing his own would be wonderful, especially if her powers involved nature too. Then they could discuss magic and create spells together like Mother could never do with Father despite their deep love.

When the Duke of Oakmoor pulled Lady Annalise close enough to kiss near the end of their dance, Dare's pulse flared, and he almost scowled at the rakehell duke. Entitled gentlemen like the duke invariably assumed Lady Annalise's potent allure meant she'd welcome their advances, no matter how scandalous. Which she clearly didn't, from how she glided back from the duke with a cool smile. Court would see her refusal as another instance supporting her nickname Lady Snow.

He suppressed a snort. For all their love of gossip, court could be remarkably blind. Lady Snow was merely a mask Lady Annalise wore at court. When carefree like at that park all those years ago, her warm and radiant smile revealed her kind heart and made her even more irresistible. But she never exhibited that genuine smile at court, probably to protect herself from gossip and overeager suitors. And since her serene mask never cracked despite court's constant scrutiny, she was stronger than a hardy ash on a riverbank. Another ideal quality in a wife.

As the dance ended with the duke bowing and Lady Annalise curtsying, Dare forced himself to turn away. Goddess help him, he *must* quit watching her the few times they attended the same court events. No one had noticed his interest yet, or if they had, they'd assumed 'twas due to the Ravenstone-Greysnowe feud rather than attraction. But one day, someone would, and 'twould engender embarrassing gossip that could only feed the feud. Because of that centuries-long feud, her parents would *never* accept him courting or marrying her, although they couldn't forbid it since he and Lady Annalise were past the age of majority.

He almost shook his head. Instead, the ambitious fools threw Lady Annalise at King Devon as well as any unwed duke or duke's heir, regardless of how those gentlemen suited their daughter. Likely so the Greysnowes could best his family with her advantageous marriage. Lady Annalise's family were always pursuing the ridiculous feud, and they'd probably never end it despite all his attempts to seek peace.

Dare grimaced. Since becoming count three years ago after Father's hunting accident, he'd approached Lord Greysnowe at the start of every season to work toward forgiving the strife of the past and building acceptance for the future, but the other count had continually rebuffed him. And Lady Greysnowe's glares whenever she saw him resembled that of an irate gorgon, so he'd never attempted approaching her. Although just eighteen and new to court, their son Lord Alexander appeared to support the feud as much as his parents—after Dare's attempt to end the feud at Aherne's this season, Lord Alexander had pestered him to cross swords.

He sighed, his heart clenching. Despite their intense affinity and attraction, he must forget the intriguing Lady Annalise, so he could court other ladies. Every season since he was eighteen except for the one after Father died, he'd visited Ormas to find a wife because none back home appealed. Yet no ladies at court had truly appealed either—except Lady Annalise. And since nature witches despised living in cities, he'd never lasted the entire six months of the season, even when Father had been alive and insisted he attend. Living around so many humans was stifling, and the magic here was too cultivated and harder for him to wield—nothing like the wild magic permeating Wilde-wall's magical glens, enchanted lakes, and vision summits.

He swallowed another sigh. If Mother was here, she might have been able to help his frustrating hunt, so he could finally quit attending court. But she'd always refused to visit Ormas, even when Father had begged her to join him. She'd visited Ormas once as a child and hated it so much that she always said nature witches didn't belong here. So Dare had never bothered to ask Mother to join him at court, despite longing for her help finding a wife. Instead, he'd obtained her advice during their weekly mirror calls like he had this morning. Although he'd never dared admit his impossible attraction to Lady Annalise. Mother didn't support the feud any more than he did, but she'd never met the Greysnowes, so she didn't understand the depth of their rancor. She'd encourage him to pursue Lady Annalise, which 'twould only feed the feud.

As King Devon took Lady Annalise's arm from the Duke of

Oakmoor, Dare scanned the ballroom for a lady he could ask to dance. He'd turned twenty-four on his natalday over a month ago, so he was now the same age Father had been when he'd been born, and Father had been married a year before that. He couldn't keep delaying marriage. Soon, all the unwed ladies at court would be much too young for him.

He set his jaw. This season he *wasn't* returning to Wildewall until he'd found a bride, no matter how much he despised town life. But he'd already been in Ormas almost three months this season, and he'd yet to find a lady he might want to marry besides Lady Annalise, whom he'd not even seen until tonight since he'd avoided events she and her family might attend. Perhaps forcing himself to remain for the rest of this season would convince his heart to settle for a suitable lady. Although those three and a half months would likely be tortuous.

His gaze landed on Miss Winston sipping sparkling wine in her habitual chair near the chaperones and dowagers. Despite her cad of a brother Herrick Winston, her nonexistent dowry, and being a few years older, Miss Winston was pleasant and enjoyed living in the country as much as he did. She was no witch, but most at court weren't, and she'd an appealing interest in alchemy that other ladies didn't. So he strode over and swept a bow. "Would you care to dance?"

Miss Winston nodded and set aside her flute of sparkling wine to accept his hand.

As they joined the other couples including King Devon and Lady Annalise, Dare grinned at Miss Winston. They'd not danced since the Campbells' first ball two months ago early on in the season. "How do you find the season so far?"

Miss Winston grimaced as he twirled her across the floor. "As dull as ever. If only I'd an excuse to return to the country. But until I magically find a husband, my parents shall never allow that."

He sighed. Poor Miss Winston to be trapped by her family and situation. If only *he* could be that magic husband. But like usual, no attraction or potential love burned between them—she felt more like a sister than anything. 'Twas why he'd never proposed to her before. He flashed a warm smile. "Perhaps you should use your interest in alchemy to your advantage. Surely in a city as large and affluent as Ormas, you can find someone to hire you. And if you earn enough money, you can move anywhere you wish."

Humming, Miss Winston tilted her head. "A lady working as an alchemist would be a scandal, but perhaps I should consider it. Since 'tis my ninth season at court, clearly no gentleman shall ever offer for me."

Dare winced and leaned toward her. Had his lack of interest hurt her? She was too nice to deserve that. "I would if I could, but..."

Miss Winston chuckled then squeezed his arm. "If you did, I'd refuse. Kissing you would be almost like kissing Herrick." She grimaced. "And making children together would be worse."

He echoed her chuckle, his chest easing. Thank the Goddess she recognized that. Then he asked her about her latest alchemy studies and offered her some advice based on his land magic involving nonliving nature. Not that he revealed the source of his knowledge. Others realizing his powers might complicate his hunt for a wife—some would fawn and become desperate for him to marry into their family, while others would shun and gossip about him. Court could never decide if they adored or despised witches for their magical powers that other humans didn't possess.

After his dance with Miss Winston, Dare escorted her to the refreshments table, but as he handed her a flute of sparkling wine, Lord Alexander charged toward them. Although his tousled hair was sandy rather than white-blond, his eyes plain blue rather than cerulean, and his expression irate rather than serene, Lord Alexander still resembled his sister Lady Annalise. The young hellion was probably about to pester him to cross swords again to further the feud. Yet on previous encounters, the boy had done so with a smirk, not a scowl.

Miss Winston eyed the seething Lord Alexander then muttered, "Excuse me." She darted back to her chair by the chaperones and dowagers. Wise of her to flee. If only he could too.

Dare inhaled and straightened. Not that he would. He'd never end the feud and build connections with the Greysnowes if he avoided them when they approached. He flashed a genial smile to placate Lord Alexander.

The young lord's eyes narrowed further. "I've always believed Father's rancor toward the Ravenstones ridiculous, but your behavior tonight makes me suspect he might be right, after all."

Dare stiffened, a chill prickling his neck. Had Lord Alexander been the first to notice his interest in Lady Annalise? Not good. He clung to his smile. "What do you mean?"

His jaw twitching, Lord Alexander leaned toward him. "You know, rakehell."

Dare winced. Damnation. Lady Annalise's brother *had* noticed. And was furious about it too. The younger gentleman probably assumed his interest wasn't sincere because of the feud.

Lord Alexander fisted his hands. "Your words of building acceptance and forgiving the past were clearly nothing more than an excuse to seduce my sister. Such cads deserve punishment." He leaned even closer, his voice deepening, "I demand satisfaction."

Dare swallowed as his stomach lurched. Another duel between a Ravenstone and a Greysnowe, especially one fueled by fraternal protectiveness, would definitely feed the feud and was the opposite of everything he sought to build as a nature witch who respected all life. He smiled and raised his palms. "I apologize for appearing to insult Lady Annalise. I didn't mean to stare, but I find her irresistibly intriguing. I'd seek to court her if your parents would accept it."

Lord Alexander growled. "They won't. So don't stare again, Ravenstone."

Dare inclined his head then pivoted and strode over to Miss Hawke, a distant cousin to Lord Treyvan who'd come out this season. Hopefully, dancing with the bubbly lady would distract both him and Lord Alexander from his interest in Lady Annalise. He couldn't allow the feud to grow.

CHAPTER 3

When Lord Ravenstone strode away from Alex, Annalise sighed and sipped the flute of sparkling wine King Devon had handed her after their dance. Given her brother's scowl, he'd been quarreling with their family's ancestral enemy. Thank the Goddess Lord Ravenstone was harmonious enough to withdraw without inflaming the feud. *Why* had Alex approached the count?

Since she'd not discover that across the ballroom, she turned to King Devon beside her. "Excuse me, I must go speak with Alex."

His commanding red aura steady as ever with its few gold motes barely visible, King Devon hummed while eyeing Alex. "Of course. Shall I escort you?"

Annalise flashed a serene smile. Not surprising the dutiful king would suggest that. He probably wished to ensure the feud wasn't endangering his kingdom. But Alex would reveal nothing if the king joined them. "Thank you, but I must speak with him alone." She curtsied then swept over to Alex and arched her brows at him. "Was that your perfectly civil challenge? It appeared irate to me. Are you *trying* to get wounded?"

Muddy-red fury pulsing around him, Alex grunted and kept

glowering at Lord Ravenstone, who was smiling as he spoke with Miss Philippa Hawke. "I had to make Ravenstone stop leering at you."

She stiffened and studied Lord Ravenstone as well. Her heart twisted. Doubtless he was asking the bubbly lady to dance. Was he considering her as his wife? Such a vivacious and sunny lady would suit the genial and kindhearted count. "Leering? Lord Ravenstone is too chivalrous to leer."

Alex scowled. "What else would you call his incessant staring? Surely you noticed, given how often you glanced at him while dancing with the Duke of Oakmoor and King Devon."

Annalise swallowed and almost blushed. Whenever she and Lord Ravenstone attended the same court events, they couldn't help but watch each other thanks to their secret encounter—although they'd managed to conceal it well enough that no one had noticed. But Alex knew her better than anyone, even Mother and Father, so of course he'd noticed the first time he saw them together. Somehow, she must convince him 'twas nothing. "Lord Ravenstone's staring is mere interest, although he'll never act on it because of our families' feud. Besides, other gentlemen are far worse—why, the Duke of Oakmoor just tried to kiss me in the middle of a crowded ballroom."

Alex grunted, his scowl deepening. "I know. None of the gentlemen at court treat you with the respect you deserve."

She laid her hand on Alex's arm, warmth filling her chest. Unlike Mother and Father, who only seemed to care when lesser lords or gentlemen imposed, Alex invariably sought to protect her despite being six years younger and new at court. "My beauty overpowers their genteel restraint."

Alex glared at her. "That's no excuse."

Annalise squeezed his arm. Perhaps not, but her irresistible aura as a soul healer did explain their reactions and was partly why she'd developed the distant manner that had earned her nickname Lady Snow. "Although I appreciate your concern, I've learned ways to protect myself after being at court for six years."

When Alex still glared, she sighed. She'd better get him to leave before he challenged Lord Ravenstone or something equally mad. "Could you escort me home? I'm weary of dancing."

Alex arched a brow but began escorting her through the crowded ballroom. "Father and Mother shall scold about you leaving so early."

She shrugged. True, so she typically remained at court events hours longer than she wanted to appease them. But preventing Alex from challenging Lord Ravenstone was more important. She jested, "I'll tell them the Duke of Oakmoor's overpowering sandalwood scent gave me a headache when he attempted to kiss me."

His aura clearing and usual grin brightening his face for the first time since Lord Ravenstone had arrived, Alex chuckled while leading her outside. "They deserve that for encouraging the rakehell duke to dance with you."

Annalise grinned back as they settled across from each other in the carriage, and her throat eased. Thankfully, she'd managed to distract Alex. "Exactly."

THE FOLLOWING MORNING, Annalise rose just after dawn then slipped out to the nearby park where she'd encountered Lord Ravenstone years ago. Since that first season, she always rose well before Mother and Father then escaped to either the park or went riding. She'd never have survived her six seasons in Ormas without centering herself every day. Until this season, she'd escaped alone—except for her angelcat Finn or her stallion Storm—but now Alex accompanied her sometimes. But today, she only brought Finn since her younger brother would just unsettle her.

Her entire body concealed in a voluminous, black cloak, she hurried to the park but peered about for the glow of approaching auras. For a lady, especially an irresistible one, walking alone in Ormas could be dangerous, but she needed the escape and should be safe enough if she took care. Although her powers as a soul healer couldn't protect her, reading auras helped her avoid others. Plus, Finn was with her, and despite their angelic appearance, angelcats were fierce when hunting their prey or protecting those they considered their pride.

Annalise exhaled when she reached the park's well-tended trees, whose verdant leaves rustled in the warming breeze. Even though no nature witch like Lord Ravenstone, the calm aura of plants and creatures settled her soul better than anything else. As she caressed the rough bark of the first tree she passed, Finn bounded into the oak's branches. Angelcats adored heights, and since they could float when they chose, leaping from branch to branch was nothing to them. With Finn prowling the branches like a white shadow, she wandered the park's familiar paths and smiled at the oaks, plane trees, and chestnuts surrounding her, the flowering honeysuckle, sweet azaleas, and wild roses perfuming the air, and the squirrels, robins, and early butterflies darting away when Finn neared. She walked around an hour or so until her chest eased and she could truly breathe again.

Then she returned to her family's townhouse and visited Storm in the stables, as she did every morning she didn't go riding. Like always, the pale-gray stallion nickered and leaned forward when she neared then nuzzled her and lipped her hair as she petted him and murmured greetings in his ear. The massive stallion could be recalcitrant with everyone else, but he was sweeter than the huge bee-like melissae's healing ambrosia with her, although he did accept Alex with little protest.

When Finn's begging became too strident to ignore, Annalise patted Storm a final time before heading to the kitchen to fetch the usual breakfast tray prepared for Finn and her faebirds. The amount of food appeared excessive, but magical pets had massive appetites due to the magical energy they generated. After thanking Cook, she glided upstairs to her chambers with the heavy tray, chuckling at Finn's antics. As wild as ever when his food was near, the angelcat meowed constantly while weaving about her and leaping atop the banister on the stairs and display tables in the hall.

She grinned but tsked as she entered her chambers. "I swear, Finn, you're worse than a ravenous manticore who's not eaten in a month."

Meowing louder, Finn sprung over to his feeding area before the fireplace. He wasn't the neatest eater, and the hearth was easier to clean than carpet. Plus, the angelcat adored the heat when a fire was burning. Not that one was burning ten days before Summerday.

She set the huge bowl of cut but not skinned rabbits and pigeons before Finn's nose and shook her head when he began bolting his food. 'Twas amazing he didn't choke. Then she whistled as she turned to the large, golden birdcage between the fireplace and her bed.

Nestled together as close as mated griffins, her two faebirds ruffled their feathers and trilled back an intricate melody. Then the sapphire male Rain and the amethyst female Aria preened each other before flitting over to Annalise with their long, flowing tails streaming behind them.

She opened the cage, and the tiny faebirds perched on her head and preened her hair. Giggling at their claws and beaks tickling her scalp and their tails brushing her neck, she set a bowl twice the size of the faebirds containing cherries, strawberries, and seeds inside their cage then poured honey into the empty cup hanging beside the water cup, which she also refilled. She plucked Aria from her head and fed the faebird a faeberry, a sweet, raspberry-like magical fruit grown by fae that faebirds adored. Once Aria trilled and devoured her treat, Annalise placed her on the food bowl in the cage, extracted Rain from her hair, and fed him a faeberry before setting him beside his mate.

Still licking his lips, Finn rubbed against her with a purring meow.

She chuckled. How could he beg for more food already? "No more until tonight, you glutton. And no eating Rain or Aria."

His blue eyes wide, the white angelcat blinked at her and meowed—the perfect picture of starving innocence. Not even close to the truth.

Annalise grinned then locked the faebirds' birdcage. Finn knew better than to hunt them, but 'twas best to ensure he couldn't succeed if he tried. Then she scooped the angelcat in her arms and scratched his chin until he purred and cuddled against her.

She sighed as light suffused her chest. How she adored Finn, Rain, Aria, and Storm. Unlike humans, they unconditionally returned her love and never sought to exploit her. They didn't care that she was a rare and powerful soul healer, the most beautiful lady in Calatini, or the daughter of a wealthy count.

When her stomach rumbled, Annalise made herself release Finn and brush the white fur from her gray-blue dress. Time to endure breakfast and face the scold Mother and Father had been brooding over since last night. She slipped from her chambers, swiftly shutting the door behind her. Mother hated Finn's begging at meals.

Only Alex was in the breakfast room when she entered. Perhaps she could eat most of her meal before the scold. His mouth full and plate half finished, Alex nodded at her as she sat beside him then filled a heaped plate of eggs, beefsteak, and toast most ladies would never finish. Like magical pets, soul healers required enormous amounts of food to fuel their high-energy auras.

She'd only just begun when Mother and Father sailed into the breakfast room. As always, Mother pursed her lips at Annalise's full plate, but she no longer complained since Annalise became gaunt if she ate less. Once they sat across the table and served themselves breakfast, Mother frowned at Annalise over her teacup and tilted her head, her white-blonde hair shimmering. "Why did you leave the Duchess of Wildewall's ball early?"

Annalise swallowed a bite of beefsteak with a small shrug. "I wasn't feeling well." Emotionally anyway, thanks to Alex quarreling with Lord Ravenstone.

Mother frowned harder, muddy-green suspicion flickering across her aura of ardent indigo with ivory motes. "Nonsense. You're never ill."

Annalise forced herself to sip her tea. Because she was a soul healer. Thank the Goddess Mother and Father had never sensed her magical powers despite being witches themselves or recognized her massive appetite and irresistible allure as signs she was a soul healer.

His cerulean eyes dark and muddy-orange contempt staining his aura of competitive red with ivory motes, Father grunted as he cut his beefsteak. "And leaving immediately after Alexander's quarrel with Ravenstone makes it appear the treacherous cad routed you."

Annalise stiffened. Why must Mother and Father continually denigrate Lord Ravenstone? Everyone at court knew the count was both genial and chivalrous. But saying so would only provoke them further, so she pursed her lips and remained silent.

Alex glowered at Mother and Father over his empty plate. "Perhaps Annalise didn't feel well because of how gentlemen treated her at the ball. King Devon kept ignoring her, the Duke of Oakmoor tried to kiss her during their dance, and most of the other gentlemen leered the entire evening."

Ignoring Alex, Mother leaned toward Annalise. "King Devon asked about you once you'd left, so dancing with the Duke of Oakmoor roused his jealousy. You must keep accepting dances with rival gentlemen. And quit hiding behind Lady Snow whenever he joins you. He'll soon realize that he can't bear to lose you, and he'll propose. Then you'll be queen like you deserve, and you can start your own family at last." She frowned and shook her head. "Despite your cool serenity, King Devon should have realized that a lady as wonderful and loving as you is rarer than a faebird's teeth and have proposed ages ago."

Her cheeks warming, Annalise sighed and finished her toast. Yet again, Mother and Father couldn't see the truth. Although she yearned to start her own family, it would never be with King Devon. He'd doubtless only asked about her because he'd escorted her to the ball and was concerned about the feud worsening after Alex's quarrel with Lord Ravenstone.

Father patted Mother's hand. "Don't fret, Emmeline. King Devon must know how perfect Annalise is. He's probably just waiting to make sure she's ready to become queen. But that shall end soon. He can't afford to still be unwed when the nightmara delegation arrives. Goddess knows if the Nightmara-Calatini Treaty would survive."

Suppressing a grimace, Annalise devoured her eggs and beefsteak. King Devon would make sure the legendary treaty continued somehow. But not by marrying her. He was too romantic to wed for mere convenience, and even if he proposed, she'd refuse him. Marrying someone who felt like a brother would be wrong.

Mother beamed, her blue eyes brightening. "True. Our Annalise shall be queen in less than two months. Exactly like we've always hoped."

Father smirked back. "Just try to see the treacherous Ravenstones best that."

As Annalise raised her gaze skyward, Alex drawled beside her, "Lord Ravenstone could marry one of the Tsarkan emperor's many daughters."

Her smile vanishing, Mother sniffed. "But that wouldn't make Ravenstone emperor. The Tsarkan emperor has just as many sons to inherit."

After exchanging a wry glance with Alex, Annalise eyed her empty plate. Should she serve herself more breakfast? She'd have to hear further matchmaking schemes if she did, and although she could eat more, she'd performed no soul-healing to need it.

Alex rose and arched his brows at her. "Care to go riding?"

Annalise leapt upright. Riding would be much better than eating food she didn't need while Mother and Father plotted their futile matchmaking.

Mother frowned at Annalise. "Make sure you're back in time to attend the Reids' tea party this afternoon."

Annalise nodded, then she and Alex darted upstairs to change into riding clothes. They met outside her chambers then strode down to the stables. As Storm nuzzled her and nibbled her hair, Alex's buckskin gelding Biscuit greeted Alex just as warmly.

Once they saddled Storm and Biscuit then mounted, Alex arched a brow and asked, "Where shall we ride?"

She shrugged and patted Storm's withers. "I don't care, as long as we ride outside of Ormas. Storm and I could use a good gallop." She rarely got the chance since Mother and Father believed galloping unladylike.

Alex chuckled then nodded, and they rode through the crowded streets of Ormas then out the southern gate before urging Storm and Biscuit to a gallop and thundering between the green and blooming fields until Storm and Biscuit began to tire.

The bright, almost summer sun heating her skin, Annalise smiled as they slowed to a trot. Goddess, galloping was wonderful. If only she could always ride so wildly.

Alex grinned at her. "We must gallop like this more often."

She beamed back. "We should ride to the royal bay next time. You've never been, and 'tis glorious around Summerday." And usually empty since riding there or the royal forest required permission from King Devon.

So when the king escorted her to the St. Claires' ball five days later, Annalise asked if she and Alex could ride to the royal bay the following morning, and King Devon agreed with a grin.

The next day, she and Alex left not long after dawn because the royal bay was further than their usual ride. And since they'd not return in time for breakfast, they ate rolls stuffed with meat and cheese as they rode through Ormas and out the northern gate. But they kept Storm and Biscuit to a trot to save them to gallop at the bay.

When they reached the royal bay, Annalise halted Storm at the edge of the verdant cliffs above the bay and grinned down at the beach. She'd not ridden here since King Devon's riding party last season, but as Lady Snow, she'd couldn't risk galloping in public. And this morning was perfect—the blazing sun shone in a white-blue sky dotted with fluffy clouds, gulls swooped in the balmy air, and frothy waves from the azure ocean crashed against the golden sand at the foot of the cliffs. Inhaling the salty breeze, she grinned at Alex. "Want to race along the waves?"

Alex grinned and jerked a nod, and they began riding down the winding path to the beach.

CHAPTER 4

A week after the Duchess of Wildewall's ball, Dare galloped along the deserted beach of the royal bay. In past seasons, he'd asked to ride on royal lands at least twice a month, so at the start of this season, King Devon had given him permission to ride at the royal bay whenever he wished, although not the royal forest. Probably because the royal forest contained Esme the Great's melissae hive, and the melissae were deadly when angered. Since then, Dare rose early most mornings to gallop at the royal bay. The scenery was tame compared to Wildewall's mountains, but the king's private bay was usually empty, so he could reconnect with nature to settle his soul and revive his physical and magical energy. 'Twas how he'd endured remaining in Ormas so long this season—hopefully, 'twould continue until he *finally* found a wife.

His black-bay stallion Ebony surging beneath him, he crouched forward in the saddle and urged his stallion faster across the wet sand before the surf. As the salty wind whipped his face and seawater sprayed him and Ebony, he gulped a deep breath and flung his powers wide to gather the natural energy pulsing around him. Not as pure and wild as the magic in Wildewall, 'twas enough to counteract the drain of living in Ormas among so many humans. Although socializing with people—who were just another facet of nature—was diverting, they did alter their surroundings and stifle the natural world around them.

Midway through his ride, two blond riders galloped along the beach toward him—Lady Annalise and her brother. His heart surging, Dare shuddered with hunger as he quit gathering natural energy. Goddess, she was glorious, galloping like that. She was wearing the warm and radiant smile she never revealed at court, making her more irresistible than an ethereal siren singing to lure sailors to shipwreck on her isle. At least the beach here was sand rather than rocks like on the Sirenuse Isles.

As everyone halted their horses to avoid crashing, Lady Annalise returned his stare, and her genuine smile dimmed.

A pang bolted through him. If only he'd been the one to create that smile rather than smother it. But at least 'twas merely her brother who'd created her delight. Patting Ebony's damp withers, he gritted a polite smile and forced a nod.

Her cerulean gaze darkening with the same impossible longing coursing through him, Lady Annalise inhaled then licked her lips and smoothed back the glowing tendrils of white-blonde hair caressing her face after her wild gallop.

Dare almost shuddered again as his body tightened further. Goddess, why must she be so irresistible? Her potent allure and kind heart made forgetting her to court other ladies difficult. Yet somehow he must.

Like whenever they met, he and Lady Annalise eyed each other, and everything else faded as desire crackled between them —including Lord Alexander scowling beside her. This was the closest they'd been since their secret encounter six years ago. He was but a few paces away from touching her.

He was about to urge Ebony forward when Lord Alexander charged between him and Lady Annalise, breaking their ardent stare. The young lord snarled, "I warned you not to stare, Ravenstone."

Both Dare and Lady Annalise jerked back, and their stallions pranced. Once he calmed Ebony, he swallowed and managed a tight smile. The young hellion would soon challenge him to another duel. And unlike at the Duchess of Wildewall's ball, no other ladies were nearby to distract everyone from his interest in Lady Annalise, so he must leave straightaway. He inclined his head at her and Lord Alexander. "I apologize again. Good morning."

Then he kneed Ebony while pulling on his left rein to pivot toward the cliffs and surge past Lady Annalise and Lord Alexander. Perhaps she could convince her younger brother to forget the apparent insult once he'd gone.

As he and Ebony galloped back to Ormas, he frowned at the winding road before them. Encountering Lady Annalise on a wild gallop in a natural area had proved again how likeminded and perfect she was for him. And being reminded of that only hampered his frustrating hunt for a wife, which he definitely didn't need.

He sighed when Ormas appeared in the distance and slowed Ebony to a walk to allow the stallion to cool down. Proper care after a hard gallop was essential. He leapt down at Ravenstone House then tended Ebony himself like always. As he left, Ebony nuzzled him and lipped his cuff before eating the hay he'd just provided.

After asking the head groom Roberts to give Ebony sweet oats in an hour, Dare strode into Ravenstone House. The moment he entered, baying howls rang through the entrance hall as his two black hellhounds thundered toward him, their eyes bursting into flame with excitement. His chest warming, he grinned and petted the massive magical pets, who leaned against his thighs like panting bags of sand. He chuckled. "Raven, Bear, you'll crush me if you aren't careful."

Although her mate Bear leaned harder, Raven immediately sat on her haunches with an adoring glance. The female hellhound was both smart and obedient—the perfect hunting companion.

Still chuckling, Dare snapped his fingers, and Bear heaved a sigh then sat beside Raven. Unlike his mate, the male hellhound often acted like an overgrown puppy—until he caught a scent.

Dare smiled then scratched Raven's and Bear's chests. He'd left them behind today because he needed a hard gallop, but he often brought them along when he went on easier rides since hellhounds loved being outdoors too. And he *always* brought them hunting—they could trace any scent and never stopped until they caught their prey. As their tails thumped against the floor, he grinned and scratched harder. "I'll bring you tomorrow. Promise."

He glanced up at a trilling meow from the base of the stairs.

Lily sauntered toward him with affected nonchalance, but the cream angelcat's upright tail quivering behind her revealed she was just as excited as Raven and Bear. She slanted the hellhounds a smirk as she passed then rubbed against his legs and meowed again, her blue eyes wide as she demanded he pet her like she deserved.

He grinned but obliged her. The daughter of Mother's previous angelcat familiar, Lily was his first magical pet. Mother had given him the adorable angelkitten when he'd returned from his first season, so he'd also have a familiar to generate magical energy. Father had given him Raven and Bear as a natalday gift three years later, not long before he'd died. As soon as the hellhound puppies had arrived, Lily had asserted her supremacy as his first pet by always smirking at them and monopolizing his bed. Although she did nuzzle them and purr once they accepted her reign. And Goddess help anyone who attempted to attack him or the hellhounds—Lily would become a whirlwind of cream fur, piercing teeth, and knifelike claws to defend them.

After being petted, Lily purred and nuzzled him then widened her eyes further and meowed several more times, obviously begging for food. Somehow, the angelcat managed to make her face appear almost gaunt.

Dare tsked. Like all magical pets, Lily adored food and required substantial amounts to generate her magical energy. But he'd fed the little liar and the hellhounds plenty of breakfast before leaving for his ride, and they weren't fed again until dinner. "If you want more food, Lily, you'll have to catch it."

He strode upstairs to his chambers with Lily, Raven, and Bear bounding behind him. As he took the usual bath his valet Thom had prepared, Lily curled on his bed and dozed while Raven and Bear lounged together before the unlit fireplace. He smiled at his menagerie of magical pets. They looked so peaceful now, but how would they react to sharing him with a wife? Once his courtship of a lady became serious, he must arrange some outdoor outings and bring them to check how they and the lady reacted. He couldn't marry anyone who didn't warm to his magical pets.

After Thom helped him dress, Dare glanced at the clock on the mantel. 'Twas late enough for his weekly mirror call with Mother. Although she also rose near dawn every morning, she preferred several cups of kahve and time alone in her garden, walking outdoors, or riding before speaking to anyone. He sat at his desk and uncovered his mirror from the pair he and Mother enchanted before he left for Ormas every season. Talking on paired communication mirrors was much easier than writing letters, especially for witches who could enchant their mirrors themselves. He chanted a brief spell and waved his hand to acti-vate the mirror, which glowed white before Mother appeared.

Her amber eyes bright as ever, Mother smoothed back her windswept brown hair with a vibrant grin. She must have been riding this morning. "Dare, I was just about to call you. How's your week been?"

He shrugged. "Well enough, I suppose." Except for not finding a potential wife and encountering Lady Annalise and her brother this morning. "I tried approaching a variety of ladies as you suggested, but I still haven't found one I want as my wife." Except the lady he couldn't have.

Mother hummed and pursed her lips. "Like all things in nature, love takes time. Your father and I courted for months before I knew I loved him. You sound as if you're not allowing matters to blossom as they should."

Dare sighed, his shoulders drooping. "Perhaps. But 'tis hard when I simply want to return to Wildewall." And the impossible Lady Annalise kept distracting him. He straightened and flashed a smile. "Enough about my frustrating hunt. Tell me about things at home."

Mother tilted her head and eyed him for a moment but then told him about the litter of angelkittens she'd visited to select a new familiar.

His heart lightening, he grinned as they talked for the next hour. Mother's vibrant presence settled his soul almost as well as escaping to nature did. And she could always see to the heart of problems and know just how to fix them, so her grounded advice was invaluable.

At the end of their call, Mother sighed, and her face tightened. "This morning, I asked Cook to prepare fish pie for dinner two days from now."

His throat clenched, but he swallowed and nodded. Doubtless Mother had requested fish pie in honor of Father's natalday. Although simple fare, fish pie had been Father's favorite, so they'd eaten it at least once a week before he died. Since then, neither Dare nor Mother had been able to eat fish pie because it reminded them Father was gone.

Mother managed a tremulous smile. "'Tis been over three years since Henry died, and he'd be horrified if he knew we'd not eaten his favorite dish for so long. Remember the time Hazel and Lily stole into the kitchen and devoured all the fish for our fish pie that evening? How Henry growled when we got chicken pie instead."

Dare echoed her smile, his chest squeezing. "And Father

blamed the switch on the Greysnowes," like he always had whenever anything went awry thanks to his adherence to the feud, "until you admitted our angelcats had done it. I don't think he forgave them until Hazel brought him that monstrous trout from the lake two weeks later."

Mother grinned. "Why else do you think I told her to catch one? Henry's glowers when we retired every evening were most uncomfortable."

He chuckled. Of course she had. Mother couldn't help fixing problems and restoring balance, probably because she respected all life as a nature witch. He smiled at her. "I'll visit a tavern with the best fish pie in Ormas on Father's natalday as well. We can honor him together then."

Mother beamed back, but tears gleamed in her eyes. "Henry would have loved that."

After he and Mother said goodbye, Dare waved his hand to deactivate the communication mirror, which turned white before clearing to reflect his face. He rubbed his beard as he set the mirror on the windowsill to recharge in the sunlight for his next mirror call. Visiting The Gold Griffin, a rowdy tavern near the docks he'd heard about from Lord Treyvan, would be enjoyable despite his somber reason. He'd not visited since last season thanks to his resolute hunt for a wife.

Two evenings later, Dare sighed when The Gold Griffin's plump barmaid slammed a glowing tankard and fish pie before him, even though his stomach rumbled at the fish pie's savory aroma. Too bad Father had never heard of this tavern—he would have adored it even more than Lord Treyvan did.

Weight crushing his chest, he tossed back his gold ale in one draft. Within moments, the plump barmaid bustled over with a fresh tankard, and he requested another before she left. He'd finish this tankard before starting his fish pie, and he'd need another while he ate.

Pleasantly blurred from the glowing gold ale's alcohol and magic, Dare was sipping his third tankard with his first bite of fish pie halfway to his mouth when Lord Alexander burst into the tavern and thrust through the crowd straight toward him.

Dare sighed and lowered his fork. How had Lord Alexander found him? From the boy's scowl, he was as irate as he'd been at the Duchess of Wildewall's ball. Clearly, Lady Annalise hadn't convinced her brother to forget their ardent stare. Wonderful.

His jaw twitching, Lord Alexander halted before Dare and leaned toward him. "You just couldn't stay away, could you, Ravenstone?"

Dare forced a genial smile and waved for Lord Alexander to sit. Somehow, he must calm the young hellion. "I didn't know you and your sister would be riding at the royal bay the other day." Since he was telling the truth, his glowing gold ale didn't dim.

Yet Lord Alexander fisted his hands and remained standing. "But you couldn't resist staring at Annalise like a manticore intent on devouring her whole, could you? You're as bad as rake-hells like the Duke of Oakmoor or fortune-hunting cads like Winston. So vain and grasping that you can't see or appreciate Annalise's true beauty."

Heat flaring in his veins, Dare stiffened. He was *nothing* like those gentlemen—Lady Annalise's inner radiance was what drew him, not her physical beauty or wealth.

Lord Alexander bent until their faces almost touched and growled, "I demand satisfaction."

Dare clenched his tankard of glowing ale and suppressed the urge to toss it in the insolent boy's face to cool him. 'Twould only infuriate the boy further. "I apologize again for appearing to insult your sister."

Lord Alexander's nostrils flared. "An apology isn't enough this time, you treacherous cad. Only a duel shall settle this."

Dare shook his head as his stomach hardened. Trouncing Lord Alexander would only feed the feud. And considering his skill with swords, he'd have no trouble doing so. "I shan't meet you."

Lord Alexander sneered. "Because you're a coward. How ashamed your father would be if he were still alive to see his son refuse a Greysnowe's challenge like a craven goblin. 'Tis fortunate he's dead."

His pulse surging, Dare leapt upright and grabbed Lord Alexander's cravat. How dare the young hellion speak about Father on his natalday? Plus, someone should teach the boy a lesson about challenging more skilled swordsmen. "You want a duel? Fine. When and where?"

Lord Alexander wrenched free with a smirk. "Summerday at dawn. The park near my family's townhouse; you know it?"

Dare almost snorted. Of course he did. 'Twas where he'd secretly encountered Lady Annalise. Appropriate he'd meet another Greysnowe there. He nodded. "Seconds?"

Cocking his head, Lord Alexander smirked harder. "No need for them. No apology they could bring would halt this duel. And I'm honorable enough to abide by the rules without anyone watching—are you?"

Dare glared as blood rushed in his ears. He clenched his hand to resist punching the provoking boy. "Yes."

Lord Alexander nodded. "Excellent. See you in two days." He whirled and thrust through the teeming tavern again.

Fire still consuming him, Dare sat and tossed back his tankard. When the plump barmaid immediately brought another, he devoured his excellent fish pie, hardly tasting it. Then he downed his fresh tankard and one more before striding from The Gold Griffin.

The following morning, he woke far later than usual with a throbbing head and queasy stomach. Goddess, what had he *done*? He should have ignored Lord Alexander's insults—they meant nothing if they weren't true. Yet he'd allowed his grief and too many tankards to goad him into that mad duel.

Dare burst from bed, his head and stomach lurching. Somehow, he must stop the duel. He couldn't visit Greysnowe House to apologize since they'd never receive him. But an unlabeled note should reach Lord Alexander. He sent a heartfelt letter of apology but received no reply.

He paced his chambers before retiring that evening. Since his apology had been rejected, he must appear for their duel at dawn. His honor depended on it. He'd attempt to apologize in person tomorrow then entreat Lord Alexander to forget the duel. If that failed, he'd fight the young hellion without wounding him until the boy was too exhausted to lift his sword. Surely Lord Alexander would agree to relent then. Please, Goddess.

CHAPTER 5

After their encounter with Lord Ravenstone at the royal bay, Alex's suspicious behavior troubled Annalise. She'd attempted to convince him her lengthy stare with the count still meant nothing, yet Alex had appeared even less convinced than before. He quit attending court events but was often out, and he avoided her whenever he was in. Plus, he'd been engrossed in several conversations with a ragged street boy. Alex must be embroiled in some mischief—doubtless involving Lord Ravenstone.

So after rising at dawn on Summerday four days later, she set her jaw as she dressed for her morning walk. She must unearth that mischief before Alex did something mad or was wounded. And since today was her natalday, she could beg him to tell her and forget whatever it was as a natalday gift. Surely, he loved her too much to deny her heartfelt plea. Her mouth drying, she swallowed. Please, Goddess.

Annalise smoothed her taupe dress with a sigh. She'd wake Alex and have him join her on her walk this morning, so they could talk without anyone overhearing. She called Finn, who glided to her side, then began to her door.

She halted at the folded note on her carpet just inside the

threshold. What the—? Her pulse surging, she seized the note and ripped it open.

Annalise—

To end Ravenstone's leering, I've challenged the treacherous cad to a duel this morning. I don't intend to kill him, just wound him enough that he never dares to look at you again. Hopefully, when gossip about the duel spreads, it shall also make the other gentlemen at court treat you with the respect you deserve. Consider it a natalday gift.

Alex

P.S. I may be late to breakfast. Could you explain my absence to Father and Mother?

Black spots flashing before her eyes and her stomach lurching, Annalise crushed Alex's note. Dear Goddess, what had he *done*? Lord Ravenstone could easily kill him—not that the genial count would. But still, accidents could happen. And no matter how the duel ended, 'twould surely inflame the Greysnowe-Ravenstone feud. She *must* find Alex and Lord Ravenstone and halt their mad duel.

She worried her lip. But how? Alex hadn't written where the duel was. And she could only use auras to locate people when they were within eyesight. Plus, her powers worked differently than most witches, so she couldn't perform ordinary magic such as tracing spells. Except for her powers as a soul healer, she could only use created spells like humans without magic.

Annalise stiffened with a ragged gasp. Those wretched tracing amulets Mother and Father had created when she and Alex were small! Since such charms could be stolen or used to create a dangerous magical connection to their children, most parents didn't have them created *unless* their child was kidnapped. Yet certain the Ravenstones would attempt that, Mother and Father had. Father kept them inside his desk in his study.

Since Finn would only hinder her hunt because she must ride to find Alex and Lord Ravenstone, she shooed the angelcat back to bed then slipped from her chambers. She darted downstairs as swiftly as she could without making a sound. She mustn't wake Mother and Father. They'd prevent her from halting the duel.

Her heart pounding, Annalise stilled before the study door. Please, please let it be unlocked. She exhaled when the door silently glided open then dashed to Father's desk. Starting with the top drawers, she yanked open each one and rooted for the tracing amulets. Fortunately, the drawers were as silent as the study door, but she had to open all of them to find the amulets, which were buried beneath a sheaf of papers and several small books. Unable to distinguish between the shades of blond hair inside the clear quartz amulets that glowed with Mother and Father's magic, she placed both of the silver necklaces about her neck.

Now that she could find Alex, she must head to the palace to ask for King Devon's help. No doubt Alex was too furious to heed her and halt the duel. But surely the king could make him stop—no one ignored King Devon when he commanded them, although he only did so when imperative.

Annalise grimaced as she quietly sprinted outside to the stables. If only she could use a communication mirror to contact King Devon rather than riding to the palace. But to call someone, communication mirrors must either be linked by being enchanted together, or the caller must know the call signature of the other's mirror. And although the king had escorted her to court events for three seasons, their relationship wasn't serious, so King Devon had never shared his mirror's call signature.

When she fetched Storm, the stallion nickered and nuzzled her hair, but she patted his neck without her usual greetings and led him from the stables. Already late since duels typically began at dawn, she leapt on Storm's back without bothering to saddle him. Thank the Goddess tales of mara riding nightmara had inspired her to teach herself how to ride without tack. And to remain in practice, she'd secretly trained Storm the summer before her first season. Mother and Father would be appalled if they knew—riding bareback was even more unladylike than galloping. And she was about to do both.

Annalise nudged Storm to a silent walk until they were beyond earshot of her family's townhouse. Then she bent over his neck and kneed him to a thundering gallop. Thankfully, the streets near the palace were all but deserted at such an early hour, so she didn't need to steer to avoid anyone. It being Summerday likely helped too—most slept later since Summerday festivities started in late afternoon and lasted through the night. At the palace stables, she flung herself from her barely winded stallion then told a sleepy groom, "Prepare the king's horse at once."

Her ribs tight, she raced inside the palace then halted at the first maid she passed. "How do I get to the royal wing?"

Gaping at Annalise, the maid blinked but told her.

Annalise nodded her thanks then bounded upstairs and down the palace halls following the maid's directions. Like her unladylike gallop earlier, Mother and Father would be appalled if they saw her running through the palace. But halting the duel was too vital to consider decorum. Disregarding the startled guards flanking it, she pounded on the door to the king's chambers. "Your majesty, open up. Please, 'tis urgent!"

The door jerked open, and King Devon gaped at her with muddy-orange shock pulsing about him and both his dark hair and dressing gown disheveled. "Lady Annalise, in the Goddess's name, *what* are you doing?"

Annalise darted a curtsy with little of her usual grace. "Alex has challenged Lord Ravenstone to a duel. Please help me stop them."

King Devon paled. "Dear Goddess." He set his jaw. "I'll dress immediately."

She sighed as he bolted inside and forced herself not to pace while she waited. Mercifully, the king returned in moments, his riding clothes askew and cravat untied.

As they pelted downstairs with the royal guards from the door, King Devon managed to tie his cravat. "Do you know where they are?"

Annalise lifted the tracing amulets about her neck as they burst outside. Hopefully, they'd not be too late. "Not exactly. But one of these can trace Alex."

King Devon hummed but didn't ask why she possessed tracing amulets. Doubtless he realized 'twas because of the feud. However, when they reached the stables, he blinked at Storm then asked, "You ride bareback?"

She vaulted atop Storm and patted his withers. "I taught myself as a girl." Why was King Devon wasting time asking about that? "Mount, please. We must go."

When King Devon nodded and leapt into the saddle, the royal guards scowled, and the brown-haired one said, "Your majesty, you can't leave without us."

While Annalise began scrutinizing the tracing amulets to determine which was Alex's, King Devon frowned at his guards. "You have until Lady Annalise activates her tracing amulet, Millier. Halting this duel is too important to delay."

Still scowling, the royal guards hurtled inside the stables.

She grimaced at the blond hair inside the amulets' clear quartz balls. Luckily for the guards, although Alex's hair was now the same sandy-blond as Father's, his hair as a boy had been almost as pale as hers, so distinguishing between the two amulets was challenging. The blood inside them didn't help either since it obscured the hair. After a moment, she sighed and chose the one with hair perhaps a shade darker. If she was wrong, activating the amulet with Alex's name simply wouldn't work, and she could try the other one. The royal guards had just joined them when she clenched her chosen tracing amulet in her fist, focused on it, and intoned, "Find Alexander Merlyn Greysnowe."

Its magic flaring, the clear quartz ball began glowing like the sun, and the silver amulet jerked from her hand to point back toward her family's townhouse.

Annalise gulped a breath. Thank the Goddess it worked. She bent forward and kneed Storm to a gallop, following the tracing amulet's pull through the still-empty streets of Ormas. They only had until the tracing spell consumed the energy stored inside the clear quartz ball to find Alex. When the amulet ceased glowing, they'd need a witch to recharge the amulet for it to work again. Tracing amulets typically lasted for several hours at least, but Goddess knew when Mother or Father had last renewed or recharged the spell.

King Devon and his guards close behind, she and Storm thundered past her family's townhouse without slowing. Then the tracing amulet began to flicker and wobble as its magic dimmed. 'Twas almost spent. She bent further forward and urged Storm even faster. Please, please last until they found Alex. But just before they reached the nearby park, the clear quartz ball quit glowing and plummeted. No! Halting Storm, she clenched her jaw and almost glared.

King Devon cursed then eyed her. "What now?"

Annalise gritted a serene smile as her stomach twisted. "Let me think a moment."

The tracing amulet had appeared to be leading them to the park, which *would* be a perfect place for a duel. Perhaps they were close enough she could find them with their auras. After all, Lord Ravenstone's aura was brighter than most due to the many bronze motes from his powerful nature magic, and Alex was her brother, so she intimately knew his aura. Focusing her powers, she peered into the park, and the faintest glow appeared among the trees. That must be Alex and Lord Ravenstone.

She turned back to King Devon. She mustn't reveal she was using soul healer magic, not even to someone as trustworthy as the king. "Alex and Lord Ravenstone must be in this park. If we ride quietly, we might be able to hear them once we're near."

Urging Storm forward, Annalise steered the stallion through the verdant trees toward the glow, and they glided through the park like morning mist. Unlike usual, the calm nature surrounding them faded as she strained to follow the glow of Alex's and Lord Ravenstone's auras. When the glow brightened into separate yellow and green, she sped Storm to a trot. They must be close. They burst into a clearing near the heart of the park with King Devon and his guards directly behind them.

In the center of the clearing, Alex and Lord Ravenstone were crossing swords with Alex turned away and the count facing her. From the sweat darkening their clothes and their slow movements, they must have been dueling since dawn over an hour ago. Yet neither bore any wounds. Thank the Goddess. She'd arrived in time. Her tight ribs began to ease as she met Lord Ravenstone's gaze across the clearing.

Like always, Lord Ravenstone stilled. Then Alex's wild thrust slipped past the count's guard to stab his chest just left of center. As Lord Ravenstone staggered back and Alex's bloodstained sword wrenched free, black swamped the Lord Ravenstone's green aura, starting at his chest then spreading. Alex had hit his heart.

No! No, no, no!

Her breath frozen, Annalise flung herself from Storm and hurtled across the clearing as Lord Ravenstone crumpled. With that fatal wound, even if a witch healer was here, she probably couldn't save him. But a soul healer could. Although 'twould cost her future happiness and husband—she'd be irrevocably soulbound to the one gentleman Mother and Father would *never* accept her marrying.

She shoved aside Alex, who was ashen with muddy-blue anguish glowing about him as he gaped at his dripping sword, to drop beside Lord Ravenstone. She pressed her hands against the count's chest to staunch his bleeding. Although brash, Alex hadn't meant to kill anyone. His duel with Lord Ravenstone had been little more than a lark to him. Yet she couldn't let Alex bear the stain of murder on his soul. Not only would he never forgive himself, but he'd be executed.

Plus, despite Lord Ravenstone having no children to perpetuate the feud, his many cousins and people back in Wildewall would retaliate fiercer than ever if a Greysnowe murdered the current head of the Ravenstones. And her family would have to face his mother, likely a powerful nature witch like her son. A curse cast by a Rhiannon-descendant nature witch grieving the murder of her only child would be dreadful. Annalise's entire family would probably be destroyed if Lord Ravenstone died, starting with Alex.

As she pressed her hands against his gushing wound, Lord Ravenstone grimaced and shuddered. His amber eyes black, he lifted them to meet hers again then rasped, "You'd best stop. I'll be unable to clean the blood this time."

Tears burning her eyes, Annalise swallowed. Like he'd cleaned Finn's blood using his nature magic during their secret encounter all those years ago. From his readiness to reveal his magic to help a nameless lady he'd just met, she'd known he was the most kindhearted and wonderful gentleman. And none had ever fascinated her like he had. How could she bear a world without him in it? So even though they could never marry or reveal their soulbond, she *must* heal him. She glared at Lord Ravenstone. "Do hush."

Blood still spurting between her fingers, she turned her glare to Alex. She must get him, King Devon, and the royal guards to leave, so she could heal Lord Ravenstone before he bled out. "Go fetch a witch healer." When Alex merely blinked, she glared harder. "Now!"

When Alex dropped his sword then bolted from the clearing, she called to King Devon and his guards, "Go with him, please, all of you. He's too distressed to find a healer alone."

King Devon nodded, and he sprinted after Alex with his guards following.

Scarlet foam staining his black beard, Lord Ravenstone

coughed a gurgling laugh. "Alone at long last. Too bad I shan't live to enjoy it." His eyes drifted shut, and his aura dimmed.

NO!

Yanking energy from her soul until it matched his green with bronze motes, she enveloped his soul with hers, and tingling swamped her when their entire souls meshed. She bit her tongue to keep from screaming at the fiery agony piercing her chest while she absorbed his wounds. Would her heart stop before she finished healing Lord Ravenstone?

Annalise set her jaw. She couldn't fail—not now. So she braced herself as agony seared her chest.

CHAPTER 6

As the blinding white glow of powerful magic flooded the darkness swallowing Dare, relief swept through him, and the flaming agony consuming his chest vanished. Then before his next heartbeat, his gaping wound knit together, and energy surged through him.

His head whirling, he opened his eyes and met Annalise's tear-bright gaze. Somehow, she'd healed his fatal wound. But how? Not even the most powerful witch healer could have managed that. And why could he sense her transparent aura with electrum motes and his green aura with bronze motes intertwined like the roots of two ferns grown in the same pot?

Annalise blinked, and her tears burst free while yellow joy flared about her. "Thank the Goddess. For a moment, I feared I wasn't strong enough."

Dare shuddered as his entire body tingled. She was even more irresistible now, and not because her hands were still pressed against his chest, but because of her radiant aura surrounding him. If only he could kiss her. But she'd not given him permission for that. So instead, he sat up and wiped the tears from her cheeks. "How..."

Her heady honeysuckle scent weaving around him, Annalise swallowed and licked her lips. "I'm a soul healer."

Dare inhaled, his body tightening as he eyed her lips. Of course she was. The Greysnowes were descended from Esme the Great, so they produced soul healers every generation or two. One had even been involved in the broken betrothal that had started the feud between their families. And her being a soul healer explained why her potent magic impacted nature and her transparent aura with electrum motes. Yet how were her powers still secret? Surely, if her parents knew, they couldn't resist proclaiming such a triumph over the Ravenstones.

Annalise swallowed again, and her gaze darted away. "And I'd not healed an intelligent creature's fatal wound before, so when I meshed our entire souls to heal you, we formed a soul-bond that can never be broken. I'm sorry, but I couldn't let you die, and 'twas no other way to save you."

He blinked. But now that they were soulbound, her parents would have to accept them marrying despite the feud. He almost grinned. He could finally quit forcing himself to court other ladies and marry *her*—the likeminded lady he'd always wanted. And as soon as they married, he and Annalise could return home to Wildewall and enjoy a wonderful life together. Smiling at that, he arched his brows. "Are you apologizing for saving my life?"

Annalise glared at him. "You don't understand, Da—Lord Ravenstone. Revealing our soulbond would inflame the feud, and our families would likely destroy each other."

His heart surging at her almost using his first name, Dare grinned and took her hand. "Call me Dare—titles are nonsensical between us now." Then he shrugged. "Our soulbond shall feed the feud at first, but a permanent connection between our fami-lies should eventually heal it. After all, our children shall be both Ravenstones and Greysnowes." He chuckled. "And 'tis fitting to end the feud with a marriage, the opposite of how it began.

Besides, we're past the age of majority, so your parents can't forbid us from marrying."

Her cerulean eyes bright with tears again, Annalise drooped and tugged her hand free. "You underestimate my parents' rancor toward your family. Despite our soulbond and age, Mother and Father shall *never* accept us marrying. If we told them, they'd probably lock you in a permanent sleep spell then betroth me to a foreign prince in a way that my refusal would start a war."

He grimaced, his ribs squeezing. Perhaps they would attempt that, rather than accepting a Ravenstone as their son-in-law. "Yet what else can we do but marry? Neither of us shall ever desire another, and the pull of a soulbond is impossible to ignore. Even now, I burn to make love to you here, despite being in the open and covered in blood." But his sense of chivalry restrained him—barely.

Annalise jerked back until they no longer touched. "You mustn't. Not only does making love risk pregnancy, but consummating our soulbond shall strengthen it. We'll only survive remaining apart if we avoid each other and never feed our soulbond."

Dare frowned at her. Doing that was doubtless impossible. "But—"

Annalise stiffened and interrupted, "Hush. I can see auras approaching. Alex and King Devon will be here with a witch healer shortly." She leaned over and grasped her brother's bloody sword then swallowed. "I must stab you again, so no one realizes I healed you. But I shan't pierce your heart, and our soulbond shall bolster you, so you'll not die."

He eyed Annalise then sighed. Revealing their soulbond would be better, but she wasn't ready for that yet. He nodded and laid back down. "Very well."

Paling whiter than a banshee before a family death, Annalise shuddered then pressed the sword to the left of his previous wound.

Dare hissed as flaming agony consumed his chest again and blood gushed from his fresh wound. Damnation, he'd only endure such agony for her.

Annalise retched, and tears coursed down her cheeks. Muddy-blue shame swamping her, she flung aside the sword and pressed her hands against his bleeding chest. "Oh, Goddess, I'm so, so sorry. But I had to."

Tenderness tempering his pain, he forced a smile. "No tears now. Lady Snow can't allow anyone to see behind her serene mask."

Her white-blonde hair glowing like the midday sun even in the dappled shade, Annalise nodded then almost returned his smile. "You're right, of course."

As Lord Alexander, King Devon, an unknown witch healer, and the royal guards burst into the clearing, Dare gathered his will and directed it toward the tears wetting Annalise's cheeks. His nature magic flooded them until they evaporated into mist, leaving her face dry before the others reached him and Annalise.

The witch healer shoved aside Annalise to press her own hands on his gushing wound. She crooned a singsong chant, and a white glow, powerful but nowhere near as potent as Annalise's, flared around her hands.

Dare shuddered as his wound closed. Unlike when Annalise had soul-healed him, the witch healer's spell was excruciating as well as draining because he was enduring months of healing in several heartbeats.

Hovering beside him, Annalise clenched her hands and blinked rapidly as her eyes brightened with tears once more and muddy-yellow fear surrounded her.

Since he couldn't outwardly comfort her and reveal their soulbond, he met her gaze and sent reassurance through his aura. Please let that be enough.

Annalise inhaled, and her hands relaxed as her aura cleared. Then Lady Snow's serene smile curved her lips. Good.

The witch healer leaned back with a sigh when her spell finished. "You're most fortunate, Lord Ravenstone. If slightly to the right, your wound would have pierced your heart, and if these gentlemen hadn't fetched me so swiftly, you would have bled out. Even so, it took all my powers to heal you."

Dare sat up and smiled at the witch healer. "Thank you, Lady..."

The melissae on her gold torc glinting, the witch healer beamed back. "Healer Althea, and no thanks necessary."

Dare stood and drew Healer Althea upright then flashed a genial grin at King Devon and Lord Alexander. "I think 'tis best we leave and forget about this morning. We've Summerday festivities to attend tonight."

King Devon frowned but slowly nodded, yet Lord Alexander paled and hunched his shoulders. Although a hellion and determined to protect his sister, the poor boy clearly hadn't meant to nearly kill him. And if Annalise's arrival hadn't distracted him, the boy wouldn't have.

Annalise threaded her arm through her brother's. "Yes, and we've my natalday to celebrate as well."

Dare blinked. Her natalday was on the festival of the Goddess celebrating fertility and courtship? How appropriate. He must secretly send her a gift. Forcing himself to ignore Annalise, he bent to collect his and Lord Alexander's swords. He tossed the bloody sword to Lord Alexander. "You'd best clean that soon. A good swordsman never lets his sword rust."

Deftly catching his sword, Lord Alexander paled further. Then he jerked a nod without meeting Dare's gaze.

Dare hummed as he strode to Ebony and heaved himself into the saddle. During their lengthy duel, the boy's skill with a sword had been impressive, and with training, Lord Alexander could one day rival him. Too bad the feud prevented him from providing it.

He rode back to Ravenstone House but kept to a slow walk,

rather than his normal brisk trot. Goddess, he was exhausted. Yet he still tended Ebony himself before trudging inside. When Raven and Bear bayed and thundered toward him, he snapped his fingers before they reached him and commanded them to sit. Their usual affection would flatten him. Once Lily sauntered over, he fed the angelcat and the hellhounds, since he'd left too early for the duel to feed them this morning.

Then Dare sank into his usual bath and scrubbed the blood staining his skin. Disregarding the clothes Thom offered, he pulled on a dressing gown and devoured the breakfast tray the valet had brought. Some of his energy returned, but not enough to bother with Summerday festivities later. Besides, dancing at a Summerday bonfire or performing other courtship rituals with a lady not Annalise would be agonizing.

Instead, he remained home and carved a heart made of beech wood. He etched the heart with honeysuckle flowers then gathered his will to infuse the heart with nature magic until Annalise's heady scent perfumed the air. He wrapped his natalday faegift in plain paper and gave it to Thom, saying, "Deliver this to Lady Annalise at Greysnowe House, but make sure you aren't seen. And tell *no one*."

After his valet left, Dare ate the traditional honey feast fare of honey-glazed chicken and oatmeal cakes, although he stuck to elderflower tea rather than mead. Then he crawled into bed with a sigh. Hopefully, Annalise enjoyed his natalday faegift. If only he could have given it to her himself.

Over the following three days, Dare attended no court events, so he could fully recover from almost dying on Summerday. He spent most of his time outdoors, although he didn't risk riding on the first day. His normal vigor had returned by the third day, yet a gnawing ache still filled his soul—hunger to see Annalise again.

He sighed as he activated his communication mirror in his

chambers to call Mother. If his soulbond with Annalise was already so strong, they'd never be able to remain apart like she wished.

After the mirror glowed white and Mother appeared, she flashed a vibrant grin. "Morning, Dare." Then her grin vanished, and she leaned forward. "What has happened? You seem... different."

Dare stiffened. He'd better tell her about the duel. Everyone adored gossiping about the feud, so word of the duel would soon reach her, either through Lord Islaye or one of the Wilde-wall families staying in Ormas. And she'd worry if he'd not already told her about it. He made himself shrug. "Perhaps because Lord Alexander Greysnowe and I crossed swords on Summerday, and he managed to wound me when my attention was distracted. But he fetched a witch healer, and I'm fully recovered now."

Mother paled. "What?"

He almost winced. Too bad he couldn't explain the true reason he seemed different, but until Annalise was ready to reveal their soulbond, he must remain silent, even to Mother. Hopefully, it wouldn't be for long—a protracted silence about such a momentous development would hurt Mother. He shrugged again. "'Twas little more than a lark, and the poor boy feels wretched for wounding me. Maybe it shall make him more willing to seek peace, unlike his father."

Her eyes dark, Mother shuddered. "Or it might make Lord Alexander more determined to cling to that ridiculous feud to excuse wounding you." She scrutinized him. "Are you certain you're fully recovered?"

Dare smiled and nodded, despite his tight throat. "I'd never lie to you about that." When Mother hummed, he asked to distract her, "Did you select a new angelkitten yet?"

Mother relaxed then inclined her head. "I did. Her name is Pearl."

He chuckled. "I'll look forward to hearing what mischief she gets into while I'm in Ormas." He glanced at the clock on the mantel. He must end their call before Mother asked about the duel again. "I should go. I've some correspondence to write before the Reids' rout party tonight."

After they said goodbye and he deactivated the communication mirror then set it on the windowsill to recharge, Dare strode downstairs to his study and dropped into the chair behind his empty desk. He'd no correspondence to write—he was a terrible son for lying to Mother so. Please let him be able to reveal the truth soon.

He straightened and smoothed his beard. Although perhaps there *was* some correspondence he should write. Annalise would only be ready to reveal their soulbond if her parents would accept him marrying her. And they'd only do that if they ended their families' feud. He'd attempted approaching Lord Greysnowe before, but maybe heartfelt letters would sway the other count. They were much less likely to escalate into blows than attempts in person might, and he could keep sending them weekly until Lord Greysnowe finally agreed.

Dare wrote his letter, making sure his handwriting was flawless. Nothing must detract from his plea.

Dear Lord Greysnowe—

As I'm certain your son has already informed you, Lord Alexander and I crossed swords on Summerday, and he managed to wound me. After almost dying, I know our families must seek peace now, before further strife feeds the feud beyond mending. For our families' future happiness and prosperity, we must forgive the past and build acceptance. As powerful Wildewall families, we have much more in common than we might care to admit. Please join me here, or any other place you desire, to discuss ending our families' centuries-long feud.

Yours respectfully,

Darius, Lord Ravenstone

He finished the letter just before dinner. He gulped a breath then asked his butler Brown to have the unlabeled letter delivered to Greysnowe House. Goddess, let it help convince Annalise's parents to end the feud.

CHAPTER 7

When Annalise slipped into the breakfast room following her morning ride on the fourth day after the duel, she beamed at Alex in his typical seat. He'd kept apart from everyone since her natalday celebration and Summerday honey feast, which they'd both struggled to endure due to the nearly fatal duel that morning. She'd been exhausted, ravenous, and distressed after soul-healing Dare, so she could barely manage her usual serenity, while Alex had been so ashamed for nearly killing Dare that he'd hardly eaten or smiled.

She scrutinized Alex as she sat beside him and heaped her plate with eggs, beefsteak, and a roll. Not actually eating, he was wan with sunken eyes, and muddy-blue shame still shrouded him like fog. "How are you?"

His gaze remaining on his full plate, Alex shrugged and poked his eggs. "Well enough."

A pang darting through her at his melancholy, Annalise began devouring her beefsteak. When would Alex be his irrepressible self again? "You appear tired."

Alex sighed as he scooped eggs onto his roll. "I've not slept much since..." He shuddered and met her gaze at last, his eyes shadowed. "I never meant to..."

She touched his hand with a gentle smile to hearten him. "I know." She leaned toward him. "But you fetched that witch healer in time, so no permanent harm was done." Except for her irrevocable soulbond with Dare. Her chest squeezed.

Alex grimaced. "As long as Father and Mother never learn of it. You've not told them, have you?"

Annalise echoed his earlier shudder. They might have realized her powers and soulbond if she had. "Goddess, no."

Alex sighed again and resumed eating. "Good. Then as soon as I gather enough resolve to apologize to Lord Ravenstone, the entire matter shall pass without inflaming the feud."

Before she could suggest he attempt to heal the feud with Dare as well, Mother and Father sailed into the breakfast room. They both beamed with muddy-orange pride glowing about them, and Mother didn't frown at Annalise's full plate for once.

Her pulse fluttering, Annalise forced herself to smile and finish her beefsteak as they served themselves breakfast. Mother and Father only appeared so smug when they'd bested the Ravenstones.

Father grinned at Alex as he cut his beefsteak. "We just learned you nearly killed Lord Ravenstone in a duel on Summerday. That shall show those treacherous Ravenstones to not trifle with us."

Mother hummed and nodded. "Why didn't you tell us?" She tilted her head. "To not eclipse Annalise's natalday, perhaps?"

Annalise swallowed as her stomach roiled. How could Mother and Father gloat that Alex had nearly killed someone, even their family's ancestral enemy? If she didn't resemble them, she'd suspect herself a fae changeling.

Alex paled further and gripped his fork. "How did you find out?"

Father smirked. "Ravenstone wrote us to seek peace. Fool."

Annalise sipped her tea to settle her stomach. Doubtless Dare had written hoping Mother and Father would accept their marriage if the feud ended. An impossible dream. If only she'd warned him not to reveal the duel.

Alex inhaled and set down his fork. "Perhaps we should seek peace."

Warmth flooded Annalise's chest. From his earnest frown, he'd not suggested that to provoke Mother and Father. The nearly fatal duel had taught her brash younger brother prudence.

Mother and Father exchanged a wide glance then chuckled. After a moment, Father replied, "With a treacherous Ravenstone? Never."

Alex bolted upright and strode from the breakfast room, abandoning his half-full plate.

Mother and Father glanced at each other again, and Mother murmured, "Why was Alexander so upset?"

Clinging to her serene smile, Annalise swallowed a snort. Perhaps because he'd nearly killed someone, and his parents were gleeful about it? Yet saying that would merely deepen the discord between them and Alex, so she asked instead, "Did Lord Ravenstone write anything else?"

Father shrugged as he resumed his beefsteak. "Not really."

Annalise sighed and set down her teacup. At least Dare hadn't mentioned her involvement. Thank the Goddess for that.

As Annalise began her eggs and roll, Mother leaned toward her. "Is King Devon escorting you to the Blakeleys' soiree tonight?"

Annalise almost grimaced. King Devon was too busy with state affairs to escort her more than once a week. Further proof he wasn't truly courting her, although Mother and Father were too blinded by their ambition and obsession with the feud to see that. "No, he's not free until the Escanas' ball later this week."

Mother hummed and sipped her tea. "You must save our natalday gift and your new deep-blue satin from Celeste's until then. The king shan't be capable of resisting you in those." Her lips quirked as her gaze flicked to Father. "He might even be tempted to start your family together early. Not that you should let him until he proposes."

As Mother and Father traded a warm glance, Annalise sighed but inclined her head. Such wiles wouldn't attract King Devon, yet waiting to wear Mother and Father's natalday gift was welcome. Like usual, they'd given her a set of elaborate jewelry, diamonds and silver this year. The pet whistle charm from Alex and the enchanted heart carving from Dare were much more to her taste, and they'd clearly created the small faegifts themselves.

She soon finished breakfast then excused herself and headed up to her chambers. To counteract the ache of missing Dare, she'd been spending all her idle hours with Finn, Rain, Aria, and Storm. She released the faebirds from their golden birdcage then curled on her bed with Rain and Aria perched on her head, trilling sweet melodies. Finn immediately cuddled in her lap and purred as she petted him and scratched his chin.

Yet despite her pets' affection, Annalise drooped, and tears pricked her eyes. As if bewitched by a siren, she slid a hand into the drawer of her bedside table and extracted Dare's faegift yet again. She caressed the flowers adorning the beech wood, inhaling the sweet honeysuckle scent wafting from the faegift that sparkled with the bronze motes of Dare's magic. Honeysuckle was her favorite because it reminded her of carefree summer afternoons in the wild forests back home. Truly the perfect natalday gift.

When warmth flooded her aching chest, she made herself shove the enchanted heart carving back into the drawer of her bedside table. She should have burned Dare's faegift as soon as she'd received it, since keeping it only fed their soulbond, but she hadn't the strength.

Annalise shuddered a sigh, causing Rain and Aria to warble and Finn to nuzzle her. Goddess, remaining apart from Dare was much harder than she'd expected. They'd only been soulbound four days, and the pull to be with him was nearly irresistible. She was accustomed to being alone except for her pets and Alex, but now loneliness almost crushed her, and her entire soul craved Dare. Yet she must resist—otherwise their soulbond would grow until 'twas impossible to conceal, and her parents would be furious if they discovered it.

She grimaced and buried her face in Finn's silky white fur. Even before their soulbond, she'd barely concealed her fascination with Dare. Seeing him at the next court event they both attended would be arduous. Fortunately, only the most influential at court, like councilors or dukes and duchesses, invited both Greysnowes and Ravenstones to their events. Others typically alternated which family they invited, so she likely wouldn't encounter Dare until the king's summer masquerade next month. Hopefully, 'twould allow her time to bolster her control.

Annalise started from her reverie when her maid Grace entered to help her change for Lady Treyvan's salon that Mother insisted she attend. Although she'd little interest in art and most of the ladies would avoid her, at least a fashionable event without gentlemen would distract her from her hunger to see Dare.

OVER THE FOLLOWING DAYS, her ache for Dare didn't abate, but Annalise managed to control it through her morning walks or rides, affection from her pets, and various court events. Yet her serene mask almost cracked when King Devon escorted her for the first time since she'd become soulbound to Dare.

Although King Devon's smile was as respectful as ever—with no attraction despite the elaborate jewelry and deep-blue satin Mother had said to wear—Annalise's skin still tightened as she made herself accept his arm at the Escanas' ball. Being escorted by a gentleman other than Dare felt as wrong as a fire witch struggling to perform sea magic. But Dare escorting her was impossible, and if she refused the king, Mother and Father would shove her at other gentlemen actually interested in courting her. She suppressed a shudder. So she must continue allowing the king's escort. Besides, 'twould surely end soon, since King Devon must have a true queen before the nightmara arrived. Perhaps she should direct him toward likely ladies when he escorted her to court events.

As King Devon led her out for the first waltz, she eyed the other ladies on the floor, but none were conscientious enough to interest a king determined to serve his kingdom well. She sighed and returned her gaze to King Devon. When he arched his brows, she said, "I was checking if Lord Ravenstone was here. Although Alex remained home tonight, Lord Ravenstone encountering me would be almost as bad."

King Devon shook his head. "I doubt it. After all, you saved his life."

Annalise swallowed, a chill skittering through her as she eyed the few weak gold motes inside the king's commanding red aura. Did he realize she'd soul-healed Dare? King Devon had inherited faint witch healer powers from Calator, Calatini's first king, who'd been an apprentice witch healer before being crowned. And witch healers could recognize soul healers when they used their healing sight on soul healers. But the king's faint powers were also untrained, so perhaps he'd doubt his suspicions if she denied it.

She forced a serene smile. "Nonsense, I did nothing extraordinary."

King Devon snorted. "You immediately staunched Lord Ravenstone's bleeding and ordered everyone to fetch a witch healer. If you'd not remained so cool, the count would have bled out—Healer Althea said as much."

She relaxed as the king twirled her in a complicated turn. Thank the Goddess he didn't suspect her powers. She glided back into his arms. "Well, I couldn't allow Alex to be executed for murdering Lord Ravenstone, even if our families are ancestral enemies."

Humming, King Devon nodded at Mother and Father across

the ballroom. "Your parents definitely wouldn't have bothered. They've been boasting about the nearly fatal duel the past few days."

Annalise winced as she followed his nod. Mother and Father were beaming as they regaled Lady Morwynne, a superior and devious countess who served on the council. Mother and Father should be careful what they told her—even if they'd already boasted to all of court about their son besting a Ravenstone. The gossip about the duel that Mother and Father had created was likely why Alex had avoided everyone by riding alone and not attending court events. If only she could join him.

King Devon arched a brow. "Although they've been silent on your part so far."

She stiffened but swept a curtsy as the waltz ended. "They don't know." She managed another serene smile as she and King Devon headed toward the refreshments table. "I hope they tire of boasting about the duel soon. Such gossip is embarrassing."

Unfortunately, Mother and Father didn't, so gossip about the duel continued to flare whenever Annalise or her parents entered. Hopefully, the king's summer masquerade would provide new scandals, so court could cease discussing the duel. Alex might never emerge if they didn't.

BEFORE HER MORNING walk a week after her discussion with King Devon, Annalise knocked on Alex's door with Finn weaving about her skirt. Since Alex was avoiding everyone, breakfast the other week had been the last she'd seen him, and she must check if he'd recovered yet.

After a moment, his door creaked open a crack, and Alex peered at her. Then he sighed and completely opened the door with a wry smile. "Morning, Annalise. I should have known it couldn't be Father or Mother so early."

She scrutinized him as Finn meowed and rubbed against his

legs. Alex still appeared wan, but his aura was almost its usual irrepressible orange again. "Care for a walk to the park?"

Muddy-blue shame swamping him, Alex hunched his shoulders while bending to scratch Finn's chin. "No, I'd rather not return there."

Annalise leaned toward her younger brother. He must return to fully face his actions, so he could heal. "Please, Alex, I've barely seen you these past days, and I miss you."

Alex winced as he straightened from petting Finn. "I'm sorry. 'Twasn't you I was avoiding. Father and Mother have been unpalatable." He blew a sigh and stepped into the hall. "Very well, I'll join you."

Once they'd slipped outside with Finn prowling beside them, she smiled at Alex. "I understand why you've been avoiding Mother and Father, but you must face them eventually."

Alex shuddered. "I know, but not while they're gloating about the duel. Once they cease, I'll quit avoiding them. Although I may continue avoiding court."

Her throat constricting, Annalise arched her brows as they reached the park's well-tended trees and Finn leapt into the branches above them. "Because of gossip about the duel or to avoid Lord Ravenstone?"

Alex sighed, but his shoulders stiffened. "Neither. I've not missed court events since I stopped attending them, so why bother?"

She hummed as she inhaled the park's sweet summer breeze. Understandable, considering Alex didn't care about being influential and was too young to want a wife. If only she could stop attending too, but 'twould upset Mother and Father. "Too bad. Your company enlivens otherwise dull events."

Alex coughed then nodded. "If you ever need me to accompany you, let me know. I'll gladly attend court events for you— once I apologize to Lord Ravenstone." He grimaced. "If I can ever figure out how."

Annalise laid her hand on Alex's arm. "Just be honest with

him. I'm certain Lord Ravenstone shall forgive you." She forced herself to smile as the ache of missing Dare crushed her chest yet again. "'Twas an accident, after all, and he's a genial gentleman."

Alex sighed. "I suppose."

To cheer him and distract herself from Dare, she tilted her head and said, "Now tell me all the exciting places you've ridden while I've been attending court events."

CHAPTER 8

When Dare strode into Lady Ducharme's well-equipped sparring hall nearly a week after his second unanswered letter to Lord Greysnowe, Lady Ducharme lifted her gaze from the sword she was inspecting and blinked. Sheathing her sword, she straightened her sword clothes then grinned at him. "Lord Ravenstone, I'm almost surprised to see you here after your ignominious defeat at the hands of young Lord Alexander Greysnowe last month."

The back of his neck heating, Dare made himself shrug. Only the most skilled swordsmen and swordswomen were invited to the fencing salons that Lady Ducharme, the baroness who served on the council as the Minister of Defense, held most mornings. He'd an open invitation, although he seldom attended because he preferred riding at the royal bay to reconnect with nature. This morning was the first he'd bothered to attend since before Summerday, but not due to the nearly fatal duel. He'd attended today because the approaching storm would make riding to the royal bay and back unpleasant.

He managed a wry smile despite his tight jaw. "The Greysnowes make too much of Lord Alexander besting me. 'Twas mere chance that he did—although the boy is skilled with a sword for his age." He nodded toward young Lord Morwynne, who was crossing swords with Lady Campbell while her husband Sir Ellis observed. "Almost as much as Lord Morwynne, and he's attended your fencing salons for the past three years."

Lady Ducharme's brows flew upward. "Intriguing. Perhaps I should invite Lord Alexander sometime. Lord Morwynne would enjoy meeting another skilled swordsman his own age." She chuckled. "Although I'll ensure Lord Alexander doesn't attend in poor weather when you're likely to join us. I don't want a nearly fatal duel in *my* sparring hall."

Dare hummed. He and Lord Alexander would never duel again. He'd been mad, and weakened by grief and too many tankards, to accept the first one. And now that he was soulbound to Annalise, he could *never* injure her brother. His chest tightened. Goddess, how he missed her. These past weeks apart, he'd felt as enervated as a marsh rabbit struggling to breathe atop a mountain.

Burying his loneliness, he gestured toward an empty sparring circle. "Shall we?"

Lady Ducharme nodded, and they entered the sparring circle and began to cross swords. As always, the baroness's superior skill and speed offset his greater size and strength, so their sword fight was intricate and lengthy, and they were both damp and panting by the end.

When he finally won with his twisting riposte slipping past her guard to touch her chest, the Campbells and Lord Morwynne, who'd drifted over to watch midway through, applauded with bright grins.

Then Sir Ellis drawled, "Amazing that you bested Lady Ducharme after recently being trounced by a mere boy."

Dare suppressed a grimace while he cleaned his sword. Why must everyone keep teasing him about that blasted duel? Hopefully, the tiresome gossip would subside after the king's summer masquerade in two weeks. With the guests disguised in costumes, such events inevitably engendered fresh scandals that court gossiped about for weeks.

Sheathing his sword, he arched his brows at Sir Ellis. "I had to prove my prowess somehow, and besting Lady Ducharme seemed the fastest way. Perhaps you could spread word of my victory at court?"

Lady Campbell chuckled, tucking silver-brown hair behind her ear. "We could, but I doubt any would believe us, given the Greysnowes' constant gloating."

Dare sighed. Doubtless true.

Tapping his fingers on his pommel, Lord Morwynne shook his head. "All these tales of court gossip make me even more determined to avoid court events, even though Mother says I should attend."

Lady Ducharme arched a brow. "You should attend court events if you intend to assume her position on the council one day. Otherwise, you'll feel overwhelmed when you do. Learning your new duties as a councilor is hard enough without also having to form alliances at court. I never would have thrived when I became the Minister of Defense twelve years ago if I hadn't formed my alliances beforehand."

Dare rubbed his beard to conceal his smile. The baroness's advice for young Lord Morwynne demonstrated why she was Calatini's best war strategist in generations, despite being born a gentry lady. Unlike the younger count, he rarely received such speeches since he'd no interest in politics. He simply wanted to return to Wildewall—with Annalise. His heart squeezed.

He sighed then said farewell before walking back to Ravenstone House through the howling deluge. Unlike normal, experiencing wild nature in the middle of Ormas didn't cheer him. He ached too much for Annalise. Plus, the storm was so strong that he was soaked when he reached the townhouse, despite his cloak spelled against rain.

Dare sighed again as he petted Raven and Bear, who'd thundered to his side as soon as he'd entered, then Lily, who'd sauntered over after them. Let his heartfelt letters soon sway Lord Greysnowe to forgo their families' feud. The other count hadn't responded so far, but perhaps his third letter, which he'd write in two days, would be the one that finally succeeded. Please, Goddess.

THE MORNING of his next letter to Lord Greysnowe, Dare galloped across the wet sand of the royal bay with his magical senses unfurled to gather the natural energy like usual. But then hooves thundered toward him, so he retracted his powers and halted Ebony before he crashed into Lord Alexander. He tensed as his heart tightened for Annalise yet again. If only she'd joined her brother like last time.

He swallowed a sigh. Although perhaps not, considering they'd conceal their attraction even worse now due to their soul-bond. Scrutinizing Annalise's brother, he inclined his head. "Good morning, Lord Alexander."

Lord Alexander inhaled then bent a bow in his saddle. "Good morning, Lord Ravenstone."

Dare blinked. The young hellion wasn't smirking or scowling this morning. Interesting.

But before he could speak, Lord Alexander straightened and leaned forward with a frown creasing his brow. "My lord, I must humbly apologize for challenging you to that duel and nearly killing you. I *never* meant to go so far."

Humming, Dare narrowed his eyes at Lord Alexander. From the younger lord's frown, he truly meant his apology. Dare's chest lightened, and he flashed a genial grin. "You sought to protect your sister. Though I've none of my own, I can under-stand that." He'd do anything to protect Annalise too. "And as far as nearly killing me, 'twas an accident. These things happen at duels—which is why sensible gentlemen avoid them."

Lord Alexander winced. "Yes." He studied Dare. "So you forgive me then?"

Dare smiled again. "Of course." He leaned forward. "Although I appreciate your apology. Only a truly decent gentleman would extend one, especially to his family's ancestral enemy."

His eyes gleaming, Lord Alexander smiled back. "And only another decent gentleman would accept that apology." He gestured past Dare. "Do you mind if we ride rather than simply staring at each other like gargoyles turned to stone by sunlight?"

Dare chuckled and pivoted Ebony the same direction as Lord Alexander's buckskin gelding. Annalise was the only person he wanted to stare at so. "I prefer being active if possible."

Lord Alexander grinned as they rode before the surf. "Me too." He slanted Dare a narrow glance. "Father mentioned you wrote him to seek peace between the Greysnowes and Raven-stones. Do you truly want that?"

Steering Ebony around some driftwood, Dare nodded. "I always have. Mother raised me to believe harming others would be akin to harming myself, so I could never embrace the feud. But after our duel," and being soulbound to Annalise, "I want peace between our families even more. The feud only destroys our families' future happiness and prosperity." By preventing the Greysnowes from accepting him as a son-in-law.

Lord Alexander leaned back in his saddle. "I agree."

Dare arched a brow. "Why do you? Both of your parents raised you to support the feud." And unlike Annalise, Lord Alexander couldn't be a soul healer since he was male, so he'd not innately oppose feuds like a healer would.

Snorting, Lord Alexander raised his eyes skyward. "Because Father and Mother are so obsessed with the feud that anyone of sense can see how ridiculous it was. Plus, Annalise has never approved of it, and we've always been close, despite our age difference."

Dare sighed and patted Ebony's neck. Having such a close sibling must be wonderful, not that he'd a chance to experience it. After Mother had almost died giving birth to him, Father had refused to risk losing her, no matter how she'd pleaded for another child. Dare forced himself to smile at Annalise's brother. "You and your sister are most fortunate, Lord Alexander. I longed for a sibling growing up, especially a close one."

Lord Alexander flashed a warm grin. "Call me Alex. Greysnowes and Ravenstones who don't embrace the feud mustn't be so formal."

Dare chuckled. Alex resembled Annalise in more than appearance—he'd her kindness as well. "Agreed. Call me Dare."

Alex leaned back in his saddle. "So, Dare, care to race to the cliffs? Winner earns a favor."

Dare grinned as his blood stirred. "Prepare to lose."

Guffawing, he and Alex thundered across the beach, sand flying everywhere. Just before the cliffs, Dare urged Ebony even faster, so he won the race by a head.

His gaze bright with laughter, Alex drooped in his saddle and moaned. "What sort of favor shall a Ravenstone demand from a Greysnowe? Walking naked through Ormas? A fortune in jewels? My firstborn son?"

Dare chuckled. "Nothing so extreme." Sobering, he arched his brows at Alex. "What advice can you give me to sway your father to end the feud?"

Alex straightened, a frown silencing his laughter. "Father despises losing. Perhaps if you make ending the feud a victory rather than surrender, he *might* listen."

Dare hummed and nodded. He could write that only a powerful gentleman could be gracious enough to end the feud. "Thank you, I'll attempt that."

He and Alex galloped back to Ormas, but to prevent feeding the feud by being seen together, Alex halted when Ormas appeared in the distance, and Dare rode the remaining stretch alone.

After tending Ebony, petting his magical pets, then changing, Dare grinned as he chanted a brief spell and waved his hand to activate his paired communication mirror. Although he couldn't reveal his soulbond with Annalise, he could at least tell Mother about his encounter with Alex. He blinked once the mirror glowed white and Mother appeared. From the trees behind her, she was out riding, rather than in her chambers like normal. They rarely carried the communication mirrors to avoid breaking them since they couldn't enchant another pair unless together. He smiled at Mother. "Out on a long ride today?"

Mother smoothed back her windswept hair. "The weather's been so fine I couldn't resist. But I didn't wish to miss your call, so I brought the communication mirror along. I insulated the mirror with an air-bubble spell before putting it in the satchel secured on my back."

He nodded. That spell *should* protect the communication mirror unless Mother fell from her mare, which she never did. "I must try the same sometime. Then I can show you places like the royal bay." He leaned forward. "Guess what happened when I was riding there this morning?"

Mother hummed. "What?"

Dare beamed and straightened. "Lord Alexander Greysnowe apologized for wounding me and wants to seek peace. He even provided advice on how to approach his father. Despite the feud, Alex and I are a lot alike, so I think we'll become excellent friends."

Her eyes flickering, Mother inclined her head. "That's wonderful." She paused then added, "Just be careful your fledgling friendship doesn't rebound and worsen the feud."

He almost winced. Which it might if Alex discovered he was soulbound to Annalise and became upset on her behalf. Like when Alex had caught him staring. He managed a smile. "How's Pearl?"

He and Mother discussed her new angelkitten's mischief then said goodbye. He sighed as he waved his hand to deactivate the communication mirror then set it on the windowsill to recharge. Hopefully, Mother's warning about Alex would never happen.

Dare headed to his study and wrote his third letter to Lord

Greysnowe, using Alex's advice. Despite that, he still heard nothing from the other count over the following week, although five days later, he did receive a note from Alex asking to ride at the royal bay the following morning.

After he and Alex had raced along the surf, Dare grimaced at the younger gentleman as he patted Ebony's damp withers. "Unfortunately, using your advice didn't encourage your father to answer my last letter."

Echoing Dare's grimace, Alex snorted and shook his head. "Somehow I'm not surprised. For some reason, Father and Mother have always been irrational about the feud. But *maybe* they'll eventually see reason if you keep trying." His tone evinced his doubt that his parents would ever end the feud.

Dare sighed and gripped Ebony's reins. Yet *something* had to succeed. He couldn't live the rest of his life with the ache of missing Annalise burning in his chest. Shoving that aside, he smiled and arched his brows at Alex. "Do you mind if I unfurl my powers to gather natural energy? I promise I shan't gather any from you."

Alex leaned forward in his saddle. "Powers? I didn't realize Ravenstones were witches too."

Dare hummed with a wry smile. Because Ravenstones weren't descended from a legendary witch like the Greysnowes. "Yes, Mother and I are Rhiannon-descendant nature witches."

Alex grinned. "Father and I are Rhiannon descendants too." He shook his head. "Although the least powerful you'll ever meet, and we're just ordinary witches. Mother is a witch as well, but not a Rhiannon descendant." He sighed. "Only poor Annalise has no powers."

Stilling, Dare eyed Alex. The younger gentleman appeared sincere, so Annalise's parents and brother definitely didn't know about her powers. No wonder Alex hadn't begged Annalise to heal him after their duel. Yet why had she never told her family? Because she didn't want them forcing a soulbond or exploiting her powers? His chest squeezing, he made himself smile at Alex. "Is gathering natural energy fine then?"

Alex waved a hand. "Of course." He chuckled. "You being a nature witch explains why the street boy I hired took days to find you—you were always riding in natural areas outside of Ormas."

Dare nodded as he unfurled his powers. "Most likely here at the royal bay since King Devon gave me permission to ride here whenever I wish." Then he fell silent as he gathered natural energy.

Once he finished, he and Alex galloped back to Ormas, again separating before anyone could see them together.

The following morning, Dare glowered at his blank paper while preparing to write his fourth letter to Annalise's father. What else could he try to sway Lord Greysnowe? Maybe she could provide advice that would help, unlike her brother's. His pulse quickened. Doubtless he'd see Annalise at the king's summer masquerade next week. But how could he approach her without anyone, especially her parents, realizing? Perhaps slipping out into the palace gardens would work. Even glances across the ballroom could arrange something so simple.

CHAPTER 9

At luncheon a week before the king's summer masquerade, Annalise suppressed a wince when Father snickered as he read then handed Mother the unlabeled letter their butler Wilson had just brought. Dare must have sent another plea to seek peace—he'd been sending them weekly since the duel. Not that they'd any impact on Mother and Father other than derision.

Reading the letter, Mother stiffened and frowned over her wine glass. "Alistair, you must do something about these letters. A Ravenstone, especially *him*, claiming to seek peace is ludicrous and must be part of some treacherous scheme. Not that we'd *ever* be so witless as to believe him. But 'tis clear he'll not quit sending them until we respond."

An ache suffused Annalise's chest. Because Dare was determined to convince Mother and Father to end the feud, so they'd accept him marrying her. If only that were possible. Why must Mother and Father be so obsessed with the feud? Couldn't they see that living in harmony would be better for everyone?

Father patted Mother's hand. "I'll devise something soon that shall make the obstinate whelp quit sending his deceitful letters." He grinned. "I already have a few ideas to discuss."

Her fingers clenching her knife and fork, Annalise forced herself to cut her baked fish with a faint smile. *Please let Father's idea not involve challenging Dare to another duel or something equally ridiculous.*

Mother flung Dare's letter on the table. "Later. We've more important matters to attend at the moment." She turned to Annalise. "Has King Devon asked to escort you to his summer masquerade yet?"

To feign serenity, Annalise swallowed her baked fish then sipped her wine. "No, but I expect he shall be at the Duke of Osbourne's card party tonight."

Mother pursed her lips. "Ensure he does. Masquerades are ideal for enticing reluctant suitors into proposing. Just ask your father."

Indigo love flaring about him, Father gave Mother an ardent glance. "I wasn't reluctant, Emmeline. I just needed time to get to know you better."

Her aura matching Father's, Mother blushed as she giggled and returned his ardent glance. "The masquerade definitely helped with that."

Warmth filling her chest, Annalise smiled at Mother and Father. For all their ambition and obsession with the Greysnowe-Ravenstone feud, they adored each other. And they loved her and Alex too, so their insistent matchmaking wasn't just fueled by their ambition and hunger to best the Ravenstones but also by their desire for their children to have the best. Unfortunately, their determination to achieve their goals often blinded them to others' natures, including hers and Alex's.

Tearing her gaze from Father, Mother turned back to Annalise. "So at Celeste's this afternoon, we must choose a costume that makes your beauty irresistible."

Annalise almost grimaced as she served herself scalloped tubers with bacon. King Devon wouldn't care about that any more than he'd cared about her natalday diamonds and deep-blue satin at the Escanas' ball over two weeks ago. She swallowed. Although the other gentlemen at court might. When not with the king, she'd likely spend the entire evening fending off unwanted advances, and such attempts were always bolder at masquerades since everyone wore masks. Wonderful.

Her heart squeezed while she finished her scalloped tubers. And to prevent feeding their soulbond, she must avoid the one gentleman whose advances she wanted. She sighed. At least her mask should conceal her reaction when she saw Dare for the first time since Summerday. Plus, Alex wouldn't be there to notice because he'd already declared his intentions to eschew the most exclusive court event of the season.

After luncheon, Annalise and Mother headed to Celeste's, the most fashionable dress shop in Ormas, likely because the influential Duchess of Childes patronized it. Although perhaps not—Celeste was a true artist, and her creations always accentuated the wearer's beauty while disguising any flaws.

Once Mother explained they required the perfect masquerade costume for Annalise, Celeste cocked her head and beckoned Annalise. "I know just the thing."

Mother remaining in the anteroom because Celeste only allowed recipients in her fitting rooms, Annalise followed the dressmaker and climbed onto the stool as her assistants closed the curtain. Hopefully, Celeste's idea wouldn't be too elaborate.

Celeste snapped her fingers at her assistants. "The sky-blue cambric, white wings, and matching feather mask." Once they scurried from the fitting room, she began measuring Annalise's shoulders. "With your coloring and beauty, you'll make the perfect siren, especially with your hair loose like theirs."

Annalise nodded. True, and her costume would be much less elaborate than some she'd endured at the king's summer masquerade during previous seasons. Once the dressmaker had finished her siren costume, she said, "Another exquisite creation, Celeste. Thank you."

When Annalise emerged from the fitting room, Mother leapt upright. "Well?"

Annalise almost chuckled. Although she only cared about clothes as part of her Lady Snow facade, Mother's delight whenever they visited Celeste's was endearing. "A siren."

Mother beamed. "Perfect!" She tapped her aquamarine necklace. "To enhance your costume's impact, don't say a word about it to anyone, not even your father or Alexander."

Annalise shrugged as they left. Enhancing the impact of a gown from Celeste was hardly necessary. "If you like."

On the carriage ride home, Mother sighed as indigo love pulsed about her. "I dressed as a siren for the king's summer masquerade the season your father courted me." Blushing, she giggled. "My costume helped him get to know me better, so he proposed the following morning."

Annalise blushed too. Please let Mother not describe further. Although Mother and Father's love was adorable, hearing details was embarrassing.

Mother reached across the carriage to squeeze her hand. "And I'm certain your siren costume shall entice King Devon to do the same. You'll be married within a month, and you'll have your own family by spring."

Humming, Annalise slid her hand free. If only she could explain that would never happen without creating discord between her and her parents.

Mother added as they alighted, "And don't forget to discuss the masquerade with the king tonight, but without revealing your costume."

Sighing, Annalise inclined her head. Although King Devon would probably ask about the masquerade tonight, he didn't care enough to quiz her about her costume, so she'd have no difficulty obeying Mother.

When Mother repeated her advice on the steps of Osbourne House that evening, Annalise sighed and nodded again before they greeted the elderly Duke of Osbourne then joined the other guests.

She blinked at King Devon as he approached—silver motes

swirled just outside his red aura, so some kind of magic was influencing him. She peered closer. But not human magic given its glittering intensity. The silver motes must be nightmara magic. Should she warn the king? She swallowed. She'd need to reveal her secret powers to do so. She eyed the powerful protection charm glowing on his left wrist. 'Twas still active, so the nightmara's magic mustn't be harming or bewitching him. Perhaps the nightmara had contacted King Devon to prepare for their treaty negotiations in a few weeks. She needn't expose herself for such a trifle. She sighed as she accepted his arm. Yet she couldn't become entangled in whatever nightmara magic surrounded him, so she really must encourage him to pursue his true queen instead of escorting her.

As he led her to a table to play cards, King Devon arched his brows. "Shall we attend the summer masquerade together?" When she nodded, he continued, "We can meet in the royal anteroom and enter the masquerade together."

Suppressing a wry smile, Annalise settled in the chair he held out for her across from the Duke and Duchess of Childes, his closest relatives. As expected, King Devon hadn't bothered to ask about her costume. "As you like."

So when Annalise entered the palace for the king's summer masquerade, she glided to the royal anteroom, while Mother and Father, dressed as desert elves, headed to the ballroom. She smoothed her siren costume as she waited for King Devon. Goddess, was she ready to see Dare again? Please let her feather mask be enough to conceal her reaction.

Then King Devon, the nightmara magic about him as strong as before, joined her in the royal anteroom, and they swept into the buzzing ballroom.

Her heart quickening and soul straining toward Dare, she couldn't help glancing across the ballroom to meet his intense gaze. She inhaled. How had he found a dragon costume that precisely matched the bronze motes in his aura? Plus, with his active air, rugged features, and costume's massive wings, he made the perfect dragon in drake form—the rare magical creatures were all born male and were exceptionally brawny and magnetic to attract mates from other intelligent creatures. Becoming a dragon's mate was a risky proposition because a dragon could only breed after transforming his mate into a female dragon through perilous magic.

A prickle skittered across her skin, but she kept returning Dare's stare, even while greeting guests with King Devon. She only forced herself to quit when King Devon led her out for the first waltz. King Devon might notice if she ignored him the entire time. Yet she stiffened when Lady Blaine approached Dare, and they began dancing as well. The fashionable and sultry countess was known to be hunting for a new husband now that her year of mourning had ended.

To distract herself from Dare dancing with Lady Blaine, Annalise encouraged King Devon to pursue a lady he wanted as his queen. She even suggested some of the ladies dancing around them, but the king rejected them all. Then near the end of their waltz, she almost winced as a dryad surrounded by a spell brighter than the sun slipped into the ballroom. Was that the reclusive Miss Keyes? When King Devon noticed her looking past him, she suggested Miss Keyes as his potential queen, even though Lord Beza Hawke was already whisking Miss Keyes into the palace gardens.

Once the first waltz ended, Annalise and King Devon began walking a circuit of the ballroom, while Lady Blaine clung to Dare's arm near the refreshments table. Her stomach hardening, Annalise swallowed and twirled her flute of sparkling wine against her lips without tasting it. She must leave before she slapped Lady Blaine or leapt into Dare's arms. Not only would such mad behavior feed their soulbond, but her parents would surely realize what had happened at the duel and discover her powers. No, she must flee and avoid Dare for the rest of the masquerade.

So when she and King Devon reached the entrance to the palace gardens, she flashed a glittering smile and said, "I'm sweltering in all these feathers. I must take a turn about the gardens to refresh myself."

King Devon handed their flutes of sparkling wine to a nearby servant. "I'll escort you."

Annalise stiffened. King Devon joining her would only make it harder to avoid Dare. "No, no. Half of court would follow if you leave too. I'll be fine alone." Before King Devon could respond, she curtsied then glided into the gardens as Dare strode away from Lady Blaine.

Inhaling the roses, gardenias, and jasmine perfuming the balmy air, she smiled while she swept through the gorgeous gardens turned to shades of gray and inky shadows by the full moon's cool light. Since the masquerade had just begun, she encountered no other guests, although she sensed Dare following her as relentless as a hellhound on the scent. Thanks to their soulbond, she could sense his aura whenever they were close, not only when she could see him like with everyone else.

Annalise hastened faster. Doubtless Dare could sense her as well, and he seemed determined to find her, so she must keep moving to elude him. She rolled her shoulders to ease the ache from wearing her siren costume. The heavy, white wings slowed her flight, made her a beacon in the darkness, and prevented her from slipping into hidden corners. Too bad she couldn't remove her wings without a maid's help.

She kept moving until she reached a romantic garden along the far edge of the palace gardens. She halted and winced away from the blinding white glow surrounding the couple dancing as one. Somehow, she'd stumbled upon Miss Keyes and Lord Beza. She squinted at the potent magic around them—whatever witch had created that spell was more powerful than any she'd met, a Rhiannon descendant like no other. She peered closer then gasped. And a *seer* from the silver motes swirling inside the magic. Seers weren't as rare as soul healers, but they weren't common. Where had Miss Keyes unearthed one? She shuddered. They were also the only class of witch besides soul healers able to read auras without a spell, so a seer would immediately recognize her as a soul healer. Hopefully, she'd never encounter Miss Keyes's seer.

Although Miss Keyes and Lord Beza were too engrossed with each other to notice anyone else, Annalise silently backed from the romantic garden until she collided with a hard body behind her. Tingling warmth flooding her, she gasped as arms covered in bronze scales wrapped about her waist.

Dare murmured in her ear, "Caught you at last." He paused. "Is that *Miss Keyes* dancing scandalously close to Lord Beza Hawke? And *what* spell are they using? Its magic is even more blinding than yours."

Annalise jerked from his embrace then darted past him into another garden. She *never* should have halted at Miss Keyes's spell. Dare wouldn't have caught her otherwise. And now that he had, he'd probably not leave. She swirled to face him, fisting her hands on her hips. "Please go. We mustn't risk feeding our impossible soulbond."

Dare strode over to grasp her hand. "I can't. We must talk."

Her heart fluttering, she swallowed. "No."

She attempted to wrench her hand free, but his grip was so firm that she rebounded into him instead. As their chests pressed together, she shivered and stared up into his amber eyes. Oh, Goddess. She licked her lips.

Dare groaned then lowered his head until his mouth brushed hers.

Annalise stilled, her pulse surging and the ache in her chest easing as their souls meshed. She should really withdraw. But instead, she wrapped her arms about his neck and deepened their kiss.

CHAPTER 10

As Annalise returned his kiss and her heady honeysuckle scent surrounded him, Dare shuddered and wrapped his arms about her beneath her snowy wings. For the first time since Summerday, the ache gnawing his chest eased while their mouths fused and souls meshed, but his body hardened and pulse throbbed at their lengthy kiss. Goddess, she was more intoxicating than the spiritmead distilled in Wildewall's mountain glens. He must taste her deeper.

When his tongue brushed hers, Annalise sighed and began echoing him. Then she jerked back and shoved his chest, while wrenching their souls apart. "No, we mustn't!"

He froze then lowered his arms. He couldn't take more than she was prepared to give. But when she started to dart away, he grasped her hand again. "Stop, we must talk, remember?"

Annalise grimaced, muddy-blue regret swirling about her. "Fine. But no touching. That only feeds our soulbond and instigates more kissing, which is even more dangerous."

Dare released her hand, his heart twisting. "I enjoyed kissing you. More than I've ever enjoyed kissing anyone."

Glancing away, Annalise swallowed and sank onto a stone bench. "'Tis why kissing is so dangerous. Plus, our souls meshed unbidden when we kissed. If we indulge, we'll soon never want to stop. And if you think our soulbond is impossible to ignore now, a consummated soulbond is *much* stronger. We'll be unable to keep our soulbond secret then—or the child I'd likely conceive."

Their massive wings almost touching, he sat on the opposite end of the stone bench as heat suffused him at Annalise carrying his child. Yet the strong-magic contraceptive charm he wore about his neck would surely prevent that—unlike standard contraceptive charms, 'twas meant to work around potent magic like theirs. His skin cooled, and he swallowed. So no point even discussing her possible pregnancy.

Instead, he arched a brow. "Are you certain we should keep our soulbond secret? We're both old enough to marry without permission. Perhaps we should simply marry then face your parents." Although they'd have to explain more than just their soulbond when they did, and her parents would doubtless be upset she'd concealed her powers, which wouldn't help her parents accept her marrying a Ravenstone. He frowned. "Facing them shan't be pleasant, but at least it shall be over. We can return to Wildewall and start building our life together."

Annalise gasped then winced. "Impossible while King Devon remains unwed. Mother and Father would consider our marriage a treacherous scheme to prevent me from becoming queen."

Dare smoothed his beard below his dragon mask. Her ambitious parents *would* likely believe that, especially since they could have used her secret powers to bind her and King Devon so she had to become queen. They'd accuse him of unearthing her powers then tricking Alex into nearly killing him to force her into forming a soulbond with him rather than King Devon. And they'd never end the feud if they thought that.

He sighed. "I suppose we can wait until King Devon marries. Doubtless it shan't be long since he must have a queen before the nightmara delegation arrives in a few weeks."

Annalise laced her fingers together in her lap. "I attempted to encourage him to pursue his true queen tonight, but he rejected every lady I suggested."

His stomach hardening, Dare gritted a faint smile. Perhaps because King Devon truly wanted Annalise—not only was she the most beautiful lady in Calatini, but she was kind and strong as well, so she'd make the perfect queen. "I'm surprised King Devon hasn't asked you to marry him."

Annalise's eyes widened behind her feather mask. "Oh, no, he'd never do that. In addition to inflaming the feud if he did, I told King Devon before he began escorting me that I'd no interest in becoming queen." She shrugged. "'Tis *why* he began escorting me."

Dare blinked at her, his tension easing. "King Devon has been escorting you to court events for over three years *because* you'd never marry him?"

Annalise shrugged again. "King Devon's supposed courtship has always been a convenient pretense. Since he knew I was uninterested, he could escort me without worrying he was raising my expectations and could abandon me whenever state affairs intruded. My presence protects him from ladies only interested in becoming queen, and his escort prevents Mother and Father from shoving me at unwed dukes or their heirs."

Leaning toward her, Dare grinned. His clever Annalise. "How did you and King Devon form that convenient pretense?"

Annalise hummed. "The season you remained in Wildewall to mourn your father's passing, King Devon rescued me from Mr. Winston attempting to kiss me on a secluded balcony to force a betrothal."

Dare almost growled, his hands fisting. Fortune-hunting cad. Not punching Winston when they next met would be near impossible.

Annalise pursed her lips. "While talking afterward, I mentioned I much preferred Wildewall to court and would never want the onus of becoming queen. Soon after, King Devon asked if he could escort me to the Duchess of Childes's spring ball as friends. I accepted because I thought 'twould allow me time to find a trustworthy gentleman who saw me as a person, not just a renowned beauty with wealthy parents."

His fists relaxing, Dare swallowed and gripped the stone bench to avoid taking her hand. "I always saw you as a person. A likeminded lady with deep kindness, serene strength, and powerful magic akin to mine."

Annalise swayed toward him as indigo tenderness glowed about her. "I know. 'Tis why I could never forget our secret encounter during our first season." The indigo about her vanishing, she recoiled. "But marriage between us has always been impossible because of the feud. And being soulbound doesn't change that, which is why we *must* avoid each other."

Dare eyed Annalise. She was clearly determined to resist their soulbond, and as a gentleman, he must obey her wishes. "Very well. We can continue avoiding each other—for now." He leaned toward her. "Although you should tell your family that you're a soul healer, so you at least don't have that secret between you." And 'twould make revealing their soulbond easier later. "Why have you never told them about your powers?"

Annalise sighed. "When I showed my former nursemaid Alice the robin I'd soul-healed, she warned me never to reveal my powers to anyone, even Mother and Father. Greysnowes have a history of forcing their soul healer daughters to form soulbonds with advantageous gentlemen, and Alice wanted me to marry for love."

A pang darting through him, he swallowed. And no matter how powerful, a soulbond wasn't the same as love. "I see. But why have you never told Alex? You two seem close, so he'd surely keep your secrets from your parents and everyone else."

Annalise shook her head. "Yes, but I couldn't burden Alex with my secrets, and more people knowing secrets makes them harder to keep." She paused and narrowed her eyes at him. "Since when do you call my brother *Alex*?"

Dare coughed. Of course she'd noticed that. "Since last week when he found me at the royal bay to apologize for the duel and nearly killing me. We're a lot alike, so I think we could become excellent friends one day."

Annalise flashed a wry smile. "Especially if you offer to teach him your best sword moves. 'Tis why he wanted to cross swords with you at first."

Dare chuckled. That explained Alex pestering him to fight despite not embracing the feud. "I'll make sure to offer when I see him next." He sagged. "I wish ending the feud with your parents was as easy as with you and Alex. Your father hasn't responded to any of my letters, and we must communicate to end the feud. Any suggestions?"

Annalise winced. "Mother and Father shall never end the feud. And they assume your letters are part of some treacherous Ravenstone scheme."

His chest tightening, he grimaced. Just like they'd assume that about his and Annalise's soulbond. What could he do to make them see the truth? Surely his letters would succeed eventually—they had to.

Annalise leaned toward him, her gaze dark. "Mother and Father are planning to respond somehow soon. Perhaps you should quit your letters to avoid provoking them."

Dare set his jaw. If he didn't attempt to end the feud, then he and Annalise could never marry and build a life together. "I'll keep sending my letters, regardless. We can't live our entire lives like this."

Annalise sighed as muddy-white loneliness surrounded her. "We should return to the masquerade. Mother and Father have doubtless noticed my absence, and we must start avoiding each other."

He grimaced. Too bad they couldn't remain in the quiet garden together rather than returning to the teeming ballroom. Masquerades just before the unveiling were raucous. "I suppose."

Sighing again, Annalise smoothed her sky-blue skirt. "Although I'm not looking forward to fending off the advances of gentleman emboldened by wearing masks and too much sparkling wine."

Dare stiffened. There would be plenty of those thanks to her siren costume. With her white-blonde hair loose, resplendent ballgown, and white wings, her otherworldly beauty was irresistible—she was more enthralling than an actual siren. And once they returned, he couldn't protect her if they were avoiding each other. "Perhaps you should remain with Alex for the rest of the masquerade."

Her brows rising, Annalise hummed. "Alex isn't here. He's decided to stop attending court events."

Dare suppressed a growl. The young hellion who'd challenged him to a duel to protect his sister should have attended a masquerade to do the same. "Well, he should have attended this one to protect you."

Annalise lifted her chin. "I can protect myself by reading auras. Not only can I sense people's moods from the color pulsing across their base aura, but when needed, I can slip away unseen then avoid them since I see the glow of approaching auras."

He frowned. Avoiding others wasn't enough to truly protect her. "Even with reading auras, you can't match a man's strength. Do you know any defense or attack spells?"

Sniffing, Annalise shrugged. "Soul healers can't do ordinary magic. We can only perform soul-healing, read auras, and communicate with the melissae. But I've protected myself just fine so far—without anyone's interference." She shooed him toward the palace. "You should return to the masquerade first and dance again to prevent gossip. To avoid unwanted advances, I'll remain hidden until the unveiling."

Dare gritted a smile. He'd not leave Annalise alone unprotected, despite her protests. He rose and extended a hand. "Only if you accompany me back to the palace. I must be near in case you require help."

Annalise rose as well but didn't take his hand. "Fine, but no touching, remember?"

As they walked through the palace gardens without speaking but with their wings brushing, tingling warmth flooded him. He clasped his hands behind his back to resist taking her arm. Yet he nearly yanked her into his embrace when she shoved him into an empty water garden, whispering, "People approaching."

His pulse surged and body tightened while they waited for the others to pass. Goddess, if only he could kiss her again and truly taste her this time.

But soon they were alone once more, so they resumed their walk—almost running now—back to the palace. Dare left Annalise in a secluded anteroom near the ballroom's main door then returned to the gardens to use a different entrance.

Once he slipped back inside the sweltering ballroom, Lady Blaine slid her arm through his and purred, "Lord Ravenstone, there you are. The last waltz is about to start. Our earlier dance was so delightful. Please say you'll partner me again."

Dare stilled and almost sighed. The sultry countess was hunting for a new husband, and even without Annalise, he'd not be interested. Lady Blaine was too much a creature of court to ever be happy living in Wildewall. Yet dancing with her would keep him from being connected to Annalise, so he forced a genial smile. "If you like."

Once they began dancing, Lady Blaine tilted her head and squeezed his shoulder. "Are you attending my water party tomorrow? 'Tis my first event since my year of mourning ended and shall be marvelous."

His heart quickening, he nodded. Doubtless the fashionable countess would invite both the Ravenstones and the Greysnowes to prove her influence, so he'd see Annalise again. Although there'd be no gardens to slip into for time alone. "I always enjoy outdoor events."

Lady Blaine flashed a coy grin. "Excellent. You must open the dancing with me."

Dare tensed. If he accepted, Lady Blaine would assume he was interested in marrying her and would never leave him alone. "A Ravenstone opening the dancing with the most fashionable lady at court would infuriate the Greysnowes and feed the feud."

Lady Blaine opened her mouth, but before she could reply, the bells began tolling midnight, and everyone stilled for the unveiling. Everyone except the sparkling mermaid, who darted past them during the final ring and careened into Annalise by the ballroom door.

As the mermaid fled, he met Annalise's wide gaze, and desire crackled between them yet again. He clenched his hands to prevent himself from approaching her. He started when Lady Blaine chuckled. Had she noticed the ardent stare between him and Annalise? "What?"

Twirling her firecat mask, Lady Blaine nodded at King Devon, who was hurtling from the ballroom after the mermaid without even acknowledging Annalise, the lady he'd escorted to the masquerade. "I suspect King Devon has fallen in love at last. Once he met that mermaid, he flirted like a rakehell and refused to release her."

Dare blinked while removing his dragon mask. How unlike King Devon. His chest lightened. But if the king married another, the Greysnowes couldn't accuse him of preventing Annalise from becoming queen. "Fortunate, considering the nightmara delegation arrives soon."

Lady Blaine chuckled again as she gestured at Annalise's parents, who glowered beside the Duchess of Wildewall. "I doubt Lord and Lady Greysnowe think so. They've been pestering the poor Duchess of Wildewall since King Devon began ignoring their daughter for his mermaid." She turned to Annalise, who was gliding toward her parents with a serene smile and her feather mask in one hand. "Lady Annalise reacted by disappearing for the entire masquerade. Watching another lady steal the king's attention must have been too difficult for her."

He hummed since he couldn't risk discussing Annalise. He'd likely reveal too much, and Lady Blaine would realize Annalise wasn't the only one who'd disappeared. And the fashionable countess mustn't connect him and Annalise—she might gossip if she did. To escape Lady Blaine, he bowed and said, "I must go. I'll see you at your water party tomorrow."

Lady Blaine swept a curtsy with another coy grin. "I look forward to it."

Dare swallowed as he strode away. At least someone was.

CHAPTER 11

When the carriage approached the royal bay holding Lady Blaine's water party, Mother said, for the fifth time since the king's summer masquerade yesterday, "Remember, Annalise, you must find King Devon as soon as we arrive. Don't let that wanton mermaid fabricated by the treacherous Ravenstones beguile him again."

Staring out the carriage window into the night, Annalise suppressed a sigh. Dare and his family had nothing to do with the king's mysterious mermaid—although doubtless the nightmara and Miss Keyes's seer did. When she and the mermaid had careened into each other by the ballroom door, she'd gawked at the nightmara's and seer's silver motes surrounding the mermaid. The glittering nightmara magic had swirled outside the mermaid's devoted indigo aura just like it had for King Devon, while the blinding magic of Miss Keyes's seer had glowed about the mermaid's enchanted ballgown.

Annalise smiled. Yet her surprise at the powerful magic surrounding the king's mermaid had transformed to delight moments later as King Devon hurtled after his mysterious lady. He'd found his true queen at last. Turning back to Mother and Father, she inclined her head as the carriage halted at the edge of the cliffs. "I'll make sure to speak with King Devon." To congratulate him.

She alighted then eyed the crowd following the white witchlights illuminating the winding path down the cliffs and across the beach. At the bay, the crowd boarded the many barges tied together and blazing with color-changing witchlights. All those witchlights must have cost Lady Blaine a fortune.

Her soulbond flaring, she glided down the path after Mother and Father. Dare was somewhere amidst the crowd. Not surprising. Although no councilor or duchess, Lady Blaine was influential enough to invite both Greysnowes and Ravenstones to her events. Annalise's stomach hardened. Would the fashionable countess corner Dare again tonight? Lady Blaine had seized both his dances at the masquerade, so she must want him as her next husband.

Annalise relaxed when they boarded the first barge. Lady Blaine was fluttering her lashes and leaning toward Lord Beza Hawke just ahead of them, so she mustn't seriously want Dare. Thank the Goddess. Although they could never marry because of the feud, watching another lady pursue Dare was like being stung by a swarm of irate melissae.

After they greeted Lady Blaine and began circulating, Father grunted while handing Mother and Annalise glasses of strawberry wine. "I see Lady Blaine invited that treacherous whelp Ravenstone."

As Mother grimaced, Annalise sipped her strawberry wine and let herself glance toward Dare, who was between Lady Ducharme and the Campbells. Her heart surged at the genial grin glinting amid his black beard as he conversed with his friends. She yanked her gaze away before their eyes met. Mother and Father were right beside her and might notice her reaction.

Father arched his brows at Mother. "Once Annalise is with King Devon, we should inform Ravenstone that his mermaid scheme shan't succeed."

Annalise swallowed and tensed. If her parents approached

Dare, Father would attempt a blow, while Mother would cheer and interject barbs. Someone, likely Father, would end up in the royal bay. She forced a serene smile. "Perhaps you should avoid Lord Ravenstone tonight. King Devon doesn't like when Greysnowes and Ravenstones brawl."

Her mouth pinched, Mother nodded. "A brawl, no matter how justified, would curb King Devon's courtship of Annalise. And we can't let a Ravenstone's schemes defeat us. We better wait to approach Ravenstone." She scrutinized the crowded barge. "I don't see King Devon here; let's continue to the next one."

Not glancing at Dare as she and her parents glided past him, Annalise twirled her glass before her lips. At least she'd prevented a brawl, but for how long? Mother and Father could never forget grievances they ascribed to the Ravenstones.

She and her parents checked the many teeming barges, but they didn't spot King Devon. At the last barge, Mother hummed and said, "Lord Treyvan might be able to tell us where King Devon is tonight."

When Father nodded, Annalise smothered a useless protest. As King Devon's cousin and best friend, Lord Treyvan should know, but interrogating him about the king was brazen. She sighed yet followed Mother and Father back to the first barge.

She almost winced when after the briefest pleasantries, Mother flashed a glittering smile at Lord and Lady Treyvan then asked, "Where's King Devon this evening?"

Although the skin about his eyes tightened, Lord Treyvan only replied, "At the palace."

Her freckled face wan, Lady Treyvan added, "He must ensure everything is prepared for his mermaid."

Annalise scrutinized Lady Treyvan. No gray darkened her bold orange aura, so she wasn't ill, and her aura was more intense about her waist—pregnant, likely three months given her aura's intensity. Surprising her mother-in-law the Duchess of Childes hadn't shared that with all of court yet.

Mother tsked and shook her head. "Surely King Devon shan't abandon Annalise after courting her for years. Anyone can see she'll make a wonderful queen and mother."

Father harrumphed. "That mermaid was nothing more than a masquerade flirtation."

As Lord and Lady Treyvan shared a glance, Annalise stiffened and drained her strawberry wine. So embarrassing. Before anyone else could speak, she murmured, "Everything shall resolve as intended in due time."

Mother pursed her lips. "We must greet the Duke of Oakmoor. Excuse us." She gripped Annalise's arm and drew her across the barge. "King Devon hearing about you flirting with the duke shall remind him that he may lose the perfect wife and queen if he keeps neglecting you."

Annalise hummed, tugging her arm free. Except King Devon wouldn't care about that. Hopefully, he'd introduce his mermaid to court soon, so Mother and Father's futile attempts to make her queen would end. Although then they'd matchmake and shove her at other influential gentlemen. She swallowed a sigh as Mother and Father greeted the rakehell duke with obsequious smiles.

His erratic magic flickering brighter this evening, the Duke of Oakmoor swept a bow and kissed Mother's then Annalise's hand. "Your and your daughter's dazzling beauty illuminate the evening more than Lady Blaine's entrancing witchlights, Lady Greysnowe."

As Mother giggled, Annalise extracted her hand. At least with Mother and Father beside her, the rakehell duke wouldn't attempt to kiss her like he had during their dance at the Duchess of Wildewall's ball. Not that his attempt had been serious— unlike Dare's kiss in the palace gardens. Tingling warmth echoed through her.

While Father grumbled at the duke for flirting with Mother, Annalise stiffened when Lady Blaine finished welcoming her guests and sashayed straight to Dare. Why wasn't she pursuing

Lord Beza instead? As Lady Blaine caressed Dare's arm, Annalise clenched her empty wine glass. If only she could shove the sultry countess over the barge railing into the dark waters below.

The Duke of Oakmoor coughed. "Lady Annalise, are you well?"

Annalise wrenched her gaze from Dare removing Lady Blaine's hand from his arm. No, she wasn't well, but she'd be even worse if she kept betraying her reaction to Dare.

Mother and Father peered at her then Mother frowned and said, "You do look flushed."

Her chest squeezing, Annalise gritted a weak smile to feign nausea. "The swaying of the barges is bothering me."

Indigo concern pulsing about them, Mother and Father exchanged a glance. Mother took Annalise's arm and replied, "We should leave at once then."

Annalise sighed. Her lie had averted Mother and Father from discovering her soulbond with Dare. Yet they'd eventually realize the truth if she kept betraying herself. Hopefully, she could learn control before she saw Dare again.

SHORTLY AFTER DAWN the following morning, Annalise slipped from her chambers with Finn for her morning walk and encountered Alex leaving his chambers as well. She beamed. Because he was still avoiding Mother and Father, she'd not seen him since before the king's summer masquerade. "Care to join me on my walk?"

His gaze darting away, Alex waved toward his riding clothes. "Thanks, but I'm riding to the royal bay."

She licked her lips as an ache flooded her chest. Doubtless he was meeting Dare. Too bad Alex would realize her and Dare's soulbond if she joined them. She couldn't burden him with that or risk Mother and Father discovering it too. Besides, she still must avoid Dare to not feed their soulbond. She smiled as they began downstairs. "A ride sounds enjoyable, but Finn requires a long walk this morning. He attempted to eat Rain and Aria yesterday."

Alex chuckled while he petted Finn sauntering on the banister beside them. "Maybe you should feed him more."

Annalise grinned. "Finn certainly thinks so, the glutton." She tsked then glanced at Alex. "By the way, you can quit avoiding Mother and Father now. They've ceased gloating about the duel because a mysterious mermaid captivated King Devon at his summer masquerade. Mother and Father are blaming the Raven-stones, of course."

Alex raised his eyes skyward. "Like they do whenever anything doesn't proceed as they planned. So ridiculous." He nodded while they headed outside. "But tomorrow, I'll join everyone for breakfast again."

Warmth flooding her chest, she embraced him. "Good, I've missed you."

Alex squeezed her then stepped back with a wry grin. "You'd miss me more if I were executed for murdering Father and Mother because they kept praising me for nearly killing Lord Ravenstone." After she chuckled at his quip, he waved and headed to the stables. "Until tomorrow."

The following morning, she beamed when she entered the breakfast room. Alex was sitting in his typical seat and devouring a full plate. She served herself plenty of eggs, beef-steak, and tubers then sat beside him and arched a brow. "How was your ride yesterday?"

Yellow happiness glowing about him, Alex grinned. "Exciting."

Annalise hid her echoing grin behind her teacup. Doubtless because, like he'd promised at the king's summer masquerade, Dare had offered to teach Alex his best sword moves. She swallowed. Dare was truly the most kindhearted and wonderful gentleman.

Then Mother and Father sailed into the breakfast room, and Mother pursed her lips at Annalise's heaped plate like always.

Annalise smiled at them despite her clogged throat. Not that Mother and Father would ever see how wonderful Dare was. He was a "treacherous" Ravenstone, after all.

Once they sat across the table and served themselves breakfast, Father nodded at Alex. "Good to see you finally. What have you been doing the past month?"

Alex shrugged as he finished his eggs and bacon. "Exploring Ormas mostly."

Cutting her beefsteak, Annalise sighed. If only she could disappear for a month with such a meager explanation.

Mother leaned forward as she stirred sugar into her tea. "You should have attended court events with us. If you'd been at the king's summer masquerade, you could have distracted that Ravenstone mermaid who beguiled King Devon."

Annalise and Alex traded a wry glance, then Alex murmured, "Could I? A future count doesn't compare to a king."

Annalise swallowed the last of her beefsteak. Although she usually remained silent when Mother and Father discussed their ambitions to prevent discord, she must prepare them for King Devon marrying another. "And given how King Devon chased after his mermaid when she fled, I doubt he would have allowed another gentleman to distract her."

Mother and Father stared at her, muddy-blue surprise flaring about them. Then Father snorted and said, "King Devon had no right to chase after another lady while courting you."

Almost wincing, Annalise made herself shrug. Perhaps she shouldn't have allowed Mother and Father to assume King Devon was courting her. They were upset on her behalf and likely wouldn't believe her if she explained his escort hadn't been serious.

After trading a frown with Father, Mother shook her head then said, "Guess what we received this morning? An invitation from the Duchess of Childes for a fete next month celebrating

Lady Treyvan expecting the duchess's first grandchild." She narrowed her eyes at Alex. "And I expect you to attend. No one refuses the Duchess of Childes."

Alex hummed while he ate his last bite then rose. "Perhaps someone should."

As he strode from the breakfast room, Annalise smiled behind her teacup. Why did Mother and Father always forget that ordering Alex to do something because everyone else did just made him refuse?

Mother scowled then turned to Annalise. "We must purchase new ballgowns for the Duchess of Childes's fete from Celeste's. I'll schedule our dress fittings this afternoon."

Annalise nodded and began her eggs. The Duchess of Childes's favorite dress shop would soon be swamped since everyone, other than Alex, attended the duchess's elaborate court events. Annalise inhaled, her heart quickening. Dare would surely be there. Would it be the next court event they'd both attend? No, his friends the Campbells were hosting a ball later this week to celebrate their wedding vow reaffirmation, and the Duchess of Wildewall's garden party was the week before the fete. She and her parents were attending both, and doubtless he would too.

So at Campbell House a few days later, she couldn't help glancing about for Dare, but he never arrived at his friends' ball. When the dancing began, she sighed and let Lord Morwynne, a count Alex's age and a friend of the Campbells like Dare, lead her onto the floor, despite Mother and Father wanting her to dance with the Duke of Oakmoor.

During her dance with Lord Morwynne, who was surprisingly affable considering his superior and devious mother, Annalise concealed her ache at missing Dare behind a serene smile. 'Twas just as well he wasn't here, given her control crumbled whenever she saw him. She really must quit hoping to see him. But how could she when her entire soul yearned for him?

CHAPTER 12

$\mathcal{A}$ week after Lady Blaine's water party at the royal bay, Dare met Alex on the cliffs there two hours after dawn for their third intentional ride together—this time with swords as they'd arranged during their previous ride. He grinned at the younger gentleman and nodded at the copse of ash trees along the rocky stream that cascaded down the cliffs at the northern end of the royal bay. "I thought we could tie Ebony and Biscuit here while we practice nearby. 'Tis the only spot of cover for them, and sword fighting on sand is messier than on grass."

Alex chuckled as he leapt from his saddle. "But I was anticipating my valet Jack's grumbles when I returned covered in sand."

Coughing to disguise his laugh, Dare shook his head and dismounted as well. Of course, the young hellion would enjoy teasing his poor valet. "How about I promise to provide some grass stains instead?"

His eyes gleaming, Alex smirked while they secured Ebony and Biscuit then strode to the flat area beside the stream. "Sounds perfect."

They faced each other and bowed, and Dare opened with a rapid feint then attack to test Alex's reflexes. Like during their duel, Alex deftly parried then riposted, and their sword fight began in earnest.

Yet Dare's thoughts kept wandering to Annalise. After their desperate kiss and intimate conversation at the king's summer masquerade, seeing her from a distance at Lady Blaine's water party had just whetted the ache filling his soul. And that had been a week ago, so he was more ravenous for Annalise than a wyvern was for gold deer after being starved a year. Perhaps hearing how she was from Alex would help. Not that he could ask directly without revealing their soulbond, and she'd not want that.

So once they'd traded several engagements, Dare arched his brows then lunged forward and asked, "How are things at home?"

Alex grunted as he parried. "You expect me to converse while crossing swords?"

Dare stilled to prompt Alex to attack. Fighting should prevent the perceptive younger gentleman from noticing his continued interest in Annalise. "Doing both sharpens your mind, which is essential to being a skilled swordsman."

His sword glinting as he thrust, Alex grimaced. "Things at home are fine, I suppose. Father and Mother have quit gloating about our duel to gripe about the king's mysterious mermaid. They blame you for her, by the way."

Sighing, Dare danced backward then advanced with a feint. Not surprising. He'd never convince the Greysnowes to end the feud at this rate. "Should I mention I know nothing about King Devon's mermaid when I write my next letter to your father?"

Alex snorted as he parried then attacked. "Don't bother. Father and Mother are too obsessed with the feud to believe you." He sighed. "Plus, they're fixated on Annalise recapturing King Devon's interest. Annalise mentioned they've been shoving her at the Duke of Oakmoor to make the king jealous."

His chest clenching, Dare almost fumbled his circle-parry. How could Annalise's parents be so witless? The rakehell duke would attempt to seduce her. And since few invited both Raven-stones and Greysnowes to their events, he couldn't rescue her when the duke made unwanted advances.

Feinting then riposting, Alex flashed a broad grin. "Although Annalise said she's managed to elude their worst matchmaking schemes by securing dances with other unwed gentlemen—but ones already pursuing other ladies or uninterested in marriage."

Dare sighed as he flicked aside Alex's sword. At least Annalise had her parents' matchmaking well in hand. Too bad he couldn't help her. "Clever of your sister."

Alex chuckled. "I know." He sighed and lunged with a thrust. "Poor Annalise. She's endured court for six years, and she's still not found a gentleman she wants courting her. I wish she would."

Dare's heart wrenched. She already had. He darted around Alex's thrust to press his sword against the younger gentleman's chest. "She shall one day."

Panting, Alex lowered his sword and grinned at Dare. "An exciting fight. Show me that last move slower."

Once he'd demonstrated and Alex repeated him until he'd mastered the evasive thrust, Dare cleaned and sheathed his sword then clapped Alex's shoulder. "Enough sword fighting for today. Let's cool down with a ride on the beach."

Alex waggled his brows but cleaned and sheathed his sword as well. "But what about my grass stains?"

Dare tsked. Outrageous hellion. "Another time, perhaps."

Alex chuckled and nodded, so they rode down to the beach. While they galloped across the wet sand by the surf, Dare unfurled his powers to gather the natural energy he needed to endure Ormas, but away from Alex to avoid absorbing the other witch's energy or magic. They slowed when they reached the stream at the northern end of the royal bay, and Dare retracted his powers as they turned their horses. "You're a skilled swordsman for your age. You should join me at Lady Ducharme's fencing salon the next time I attend."

Alex beamed and patted Biscuit's damp neck. "Really?" Then he sighed. "I'd love to, but I can't. Father and Mother might discover our friendship then." He shook his head. "They'd erupt worse than the crazed chimera that razed the Goddess's Great Temple during the Stone Wars."

Steering Ebony around some driftwood, Dare hummed and arched his brows. So Alex avoided upsetting his parents like Annalise. He'd not have expected that of the brash younger gentleman. "Worried they'll disinherit you?"

His eyes narrowing, Alex set his jaw. "No, although I'm certain they would." He sighed again. "And when they did, Annalise would have no allies at home if she required help to elude their matchmaking schemes."

Dare stiffened and clenched Ebony's reins. He forced himself to drawl, "Does she require help? You mentioned her clever maneuvers earlier."

Alex shrugged. "Not generally, but I want to be nearby if she ever does." He grimaced as he turned Biscuit toward the cliffs. "Until I attended court this season, I never realized how different Father and Mother were in Ormas. They've always been ridiculous about the feud, but here 'tis practically all they discuss. And they're forever scheming to use Annalise to improve our standing at court. In Wildewall, they don't bother to matchmake, and we enjoy quiet evenings together as a family. Annalise and I both miss that."

Dare inclined his head as they began up the cliffs. Father had always been worse about the feud when in Ormas too. Perhaps because encountering the Greysnowes kept reminding him about it. "I miss living in Wildewall as well. Once I get married," to Annalise, "I intend to return there and build a wonderful life with my wife, full of abiding love and outdoor pursuits as well as our family of magical pets and boisterous children."

Alex hummed, slanting him a narrow glance as they left the royal bay. "Shall we gallop back to Ormas again?"

Dare nodded, and they thundered down the winding road.

As always, they separated when Ormas appeared in the distance. Dare sighed while he continued alone. Discussing Annalise with Alex hadn't soothed him—now he burned to rescue her from her parents' matchmaking in addition to kissing her again.

To distract himself from Annalise, Dare spent the following few days visiting natural areas within a day's ride of Ormas, except for the royal woods since that required permission from King Devon. He went hunting in Blacke Woods with Lily, Raven, and Bear. He rode to Column Caverns and explored the sprawling limestone caverns with them as well. He chartered a ship then sailed along the coast to fish and watch for whales and puffins. Every day he left at dawn and didn't return to Raven-stone House until dark, so he collapsed into slumber shortly after devouring dinner. Yet none of his adventures helped. He still ached for Annalise and often imagined her warm and radiant smile at the sights if she'd joined him.

A deluge from dinner through the following dawn thwarted his plans to ride to Glass Lake. The roads past Ormas would be a sodden mess. So he headed to Lady Ducharme's fencing salon instead.

As soon as Dare arrived, Sir Ellis beckoned Dare from the sparring circle he was sharing with his wife Lady Campbell. "Care to cross swords, Lord Ravenstone? We've not fought in ages."

Dare flashed a genial grin. A strenuous sword fight with Sir Ellis might help him forget Annalise for a time. "Gladly."

Like whenever they sparred, their sword fight fiercely employed their matching strength. They were both gasping, sweating, and aching, with their clothes and hair askew, when Dare finally wrenched Sir Ellis's sword free with a twisting thrust.

While Lady Campbell handed him his sword, Sir Ellis

grinned at Dare. "Vigorous as ever." He squeezed Dare's shoulder once they'd cleaned and sheathed their swords. "I hope you weren't insulted that Helena and I didn't invite you to our ball last week celebrating our wedding vow reaffirmation. We're not influential enough to invite both Ravenstones and Greysnowes to our events, and we thought you'd enjoy attending the kelpie races with us in a few days instead."

Dare smiled as he redid his queue. Since kelpies raced on both water and land, the sports-mad at court, like the Campbells, adored the exciting and unpredictable kelpie races. He did too. He chuckled and finished straightening his clothes. "What gentleman wouldn't? Unless they were courting a lady, of course." His heart twisted. Except he couldn't court Annalise.

Lady Campbell pursed her lips. "Perhaps we *should* have invited you to our ball then. You do need a wife."

He shrugged. Only swaying the Greysnowes to end the feud would accomplish that. "I'm sure I'll marry one day soon." He might go mad if he didn't. Distracting himself wasn't helping.

So once he returned from Lady Ducharme's fencing salon, Dare wrote another heartfelt letter to Lord Greysnowe begging to end the feud. Before riding to the royal bay the following morning, he reread his letter then asked Brown to have it delivered.

Then like Mother had been doing for the past month, he insulated his communication mirror with an air-bubble spell and slid it into a satchel he tied to his back. He activated the mirror at the royal bay and showed Mother its beauties.

Afterward, Mother beamed at him. "What a perfect natural retreat so close to Ormas. Thank the Goddess King Devon gave you permission to visit whenever you wish."

Dare grimaced. "Yes, reconnecting with the nature here and at the other natural areas within riding distance of Ormas has made this season more bearable." But not enough to ease his ache for Annalise.

Mother hummed and tilted her head. "You look tired though. Are you certain you're recovered from that duel?"

Rubbing his chest, he flashed a grin. His stifled soulbond with Annalise was the problem, not the duel. "Of course. 'Tis my hunt for a wife that's exhausting me. Nothing I've tried has succeeded." He paused. Maybe Mother could help him sway Annalise's parents. "Plus, I've been attempting to convince Lord Greysnowe to end the feud, and I can't even get him to respond to my letters. Any suggestions? What did you attempt when Father was being mulish?"

Wincing, Mother swallowed. "I *never* could get Henry to listen about that feud. But for other matters, appealing to his reason and kind heart worked—eventually."

Smoothing his beard, Dare nodded. In his next letter, he'd invoke the Greysnowes' love for Annalise and Alex. "I'll attempt that when I write again next week. Thanks, Mother."

He and Mother talked for a bit longer about her angelkitten and Wildewall then said goodbye. When he returned to Ravenstone House, Brown handed him an invitation from Lady Blaine to a family card party the following evening. Dare winced and immediately wrote back to decline the invitation. The fashionable countess was definitely pursuing him as her next husband, so he must avoid her as much as possible.

He continued eschewing court events in the days before the kelpie races with the Campbells, although he quit attempting to distract himself to exhaustion. Nothing could make him forget Annalise. He simply must endure until she was ready to reveal their soulbond.

CHAPTER 13

$\mathcal{W}$hen Grace sailed through the door, Annalise was curled in a chair by her bed, caressing the enchanted heart carving from Dare while scratching Finn's chin with Rain and Aria singing in her hair.

Grace smiled as she headed to the wardrobe. "Time to dress for the Duke of Golddell's soiree, my lady."

Sighing, Annalise nodded then scratched Finn once more and rose despite his grumbled meow. As he stalked to the bed, she slipped Dare's fragrant faegift into her bedside table then deposited Rain and Aria in their golden birdcage. She allowed Grace to help her into her violet satin but refused the matching amethysts. Then she stroked the faebirds' chests through their cage, and they trilled a sweet farewell, before she petted Finn curled on her pillow. When the disgruntled angelcat didn't stir except for his twitching tail, she kissed his head and murmured into his silky fur, "I'd rather stay, but Mother and Father would be upset if I missed the soiree in honor of the nightmara delegation's arrival. King Devon should attend, you know."

She smiled when Finn continued ignoring her. Such excuses meant nothing to an angelcat, rightly so. She petted him then straightened. "We can cuddle after the soiree—if you've forgiven me by then."

With another sigh, Annalise smoothed her gown then glided from her chambers. She brightened when Alex joined her in the hall. "Are you attending the young Duke of Golddell's soiree tonight?"

Alex shuddered. "Goddess, no. A friend mentioned some kelpie races on the coast south of Ormas."

She licked her lips as her heart squeezed. A friend? Dare, perhaps? She managed a smile. "Kelpie races sound more exciting than a stuffy soiree. Too bad I can't attend too."

An impish glint flickering in his blue eyes, Alex grinned at her. "You should, simply to provoke a reaction from Father and Mother."

Annalise tsked as they began down the stairs. Only Alex would suggest that. "I know how they'd react. Badly. They expect King Devon to be there tonight, as well as the Duke of Oakmoor and the Duke of Golddell."

Blinking, Alex eyed her askance. "The Duke of Golddell? But he's just fifteen. Surely Father and Mother don't mean to match you with him."

She tilted her head and drawled, "What's a mere nine years between husband and wife? Although it does help if both are above the age of majority." She giggled when muddy-yellow disgust flared about Alex. "No, Mother and Father shan't shove me at a mere boy."

Alex relaxed as they reached the entrance hall. "Good. Don't forget to let me know if you need me to attend a court event. I'll gladly cancel my plans. Even exciting kelpie races."

Annalise beamed at him, warmth suffusing her chest. "I know, but I can handle Mother and Father." As long as they never discovered her soulbond with Dare. She waved when Alex began toward the door. "Place a wager for me."

Glancing back over his shoulder, Alex waggled his brows. "On a kelpie with a blaze, right?"

She chuckled. Just like Blaze, the gelding she'd ridden as a little girl. Much to Mother and Father's displeasure, she'd galloped everywhere on him until he'd died. And since then, she only wagered on horse-like creatures with blazes to honor his memory. "Right."

Mother and Father swept into the entrance hall just as Alex left. His eyes narrow, Father asked, "Was that Alexander?"

Annalise inclined her head as they descended the front steps. Fortunate Alex had escaped before Mother and Father could delay him. "He's attending the kelpie races tonight."

Mother sighed while Father handed them into the carriage. She said, "He should have joined us. The nightmara delegation's arrival is important. The Nightmara-Calatini Treaty is only renewed every twenty-five years, and nightmara avoid Ormas except for the treaty."

Settling in the backward seat across from Mother and Father, Annalise laced her fingers in her lap. Only the king, the councilors, and those interested in politics cared about the nightmara delegation's arrival. Which Alex definitely wasn't, and neither were most of court. The Duke of Golddell's soiree would likely be small—many would attend either the kelpie races or the Westons' musical evening tonight. After all, the duke wasn't old enough to marry, while kelpie races were exciting and the Westons' musical evenings superb.

As expected, the drawing room at Golddell House was nearly empty when she and her parents greeted the young Duke of Golddell.

The gangly duke stuttered a bow while he muttered a return greeting. His guardians, Lord and Lady Farson, observed from nearby but didn't approach. Doubtless they wanted him to practice managing court on his own.

Mother beamed at the duke. "Has King Devon arrived yet?"

The Duke of Golddell blinked like a moonowl caught in sunlight. "N-no, Lady Greysnowe. Farson said King Devon is too busy preparing for his first meeting with Lady Moonbud, the nightmara queen-heir, to attend my soiree."

Annalise almost sighed when Mother hummed then said, "Well, at least you didn't invite Lord Ravenstone."

As Father nodded beside Mother, the young duke tugged on his cravat. "Elise—Lady Farson—invited everyone at court, although she did warn me most weren't likely to attend. Not that I minded." He paused. "I believe Lord Ravenstone declined because he was already attending kelpie races with the Campbells."

The Duke of Golddell winced back when Mother and Father glared. Hopefully, they'd not connect both Dare and Alex attending the kelpie races tonight.

To rescue the poor boy and distract her parents, Annalise smiled then asked, "Since there are no guests behind us, your grace, would you mind escorting me to the refreshments table?"

A flush staining his smooth cheeks, the Duke of Golddell jerked a nod and extended his arm. "O-Of course, Lady Annalise."

She almost chuckled when the duke yanked her across the room. He was clearly desperate to escape. She smiled at him as he handed her a flute of sparkling wine. "How do you like Ormas so far?"

The young duke grimaced when the servant gave him lymonade instead of sparkling wine. Probably at Lord and Lady Farson's behest. "I don't like it and can't wait to return to Golddell." He sighed. "I miss the plains."

Annalise twirled her flute against her lips as muddy-white loneliness pulsed about him. "Do you visit the Nightmara Plains often?"

Gulping his lymonade, the Duke of Golddell brightened as they began toward Lord and Lady Farson. "Yes. As the councilor representing Golddell, Farson visits the Nightmara Plains at least once a year, and Elise and I always accompany him. Just last autumn, we visited the Flower Herd and their mara clan to meet Lady Moonbud."

Annalise smiled while they halted beside the Farsons. From his blush and indigo tenderness glowing about him, the young duke had enjoyed more than the visit. "What's the nightmara queen-heir like?"

The duke hummed and glanced at Lord Farson. "Intense but gracious. She'll treat Calatini fairly despite us having no queen, right, Farson?"

Lord and Lady Farson glanced at each other, then Lord Farson smoothed his beard and replied, "I certainly hope so."

A pang darted through Annalise. Dare often did the same when he was thinking or concealing something. Shoving that aside, she flashed a smile. "'Tis unfortunate that King Devon hasn't found his mermaid yet. Surely Lady Moonbud wouldn't mind negotiating with our future queen."

The Farsons stared at her, then Lady Farson nodded and murmured, "True enough."

Annalise swallowed her sigh as she sipped her sparkling wine. Thanks to Mother and Father's ambitions, no one believed her uninterested in becoming queen. Doubtless the king's mermaid would suspect her as well. Too bad. A lady possessing such a devoted indigo aura could be a wonderful friend.

Clinging to her smile, Annalise asked the Farsons and the Duke of Golddell about visiting the nightmara and mara clans. Remaining with their hosts should prevent Mother and Father from shoving her at the Duke of Oakmoor again.

AT BREAKFAST three days after the Duke of Golddell's soiree, Father scowled when he read the unlabeled letter Wilson handed him. Surely another from Dare.

Annalise sighed into her tea. Not that Mother and Father would heed this one any more than they had his previous seven letters. Why must they be so obsessed with the feud? No one but a truly decent gentleman would continue sending pleas to seek peace when none of his letters were answered.

Muddy-red fury swirling about him, Father crumpled the letter then thrust it at Mother. He growled, "The effrontery of that—that treacherous *Ravenstone*."

Stiffening, Annalise exchanged a wide glance with Alex as she set down her teacup. What could Dare have written that infuriated Father so?

Her aura turning the same shade as Father's, Mother flushed scarlet and pursed her lips until they disappeared. "How dare that cad suggest we'd end the feud if we loved Annalise and Alexander?"

Annalise swallowed as she and Alex traded another glance. Doubtless Dare hadn't meant to imply Mother and Father didn't love them, but that the feud harmed everyone's futures. Which it did by preventing her and Dare from revealing their soulbond. And the feud had almost made Alex a murderer. Anyone not blinded by the feud could see how harmful it was. Yet saying that would only upset Mother and Father further.

Father snorted, the brown in his aura fading. "Plus, Ravenstone has no right to adjure us to end the feud. Not after he fabricated that mermaid to beguile King Devon at the king's summer masquerade."

Suppressing a grimace, Annalise began her beefsteak. Why must Mother and Father continue to harp on King Devon's mermaid? Only *they* could believe a genial gentleman like Dare would be behind such a convoluted scheme.

Alex arched a brow while buttering a roll then echoed her thoughts, "Are you certain Lord Ravenstone had anything to do with the king's mysterious mermaid?"

Mother scowled. "Of course he did. The appearance of an alluring yet unknown lady at the most exclusive court event of the season couldn't be mere chance." She smirked and sipped her tea. "But Ravenstone's scheme shan't help. Word at court is that the nightmara talks have foundered because the nightmara refuse to negotiate with anyone but Calatini's queen. So King Devon must find a queen at once, and Annalise is his only choice because that mermaid is nowhere to be found."

Her heart twisting, Annalise clenched her knife and fork over her beefsteak. How could Mother and Father want such a life for her? *They'd* married for love. "You want me to endure a loveless marriage forced by convenience?"

Mother blinked with a faint frown furrowing her brow. "Don't be daft. You wouldn't have allowed King Devon to court you for years if you didn't love him."

Swallowing, Annalise lowered her gaze. Yes, she definitely shouldn't have allowed Mother and Father to assume King Devon's escort was serious. Somehow, she must prepare them for him marrying another.

Mother continued, "And King Devon shall learn to love you once he knows the true you." She hummed. "You hide too much behind Lady Snow."

Annalise sighed as she resumed eating her beefsteak. Because if she didn't, someone might realize she was a soul healer. To help Mother and Father see she and King Devon were nothing more than friends, she raised her gaze with a serene smile and said, "From his absorption at his summer masquerade and his determination to find her since then, I suspect King Devon shall always want his mermaid."

Father bit into his roll slathered with raspberry preserves then snorted. "Bah, he'll forget that wanton creature in time." He turned to Mother. "Although King Devon wouldn't have to, if not for that treacherous whelp Ravenstone. I must confront Ravenstone about his mermaid scheme and deceitful letters when we attend the Duchess of Wildewall's garden party."

Mother beamed at him. "Excellent idea, Alistair." Her blue eyes darkened. "The slurs in his letter today mustn't go unanswered."

Tensing, Annalise quit eating. She couldn't allow Mother and Father to attack Dare. Yet they'd been brooding over the mermaid for weeks, and whatever Dare had written today had only provoked them further. Perhaps her earlier persuasion would succeed again. She leaned forward. "King Devon shan't approve of you attacking Lord Ravenstone."

Alex quirked a wry smile. "Plus, given his physical prowess, Lord Ravenstone could easily trounce you."

Father glowered at him. "*You* beat him at your duel."

Annalise's stomach clenched. Only because she'd distracted Dare.

Muddy-blue shame flickering about him, Alex shook his head. "A mere accident. Before that thrust, Lord Ravenstone had been controlling my every move for almost two hours without slowing. So, believe me, you'll lose if he fights back."

As Father's glower blackened, Annalise almost winced. Although true, saying that would only inflame Father. He despised losing more than a firecat despised the sea. Odd that Alex had attempted that tack—her brother was never so maladroit. His shame over the duel must have distracted him.

Mother frowned at Alex over her teacup. "Your father can handle Ravenstone." Her jaw tightened. "We've been handling his family's treacherous schemes for years."

Annalise and Alex glanced at each other then sighed. Mother and Father were as mulish about the feud as ever. Why could they never listen to reason about the Ravenstones?

So 'twas little surprise when Father stormed toward Dare, with Mother close behind, as soon as they entered the Duchess of Wildewall's lush garden a few mornings later.

Her soulbond flaring at Dare's nearness, Annalise darted after her parents. Oh, Goddess. How could she stop them this time? Whatever she attempted mustn't hint at her soulbond with Dare. Discovering that would only inflame Mother and Father's fury.

CHAPTER 14

When his soulbond burgeoned at Annalise entering the Duchess of Wildewall's verdant garden, Dare's breath quickened, and he couldn't help turning to see her. Then he tensed. Lord and Lady Greysnowe were charging toward him with Annalise close behind. Given her parents' glares, they weren't approaching to end the feud. And Lord Greysnowe's fists were already clenched to deliver a blow.

Dare smoothed his beard. Somehow, he must prevent this confrontation from escalating to a brawl—while not betraying his burning ache for Annalise. Nearly impossible with her being so close. When her parents halted before him, he flashed a genial smile without glancing at her. "Good morning."

As the other guests turned to stare like curious ghosts, Lord and Lady Greysnowe glared harder at Dare. Lord Greysnowe said, "Don't smirk at us to feign courtesy. We know what you've done."

His pulse surging, Dare clung to his smile as the Duchess of Wildewall joined them. From the lack of panic in Annalise's radiant aura, her parents didn't mean his soulbond with her. Had they discovered his rides with Alex? "What I've done?"

Lady Greysnowe glaring beside him, Lord Greysnowe leaned

forward and growled, "The king's mermaid. You fabricated her to beguile King Devon from Annalise."

Dare sighed. Of course, they meant that nonsense. "You overestimate me. I wasn't behind King Devon's mermaid. Choosing a suitable masquerade costume for myself was hard enough."

Her gaze dark, Lady Greysnowe snorted. "Fabricating a mermaid would be nothing to a treacherous Ravenstone. What kind of spell did you purchase for that mermaid? Only a powerful one could have beguiled King Devon from our daughter."

While Dare stiffened, Annalise gaped at Lady Greysnowe, and muddy-blue embarrassment swirled about her. "Mother!"

The Duchess of Wildewall frowned. "Your accusation is hardly fair, Lady Greysnowe." As the Minister of Justice and the head of their duchy, the duchess always strove to keep interactions between the Ravenstones and Greysnowes fair. "The protection charm King Devon wears defends him from any enchantments, no matter how powerful."

Her white-blonde hair shimmering like her daughter's, Lady Greysnowe tossed her head then scowled at Dare. "A treacherous Ravenstone could have subverted that." Scowling too, her husband nodded beside her.

As a blush stained Annalise's cheeks, Dare inhaled then replied, "Again you overestimate me. Attempting to subvert a protection charm created by Lady Juliet, the most illustrious witch in Calatini, would be futile." Even for another Rhiannon descendant like him. "Not to mention treasonous." He smiled at Annalise's parents. "Besides, why would I attempt such schemes when I simply seek peace with the Greysnowes?"

Lord Greysnowe clenched his fists. "As if we'd believe that lie. A Ravenstone would no sooner seek peace with us than a naga would with harpies." And the serpent-human naga and bird-human harpies had been enemies since before the Stone Wars and relished harassing each other. "'Tis unnatural."

His chest squeezing, Dare exchanged a heavy glance with

Annalise. Not surprising her father admired those feuding magical creatures. When her cerulean eyes darkened and their souls strained to mesh, he began leaning toward her. He stilled then wrenched his gaze free. Goddess! Their stifled soulbond was so ravenous that even a brief glance almost overwhelmed them.

Yet unlike Alex, Annalise's parents didn't notice their ardent stare. Too blinded by pursuing the feud, no doubt. Their scowls remained steady as Lady Greysnowe said, "You might as well quit sending those deceitful letters."

While the Duchess of Wildewall blinked and eyed him, Dare set his jaw. He couldn't quit sending those letters. They were his only chance to convince Annalise's parents to end the feud and accept him marrying her. "Yet the Ravenstones and Greysnowes must communicate with each other to build acceptance and forgive the strife of the past."

Lord and Lady Greysnowe snickered, then Lord Greysnowe said, "Only a miracle could manage that." He took his wife's arm. "We should greet the Duke of Oakmoor. Come, Annalise." After a final scowl at Dare, the Greysnowes swept across the duchess's garden, and Annalise followed without glancing at him again.

Dare swallowed as his heart twisted. He and Annalise couldn't continue avoiding each other and stifling their soul-bond. Their hunger would consume them, and they'd betray their soulbond in public before they swayed her parents.

The Duchess of Wildewall hummed. "You've been writing the Greysnowes?"

He started and yanked his gaze from Annalise giving the Duke of Oakmoor a cool smile. Hopefully, the duchess assumed his stare had been due to the near brawl, not hunger for Annalise. He nodded at the duchess. "I've been writing to seek peace since young Lord Alexander nearly killed me. The feud must end before further strife feeds the feud beyond mending."

The duchess inclined her head, the frost in her auburn hair gleaming. "I pray that you succeed, Lord Ravenstone. The

Greysnowe-Ravenstone feud has blighted enough lives. Excuse me, I must return to greeting my guests."

Once the duchess left, his gaze drifted back to Annalise, who was now conversing with Lady Ducharme, even though her parents were still with the Duke of Oakmoor. Dare sighed as he strode to the refreshments table. He and Annalise must slip away to talk privately about their soulbond. After the confrontation with her parents, they couldn't risk today, so they must wait until they next attended the same court event. But when?

He'd just accepted a cup of tea when Lady Blaine slid her arm through his and purred, "Lord Ravenstone, finally. I've not seen you since my water party. Are you avoiding me?"

Freeing his arm, Dare gritted a genial smile. 'Twould be rude to admit to avoiding the husband-hunting countess, so instead he replied, "I've been busy visiting the natural areas around Ormas."

Lady Blaine moued. "I see. Well, I hope you still mean to attend the Duchess of Childes's fete next week celebrating Aragon and Selena's pregnancy. No one refuses an invitation from the duchess."

He sipped his tea, his pulse stirring. Annalise would doubtless attend, and they could easily slip away from the Duchess of Childes's crowded ballroom. Surely they could manage to endure until next week. He nodded at Lady Blaine. "Of course, I'm eager to celebrate Lord and Lady Treyvan's good fortune."

Fluttering her lashes, Lady Blaine slanted him a coy smile. "Wonderful. I expect more delightful dances like at the king's summer masquerade."

Dare sighed. No doubt she did. "I'm certain you'll be much in demand." He drained his tea then nodded at Lady Blaine again. "I must be off. Until the Duchess of Childes's fete."

He strode from the verdant garden. To avoid Lady Blaine and not provoke his stifled soulbond, he'd eschew further court events until the fete. He'd resume visiting the natural areas around Ormas instead.

. . .

OVER THE FOLLOWING FEW DAYS, Dare visited the natural areas around Ormas as planned, starting with the ride to Glass Lake he'd skipped last week. But like before, his beloved nature couldn't distract him from Annalise.

Yet the closest he got to Annalise was crossing swords with Alex at the royal bay. So once they'd traded several parries and ripostes, he asked Alex, "Things still well at home?"

Alex snorted as he lunged toward Dare. "I suppose so. Father and Mother were more gleeful than bloodthirsty orcs after defeating an enemy clan when Annalise mentioned King Devon would escort her to Lady Staghorn's ball last night."

His stomach hardening, Dare danced backward then parried. Why was King Devon escorting Annalise again? Had the king abandoned finding his mysterious mermaid? And how could Annalise bear to allow another gentleman to escort her with their stifled soulbond so ravenous?

Alex grimaced and feinted an attack. "Of course, Father and Mother assume King Devon shall offer for Annalise and are planning her triumphant reign as queen. They're gloating that 'your' mermaid scheme failed."

Dare grunted while he thrust. Why must Annalise's parents be so blindly mulish? "I told your parents I wasn't behind King Devon's mermaid."

His sword glinting, Alex parried and shook his head. "I know, but Father and Mother refuse to believe that. They can't imagine a Ravenstone or Greysnowe seeking peace."

Dare sighed as he twisted his sword around Alex's. "That was apparent. They said only a miracle could get them to end the feud. And I doubt the Goddess shall provide one when ending the feud simply requires acceptance and forgiveness." He slipped past Alex's guard to win their sword fight.

Alex lowered his sword with a wry grin. "If not a miracle from the Goddess, something equally dramatic should do."

Dare sighed again. His soulbond with Annalise was dramatic. Although until her parents were ready to end the feud, they'd be furious if they discovered that. He must continue his letters, but reasoned pleas weren't enough. Perhaps detailing the strife of the past would help—those were certainly dramatic.

As they cleaned their swords, he tensed at the thunder of approaching hoofbeats. No one could see him and Alex together —gossip about their friendship would feed the feud and infuriate the Greysnowes. "Riders approaching."

Alex stilled too. "I hope they're discreet. We've nowhere to hide."

Dare shook his head. "You don't. Stay here and pretend you're practicing sword moves alone. The riders might have already seen us and wonder why no one is here."

As Alex nodded, Dare ran to Ebony tied to an ash tree. He gathered his will and flung his nature magic around them until they faded into the ash trees behind them. Then he scratched Ebony to keep the stallion still and quiet. Even with his nature mimicry spell, others might notice any movement or sound.

Within moments, Lord and Lady Farson and the teenage Duke of Golddell halted their horses beside Alex. Dare stiffened. Of course, it had to be people who knew about his frequent rides to the royal bay. He'd encountered the Farsons and their ward several times here. From Golddell where the horse-like nightmara lived, they were all avid riders, so they enjoyed early rides together, unlike many at court. And since Lady Farson and King Devon shared the same cousins and were practically family, the Farsons and the Duke of Golddell rode to the royal bay several times a month.

Sheathing his sword, Alex grinned at the Farsons and the young duke, and everyone exchanged greetings.

Then the Duke of Golddell beamed at Alex. "You're Lady Annalise's brother."

Dare smiled. From the boy's reverent tone, Annalise had completely charmed him when they'd met recently. Not surprising. Fortunately, the duke was much too young to be a serious suitor.

Alex chuckled. "Yes, I am. I was practicing my sword moves here because not many ride so close to the royal bay."

Lord and Lady Farson traded a glance, then Lord Farson smiled at Alex. "You should join our ride along the ocean. 'Tis a lovely morning."

Grinning, Lady Farson nodded. "Yes, King Devon shan't mind us inviting another."

Alex bent a brief bow. "I'd enjoy that." He strode over to Biscuit beside Dare and Ebony. As he untied his gelding, he muttered, "I should join them to prevent questions. I'll trounce you next week."

Dare snorted in reply then almost laughed at Alex's answering smirk. Brash hellion.

After Alex and the others rode down the cliffs, Dare sheathed his sword and mounted Ebony. Then he gathered natural energy, which was harder than usual while maintaining his nature mimicry spell. He couldn't risk dropping that until well away from the royal bay.

As he and Ebony rode back, he frowned at Ormas in the distance. He and Annalise must definitely talk at the Duchess of Childes's fete. Hearing about another escorting her, especially the king her parents wanted her to marry, was wrenching.

To distract himself, he spent the day hunting with Raven and Bear coursing beside him and Lily perched on his saddle. Then after dinner, he scoured the family histories kept in Ormas for the most dramatic and dire incidents in the Ravenstone-Greysnowe feud.

However, the histories in Ormas were sparse, so during his mirror call with Mother the following morning, Dare asked, "Could you send me the family histories from Ravenstone Castle with a transportation spell? I'm researching the feud to enhance my letters to Lord Greysnowe. Appealing to his reason and heart didn't succeed."

The leaves behind her rustling in the breeze, Mother hummed and tilted her head. "'Tis a lot of volumes. Perhaps you should perform a library spell instead."

He grimaced but nodded. Although that spell was involved, one book enchanted to display any book in Ravenstone Castle's library *would* be more convenient. "Very well. I should go so I can do that. Until next week."

After deactivating the communication mirror and setting it on the windowsill to recharge, Dare headed to his study with Lily, Raven, and Bear. Since the library spell didn't involve nature, performing it would be harder, and setting its cost could be tricky. But having his magical pets act as familiars would help.

In his study, he collected a blank book, a charged clear quartz crystal, and his spell ingredients of dried sage, powdered clear quartz, and faedust. Then gathering magical energy from Lily, Raven, and Bear, he mixed the spell ingredients while crooning a singsong chant. He soon began panting, but he sprinkled the magical powder over the book and charged quartz, focused his will, set the spell cost to the energy in the quartz, then finished the chant. Even with his magical pets' help, performing the library spell had been demanding.

Yet once he'd completed the library spell, he perused several of the more detailed family histories from home then wrote his ninth letter to Lord Greysnowe. Goddess, please let this one curb Annalise's parents' obsession with the feud.

CHAPTER 15

$\mathcal{A}$nnalise and her parents were in the entrance hall and about to leave for the Landrys' ball when Wilson handed Father another unlabeled letter.

His brows flying upward, Father tore open the letter then glared as he read. "Damn that whelp Ravenstone. How dare he write after our confrontation the other day?"

Annalise sighed, her chest squeezing. Because Dare was set on winning Mother and Father's acceptance, so they could quit concealing their soulbond and marry one day. An impossible dream, but he was still determined.

Mother scowled while reading over Father's shoulder. "And to brandish past strife too. Smug cad. You *must* make him quit sending these deceitful letters."

Muddy-orange smugness flickering about him, Father smirked as he ripped Dare's letter into pieces then dropped them. "That idea we discussed yesterday should suit."

As Mother echoed Father's smirk and took his arm, Annalise swallowed. What scheme had they concocted now? She must discover the details, so she could warn Dare somehow. "What idea?"

Father harrumphed. "Nothing that concerns you. I can handle

Ravenstone. A sweet girl like you mustn't become involved with such a treacherous cad."

Annalise almost winced. Except she already was. And Dare wasn't a treacherous cad. If only she could defend him without provoking Mother and Father.

Mother beckoned her. "Come, we must attend the Landrys' ball. King Devon is waiting."

Annalise suppressed a grimace. Yes, he was, although not for the reason Mother and Father assumed. Unfortunately, her attempt to explain why King Devon was escorting her again had foundered when she'd mentioned his escort to Lady Staghorn's ball two days ago. So she followed Mother and Father into the carriage without another word.

Father's arm draped about her shoulders like usual, Mother chuckled and leaned against him as the carriage rumbled forward. "We really shouldn't allow Ravenstone's futile schemes to upset us. After all, King Devon has escorted Annalise two evenings in a row." She beamed at Annalise. "He's finally seen past your cool serenity and realized what a loving wife and queen you'll be. Surely he's about to propose, and soon you'll start your own family together."

Clenching her hands in her pale-lymon skirt, Annalise hummed and glanced out the carriage window. She was no closer to starting her own family than she'd been before. She was soulbound to Dare, and King Devon didn't want to propose to *her*. He was only escorting her again so she could help him hunt for his mermaid. Not that they'd any success yet.

Mother and Father continued gloating about King Devon's supposed proposal for the rest of the ride, so Annalise leapt from the carriage as soon as it halted at Landry House. Their gloating grew more unpalatable every day. Hopefully, King Devon would find his mermaid soon. Then Mother and Father would have to see she'd never become queen.

Once she and her parents greeted Mr. and Mrs. Landry, King Devon captured her arm, and she and the king began circulating.

She scrutinized the ballroom for his mermaid's devoted indigo aura while they spoke to the other guests. She sighed after they'd circled twice. "I don't see your mermaid here tonight either. I'm sorry, your majesty."

Muddy-white loneliness swamped King Devon, and the silver motes of nightmara magic around him swirled faster as he echoed her sigh. "*Where* is she? The nightmara shan't wait forever for me to find her. But having met her, I can't marry another."

Annalise forced a serene smile even though her heart twisted. And *he* wasn't even soulbound to his mysterious mermaid. "You'll find her eventually. Shall we dance?"

Sighing again, King Devon nodded and led her onto the floor, but he left soon after. Yet since he'd arranged to escort her tomorrow, she convinced Mother and Father to allow her to leave early as well. Their assumptions were good for that at least.

King Devon kept escorting Annalise to court events over the following days, but they still had no luck finding his mermaid. Annalise exhaled when she and her parents arrived at the Duchess of Childes's fete. Although perhaps 'twould change tonight—all of court, except Alex, should attend the duchess's fete.

She swallowed as they greeted the Duke and Duchess of Childes. And Dare would definitely attend, so she'd see him for the first time since his confrontation with Mother and Father, where a simple glance had nearly betrayed their soulbond. Could she manage Lady Snow's serene mask tonight? She burned to see Dare again, even more than ever.

Her throat tightened as King Devon escorted her across the ballroom. And even if she controlled herself, would Mother and Father do the same? Or would they behave as outrageously as at the Duchess of Wildewall's garden party? Please let them not corner Dare tonight.

When her soulbond flared at Dare entering the Duchess of Childes's ballroom, Annalise tensed but refused to glance toward him, so they'd not stare at each other again. Instead, she eyed Mother and Father, but they were gossiping with the devious Lady Morwynne and didn't notice Dare's arrival. Thank the Goddess. She swallowed a sigh and turned to King Devon beside her. "Before the dancing starts, shall we circulate to hunt for your mermaid?"

King Devon nodded, and they began greeting the other guests, but she ensured they avoided both Dare and her parents. They were halfway through, with no sign of the king's mermaid, when the Duke and Duchess of Childes headed to the front and thanked everyone for attending. Yet instead of the first dance, they announced their family was performing a play written by Miss Keyes.

Annalise winced as she faced the cerulean curtain beneath the musicians' balcony. The white glow with silver motes that still surrounded Miss Keyes and Lord Beza Hawke was as blinding as at the king's summer masquerade last month. Miss Keyes's seer was *definitely* a Rhiannon descendant like no other. Plus, a potent spell lasting so long must have a hefty magical cost.

After Miss Keyes's delightful play, the duchess opened the dancing, but Annalise and King Devon returned to circulating, although they didn't find his mermaid. When the third dance began, King Devon sighed and asked, "Care to dance? I think we've greeted nearly everyone."

Annalise inclined her head, but her gaze caught on Dare leading Miss Philippa Hawke onto the floor. Her stomach hardened. Even though he couldn't be pursuing another because of their soulbond, somehow him dancing with the bubbly younger lady was more wrenching than his previous dance with the country-loving Miss Winston. She wrenched her gaze free then made herself turn to King Devon. "After our dance, we should visit the refreshments table. I'm parched."

King Devon chuckled as they began dancing. "Of course."

Throughout her dance with King Devon, she kept slanting glances at Dare and Miss Hawke across the ballroom. Was he holding Miss Hawke closer than normal? Was his genial grin warmer? He'd said neither of them could desire another, but perhaps he wished he could court a lady without a feud between them, so he could actually start his own family.

Near the end of their dance, King Devon frowned and eyed her. "Are you well, Lady Annalise?"

Annalise swallowed. She was already betraying her soulbond with Dare and must devise an excuse to slip away soon. She flashed a serene smile. "I've been watching the other dancers in case your mermaid arrived late like she did at your summer masquerade."

King Devon sighed as he bowed and she curtsied at the music fading. "If only. But no one would dare arrive late to one of the duchess's events."

King Devon was handing her a flute of sparkling wine at the refreshments table when the Duchess of Childes and her youngest son Lord Beza joined them. Annalise muffled a sigh. She couldn't slip away with the perceptive duchess so near. But at least the magic surrounding Lord Beza wasn't blinding without Miss Keyes beside him.

While she and the duchess discussed their ballgowns from Celeste's, Lord Beza murmured something to King Devon, which King Devon explained when he escorted her across the ballroom, "Hawke asked us to check on Wren. She's on the balcony."

Annalise hummed. Not surprising Lord Beza was solicitous of Miss Keyes. And she could slip away while King Devon was distracted by his cousin's lady. But then she stiffened when Mother and Father sailed over and waylaid them just before the balcony.

Mother beamed at them. "You two make the most perfect couple and should announce your betrothal soon. I'm sure you're both eager to start your family."

Father nodded. "I'm available to discuss Annalise's dowry whenever you wish, your majesty."

A blush heating her neck, Annalise made herself smile at Mother and Father. Why must they be so grasping? "King Devon has no need to discuss my dowry. Excuse us; I require air." She tugged King Devon toward the balcony. "I apologize, your majesty."

King Devon shook his head, but his reply was halted when they interrupted Mr. Winston attempting to kiss a struggling Miss Keyes on the balcony. No doubt the fortune-hunting cad was attempting to force a betrothal—just like he had with Annalise years ago. Poor Miss Keyes. Thankfully, King Devon routed Mr. Winston as swiftly as he had for Annalise then escorted her and Miss Keyes back inside.

As King Devon left to fetch tea for Miss Keyes, Annalise glanced across the ballroom where Dare was grinning at the Duchess of Childes and Lord Beza. Her heart fluttered. He was more irresistible than the most seductive siren. Then she tensed at the silence between her and Miss Keyes. Goddess, how long had she been staring at Dare? She must explain before Miss Keyes realized her interest. "I suppose the Duchess of Childes *had* to invite Ravenstone."

Her seer's potent spell brighter around her than Lord Beza, Miss Keyes glanced across the ballroom for a moment before turning back to Annalise. "The duchess is powerful enough to disregard the Greysnowe-Ravenstone feud if she likes. And apparently, she does."

Annalise pursed her lips to feign disdain. "I suppose, but I hate encountering the wretch." Somehow she must distract Miss Keyes from Dare. She eyed Miss Keyes's dark-green ballgown with gold wrens. That might do. Court gossip said 'twas made of magical fabric, and although the fabric did possess a peculiar luster indicating a magical nature, the glimmer of residual magic was eclipsed by the potent spell surrounding Miss Keyes.

Even so, 'twas magnificent and far surpassed her own cerulean silk ballgown from Celeste's. Mother would be annoyed.

Flashing a glittering smile, she said, "Your ballgown is magnificent—even better than your dryad costume at the king's summer masquerade. The fabric is arachne silk, yes? The one Lord Beza just imported."

Muddy-yellow panic pulsing about her, Miss Keyes inhaled then lifted her chin. "Yes, 'tis arachne silk, but I didn't attend the masquerade."

Annalise arched her brows at Miss Keyes's lie. Was it connected to her seer's potent spell? "If you count gracing the ballroom as attending, then yes, you didn't attend. But you were in the gardens dancing scandalously close to Lord Beza."

Miss Keyes paled but met her gaze. "I'm afraid you're still mistaken, but gardens at night are too dark for clear sight, hence their affinity for dalliance. I'm surprised you ventured into one."

Annalise stilled. She shouldn't have admitted that she had. If gossip about that spread, someone might realize Dare had joined her. "After the king met his mermaid, I required air." Before Miss Keyes could probe further, Annalise flicked a wave. She must leave before King Devon returned. "'Tis been pleasant talking with you, Miss Keyes, but I must go refresh myself. I look forward to your happy announcement with Lord Beza."

She slipped from the crowded ballroom and out into the quiet garden. Inhaling the sweet, balmy air, she relaxed and sank onto the stone bench in an alcove behind the trellis of climbing roses. She could finally quit clinging to her Lady Snow mask. Then she stilled as her soulbond surged at Dare entering the garden. Perhaps he'd leave if she didn't acknowledge him.

Yet Dare strode straight to the concealed alcove. Halting before her, he flashed a warm smile as indigo tenderness glowed about him. "Evening, Annalise."

Tingling warmth suffused her, but she lifted her chin and frowned. She must encourage him to leave before she leapt into his arms. "You should return to the fete. We agreed to avoid each other."

Sighing, Dare rubbed his beard. "True, but we can't continue as we have been. Stifling our soulbond is making it too ravenous. Soon it shall overwhelm us—like it almost did at the Duchess of Wildewall's garden party."

Annalise slid to the far end of the stone bench when Dare sat beside her. If she touched him, her control would crumble. "Then we must avoid each other in public too. Feeding the soulbond shall make it impossible to conceal."

Dare leaned toward her. "Stifling the soulbond is worse. I ache for you constantly, and 'tis escalating as the days pass."

She shivered and fisted her hands in her lap as her pulse quickened. She felt the same, but what else could they do? "We'll become inured in time."

His jaw tensing, Dare snorted. "No, we won't. Consider this; if you starve angelcats or hellhounds long enough, they'll savage the first creature they encounter—even if 'tis their beloved owner. But if their owner feeds them every day, they remain sated and would never dream of doing so. Our soulbond is no different."

Her soul straining toward his, Annalise swayed until their mouths almost met. Then she leapt upright. She'd nearly kissed him, and he'd not even been flirting. She must escape at once.

But before she fled, Dare grasped her hand, and she stilled as their souls meshed at that simple touch. Hunger throbbing in her veins, she tumbled into his lap and twined her arms about his neck then kissed him. More, she needed more. She buried her hands in his long hair, pressed her body closer, and parted her lips to deepen their kiss.

CHAPTER 16

When Annalise kissed him harder and her heady honeysuckle scent swamped him, Dare shuddered and pulled her even closer. At last. His burning ache for her eased as their souls remained meshed, but his body hardened painfully at their ravenous kisses. He must have more.

Unlacing her ballgown, he caressed her bare back then shuddered again as she purred and undulated against him. More, Goddess, more. His pulse throbbing, he began sliding his hand up her legs beneath her skirt.

"Annalise, are you out here?"

Dare and Annalise froze mid-kiss at her mother's call. Lady Greysnowe would spot them once she passed the rose trellis. She, and Lord Greysnowe who was likely with her, would have a fit if they saw their ancestral enemy seducing their daughter. *Not* the way to reveal his soulbond with Annalise.

Gathering his will, he flung a nature mimicry spell around him and Annalise until they faded into the stone bench as well as the ivy and jasmine in the alcove. He muttered against Annalise's lips, "Remain absolutely still until they leave."

Annalise blinked her consent, and they barely breathed as

her parents checked the garden. Eventually, she relaxed with a heavy sigh and separated her soul from his. "They're gone."

Dare sagged while dropping his nature mimicry spell. She'd know since she could read auras. He swallowed then relaced her ballgown and set her on the stone bench beside him. "I apologize for mauling you like a lusty satyr."

Licking her lips, Annalise sighed. "I kissed you first, so I'm just as responsible."

He eyed her lips, his body hardening again. He fisted his hands to not yank her against him and kiss her senseless once more. "This is why stifling our soulbond is dangerous. We're too ravenous to control ourselves when we meet. If your parents hadn't interrupted, I'd have made love to you."

Annalise paled whiter than the marble statue beside the stone bench. "Which would be devastating. Not only would I likely become pregnant, but consummating our soulbond would make its pull excruciating to resist."

Dare smoothed his beard to conceal his grimace. Her becoming pregnant was impossible thanks to his strong-magic contraceptive, and their soulbond was already excruciating to resist. So he only replied, "Feeding our soulbond is the only way to retain control. Perhaps if we meet privately—but to talk, no touching or kissing. Even with our soulbond sated, I doubt we can manage those without going too far."

Violet longing swirling about her, Annalise rubbed her chest. "I suppose we'd better try private meetings. You were right that we can't continue as we have been."

Energy surged through him. Thank the Goddess she'd agreed. He grinned at her. "How should we meet?"

Annalise hummed and twisted her hands in her lap. "Meeting in the park near my family's townhouse like we did during our first season should do. I still walk there most mornings. Or I ride, so we could do that as well. Although we can't ride as far as the royal bay very often—Mother and Father might notice if I miss breakfast too frequently."

Aching to take her hand, Dare nodded. "I'd prefer to meet every morning, but I think we must keep to every other. If I don't ride to the royal bay or similar areas to gather natural energy, I'll be unable to endure living in Ormas for longer than a month. Plus, I'm still riding with Alex every week or so, and we must skip those mornings unless you want to reveal our soulbond to him."

Her hands stilling, Annalise frowned. "I'd like to, but we can't. I already told you that."

He nodded but sighed. Keeping secrets from a close friend like Alex had become over the past two months was distasteful. Yet he'd continue remaining silent for Annalise. "As you wish. I'm riding with Alex the day after tomorrow, but I'd rather not wait three days to see you again. So shall we meet tomorrow not long after dawn? Then we can start meeting every other morning."

Annalise smiled at him. "Sounds good."

Dare swallowed as tingling warmth filled him at her radiant smile. Goddess, she was more tempting than bee balm to melissae. He could drink her nectar forever.

Annalise tilted her head, her white-blonde hair shimmering in the moonlight bathing the garden. "We should return to the fete." She grimaced. "But I've little interest in returning to the crowded ballroom."

He leaned toward her. If only he could twine her silken tresses about his fingers. "I don't want to return to the fete either." There, he must feign interest in other ladies.

Annalise sighed and smoothed her cerulean skirt. "Doubtless Mother and Father are still looking for me. You should leave before they check the garden again."

Dare tensed. He couldn't leave her unprotected. Another gentleman might find her and attempt a kiss. Besides, he needed this time alone with her. He smiled at Annalise. "I doubt they'll return for a while, and I can recast my nature mimicry spell when they do."

Sighing again, Annalise lifted a shoulder. "I suppose." She hummed. "I wonder if Mother and Father were looking for me because King Devon was leaving."

He stiffened, his stomach hardening. Did she care if the king left? "With our soulbond, how can you bear to allow King Devon to escort you? Your parents assume you'll marry him."

Annalise pursed her lips. "I know, but King Devon shall only marry his mysterious mermaid." She glowered at him. "And how can *you* bear to dance with Miss Winston, Miss Hawke, or Lady Blaine?"

Dare snorted. Not easily. "I've no choice. All of court knows I'm only in Ormas to find a wife, and that means dancing at court events, and I can't dance with you."

Her glower fading, Annalise sagged. "True enough."

Burning to pull her into his arms, he clenched his hands to remain still. "I've attempted to dance with ladies uninterested in marrying me as much as possible. Miss Winston and I both recognize we feel too much like siblings to marry. And Miss Hawke only wants Lord Blaine, who's been quietly courting her since her come out this spring."

Annalise brightened. "Really?" When he nodded, she smiled. Then she tsked. "The husband-hunting Lady Blaine can't possibly be uninterested in marrying you."

Dare winced and suppressed a shudder. Unfortunately true. "She's not, but she's forceful in her flirtations. She makes it impossible to refuse without drawing unwelcome attention. I accepted her pursuit at first since it helped conceal our soulbond, but I've been attempting to avoid her since then, although she still corners me on occasion."

Flashing a wry smile, Annalise reached for his clenched hand but halted just before she touched him. "Forceful suitors can be vexing." She sighed and laced her fingers in her lap. "After your near brawl with my parents, King Devon only asked to escort me again to appease them until he found his mermaid. Plus, he wanted my help finding her."

His chest easing, Dare grinned. So another convenient pretense. "I should have realized 'twas something like that, but I was too jealous to think clearly."

Annalise grinned back. "Understandable—I was just as jealous about you dancing with other ladies, even though I knew you couldn't be pursuing them because of our soulbond. But having discussed it should ease our jealousy." She grimaced. "Although I do hope King Devon finds his mermaid soon. Mother and Father's behavior becomes more outrageous every day. Tonight they waylaid me and King Devon then practically demanded he discuss marriage settlements."

Dare echoed her grimace. Of course the grasping fools did.

But before he could reply, Annalise threw up a hand and hissed, "The Duke of Oakmoor and Lady Juliet just entered the garden."

He swiftly recast his nature mimicry spell about him and Annalise. Why were the Minister of Foreign Relations and the royal witch entering a garden together? According to court gossip, the two disliked each other.

Once the Duke of Oakmoor and Lady Juliet disappeared into an alcove across the garden and began quarreling, Annalise grasped Dare's hand and tugged him back to the ballroom. She was right; they should return while the duke and royal witch were engrossed in their quarrel and before anyone else entered the garden.

At the door, Dare dropped his spell then whispered, "I'll wait here for a bit, so no one connects our returns. See you tomorrow in the park."

Annalise squeezed his hand before slipping inside, and he set his jaw while he remained behind. Letting her go was wrenching. After waiting the length of several dances, he strode back to the ballroom.

As soon as he entered, Lady Blaine slid her arm through his with a coy grin. "Lord Ravenstone, there you are. Why do I always find you returning from gardens?"

Dare stiffened. Had the fashionable countess noticed Annalise had also returned from the same gardens both times? He made himself smile. "Because I miss the country while living in Ormas."

Lady Blaine moued. "What's the country to the delights available here?" Her coy grin deepened. "Come, the next song is starting, and we've not danced yet."

He almost grimaced but led the sultry Lady Blaine out onto the floor. If he refused, she might wonder why and think about his return. Then she might connect it to Annalise's. And if the fashionable countess did, the rest of court would know within a fortnight. At least he could cling to his walk with Annalise tomorrow while enduring his dance with Lady Blaine.

AT DAWN THE FOLLOWING MORNING, Dare leapt from bed then yanked on his clothes without calling for Thom. He was finally about to see Annalise alone again. Not eating or disturbing Lily, Raven, and Bear, he strode to the park near Greysnowe House. Then he forced himself to lean against an oak near where Annalise should enter the park, even though he burned to pace to expend his energy. Although most of court was still abed, pacing would attract attention if anyone passed him.

Thankfully, Annalise soon swept into the park, her entire body concealed in a black cloak with Finn prowling beside her. Doubtless both were to protect her from unwanted advances.

His pulse quickening, he grinned and thrust from the oak then held his hand out for the white angelcat to inspect. "Finn is much larger than when we first met."

Annalise grinned back as Finn sniffed then purred and rubbed his head against Dare's hand. "And much less bloody. I'd just healed his fatal wound, you know."

Dare chuckled and petted the angelcat. Of course, that explained the blinding magic glowing around her the morning they'd met. "So I'm not the only one you've saved from death in this park. We must make sure it doesn't become a habit."

While Finn bounded into the branches of the oak Dare had leaned on earlier, Annalise hummed and slanted Dare a coy glance. "That depends on if you lose any more duels here or not."

Warmed by her flirting like he'd not been by Lady Blaine's, he waggled his brows at Annalise as they began walking through the park's well-tended trees. "We needn't worry then. I'm one of the most skilled swordsmen in Calatini. I've even an open invitation to attend Lady Ducharme's fencing salons."

Annalise giggled. "Impressive—or at least 'twould be if my eighteen-year-old brother hadn't trounced you."

Dare gasped and clutched his chest to tease her, and her face lit with her warm and radiant smile as she giggled again. Heat surging in his veins, he forgot to breathe for a moment. Goddess, 'twas glorious being the one to create that genuine smile.

He gulped a breath then jerked his gaze free from Annalise. Glancing at Finn prowling in the branches above them, he said, "I've an angelcat now too. Her name is Lily because of her cream fur." He quirked a wry smile. "Although perhaps I should have called her Queenie since she reigns over everyone. Mother gave Lily to me when I returned home after my first season, so I'd have a familiar to generate magical energy."

Somehow Annalise's beam glowed brighter. "I'd love to meet her. Bring her on our next morning walk."

His heart swelling, he grinned at Annalise. How like her to request that. He arched a playful brow. "Would Finn be all right with that?"

Annalise hummed and tilted her head. "Probably not at first, but meeting Lily would do him good." She sighed. "He's always been skittish of other angelcats. Three adults had him cornered when I discovered him as a kitten."

Dare nodded. Which explained the fatal wound she'd healed. "'Twas fortunate you discovered him when you did."

Annalise's eyes darkened as muddy-white loneliness pulsed

about her. "I know. My life would have been so much emptier without Finn."

He swallowed. Goddess, if only he could wrap Annalise in his arms. But he'd not resist kissing her if he did, and that was too dangerous. Yet at least with their soulbond, she'd never be so alone again. Clasping his hands behind his back to avoid reaching for her, he leaned toward her with a warm smile. He must distract them from her past loneliness. "What other animals do you have besides Finn and your stallion?"

CHAPTER 17

 er chest warming at Dare's tender smile, Annalise licked her lips. Goddess, when he smiled at her like that, 'twas nearly impossible to resist kissing him. But kisses would soon lead to more, and they mustn't consummate their soulbond. She inhaled then made herself answer his question, "Besides Finn and Storm, I've two mated faebirds—a sapphire male named Rain and an amethyst female named Aria."

Dare grinned. "I suspected you might. You wear their feathers in your hair sometimes."

She blinked to clear her blurry vision. Of course he'd noticed that. He was always so attentive. She managed a wry smile. "I'd have more animals if Mother and Father would allow it. Animals unconditionally return your love and never seek to exploit you."

His amber eyes darkening, Dare stilled and stared at her for a moment. Then he shook himself and winked. "I always knew you wanted a growing menagerie too. How do you like hellhounds?"

Annalise swallowed as her heart fluttered at his attempt to cheer her. "I adore them, but Mother and Father won't allow me to have any. They say they're not proper pets for ladies."

Dare chuckled. "They *are* rowdy. I've two—Raven and her mate Bear. They were the last natalday gift Father ever gave me."

Aching to take his hand, Annalise smiled at him instead. "Raven and Bear must be especially dear to you then." She paused. "When *is* your natalday?"

Dare arched his brows. "In spring, exactly halfway between Plantfete and Summerday. Why do you ask?"

She blushed but shrugged. "I owe you a natalday gift for that perfect faegift you gave me. Honeysuckle is my favorite scent—it reminds me of carefree summer afternoons in Wildewall."

Dare swallowed then rumbled, "It's become my favorite scent too, although not because of home." As she blushed harder, he coughed and resumed his normal voice, "But you don't owe me a natalday gift. You saved my life, after all. That's gift enough."

Her blush fading, Annalise pursed her lips. Not hardly. He deserved the perfect natalday gift, although she couldn't create a faegift like he had. She'd decide what before their next walk. "Can I thank you at least?"

Dare hummed. "Thank me how?"

The words "a kiss" burned on her tongue, but she swallowed and made herself reply, "The normal way, with words." When he gestured for her to continue, she beamed at him and said, "My deepest thanks for your lovely faegift, Dare. I truly treasure it."

Dare inclined his head. "I'm glad." They smiled at each other for a moment, then he sighed. "We should probably return. 'Tis surely almost breakfast."

Sighing as well, Annalise nodded, and they turned around. They both remained silent on the return walk. Doubtless he ached as she did that their time alone was nearly over.

However, just before she left the park, Dare halted and asked, "Here at the same time the day after tomorrow?"

Weight squeezing her chest, she smiled at him. "I look forward to it. Have fun riding with Alex tomorrow."

Dare remaining behind so no one would see them together, she hurried back to her family's townhouse. Since she was late, she kept her visit to Storm in the stables short before hastily feeding Finn, Rain, and Aria in her chambers.

When she glided into the breakfast room, Mother and Father were already eating. Wonderful. She swallowed as she sat beside Alex and heaped her plate with food.

Mother pursed her lips. "Annalise, there you are. Finish that mountain of food quickly. I've arranged appointments at Celeste's this morning, but the only ones left were early, so we must leave soon."

Annalise blinked as she buttered her toast. Mother must be desperate to accept an early appointment. "Why do we need new gowns?"

Mother frowned at her. "Didn't you see that arachne silk ballgown Miss Keyes wore to the fete yesterday? She was stunning, *and* Lord Beza Hawke nearly kissed her in the middle of the ballroom because of it."

Annalise sighed while she began her beefsteak. As she'd expected, Mother was annoyed that Miss Keyes's arachne silk surpassed her cerulean ballgown. Although the arachne silk had little to do with Lord Beza almost kissing Miss Keyes, considering their ardent embrace at the king's summer masquerade.

Mother leaned toward her. "We *must* have ballgowns from that magical fabric. King Devon shall propose as soon as he sees you wearing it."

Suppressing a grimace, Annalise devoured her beefsteak, eggs, and toast as if she were a starving werebear after a winterlong nap. If she didn't finish before 'twas time to leave, she'd be ravenous the rest of the day. And thanks to their appointments at Celeste's, she'd have no time to hunt for the perfect natalday gift for Dare. How vexing.

WHILE WALKING in the park the following morning with Finn, Annalise realized the perfect natalday gift for Dare. She'd a half-completed embroidery of her favorite Wildewall lake. If she embroidered every spare moment, she might complete it before their walk tomorrow, and he'd surely love it. So she raced back to the townhouse, fed her magical pets, grabbed her embroidery bag, bolted breakfast, then headed to the stables. Mother and Father would never think to look for her there.

After asking the grooms for a blanket, she laid it on the straw in Storm's stall then sat and began embroidering while Storm nickered and nibbled her hair. The stallion was clearly thrilled she'd joined him. She patted him every few stitches to distract herself from her painstaking embroidery.

She'd just completed the lakeshore when Alex coughed then said, "Annalise, the grooms said you were hiding in here. Why?" He paused. "Are you *embroidering*? You despise it."

Without glancing up, Annalise grimaced and rubbed her sore fingers. Yes, she did, even though her embroidery was flawless thanks to Mother. She threaded her needle with blue thread for the lake and replied, "I needed to escape Mother and Father's gloating about King Devon's supposed proposal, and Mother shall likely forgive my disappearance if I've embroidery to show for it."

Alex snorted. "I suppose embroidery is ladylike enough for her."

So he'd not quiz her further, Annalise asked as she began embroidering the lake, "How was your ride to the royal bay?"

After a lengthy pause, Alex hummed. "Fine. How did you know I rode there today?"

She froze. Because he'd ridden with Dare—not that she should know about those rides. She forced herself to resume embroidering. "A groom mentioned it."

Alex hummed again. "Ah. Well, I'd best go. Have fun embroidering."

Annalise sighed. Impossible, but she must complete this natalday gift for Dare. She kept embroidering until her stomach began gnawing her insides. However, when she slipped inside to grab luncheon, Mother found her and insisted she attend Lady

Islaye's salon that afternoon then the Escanas' card party that evening.

As she slid into bed, she glowered at her three-quarters-completed embroidery. She couldn't give that to Dare tomorrow. She sighed. Well, a belated natalday gift could wait a couple of extra days.

THE FOLLOWING morning when she met Dare in the park, Annalise's soulbond quivered, and her heart quickened, but her reaction wasn't near as desperate as before. His plan to meet to keep their soulbond sated must be succeeding. She grinned at the cream angelcat weaving about his ankles. "Is that Lily?"

Dare nodded as Lily stilled then trilled at Finn, who froze and eyed her.

Her throat tight, Annalise knelt and petted Finn's bristled fur to hearten him. "Go on, she shan't hurt you."

Finn crept to Lily with his tail low and stiff, and the two angelcats sniffed each other. Then Lily purred a meow and bounded into the oak branches above them. His now upright tail twitching, Finn bounded after her.

Annalise grinned at Dare. Amazing that Lily had cured Finn's nerves with one sniff. "Thank the Goddess they're already friends."

Dare hummed as he peered into the branches after the angelcats. "Perhaps more than that. Lily's never chosen a mate."

Warmth filled her chest. How perfect. "Neither has Finn."

Dare smoothed his beard while they began following the angelcats through the park. "Your parents better accept our marriage before Lily's litter is born. I'm not raising a riotous litter of angelkittens alone."

Annalise swallowed. 'Twas little chance Mother and Father would relent before then. "Could you cast a contraceptive spell on Lily?" Although witch healers usually handled that, nature witches often could too.

Red determination flared about Dare. "I could, but I won't. I refuse to give up hope that my letters seeking peace shan't succeed."

Sighing, she nodded. Then to cheer them both, she asked, "How was your ride with Alex?"

Dare grinned and described his morning with Alex then asked about hers. Talking the entire time, she and Dare walked in the well-tended park for around an hour before returning, so they'd not be late like last time. Finn grumbled when she separated him from Lily. Quite a change from his earlier nerves.

After their walk, Annalise embroidered Dare's natalday gift every moment she was free. Although she still attended the court events Mother wanted, including watching King Devon decide petitions at court the following afternoon. After the petitions, King Devon escorted Annalise about the throne room, even though they didn't bother to look for his mermaid since no one mysterious attended court petitions.

Lady Blaine sashayed over with the odious Mr. Winston. The fashionable countess must be desperate for a husband if she allowed that cad to escort her. Lady Blaine leaned toward King Devon. "Have you heard the scandalous news about poor Wren?"

King Devon frowned, probably not wanting to encourage gossip about his cousin's lady. "No."

Lady Blaine's smoky eyes gleamed. "Apparently she's *pregnant*."

Annalise almost shook her head. Not terribly surprising, given Miss Keyes and Lord Beza's behavior recently. Yet she'd not noticed the glow of Miss Keyes's pregnancy at the Duchess of Childes's fete, likely because the seer's potent magic about Miss Keyes had eclipsed it just like it had the arachne silk's residual magic.

Lady Blaine tsked. "And Wren is refusing to reveal the father. No doubt Sir Alaric and Lady Keyes shall send her to the country at once."

As King Devon scowled, fire flared through Annalise. Miss Keyes didn't deserve such gossip. Although they'd not spoken often, the reclusive lady seemed sweet, and she'd despise all of court gossiping about her. So Annalise chuckled and drawled, "Unlikely. I expect Miss Keyes and Lord Beza Hawke shall announce their wedding within a fortnight instead." While Lady Blaine gaped at her, Annalise turned to King Devon, who now smiled. "Mother and Father are beckoning me. Could you escort me, your majesty?"

After reaching her parents, she convinced them to leave, so she could resume embroidering Dare's natalday gift. She *must* complete it tonight. As soon as they returned to the townhouse, she darted up to her chambers and locked the door. Fortunately, she completed Dare's gift just before dinner and wrapped the embroidered lake in green paper with gold flecks—exactly like his lush aura.

The following morning, Annalise leapt from bed and darted to the park with Finn, arriving before Dare this time. When he joined her with a warm smile, she beamed back and thrust the wrapped gift toward him, while Finn and Lily bounded into the trees together. "For you. A belated natalday gift."

Indigo tenderness swirling about him, Dare accepted it but shook his head. "You didn't need to do this."

She leaned toward him, her heart surging. Silly man. "I wanted to. Open it, please."

Dare unwrapped the green and gold paper then inhaled. "'Tis exquisite. Is it Doimhn Lake?"

Grinning, Annalise almost giggled. Of course, a nature witch like Dare recognized it at once. "Yes, 'tis my favorite lake back home."

Dare swallowed then folded the paper back over his gift and tucked it beneath his arm. "Mine too. 'Tis the deepest in Calatini and has excellent fishing and stunning walks. We must visit together one day." He leaned forward. "Thank you, Annalise. I'll cherish it always."

She quit breathing as he bent his head. Goddess, he was about to kiss her. She should be stopping him. Instead, she swayed closer.

When their lips brushed, they both shivered, and the edges of their souls began to mesh.

But then Dare sighed and stepped back while separating their souls. "We'd better not."

Annalise swallowed but forced a wry smile. "I know." To distract them as they strolled after Finn and Lily, she asked, "Have you heard the latest court gossip?"

Dare echoed her smile. "About Miss Keyes? Yes. I expect she and Lord Beza Hawke shall marry within a fortnight."

Annalise frowned as her neck prickled. Exactly what she'd said. "You didn't say that to anyone, did you?"

Blinking, Dare eyed her. "No, why?"

She nibbled her lip. "We must be careful about revealing information only the other knows. I slipped and asked Alex about your ride together the other day." She grimaced. "A few more slips like that, and Alex shall discover our soulbond. He's perceptive and knows me too well."

Dare sighed and adjusted his gift beneath his arm. "True." He grinned at her. "Tell me about your favorite visit to Doimhn Lake, then I'll tell you mine."

Warming at his obvious attempt to hearten her, Annalise smiled back and described her visit with Alex two autumns ago when they'd found a river otter and her pups along the shore.

CHAPTER 18

During his sword fight with Alex on the cliffs above the royal bay a few mornings later, Dare grinned when Alex jerked aside to avoid a twirling thrust. Alex's skill was improving.

Alex grunted as he parried and riposted. "Dare, why do you bother to attend court every season? 'Tis obvious you much prefer Wildewall over Ormas."

Dare sighed and feinted then thrust. "Because I need a wife, and no one back home appeals. This season I swore not to return unwed." His heart squeezed. Then he'd become soulbound to Annalise and couldn't leave without her. Yet her parents refused to forgive the past and end the feud, despite his many letters seeking peace. He leapt forward then knocked aside Alex's sword to press his own against Alex's chest to win.

Alex chuckled as they cleaned and sheathed their swords. "You could always marry Lady Blaine. Even *I've* heard she's pursuing you."

Shuddering, Dare leapt into Ebony's saddle. "Goddess, no. I need a kind lady who loves nature, outdoor pursuits, pets, and children." Annalise, even if they weren't soulbound.

Alex hummed as he mounted. "How specific." He flashed an

irrepressible grin. "Race you to the path to the beach." He spurred Biscuit to a gallop.

Dare urged Ebony to a gallop as well, but Alex and Biscuit still beat them. After riding down the winding path, they galloped along the beach for an hour or so while he gathered natural energy before they returned to Ormas.

At Ravenstone House, Dare tended to Ebony, who nuzzled him when he left. As soon as he entered the townhouse, Raven and Bear bayed and thundered toward him with Lily sauntering close behind—expected when he returned from a ride. Yet his butler approaching with a lanky footman wasn't.

Brown coughed and gestured toward the fidgeting footman beside him. "Young James has some information I think you should hear, my lord."

Dare arched his brows at James but continued petting Lily and Raven with Bear leaning against his thighs. Perhaps remaining kneeling would encourage the nervous footman to talk. "Go on."

James swallowed. "Me and some mates was meetin' at The Fox, and we happened to see a most unexpected visitor, my lord."

When Dare frowned, Brown explained, "The Fox is a common tavern a few streets over. 'Tis the closest to Ravenstone House, so many of the servants visit on their days off."

Dare nodded then scratched Lily's chin when she butted his hand. Ah yes, Thom had mentioned the place—said The Fox's spiritmead was watery compared to that brewed back in Wilde-wall, but 'twas still the best in Ormas. "I see. And who was this unexpected visitor?"

James leaned forward, his voice lowering, "Lord Greysnowe, my lord. He was meetin' with a shady man that nobody had seen before, and Betsy, the barmaid who's a friend of mine, said she overheard Lord Greysnowe talkin' about unexpected accidents when she brought them their ale."

Stiffening, Dare ceased petting Lily and Raven. What scheme

was Annalise's father plotting now? Clearly something clandestine—Lord Greysnowe was too obsessed with status to visit a common tavern otherwise. Dare set his jaw and rose. "Did Betsy overhear anything else?"

James lowered his gaze and twisted his hands. "Not really. The shady man stormed from The Fox not long after. Whatever Lord Greysnowe said must of insulted him. But Betsy did say the count's been in the tavern a couple times during the past week meetin' other shady men, and that he must be annoyin' because his companions always leave angry."

Dare frowned, a chill prickling his neck. Lord Greysnowe must be determined then, but *what* were his intentions? Dare made himself smile at James. "Thanks for telling us about Lord Greysnowe. We'll figure out his suspicious behavior soon. Brown, please make sure James is suitably rewarded."

James jerked a bow. "Thanks, my lord."

Once the footman bolted from the entrance hall, Dare sighed and let his smile fade. He turned to Brown. "Two servants should visit The Fox every night to watch for Lord Greysnowe and report back his doings. And pay Betsy and the other tavern staff to report back as well." Please let that be enough to discover Lord Greysnowe's scheme before it unfolded.

Frowning, he smoothed his beard as he strode upstairs with Lily, Raven, and Bear close behind. Should he tell Annalise about her father's suspicious tavern visit during their walk tomorrow? He sighed. No, they knew too little right now, and she'd only worry. He'd tell her once he'd discovered Lord Greysnowe's scheme.

So the following morning, Dare brought Raven and Bear along with Lily to the park. Introducing Annalise to his hellhounds would make sure he didn't mention Lord Greysnowe meeting shady men in The Fox.

Yellow joy glowing around her, Annalise beamed when she

joined him. As Lily and Finn bounded into the oak branches together like always, she knelt before the hellhounds and offered them her hands. "These beauties must be Raven and Bear."

Their black tails thumping against the ground, Raven and Bear sniffed then licked Annalise's outstretched hands. When she giggled and scratched their chests in that spot they loved, their eyes burst into flame with excitement, and they leaned against her.

As Annalise giggled harder and continued scratching, warmth flooded his chest and his soulbond burgeoned, like it had when she'd first met Lily. Not surprising his magical pets and Annalise had adored each other at once. One day, they'd probably adore her *more* than him. Chuckling, he nudged Raven and Bear aside then pulled Annalise upright. "Beauties that shall crush you if they aren't careful."

Her hair shimmering in the dappled shade, Annalise tilted her head and flashed a brilliant grin. "Nonsense. Raven and Bear know their own strength."

Burning to pull her against him then kiss his radiant and kind lady, Dare released her and clenched his hands together behind his back instead. "But they don't understand human limitations. Even Raven, the more perceptive of the two, appears confused that I can't trace a scent when we're hunting."

As they began walking with Raven and Bear pausing to sniff every tree and bush, Annalise hummed then shrugged. "There are always misunderstandings between different creatures."

He tensed. And between humans as well—like suspicious visits to a common tavern. He muttered, "Or between families."

Annalise's cerulean eyes darkened, but she smiled. "Or even between ladies and the gentlemen they love. Apparently, the misunderstanding between Miss Keyes and Lord Beza Hawke has been resolved, and they're marrying this week in a private ceremony."

Dare relaxed at her attempt to lighten their discussion. Wise of her. "Not at all surprising. I'm happy for them." Yet he couldn't help adding, "I only hope we can share the same good fortune soon."

Annalise hummed and pursed her lips. "A scandalous pregnancy?"

He grinned at her, his pulse quickening. He couldn't wait until she was carrying his child. "No, the hasty wedding. Soulbound or not, your parents would probably never end the feud if I made you pregnant before we married."

Her shoulders drooping and muddy-yellow despair swamping her, Annalise hummed again but said nothing.

Dare swallowed as his chest clenched at her silence. Doubtless she was thinking her parents would never end the feud regardless. To distract them, he nodded toward Raven and Bear then asked, "Do you think you can risk a longer morning outing one day? Hunting with Raven and Bear in Blacke Woods is exhilarating."

Annalise brightened for a moment then sighed. "Not yet. Mother and Father are too determined for me to catch King Devon to not mind me missing for an entire morning. But I can once he finds his mermaid."

He winked to hearten her. "Then Raven, Bear, and I pray that King Devon finds his mysterious mermaid soon."

Annalise grinned back. "So do I."

OVER THE FOLLOWING TWO DAYS, Dare's servants kept visiting The Fox, but Lord Greysnowe never returned, so Dare still said nothing to Annalise about her father's suspicious behavior during their next morning walk. Instead, he brought Raven and Bear again, and they chuckled over the hellhounds' rowdy antics, especially Bear daring to lick Annalise's cheek when she bent to pet him and Raven.

After his walk with Annalise, he returned to Ravenstone House and wrote his weekly letter to her father, making sure not to hint at the other count's suspicious visits to a common tavern.

Revealing that would only make Lord Greysnowe feel defensive and less likely to end the feud. Plus, he'd quit his visits before Dare's servants could discover his scheme.

Once Brown took his unlabeled letter, Dare uncovered his paired communication mirror then chanted the brief spell and waved his hand to activate it.

The mirror glowed white before Mother appeared, sitting in a clearing with her brown mare Willow grazing behind her. She smoothed back her windswept hair with a vibrant grin. "Morning, Dare. How's your week been?"

He swallowed. Since telling Annalise about her father's suspicious visits would only worry her, perhaps he could tell Mother instead and ask her advice. "A bit troubling. Some servants have seen Lord Greysnowe visiting a common tavern and meeting with shady men. But they couldn't tell why, although Lord Greysnowe doesn't visit often or stay long. I've had servants watching since then, yet they've learned nothing new. Any thoughts?"

Her gaze shadowed, Mother frowned. "Troubling, indeed. Although we've never met, I've heard that Lord Greysnowe is much too conscious of his status to ever visit a common tavern without a serious motive. Whatever he's doing involves the feud."

Dare grimaced. That much was obvious and not helpful. "Yes, but what? Apparently, all the men he's met with have left angry. Yet he returns every few days."

Still frowning, Mother shook her head. "Maybe he's hiring them for an underhanded task, and they don't like his terms? Someone shall have to overhear their conversations to be certain. Perhaps you can provide the servants listening spells?"

Rubbing his beard, he frowned. Except Lord Greysnowe was a Rhiannon-descendant witch, so he'd surely sense most listening spells—even if Alex said he and his father weren't that powerful. "Except Alex told me he and his parents are witches."

Mother's brows rose. "What about Lady Annalise? Although

witches can have children without powers, given her lineage, I'd be surprised if she didn't have any."

Dare swallowed but forced a shrug. "Alex said she didn't."

Mother hummed and eyed him, her frown almost returning.

He swallowed again. Could she sense his lie buried beneath the truth? They must quit discussing Annalise before he said too much, if he hadn't already. He leaned forward. "But we've digressed. Providing the servants with listening spells wouldn't work since Lord Greysnowe would likely sense them and either block or destroy them."

Mother inclined her head. "Unless you provided the servants *another* spell to distract his magical senses."

Tapping his finger on his desk, Dare nodded. "I'll risk that if my servants don't discover Lord Greysnowe's scheme in a week or so." He couldn't hide something from Annalise much longer than that. To divert Mother from Annalise's family, he smiled at Mother and asked, "So how's Pearl?"

He and Mother talked about her angelkitten then said good-bye, so Mother could continue her ride. He sighed as he waved his hand to deactivate the communication mirror then set it on the windowsill to recharge. Hopefully, he'd not need to use Mother's advice.

THE FOLLOWING MORNING, a kitchen servant named George told Dare that Lord Greysnowe had visited The Fox the previous evening. Unfortunately, George and the others had learned nothing new, although last night's shady man had tossed his ale in Lord Greysnowe's face before storming from the tavern—the most dramatic reaction by far.

Dare sighed but thanked George. Had Lord Greysnowe visited The Fox because of the letter seeking peace Dare had sent earlier that day? Perhaps Annalise would know.

So during their walk at the park the following morning, he asked Annalise, "How have your parents been lately?"

Annalise grimaced as she tossed a stick for Raven to fetch. "Smug about King Devon's supposed proposal, although they're becoming impatient that he's not proposed yet. Why do you ask?"

His stomach twisting, he managed a shrug. "Because your father still hasn't responded to any of my eleven letters." And was acting suspicious.

Annalise winced and nibbled her lip. "Over two weeks ago, my parents mentioned some idea to make you 'quit sending those deceitful letters.' But they refused to explain, and I forgot to warn you when we—spoke at the fete. Your ravenous kisses made me forget everything else."

Heat flared in his veins, and his body tightened. If only he could kiss her like that again. But although seeing her frequently helped ease their soulbond, even one kiss would be like a spark falling on a forest floor after a summer of no rain. He sighed. "Understandable. I forget everything else too."

Red passion and indigo tenderness swirling about her, Annalise swayed toward him then jerked back with her hands clenched at her sides. "I must go. See you the day after tomorrow." She called Finn then darted from the park.

Dare stared after her, his chest squeezing. Goddess, how he burned to chase after her and tumble her into his arms where she belonged. But he couldn't. Not until her parents accepted their soulbond and marriage.

CHAPTER 19

When Annalise slipped into the park to meet Dare for their next morning walk, she gulped a bracing breath. They mustn't discuss kissing again—just thinking about their ravenous kisses at the fete had almost made her control crumble, and her dreams the past two nights had all involved kissing Dare. Not ideal for restful slumber.

Shoving that aside when she joined Dare, she knelt to scratch Raven's and Bear's chests and smiled at Lily and Finn rubbing against each other with purring meows. Definitely mates. Then Bear took advantage of her distraction to lick her cheek like before, until Raven wedged herself between them. Chuckling along with Dare, she rose then tossed sticks for Raven and Bear to chase.

As the hellhounds coursed away, Lily smirked after them then nuzzled Finn again before bounding into the oak branches with a coy glance. Finn leapt after her, his gaze intense and tail quivering. Quite a change from his slinking about Annalise's chambers earlier.

She grinned at Dare. "I swear poor Finn mopes the rest of the day without Lily."

No longer chuckling, Dare managed a faint smile, but his eyes remained shaded. Not like him at all. "So does Lily."

Annalise leaned toward Dare, her chest tightening. His movements lacked their usual energy too. "What's wrong?"

Sighing, Dare rubbed his beard as muddy-yellow sadness flared about him. "I suppose concealing our soulbond and your parents' mulish refusal to end the feud are upsetting me. I don't understand why people can't just accept each other."

She swallowed and clenched her hands to remain still. Goddess, if only she could wrap him in her arms to comfort him. But 'twas almost as dangerous as kisses. "I know."

Dare shuddered as they began following Raven and Bear. "Plus, the Dabars' rout party yesterday was painful. I merely attended because I thought you might be there."

Annalise grimaced. If only Mother and Father had chosen the rout hosted by the Minister of Transportation and his wife. "We attended Lady Morwynne's card party instead." For some reason, since the king's summer masquerade, Mother and Father had become close with the superior and manipulative countess who served as the Minister of Health and Community.

Dare sighed then tossed Raven's stick when she dropped it at his feet. "Well, not long after I arrived at the rout, Lady Blaine cornered me then clung to me like a hungry python the entire evening, despite my frequent hints she should leave." He shuddered again. "Last night, she was almost desperate—as if with Lord Beza Hawke now married, I was her only option for a husband."

Fire flashed through Annalise. How dare Lady Blaine attempt to steal Dare? Couldn't the sultry countess find an unattached gentleman to pursue? She inhaled to calm herself. Such jealous thoughts couldn't benefit Dare. "Somehow, you must prove you aren't an option. Perhaps when she next corners you, mention that you prefer the country over court, so you'll rarely leave Wildewall once married, and you shan't live apart from your wife. A fashionable court lady like Lady Blaine wouldn't want to be buried in the country."

Dare shook his head before tossing Bear's stick again. "I hinted that several times last night, but Lady Blaine ignored me. Although maybe being blunt shall succeed."

Annalise hummed and tilted her head. The countess must have been desperate indeed to have ignored being buried in the country. "Just keep reminding Lady Blaine the reasons you aren't an option every time she pursues you, and don't let her trick you into a betrothal. Always attempt to steer her toward other suitable gentlemen, and slip away as soon as you've an opportunity. Not even a hellhound would continue such an obviously futile hunt."

Straightening, Dare chuckled. "Don't be too certain about that. One early spring morning, Raven and Bear chased a marsh rabbit in the freezing rain through a swamp for hours until they finally caught it. Nothing I attempted persuaded them to quit. 'Twas miserable, and I nearly caught lung fever."

She eyed Raven and Bear, who were sniffing the ground while still carrying their sticks. Hellhounds were renowned as tireless hunters who'd not stop until they caught their prey, but through a swamp in freezing rain? "'Tis fortunate that Lady Blaine isn't a hellhound then."

Dare flashed a wry grin. "I don't know. I'd not mind adding another hellhound to our menagerie. Another wife, however... no."

Suppressing an echoing smile, Annalise arched her brows. Of course, Dare wanted more pets—a nature witch like him would doubtless keep adding plants and animals until his residences could hold no more. Not that she'd mind—she adored plants and animals too. "Having two wives *is* illegal in Calatini and most of Damensea. Only the Tsarkan Empire allows men to have multiple wives."

Dare tsked. "I pity the men of the Tsarkan Empire." He whistled for their angelcats and his hellhounds. "We should be heading back. 'Tis almost breakfast."

She sighed as weight squeezed her chest. So it was. Why must their morning walks always seem so short? "I suppose so."

They retraced their steps in silence with their magical pets close behind, but at the edge of the park, Dare said, "See you here next time. I'm riding with Alex tomorrow, but I promise not to reveal anything only you should know."

Aching to touch his hand or kiss him, Annalise pursed her lips instead. "Hopefully, I can do the same. Come on, Finn."

She glided from the park as Finn grumbled and slunk away from Lily. She sighed. She understood exactly how the angelcat felt. Leaving Dare was always hard, especially since they must feign indifference elsewhere.

AFTER WALKING in the park the following morning with Finn, who moped and meowed for Lily the entire time, Annalise bolted breakfast before Mother and Father arrived. She fetched Finn and a book from her chambers then slipped out to the stables and into Storm's stall. As Finn disappeared to chase mice, she groomed Storm, who nickered and leaned into every stroke. The massive stallion adored when she groomed him.

She'd finished that and was reading, curled on a blanket in his stall, when Alex coughed then drawled, "Hiding from Father and Mother again, I see. No embroidery this time?"

Closing her book and rising, she pursed a wry smile and shook the straw from her blue-gray skirt. "I finished that piece, and I don't think I can start another for a year at least." Forcing herself to sound casual and *not* mention the royal bay this time, she asked, "How was your ride?"

Alex grinned and leaned against the stall door then scratched Storm's muzzle when the stallion craned toward him. "Exciting. I galloped at the royal bay again."

Her heart aching at Alex galloping with Dare like she couldn't, Annalise arched her brows to continue feigning indifference. "You've been riding there a lot lately."

Alex shrugged. "The scenery isn't as wild as at home, but 'tis the best near Ormas." He cocked his head. "So why are you hiding today? Is Father and Mother's gloating worse?"

She grimaced then sighed. "No, Mother and Father are beginning to fret that King Devon hasn't escorted me to, or even attended, any court events since before Lord and Lady Beza Hawke's wedding several days ago." Which hadn't been unusual before he'd asked her to help hunt for his mermaid. Yet he'd not written to disclose why he'd quit his hunt. Perhaps something had happened when he attended his cousin's wedding.

She shook her head. "Mother talked about attending Miss Hawke's embroidery party this afternoon, in case King Devon stops by his cousin's event."

Orange mirth swirling about him, Alex chuckled. "And you can't start another piece for a year." He tsked. "But if you keep hiding in the stables, Father and Mother shall discover you. The grooms do work for them, after all."

Annalise grimaced again as her stomach twisted. The grooms wouldn't dare lie to Mother and Father, who'd doubtless start hunting for her soon. "I know, but my chambers are too obvious, and where else can I hide?"

Alex hummed with a grin. "You need an activity that removes you from the townhouse—like your brother taking you on a long ride."

She blinked at him. Did he mean now? "But you just finished a long ride."

Winking, Alex shrugged. "To save my beloved sister from embroidery, I can manage another. I'll go have Cook pack luncheon for us, so we can remain out the entire afternoon. You get Storm and Biscuit ready."

Warmth filling her chest, Annalise grinned while she saddled their horses. Alex was truly the best brother. If only she could tell him about her powers and soulbond with Dare.

So she and Alex rode along the coast south of Ormas and spent a delightful day riding and basking beneath the late summer sun. Fortunately, as a soul healer, her high-energy aura instantly repaired her minor ailments—otherwise, her pale skin would have been redder than a boiled krab after so much time in the sun. Alex didn't share her powers, but he wore a sunshield charm from his healer which did the same.

When they returned just before dinner, Wilson handed her a letter from the new Lady Beza Hawke. Annalise blinked at the polite invitation to a private luncheon a few days before Harvestfete. The most she and the reclusive lady had ever spoken had been at the Duchess of Childes's fete. Perhaps Lady Beza wanted to thank her for not spreading rumors about her and Lord Beza's ardent embrace at the king's summer masquerade.

Despite not knowing the reason behind Lady Beza's invitation, Annalise still penned her acceptance after she and her parents returned from the Duke of Oakmoor's ball that evening, which King Devon hadn't attended, much to Mother and Father's frustration. Perhaps King Devon was pursuing the new rumors about his mermaid being a lost princess rather than bothering with the court events his mermaid hadn't attended since his summer masquerade.

Over the following few days, Mother and Father kept dragging Annalise to various court events, hoping to encounter King Devon, but the king remained elusive until they attended petitions at court. Annalise blinked when they entered the throne room—the glittering nightmara magic about King Devon had vanished. Was *that* why he'd quit his hunt for his mermaid? But she never got to find out because he left before she and her parents could speak with him. When she told Dare the following morning during their walk, he was relieved that King Devon was no longer escorting her, although she still wished she knew why. Until King Devon found his mermaid, Mother and Father would never quit shoving her at him.

When King Devon's invitation to his Harvestfete masquerade arrived that afternoon, Mother scowled at the black vellum letter with gold lettering. "*Another* masquerade, and in less than two weeks? How are we supposed to have new costumes by then? We don't even have the arachne silk ballgowns we ordered from Celeste's after the Duchess of Childes's fete, and we should have received those last week."

Annalise hummed. Considering King Devon only held his summer masquerade since 'twas tradition, this masquerade must involve his mermaid. Perhaps he was hoping to coax her from hiding with another masked event. Annalise smiled at Mother. "Our maids can help us assemble suitable costumes."

Mother scowled harder, muddy-red annoyance surging about her. "Nonsense. We *need* costumes from Celeste's. I'll write to see if they've appointments tomorrow. And let her know we'll fetch our arachne silk ballgowns then too."

That evening when Mother received the reply from Celeste, she almost growled then crumpled the letter. "The Duchess of Childes secured all of Celeste's appointments for tomorrow. Why in the Goddess's name does she need so many?"

Annalise blinked. That *was* odd. "Maybe the Duchess of Childes wanted to ensure her daughters-in-law and other female relatives had appointments."

Mother pursed her lips. "Why? None of them want to catch King Devon." She huffed a sigh. "At least Celeste had appointments for us first thing the day after tomorrow. I just hope eleven days is enough time for Celeste to finish our costumes."

Annalise stilled, her chest squeezing. She'd another walk with Dare that morning. "How early is first thing?"

Mother frowned at her. "Straight after breakfast, so you'd better not sleep late."

Inclining her head, Annalise lowered her gaze. She never

slept late because soul healers required less sleep than most. 'Twas why she could rise at dawn to escape and center herself, even after staying at most court events until midnight. She sighed. But she'd need to shorten her morning walk with Dare. Wonderful. She forced a cool smile. "Of course, Mother."

CHAPTER 20

$\mathcal{W}$hen Annalise joined Dare in the park for their next morning walk, his soulbond stirred, and his soul strained to touch hers. Like always, he yanked his soul back then clasped his hands behind him. Their morning walks the past three weeks had mostly eased their soulbond, but he still ached to hold her every day. Yet he couldn't risk touching or kissing her—once he started, he'd likely not stop until he made love to her. Burying his hunger, he made himself grin. "Morning."

As Lily and Finn bounded into the trees, Annalise sighed then bent to pet Raven and Bear panting at her feet, but she rose before Bear could lick her cheek. "I can't stay long today. Mother and I have an early appointment at Celeste's for costumes to wear at the king's Harvestfete masquerade."

He swallowed, his pulse quickening at her siren costume from the previous masquerade. She'd been so enthralling that evening. Would he survive another such costume without betraying their soulbond? "What do you intend to dress as?"

Annalise tilted her head, her white-blonde hair shimmering. "A magical creature less striking, and one fitting Harvestfete."

Aching to bury his fingers in her radiant hair, Dare nodded

and tossed some sticks for Raven and Bear. The festival of the Goddess marking the start of autumn celebrated both the harvest and deceased ancestors. But a harvest creature would still be too irresistible. "How about a banshee? Like sirens, they're known for their voices."

Annalise hummed. "Except to portend death, not charm anything. And since they're pallid with tangled white hair, I resemble one already—except for their red eyes. All I truly need is a tattered ballgown and perhaps a bit of powder to enhance the resemblance." She flashed a grin. "I like it—'tis simple and fitting—although Mother shall doubtless complain."

His chest eased. Dressing as a magical creature involved with death might make other gentlemen nervous to approach her. He smiled at Annalise while he tossed Raven's stick again. "I'm certain you can withstand her complaints."

Annalise chuckled. "Maybe I can convince her that King Devon shall approve of costumes fitting Harvestfete." She arched her brows at him. "What shall you dress as?"

Dare swallowed as his soulbond twisted. Matching costumes would help soothe the ache of seeing her dance with anyone but him. Yet it must be subtle enough that no one else realized it. "I'll be a thanatos." The magical creature collected souls of the dead for the gods. He grinned at Annalise. "'Tis an even simpler costume than yours—all I need is a black robe and a scythe. I can even wear ordinary evening clothes beneath my robe."

Annalise pursed her lips as muddy-yellow worry flared about her. "Should we both wear costumes embodying death? Someone might realize our... involvement."

He shrugged as Bear returned with his stick. "No one shall connect our costumes if we remain apart in public, which we must do regardless." Damn her parents' obsession with the feud. "Besides, plenty of others shall wear costumes fitting Harvestfete."

Annalise hummed. "True enough." She grimaced then sighed.

"I must go. Mother shall be furious if I'm late. Have fun riding with Alex tomorrow. Come on, Finn."

His heart squeezing, Dare stared after Annalise gliding from the park with the grumbling Finn. Goddess, why must separating always be so wrenching? Shoving that aside, he turned and headed deeper into the park. With Raven and Bear coursing after the sticks he tossed them and Lily meowing for Finn in the trees above his head, he strolled through the park for another hour to help settle his soul with the tame bit of nature there before returning to Ravenstone House.

When Dare strode inside with his magical pets, the young groom Stephen pacing in the entrance hall halted and jerked a bow. "Thank the Goddess you're back, my lord. I've news about Lord Greysnowe's visit to The Fox last night, but you left before I could tell you."

Dare stiffened but smiled at Stephen, who strongly resembled the head groom Roberts, the young man's father, in both looks and temperament. No doubt one day Stephen would assume his father's position. "Go on, Stephen."

Stephen frowned and leaned forward. "I managed to sit at the table beside Lord Greysnowe, so I could overhear his conversation. He asked the shady man his price, which the shady man said depended on the job but started at five gold. Then Lord Greysnowe asked what was the price for killing someone at court, and the shady man growled he didn't accept jobs from people stupid enough to discuss them in a crowded tavern where anyone could overhear. Then the shady man stormed from The Fox, just like the others on previous nights."

Dare stiffened as a chill froze his chest. Was Annalise's father contacting *assassins*? Dear Goddess. Since the feud had begun eleven generations ago, no Ravenstone or Greysnowe had ever stooped to that. Forcing a smile, he clapped Stephen's shoulder. "Thanks for your report. Don't mention what you overheard to anyone, not even your father."

Stephen blinked but nodded. Then the young groom bowed and hurried back to the stables.

Striding from the entrance hall with Lily, Raven, and Bear close behind, Dare scoured Ravenstone House until he found Brown in the wine cellar. He nodded at the butler. "Morning, Brown. We must adjust the servants' monitoring of Lord Greysnowe." With assassins involved, 'twasn't safe. "The servants should still visit The Fox every night, but *none* are to approach Lord Greysnowe or obviously watch him. And quit paying the tavern staff to help."

Brown frowned, setting down a second bottle of wine. "Of course, my lord, but why?"

Dare plucked Lily from the narrow table when she began sniffing the wine bottles—in another moment, she'd be swatting them to watch them fall. "Because Lord Greysnowe might be hiring assassins." He narrowed his eyes at Brown. "But *don't* mention that to anyone. Such rumors would feed the Raven-stone-Greysnowe feud beyond mending." Plus, a healer like Annalise would be devastated to learn her father sought to hire assassins since murder was anathema to them. And a decent gentleman like Alex would be appalled too.

Swallowing, Brown paled but nodded.

Dare sighed and dropped Lily to the floor between Raven and Bear. He must report Lord Greysnowe's activities to King Devon, although he required further information before he did. Stephen's report had been damning, but the shady man wasn't confirmed to be an assassin. And who was Lord Greysnowe attempting to eliminate—Dare or the king's mysterious mermaid if she ever reappeared? Dare frowned at Brown. "Hire someone to confirm if the shady men Lord Greysnowe has been meeting with are assassins. And see if they can unearth his target as well. Make sure they know their inquiry must remain secret. And pay them whatever necessary."

Brown inclined his head as they headed upstairs. "I'll hire someone at once, my lord."

Trudging to his chambers with his magical pets bounding before him, Dare grimaced and rubbed his beard. Goddess, Lord Greysnowe's scheme was so much worse than he'd ever suspected. Please let him be able to handle it without devastating Annalise or feeding the feud.

WHEN DARE AWOKE at dawn the following morning, he glowered at the deluge out his window. He'd been anticipating his ride and sword fight with Alex to work through his upset before he faced Annalise again. He couldn't betray their father's involvement with assassins to her. Yet riding to the royal bay in that deluge would be unpleasant, even for a nature witch.

He tapped his fingers against his thigh. He could attend Lady Ducharme's fencing salon like he usually did in such weather, but rearranging his meeting with Alex wasn't ideal. The younger gentleman might want to meet on a morning he was supposed to walk with Annalise, and only seeing her every other morning was hard enough. So he sent an unlabeled letter to Greysnowe House, asking Alex to meet him at the nearby park instead.

Covered in a cloak spelled against rain, Alex arched his brows when he met Dare beneath the well-tended trees. "Meeting here with our swords seems ominous. Are you challenging me to another duel? Not the best idea in this rain—our swords might slip."

Dare smiled at Alex's teasing. Young hellion. "No, I thought we could attend Lady Ducharme's fencing salon since riding to the royal bay isn't feasible. She's sent you an invitation by now, hasn't she?"

Alex straightened in his saddle. "Yes, but I've not attended because I was concerned I might betray our friendship through some of the moves you taught me." He paused. "Lady Ducharme also wrote I should only attend in fair weather."

Dare grinned and shrugged, water spraying from his cloak spelled against rain. Of course, the farsighted baroness had. "'Tis because I often attend in this sort of weather, and she wants to prevent us from meeting. She doesn't want another nearly fatal duel."

Alex grimaced. "Only Father and Mother are senseless enough to want that." He twisted his reins about his fingers. "If we attend together, Lady Ducharme and the others shall know we're friends, and Father and Mother might discover it too. I can't risk that."

Warmed by Alex's determination to protect Annalise, Dare kneed Ebony to leave the park. "If we tell them our friendship is secret, none of them shall mention it. Plus, you'll enjoy meeting everyone."

Alex hummed but urged Biscuit to walk beside them. "Very well."

While they rode to Lady Ducharme's, Dare eyed Alex. He should see if Alex knew anything that would help explain his father's assassins. But he couldn't let Alex discover why to avoid damaging Alex's relationship with his father. "Have you noticed anything odd with your father and mother in the past month or so?"

Alex snorted. "Other than their ridiculous fury whenever they receive one of your letters seeking peace? Not particularly."

His chest tightening, Dare gripped Ebony's reins. Doubtless that fury had inspired Lord Greysnowe's scheme with the assassins. The opposite of what he'd wanted when he began sending his letters. Why must Annalise's parents be so mulish? He'd better quit sending his letters to avoid further infuriating them. But what else could he do to convince them to end the feud?

Once they leapt from their saddles at Ducharme House, he forced himself to grin at Alex. "Enough of the feud. Ready to cross swords with the best swordsmen and swordswomen in Calatini?"

Alex grinned back and nodded, his blue eyes wide and glowing.

A pang darted through Dare. Just like Annalise's when riding at the royal bay or meeting his magical pets. He waved for Alex to precede him up the front steps. After they handed their dripping cloaks to Lady Ducharme's burly butler, he led Alex to the sparring hall. When they strode inside, everyone froze and gaped at them. Grinning, Dare clapped Alex's shoulder. "My secret friend here has come to sharpen his already excellent skill with swords."

Her hand resting on her pommel, Lady Ducharme strode forward with a faint smile. "I suppose by secret you mean Lord and Lady Greysnowe don't know of their only son's friendship with their ancestral enemy."

As Dare nodded, Alex grimaced and raised his eyes skyward. "Exactly. And if they ever discovered it, they'd be worse than crazed chimeras."

Lady Ducharme's mouth twitched. "No doubt they would. Well, they shan't discover your friendship from us. Allow me to introduce you to everyone." She took Alex's arm and escorted him around the sparring hall, starting with the Campbells.

Following them, Dare almost laughed when Lady Ducharme finally introduced Alex and young Lord Morwynne. As expected, the two younger gentlemen began a lively conversation then stepped into a fencing circle to cross swords. Definitely likeminded souls.

Lady Ducharme glided over to Dare to watch Alex and Lord Morwynne's sword fight. She chuckled. "Only you, Lord Ravenstone, would befriend the ancestral enemy who nearly killed you."

Dare shrugged, grinning when Alex used the evasive thrust he'd taught him. "'Twas an accident, and Alex apologized. Plus, we share the same interests—Wildewall, riding, swords." Annalise. "And we both believe our families' feud should end. How could we not become friends?"

Lady Ducharme hummed, and they silently watched the rest of Alex and Lord Morwynne's sword fight, which Lord Morwynne barely won when he and Alex were both gasping.

The Campbells joined Dare and Lady Ducharme. Sir Ellis grinned at Dare. "Shall we show those boys how 'tis done?"

Dare grinned back. A strenuous sword fight was exactly what he needed before he faced Annalise again. "Gladly."

THE FOLLOWING MORNING, Dare managed a warm smile for Annalise when she joined him in the park. Hopefully, his aura didn't betray his upset over her father's assassins. "We must stay on the gravel paths today. The ground is like a swamp after yesterday's deluge."

Annalise smiled back as she bent to pet Raven and Bear while Lily and Finn disappeared into the trees. "Not very adventurous for a nature witch. Couldn't you make the ground solid with your magic?"

He shrugged. A stone spell was easy enough. "I could, but why waste my magic when we can avoid the mud by simply remaining on the paths?"

Annalise tsked and straightened with a saucy grin. "So lazy."

Tingling warmth surged through Dare at her teasing. He leaned forward. Goddess, he burned to kiss her again.

Annalise licked her lips, and her eyes deepened to navy as she swayed toward him. Then she jerked back, and her gaze skittered away. "Given the deluge, what did you and Alex do yesterday?"

He made himself walk calmly beside Annalise rather than pulling her into his arms. She was right to avoid kisses, no matter how they both burned for them. "I took him to Lady Ducharme's fencing salon. Now that he knows our secret friendship is safe there, I suspect he'll attend often."

Annalise chuckled, her face softening and indigo tenderness swirling about her. "Every morning probably, except the ones he's meeting you."

Dare swallowed at Annalise's obvious love for her younger brother. She was the most loving lady he'd ever met. He burned to kiss her even more now. He halted, and they turned to face each other.

As they swayed closer, a yowl then a strident hiss shattered the quiet morning. Lily and Finn! What trouble had the angelcats run into?

Dare and Annalise whirled toward the fight and darted through the trees, their feet squelching in the mud. As they ran with Raven and Bear coursing beside them, another vociferous yowl echoed through the park, and they raced faster.

They halted when they reached the chestnut tree containing the fighting angelcats. Crouched in front of Lily, Finn growled at the massive, light gray angelcat standing before a smaller, white angelcat. Lily and Finn must have stumbled across another mated pair, and Finn and the other male had begun fighting to protect their mates.

Lily hissing behind him, Finn growled louder and slunk closer to the gray angelcat then raised his paw, and the gray angelcat yowled back and raised his paw as well.

Then Raven and Bear flung themselves at the chestnut tree, baying with their eyes bursting into flame.

The gray angelcat jerked from his predatory crouch, then he and his mate skittered away through the trees. Finn immediately relaxed, and Lily rubbed against him.

Annalise turned to Dare, her eyes wide. "Did you see how Finn was protecting Lily? He used to hide whenever we encountered other angelcats. But not today."

Dare forced a shrug. "Finn had to protect his mate." He'd do the same if he was the angelcat.

He eyed Lily and Finn nuzzling each other in the chestnut tree. He'd better cast a contraceptive spell on Lily when they returned to Ravenstone House. She wasn't pregnant yet, but it wouldn't be long before she was. And since Annalise's parents clearly wouldn't end the feud soon, he'd end up raising a litter of angelkittens alone. He almost shuddered.

Returning his gaze to Annalise, he gritted a smile. "We should leave, so you're not late for breakfast."

Annalise grimaced at her muddy skirt and shoes. Like him and the hellhounds, she was splattered with mud from their run through the park. "I hope I can change first without Mother and Father noticing."

He almost winced. He should have cast a stone spell like Annalise had teased him about earlier. "I'll remove the mud for you." Gathering his will, he directed it at the mud covering Annalise and called it to rejoin the ground where it belonged.

Grinning, Annalise shook out her now spotless skirt. "Amazing. You nature witches know the neatest spells. Thanks, Dare." She called Finn, but he and Lily ignored her and kept nuzzling each other. She glanced at Dare. "Any idea how to separate them?"

Dare sighed. If only he didn't need to. He called Lily and Finn with his nature magic, and after a moment, the angelcats grumbled but separated. Once Finn leapt into Annalise's arms and Lily into his, he cast a stone spell on the ground around him and Annalise, so she could return to the gravel paths without becoming muddy again. "Shall we go?"

Annalise nodded, and they returned to the paths. Just before they separated, she beamed at him while petting Finn. "See you the day after tomorrow."

Dare swallowed and gripped Lily in his arms. Goddess, Annalise's warm and radiant smile was so tempting. His throat tightened. Yet she didn't know he was concealing the truth about her father's assassins. Too bad he couldn't share that without devastating her. He should go before he either kissed her or blurted the truth. His soulbond aching, he made himself nod then whistled for Raven and Bear before turning and striding from the park.

CHAPTER 21

As Dare bolted from the park with Lily, Raven, and Bear, Annalise frowned at the muddy-green staining his lush aura. What was troubling him? Lady Blaine still? Something with Alex or Mother and Father? Or had the ache of their unfulfilled soulbond almost overwhelmed him, and he'd fled to avoid pulling her into his arms and kissing her?

Her heart squeezing, she sighed then drifted back to her family's townhouse with Finn grumbling beside her. After visiting Storm then feeding Finn, Rain, and Aria, she headed downstairs for her own breakfast. When she entered the breakfast room, Alex was in his usual seat, devouring his food with a grin and his irrepressible orange aura brighter than it had been since before the duel. She heaped a plate with beefsteak, eggs, and tubers then sat beside him. "You appear cheerful this morning."

Alex grinned over his nearly empty plate. "As soon as I finish eating, I'm heading to Lady Ducharme's fencing salon. I went for the first time yesterday, and 'twas exciting."

Adding lymon and honey to her tea, Annalise arched her brows to feign surprise. She couldn't betray that Dare had already mentioned that. "Really? Lady Ducharme only invites the best swordsmen and swordswomen to her fencing salons."

Alex beamed and finished his beefsteak. "I know. And everyone was so convivial. I finally found a court event worth attending. Even though I did lose my first sword fight there—barely."

Smiling into her teacup, she hummed. He'd not crossed swords with Dare then. "Who was your opponent?"

Alex chuckled and rose. "Arthur, Lord Morwynne. But he's promised another sword fight today, and I'm determined to win this time."

Annalise almost laughed when Alex bounded from the breakfast room. He was as excited as a child about to open his Longnight gifts. Dare was so wonderful to have taken him to Lady Ducharme's fencing salon. She bolted her breakfast then headed to the stables to avoid Mother and Father. They likely had another tedious court event they'd want her to attend to pursue King Devon. Or Mother would complain all morning again about her banshee costume for the Harvestfete masquerade and attempt to convince her to wear her arachne silk ballgown instead. Not that she could risk wearing that ballgown at court—the arachne silk would only enhance her irresistible allure as a soul healer.

WHEN ANNALISE ROSE at dawn for her next morning walk with Dare, she grimaced at the heavy rain lashing her window. Walking in that wouldn't be pleasant. If she wasn't meeting Dare, she'd skip her walk today.

She sighed again then dressed and wrapped herself in her cloak spelled against rain. Not that it would keep her dry in the tempest outside. She slipped downstairs but halted when she opened the front door.

Hidden but for the glow of his aura and enchanted cloak,

Dare was huddled beneath his cloak between two townhouses across the street. As she met his gaze, he shook his head and shooed her inside.

Warmth suffused her chest. Of course, he'd risen early then endured the tempest for Goddess knew how long to ensure she didn't. Giving him a tender smile, she nodded then returned to her chambers. Hopefully, he'd hurry back to Ravenstone House and take a hot bath.

With the rain, Annalise and her parents remained home all day rather than attending tiresome court events. At dinner, Father smirked as he served Mother redkrab soup. "Ravenstone didn't send his weekly letter today. My idea must have succeeded, although I'll continue visiting The Fox for a bit longer to make sure."

As Mother beamed and nodded, Annalise's stomach tightened, and she exchanged a glance with Alex. What had Father done to make Dare quit writing? Not that she could ask Father. He'd just say again that it didn't concern her. She must ask Dare during their next morning walk.

So two mornings later, Annalise leaned toward Dare as they strolled after Raven and Bear with Finn and Lily leaping in the branches above them. "What did Father do to make you quit writing your letters seeking peace?"

Dare rubbed his beard then sighed. "My letters were only goading him, and his schemes were escalating. I had to quit before your father went too far."

She frowned at Dare. But *what* had Father done? After a moment, she sagged. From his set jaw, Dare wasn't going to say, probably to protect her.

Muddy-yellow despair flaring about him, Dare grimaced and shook his head. "I'm not sure I'll ever be able to convince your parents to end the feud. So I took your advice and cast a contraceptive spell on Lily the other day that shall last until the new year. I can't raise a riotous litter of angelkittens alone."

Annalise swallowed. For Dare to be so disheartened, whatever Father had done must have been terrible. Perhaps it was better she didn't know. To distract Dare, she chuckled and said, "Look at that monstrous stick Bear is dragging over. Think you can manage to throw it?"

AT BREAKFAST THE FOLLOWING MORNING, Mother pursed her lips at Annalise. "You *must* recapture King Devon's interest at his Harvestfete masquerade. Otherwise, you'll never become queen like you deserve, nor be able to start your own family."

Beside Mother, Father nodded over his nearly empty plate. "Yes, Harvestfete usually marks the end of the season, so who knows how many court events there shall be afterward?"

Annalise hummed. No doubt there'd be plenty. The council wouldn't adjourn until the nightmara renewed their treaty, and most at court wouldn't return home until the council adjourned.

However, Mother echoed Father's nod and said, "You need something more becoming than that wretched banshee costume you wanted. Since you shan't wear your arachne silk ballgown because 'tisn't a costume, we'll visit Celeste's before the Valcrests' garden party to have her create a new costume for you. Four days should give her just enough time for a simple one."

Annalise sipped her tea to hide a grimace. Not that again. "I can't. Lady Beza Hawke invited me for luncheon today, remember? And I can't insult the Duchess of Childes's newest daughter-in-law by canceling."

Mother and Father exchanged a glance, then Mother sighed and said, "True. King Devon better like your banshee costume as much as you thought." She frowned at Annalise. "Just make sure you leave early enough to still attend the Valcrests' garden party."

Annalise inclined her head. That shouldn't be a concern— doubtless Lady Beza and her husband would keep luncheon brief since newlyweds craved time alone.

However, when Lady Beza ushered her into their dining

room, Annalise glanced about for Lord Beza, but he was absent, unless he was hiding behind the painted screen along the far wall. Curious.

No longer surrounded by a blinding white glow, Lady Beza beamed at Annalise. Whatever potent spell she'd purchased from her seer had ended at last. Hopefully, its magical cost hadn't been too dear. Lady Beza said, "Thanks for attending luncheon, Lady Annalise."

Annalise eyed Lady Beza's creative violet aura with ivory motes. Without her seer's spell eclipsing it, 'twas clearly more intense about her waist, even greater than it should be for being two months pregnant. Had Lord Beza seduced her before the king's summer masquerade? Annalise blinked then returned Lady Beza's grin with a serene smile. "I was glad to attend, Lady Beza, although thanks for not spreading rumors about you and your husband was unnecessary."

Lazy Beza halted before the painted screen, white sincerity glowing about her. "Wren, please. I'm grateful just the same."

Light filling her chest, Annalise let her smile warm. Wren was as sweet as she seemed to offer friendship for simple discretion. Too bad they'd not socialized much until now. No lady at court had ever wanted to befriend her before—most only saw her beauty and avoided her. She tilted her head. "Where's Lord Beza? From your invitation, I assumed he'd join us."

Her face radiant at her husband's name, Wren chuckled. "I banished him to the orphanage. Today's luncheon is only for ladies."

Annalise hummed. Ladies? Were others joining them? Wren's sister-in-law Lady Treyvan, perhaps? "Orphanage? I suppose you mean the one you support."

Wren grinned and bobbed a nod. "I do." She paused. "Speaking of Waterstreet Orphanage, I'd like to introduce you to my dear friend from there." She beckoned the lady emerging from behind the painted screen. "Kiera, this is Lady Annalise Greysnowe. Lady Annalise, this is Kiera."

Her devoted indigo aura no longer surrounded by glittering nightmara magic, Kiera smiled and inclined a regal nod. Undeniably a lost princess, despite being from an orphanage. And her lustrous arachne silk dress that resembled ocean eddies and glimmered with residual magic only enhanced that. Her regal smile somehow still warm, she said, "Lady Annalise."

Annalise gawked at Kiera. "You're the king's mermaid." No wonder she and King Devon hadn't found Kiera at court events. She glided closer. "Goddess, does he know?"

Kiera flourished her left hand, the Vireni betrothal ring sparkling. "Of course."

Annalise grinned. King Devon must have found Kiera when he attended Wren's wedding, which explained why he'd quit his hunt since then. "How wonderful. King Devon must be thrilled."

As Wren's brows rose, Kiera blinked then asked, "You're not upset?"

Annalise tilted her head. "Why would I be? The king has been mad about you since his summer masquerade." And would surely marry her soon—he could marry whomever he wished. Unlike her and Dare. She swallowed. "I'm glad he's fallen in love at last."

Kiera and Wren eyed her, then Kiera pursed her lips and replied, "Truly?"

Annalise almost winced. Her beauty always made other ladies suspect her intentions. Mother and Father's ambitions didn't help either. She firmed her jaw. Somehow, she must convince Kiera to believe her—befriending a lady with such a devoted aura would be amazing. She managed a smile. "Of course. I love King Devon like a brother, albeit one much less annoying than my own. *He* never dipped my hair in ink growing up like Alex did." She tsked. "Younger brothers..."

Kiera and Wren exchanged a glance, obviously not convinced.

Flicking her fingers, Annalise leaned toward Kiera. What else could she say to convince them? "You're aware of the feud between my family and the Ravenstones, yes?" When Kiera nodded, she continued, "Then you know I could never be queen, even if I loved King Devon, which I assuredly don't."

Kiera studied her for a long moment then smiled. "I believe you." She arched a teasing brow. "Although I mightn't if you keep protesting."

Annalise blinked. Most ladies didn't tease Lady Snow. But friends would. Warmth flooding her, she chuckled and grinned. "I'll endeavor to remember that." Her grin turned wry. "I'm simply not accustomed to other ladies believing I'm uninterested in their gentlemen."

Kiera and Wren traded another glance, and indigo sympathy pulsed across their auras. With their kind hearts and candor, they'd be the most marvelous friends.

Her heart twisting, Annalise clenched her hands in her lap. If only she could risk being equally candid, but her parents discovering her powers and soulbond with Dare would be too disastrous.

Wren smiled and waved toward the table. "Shall we eat?"

Over luncheon, after devouring their shokolat torte first, Annalise and her new friends discussed Kiera's introduction to court, and she agreed to help Kiera decipher court ties. Then she nearly gaped when Kiera said King Devon had concocted the rumor she was a lost princess and that their betrothal was fake to negotiate with the nightmara. Given his determination to find Kiera then concocting such a grand deception, King Devon loved Kiera terribly, so their betrothal couldn't be fake. Besides, the nightmara wouldn't believe a fake betrothal due to their power over dreams and the mind. And nightmara magic had surrounded both Kiera and King Devon at the masquerade, so surely the nightmara were involved in their betrothal.

Annalise almost chuckled. King Devon must be using a "fake betrothal" to woo Kiera. To avoid spoiling his romantic plan, she winked at Kiera and said, "It shall be nice having a friend at court, especially a lady. Lady Snow must usually eke by with the few animals her mother allows—but only in private."

Wren blinked. "You know everyone calls you that?"

Her throat tightening, Annalise made herself smile as she finished eating. "I ensured they did."

While Wren tsked, Kiera chuckled. "Despite your lesser years, I suspect you may be more adept at managing court than the duchess."

Annalise forced a grin. To keep her powers as a soul healer and her soulbond with Dare secret, she had to be. "Which means I'm *definitely* the ideal lady to help you at court." She rose. "When's your introduction?"

Kiera rose as well. "The Harvestfete masquerade."

Tilting her head, Annalise almost laughed. She'd been right; that masquerade *did* involve King Devon's mermaid. "I should have realized." She sighed. "Unfortunately, I must depart. Mother insists I attend the Valcrests' garden party this afternoon."

Annalise glided from Wren's dining room, her chest light. It had only taken six seasons, but she'd finally made friends in Ormas. Perhaps attending court events would be less tiresome now. She quirked a wry smile. And once they accepted her not marrying King Devon, Mother and Father would be pleased she'd befriended Calatini's future queen.

CHAPTER 22

When Annalise joined him in the park for their next morning walk, Dare gulped a ragged breath at her warm and radiant smile. Goddess, if only he could pull her into his arms and kiss her to taste her joy. As the angelcats disappeared into the trees and the hellhounds chased sticks he tossed, Annalise described making her first friends in Ormas—Lady Beza Hawke and the king's mysterious mermaid Lady Kiera.

Annalise was telling him all about her luncheon with her new friends yesterday when they entered the clearing ahead. Then she fell silent, and they both froze. His back to them, the Duke of Oakmoor was at the center of the clearing, practicing magic from the white glow about him.

Using his nature magic, Dare silently called Raven and Bear, who were bounding toward the duke. Hopefully, the duke wouldn't notice since he was engrossed in his own magic. The hellhounds halted then returned with drooping ears. They always loved greeting strangers.

Once he and Annalise left the clearing, Dare murmured, "I didn't know that the Duke of Oakmoor was a witch too."

A faint frown creasing her brow, Annalise hummed. "He wasn't until his erratic magic appeared last year."

Dare blinked. The duke possessed magic that appeared nearly thirty years late? "Unusual. Erratic how?"

Still frowning, Annalise shrugged. "Some days, the duke's magic is so faint 'tis barely noticeable, while other days, 'tis almost as bright as a Rhiannon descendant's. I've never seen another witch's powers change like that."

Tossing a stick for Bear, he arched a brow at Annalise. "I wonder if the Duke of Oakmoor's erratic magic is why he and Lady Juliet met at the Duchess of Childes's fete last month."

Annalise tilted her head. "Most likely. Although I doubt it helped much, considering their quarrel when we left. I suspect he's practicing here so that no one sees him. Possessing magic he can't control shan't enhance his suave reputation."

Dare grimaced. "We must watch for him on future walks then." Wonderful. To distract them from that, he smiled at Annalise and said, "Finish telling me about your luncheon with your new friends."

Beaming again, Annalise did. Then she sobered. "I just wish I could risk revealing my powers and our soulbond to Kiera and Wren. They were so candid with me, and me keeping secrets might upset them."

Dare almost winced. Because close friends, even new ones, deserved the truth. But saying that would only upset Annalise. So to hearten her, he stepped closer and said, "Perhaps, but they'll understand why you did. Everyone knows how ridiculous our families are about the feud."

Annalise flashed a wry smile. "Everyone except our families."

He sighed then tossed Raven's stick. And their families' obsession was why Annalise's father might have stooped to contacting assassins. Although Reynolds, the man investigating for him, would hopefully refute that soon. Shoving that aside, he echoed her smile then said, "Not all of our families. Alex knows too."

Annalise hummed. "True. How are your sword fights going?"

Chuckling, Dare grinned. "Well. Alex's skill is improving,

especially since he began attending Lady Ducharme's fencing salon most mornings. He keeps promising to trounce me, but he hasn't yet. I'm meeting him tomorrow for another chance."

LIKE HE'D TOLD ANNALISE, Dare met her brother at the royal bay the following morning. They exchanged grins then began crossing swords by the copse on the cliffs.

After a few engagements, Alex lunged forward with his sword extended and asked, "Why did you quit writing letters to Father seeking peace?"

His chest clenching, Dare flicked aside Alex's sword then riposted. "Because you said your parents became infuriated whenever they received one. I was concerned they'd soon do something unforgivable." If they hadn't already by contacting assassins.

Arching a brow, Alex danced back from Dare's thrust. "So how shall you convince them to seek peace and end the feud?"

Dare grunted then feinted an attack. "I don't know. Everything I've attempted so far has only infuriated them. At this rate, I'll never convince your parents to end the feud."

Grimacing, Alex parried. "We could simply end the feud when I become Lord Greysnowe."

Dare circled his sword beneath Alex's as his throat tightened. "I can't wait until they *die* to end the feud." He and Annalise might be old by then and not be able to have a family.

Alex narrowly eyed him, but the thunder of approaching horses interrupted them before he could reply.

Dare withdrew his sword and began toward Ebony tied to an ash tree behind them. "I'll conceal myself again."

Alex followed him. "I'll join you. We can't have people realizing I frequently visit the royal bay too. They might connect our visits."

Frowning, Dare jerked a nod. Hopefully, whoever were approaching hadn't already seen them. After he and Alex reached Ebony and Biscuit, he cast a nature mimicry spell about them all then said, "Hold still, and don't talk."

He and Alex remained unmoving as the Duke of Childes and Sir Alaric Keyes galloped to the path leading to the royal bay then rode down the cliffs. Once the duke and baronet were racing before the surf, Dare and Alex sheathed their swords and led Ebony and Biscuit back toward Ormas. He released his nature mimicry spell after the royal bay was out of sight.

As they began riding back, Alex arched his brows at Dare. "Why such hurry to end the feud? 'Tis lasted over three hundred years; a few more shan't hurt."

Dare almost scowled. Except 'twould destroy his and Annalise's life. "The feud between our families has lasted long enough, and all over a tragic situation that couldn't be helped."

Alex hummed. "I doubt many other Ravenstones share your outlook. 'Twas your ancestor who was spurned, after all."

Dare shrugged and urged Ebony to a trot. "True, but 'tis the only sensible outlook. Your ancestress was a healer, and my ancestor's cousin was dying. What else could she do but heal him? And once they were soulbound, 'twas impossible for her to marry anyone else." His heart twisted. Just like with him and Annalise. He managed another shrug. "My ancestor was a bitter fool for not forgiving them and marrying another. Instead, he declared eternal enmity for your family, became a sullen recluse, and died alone not long after his cousin and erstwhile betrothed disappeared."

Narrowly eyeing him again, Alex cocked his head. "My family always claimed he killed them."

Dare snorted a laugh. "'Twas no evidence of that, but I'd not be surprised." He'd better distract Alex before the younger gentleman asked about his tenderness toward soul healers. "Shall we race back to Ormas?"

Alex grinned. "Yes. I can win at that."

Dare chuckled and returned Alex's grin. "Only sometimes."

After their race, which Alex barely won, Dare continued to

Ormas alone. From Alex's probing glances earlier, the younger gentleman was suspicious about his urgency for peace. Yet he couldn't explain until Annalise was ready to tell her brother about their involvement. He should encourage her to do that again. If they told Alex rather than him realizing it, he'd likely not be upset on her behalf and begin supporting the feud.

So during his walk with Annalise the following morning, Dare rubbed his beard and said, "With Alex knowing you so well and becoming my close friend, I think he's beginning to suspect our involvement. Perhaps we should just tell him."

Annalise glowered at him as she straightened from petting Raven and Bear. "No. I already told you we can't tell anyone. Not even Alex, nor Kiera and Wren. Mother and Father discovering our secrets is too disastrous."

Dare sighed, his ribs tightening. From her set jaw and the red resolve flaring about her, Annalise wouldn't relent. Too bad. Revealing their secrets to close friends would make them easier to bear. "Very well."

He and Annalise began walking while discussing their magical pets' recent antics. Eventually, Annalise blew a sigh then said, "I should go."

He echoed her sigh. Why must their morning walks always seem so short? "I'll see you at the Harvestfete masquerade tomorrow. Shall we slip out to the palace gardens when everyone is watching Lady Kiera?" Like their matching costumes, that should help soothe the ache of seeing her dance with gentlemen her parents would accept her marrying.

Annalise licked her lips, and tingling warmth flooded him. How he burned to kiss her. Then she said, "We shouldn't, but I don't have the strength to resist. Although we must keep our time alone brief—unlike at the king's summer masquerade."

Suppressing his hunger, Dare inclined his head. "Makes sense. Until tomorrow evening."

To settle his soul, he spent another hour in the park with

Raven and Bear coursing before him and a meowing Lily in the branches above him. Then he strode back to Ravenstone House.

Brown brightened as he opened the front door. "Thank the Goddess you returned, my lord. Reynolds arrived nearly an hour ago with news. He's waiting in your study."

Dare nodded, his stomach tensing. Please let Reynolds have proved Lord Greysnowe's scheme didn't involve assassins. He hurried back to his study then settled behind his desk with Raven and Bear flopping against his chair and Lily curling in his lap. "What news do you have, Reynolds?"

The former law marshal, an agent who policed non-magical crimes for the Ministry of Justice, inclined his grizzled head. "I've unearthed the shady men that Lord Greysnowe approached at The Fox and confirmed they're all assassins."

Dare winced as his chest froze. Damnation, Annalise would be devastated. "Did you unearth his target as well?"

Reynolds grimaced. "Unfortunately not. The assassins were incensed that Lord Greysnowe openly approached them in a busy tavern, so none stayed to learn his target." He arched his brows. "If you like, I could contact Lord Greysnowe as an assassin and offer my services to find out."

Petting Lily to remain calm, Dare sighed. "Don't bother. I'll tell King Devon about Lord Greysnowe's assassins this afternoon, so royal agents shall take over your inquiry." He smiled at Reynolds and rose despite Lily's grumbled meow. "Thank you for all your help. You've been invaluable. Please see Brown before you leave for your fee."

After bolting breakfast, Dare strode to the stables, leaving Lily, Raven, and Bear inside. He needed a hard gallop in a natural area to clear his head before he visited King Devon. After saddling Ebony, he and his stallion thundered to the royal bay and galloped along the beach for over an hour. Then they returned to Ormas, and he devoured luncheon before heading to the palace to report Lord Greysnowe's scheme.

King Devon wasn't pleased to hear about assassins becoming involved in the feud, but he remained calm. Assured the king would handle matters, Dare sighed as he returned to Ravenstone House. If only he could tell Annalise about this without devastating her. Perhaps telling Mother during their mirror call tomorrow would soothe his hunger to tell Annalise.

AFTER RETURNING from the royal bay the following morning, Dare activated his paired communication mirror. Once he and Mother talked about harvest plans back home and her angelkitten's latest mischief, he swallowed and said, "Yesterday, I learned who Lord Greysnowe's shady men were—assassins."

Her mouth gaping, Mother paled. "What?!" She leaned toward the mirror. "Who does he want dead?"

Dare grimaced with a heavy sigh. "I'm not sure, but doubtless either me or King Devon's mermaid. I told King Devon about the assassins, so royal agents are handling it. But I'll be on guard as well—I've no intention of falling prey to a Greysnowe-hired assassin."

Mother shuddered. "Perhaps you'd best quit your rides with Lord Alexander. If the Greysnowes discover your friendship, they'll surely be furious, and since they're stooping to hiring assassins now, Goddess knows what they'll do."

Tapping his fingers on his desk, he set his jaw. Except his friendship with Alex was nothing compared to his soulbond with Annalise, and he could never surrender her. So why bother to quit seeing Alex? "I'm not abandoning my friendship with Alex. Building such connections is the only way the feud shall ever end."

Mother worried her lip. "I suppose. Just be careful, please." She sighed. "I should go. Talk to you next week."

Dare echoed her goodbye then deactivated his communication mirror and set it on the windowsill to recharge. Perhaps by next week, Mother would be resigned to his continued friendship with Alex. If not, he could distract her with news about Lady Kiera being introduced at tonight's Harvestfete masquerade.

After dinner, his pulse quickened while he donned his thanatos costume of a black robe over his evening clothes. He couldn't wait to see Annalise in her matching banshee costume and for their time alone in the palace gardens. He sighed as he accepted his scythe from Thom. Please let her not need to dance with too many other gentlemen first.

Almost as soon as he entered the palace's teeming ballroom, the sultry Lady Blaine, wearing revealing Tsarkan veils and bedlah, grasped his arm with a coy smile. "Lord Ravenstone, how lovely to see you."

He stiffened but suppressed his grimace. 'Twould be rude. "Good evening, Lady Blaine."

Fluttering her lashes, the fashionable countess squeezed his arm. "You must dance the first waltz with me."

Dare freed his arm then waved his well-sharpened scythe. "My scythe makes dancing impossible." Thank the Goddess.

Lady Blaine moued. "But I was so looking forward to our dances." She sighed and leaned toward him. "Although I *suppose* we could stand together instead."

His soulbond burgeoning at Annalise entering the ballroom, he forced himself to not turn toward her. He couldn't risk Lady Blaine noticing. Instead, he nodded toward two unwed gentlemen his rank or higher. "You should dance. Perhaps the Duke of Oakmoor or Lord Meade would wish to partner you."

Lady Blaine's smoky eyes glinted, but before she could reply, King Devon and Lady Kiera swept into the ballroom, which hushed as everyone turned to gawk at the king and his future queen.

When King Devon and Lady Kiera began the first waltz alone, Dare edged toward an entrance to the gardens. He must slip away to meet Annalise while everyone was distracted. But Lady Blaine clung to him like ivy on an oak. He'd better wait until another gentleman asked the husband-hunting countess to dance.

Other couples began dancing after the first waltz, but Lady Blaine still clung to him. Definitely like he was her only option. He sighed. At least Annalise wasn't dancing either—although radiant as ever despite her loose, tangled hair and tattered, reddish black ballgown, her costume embodying death must be deterring other gentlemen.

After the third dance, King Devon introduced Lady Kiera to court before the Harvestfete pantomime, but even those didn't distract Lady Blaine enough for Dare to slip out into the gardens. And when the dancing resumed, she remained beside him. He clenched his scythe. His chance for time alone with Annalise was dwindling.

But then King Devon and Lady Kiera approached, and Lady Blaine stepped back to eye Lady Kiera. "You're Wren's orphanage friend."

Lifting her chin, Lady Kiera flashed a regal smile. "And you are?"

Dare almost smiled. Although from an orphanage, Lady Kiera already possessed the air of a queen. Impressive.

Flushing, Lady Blaine said to Lady Kiera, "Kit, the Countess of Blaine. Wren and I grew up together."

Lady Kiera arched her brows. "Oh, she never mentioned you. Although you do appear *vaguely* familiar—you attended her last orphanage play, didn't you?" King Devon's lips twitched when she beamed and added, "'Twas delightful, wasn't it?"

Straightening his robe, Dare nearly laughed too. That needling must be because Lady Kiera and Lady Beza Hawke were friends and Lady Blaine had told all of court about Lady Beza's scandalous pregnancy. A loyal lady like Lady Kiera would make a perfect friend for Annalise.

Lady Blaine stiffened. "Wren's plays always are." She performed a graceful curtsy before she swept away.

Dare chuckled as his shoulders relaxed. Lady Kiera had

managed to rout Lady Blaine. Now he could finally slip out to meet Annalise. "I'm grateful for your assistance, Lady Kiera. I was almost tempted to use my scythe as more than a prop."

As Lady Kiera blinked at him, King Devon arched a brow then drawled, "Somehow I doubt that."

Dare grinned. "*Almost* tempted, your majesty, not actually tempted." As his soulbond burgeoned further, he glanced beyond the royal couple and tensed to conceal his longing. "I see the Greysnowes approaching. I must be off to prevent feeding the feud. A pleasure to meet you, Lady Kiera."

He bowed then strode away and slipped out into the palace gardens to wait for Annalise. Hopefully, she'd not be too long.

CHAPTER 23

Forcing herself to not stare at Dare as he slipped out into the palace gardens, Annalise embraced Kiera with a fond smile. Her new friend had behaved like a perfect queen tonight—regal and insightful yet warm. If only she could say that without upsetting Mother and Father behind her. "Evening, Kiera."

Kiera grinned and kissed her cheek. "Evening, Annalise. Why are you dressed as a banshee?"

Annalise shrugged while she stepped back and King Devon recaptured Kiera's arm. "I thought a banshee costume fitting for a Harvestfete masquerade." Plus, her tattered ballgown the color of dried blood and loose, tangled hair had dissuaded gentlemen from asking her to dance. She should have worn a costume embodying death before.

His sultan's robes rustling, Father glared at Kiera and pulled Annalise between him and Mother. "Or perhaps she foresaw the death of her dreams."

Annalise suppressed a wince. Must Mother and Father keep mentioning that? They were being unforgivably rude to her friend and Calatini's future queen. Somehow, she must get them to realize her becoming queen was impossible. She tsked and glided back to Kiera. "King Devon was no dream of mine. Kiera suits him better than I ever could."

As Father stiffened, Mother narrowed her eyes then asked, "And you know this *how*?"

Annalise flashed a cool smile. "Because we met at Lady Beza Hawke's several days ago and became fast friends." And she could see how well Kiera's and King Devon's auras matched. As Mother and Father gaped at her, she turned back to Kiera. "Are you nervous about meeting the nightmara queen-heir tomorrow?"

Muddy-yellow apprehension flaring about her, Kiera grimaced. "Dreadfully."

As King Devon squeezed Kiera's arm, Annalise beamed and grasped Kiera's free hand. Considering the glittering nightmara magic that had swirled around Kiera and King Devon, the night-mara doubtless knew about Kiera and approved of her becoming queen. Yet she couldn't say that without revealing her powers. Instead, she said to reassure her friend, "Let me know if you need my aid." She swept a curtsy at King Devon. "Your majesty."

Annalise and her parents glided away, but as soon as they were out of earshot, Mother grasped her elbow and pulled her to a halt then asked, "Are you truly all right? How dare King Devon abandon you for that Kiera creature after courting you for years. Why didn't you tell us about her?"

Father scowled. "Yes, we could have done something to stop her from stealing your rightful place."

Stiffening, Annalise freed her arm. What did they mean by that? Whatever they'd done to make Dare quit sending his letters seeking peace? She must be blunt to ensure they finally saw the truth. "I was never meant to be queen—Kiera was. Anyone can see how perfect she and King Devon are together. But I never mentioned meeting her because King Devon wanted Kiera to remain a secret until he introduced her tonight."

While Mother and Father narrowly eyed her, Annalise swept toward the refreshments table, and they soon followed.

Somehow she must escape them, so she could meet Dare in the palace gardens. Perhaps she could slip outside after dancing with someone? She sighed. Except she didn't want to dance with anyone except Dare. So she needed an excuse to be alone. A costume repair might work since Mother hated when she appeared less than perfect in public.

As they reached the refreshments table, she made herself stumble then step on her tattered ballgown until the creak of ripping fabric pierced the first strains of the next waltz. "Oh, dear. I must find a maid to repair my costume." When Mother began to follow, she gestured toward the dancing couples. "No, no. I can manage that alone. You and Father should dance. Since no one has partnered me tonight, you've not danced yet, and I know how you enjoy it."

Mother and Father exchanged a hungry glance. Then Mother sighed and turned back to Annalise with the indigo in her aura deepening. "Fine, but if you're not back before this waltz ends, I'll come find you."

Annalise almost winced. She and Dare must keep their meeting brief, but they couldn't manage half a waltz. Please let Mother and Father become so enthralled with dancing that Mother would forget to find her. "Of course."

She slipped into a nearby anteroom then circled around to enter the palace gardens. Her soulbond flaring at his nearness, she headed straight to Dare. She licked her lips then managed a wry smile. "We haven't long. Mother and Father are dancing now, but she said she'd come find me after this waltz."

Red passion and indigo tenderness swirling about him, Dare grasped her hand. "Then we must ensure she can't find you."

Tingling warmth darting up her arm at his first touch in over three weeks, Annalise swallowed but threaded her fingers through his even though she should be freeing her hand. Touching was too dangerous—it only made her ache for more.

Dare led her into a nearby rose garden then waved at the gate with his scythe, and the roses grew across the opening. "There.

No one shall find us now." He flashed a grin. "But we're still close enough to hear the music."

Humming, she tilted her head. Her heartbeat in her ears was louder than the waltz's final strains. "Barely."

Dare chuckled and leaned his scythe against a rose trellis while another waltz began. "But enough." Still holding her hand, he swept a bow that swished his black robe. "Shall you honor me with your first dance tonight? Although no other gentlemen were brave enough, a thanatos need not fear a banshee's power, and I burn to dance with you."

Her pulse quickening, Annalise gulped a breath, and the sweet scent of the roses surrounding them swamped her. She burned to dance with him too. But dancing could easily lead to kissing, which could easily lead to consummating their soulbond and her becoming pregnant. Her heart twisted. And they couldn't risk that. She tugged on her hand. "We mustn't."

His amber eyes dark and ardent in the moonlight, Dare stepped closer and pressed a kiss against her palm. "Please, Annalise. Despite our soulbond and all our private meetings, we've never danced together. Instead, we've had to suffer watching each other dance with others. All I'm asking for is one dance."

Shivering as her pulse surged again, she caressed his face, and tingling swept through her at his beard tickling her palm. Perhaps they could risk one dance. She licked her lips and whispered, "Very well, just one dance."

Yellow joy glowing about him, Dare grinned and drew her into his arms. "I'll even hold you at a proper distance, unlike others we've seen dancing in these gardens."

Annalise sighed as they began twirling about the rose garden. Dancing pressed together as one like Wren and Lord Beza had would be glorious. But much too dangerous.

The distant music guiding their steps and the roses' fragrance enveloping them, she raised her gaze to meet his, and warmth suffused her chest. As they danced together while staring into each other's eyes and without any complicated twirls that would separate them, the edges of their souls meshed, and their hearts beat in rhythm.

Then their waltz faded, and they stilled without breaking their locked gaze. As the next waltz began, Dare lowered his head and brushed his lips against hers.

Sighing against his mouth, Annalise slid her arms about his neck then threaded her fingers in his long hair. Goddess, his kiss felt so right, better than any dream. Tingling swamped her as their entire souls meshed like two halves becoming one.

Dare groaned and deepened their kiss for several heartbeats then jerked his head back. He rasped, "We'd best stop before our kiss becomes too heated. No doubt your parents are looking for you."

A shudder wracking her, she lowered her arms then separated their souls and stepped back. How could she have forgotten that? His kiss had driven everything else from her mind. "I should return to the masquerade."

Dare nodded and grasped his scythe. "I'll escort you." He took her arm then waved his scythe at the gate, and the roses retreated from the opening.

As he led her through the palace gardens, her chest squeezed at the silence echoing between them. If only she could tell him how she ached to stay. But doing that would only make separating worse.

At the secluded anteroom near the ballroom's main door, Dare kissed her palm again. "I'll see you tomorrow in the park."

A pang darting through her, Annalise swallowed. "You're leaving?"

Dare released her with a tight smile. "After our romantic dance, I don't think I can bear to see another gentleman dancing with you tonight."

She fisted a hand before her throat as he strode from the anteroom. She couldn't bear that either. Perhaps she could convince Mother and Father to leave.

When she joined them, Mother exhaled but frowned. "There you are. What took so long?"

Annalise sighed and forced a shrug. Hopefully, she didn't appear too guilty. "I rested a bit before returning. I'm not feeling well."

Indigo concern pulsing about them, Mother and Father peered at her, then Mother said, "You do appear flushed."

Father nodded. "We should leave at once." He glowered at King Devon and Kiera talking with the Farsons, doubtless about the nightmara. "We'll decide how to handle that creature fabricated by the Ravenstones later."

Annalise sighed again as Mother and Father swept her from the ballroom. Why couldn't they forget their obsession with her becoming queen? The only gentleman she wanted to marry was Dare—not that she could ever tell them that.

When Annalise met Dare in the park the following morning, she bent to pet Raven and Bear then blinked at the hand Dare offered, her breath quickening. He'd not done that during their walks since the hellhounds had almost knocked her over when first meeting her.

As she glanced up at him, Dare smiled. "We danced last night without going too far. I think we can risk touching each other now. And touching often might accustom us to it."

She swallowed. Perhaps... She nodded then placed her hand in his. Tingling warmth flooded her as he pulled her upright and tucked her hand against his arm.

Dare tossed some sticks for Raven and Bear, and they followed the hellhounds in silence for several moments. Then he smiled at her and asked, "Are you attending the Duchess of Childes's dinner tonight?" When she nodded, he grinned and squeezed her arm. "Did you want to meet in the garden like we did at her fete?"

Annalise sighed. If only she could. "I can't. Mother and

Father shall wonder about my disappearance at last night's masquerade if I do. Plus, I suspect the dinner is in Kiera's honor, so I must remain with Mother and Father to ensure they don't do something outrageous."

Violet longing pulsing around him, Dare grimaced. "Makes sense. I'll try not to stare at you too much."

Annalise sighed again, her chest aching. "Me too." Then she asked him when he'd next go riding with Alex, and they discussed that for the rest of their walk.

The Duchess of Childes's dinner was, indeed, in honor of Kiera. But fortunately, Mother and Father did nothing worse than grumble to each other. Plus, Dare was free of Lady Blaine for once, and Annalise managed to glance at him only a few times. Not that anyone noticed—all of court was too engrossed with watching their future queen.

Court's fascination with Kiera continued, so when Kiera leaned toward Annalise with a tight smile at the Dracwyns' ball three days later, Annalise assumed her friend wanted to discuss court rumors. Instead, Kiera invited her to a nightmara ride in a few days. Her chest buoyant, Annalise eagerly accepted and beamed for the rest of the ball. She'd never met any nightmara in person, but riding them was said to be smooth as silk yet full of vigor—as close to flying as a human could experience, which usually only the mara, the nightmara's human partners, ever got to enjoy. When she and her parents returned to Greysnowe House, she was still beaming.

Returning at the same time from a tavern or Lord Morwynne's, Alex eyed her. Once they were alone on the stairs, he asked, "You look excited. What happened?"

She beamed brighter. "Kiera invited me to go nightmara riding."

Alex whistled. "I'm jealous. Riding nightmara is supposedly exhilarating." When she nodded, he flashed a grin. "Any way I could become friends with our future queen?"

Annalise giggled. Her brash brother *would* ask that. "You'd need to attend court events."

Alex grimaced just before they entered their chambers. "Never mind then."

She floated to bed then swept to the park the following morning to meet Dare. Accepting his arm with a grin, she soon shared her upcoming nightmara ride with him.

Dare squeezed her arm. "How exciting. If only I could join you." He paused with a faint frown. "Wait, with their power over dreams and the mind, shan't the nightmara realize you're a soul healer and our soulbond?"

Still smiling, Annalise tilted her head. "Of course, but they shan't tell anyone. The nightmara have held a special regard for soul healers since the first soul healer Brigid healed Nightstone, the nightmara queen's mate, from a deadly case of dream-sickness."

So when she and Kiera followed the mara woman and her nightmara partner in the nightmara paddock a few mornings later, Annalise almost gasped at the nightmara and their mara partners spread about the paddock in clusters. Goddess, the nightmara were stunning. Every dark color imaginable, they almost resembled wild horses, except more intelligent and beautiful with potent auras adorned by glittering, silver motes revealing their powerful magic.

They headed straight toward a saddled midnight mare who was nestled against a saddled black stallion. Annalise blinked at the mare's puissant red aura blazing with silver motes. She'd never seen another as strong, so the mare must be Lady Moon-bud, the nightmara queen-heir. And from their aligned auras, the stallion must be her mate.

Once everyone exchanged greetings, Kiera introduced Annalise to the three nightmara and the mara woman.

Her powers pressing against Annalise's mind, Lady Moonbud nodded then said, :*A pleasure, Lady Heart.*:

Warmth burning her cheeks, Annalise returned the nightmara queen-heir's nod. Since they healed with their souls, acknowledged soul healers wore a healer's torc made of electrum with hearts as the terminals. So Lady Moonbud's nickname alluded to her being a soul healer.

Kiera frowned and glanced at Annalise. "I thought your nickname was Lady Snow."

Annalise blushed harder. "At court. But some at home," her nursemaid Alice, "call me Lady Heart." But only when no one could overhear.

Fortunately, Kiera simply studied her for a moment before turning to eye Lady Moonbud's saddle like a maddened orc on a rampage. Poor Kiera must be nervous about her riding lesson.

Lady Moonbud nodded at Annalise again. *:Darkthorn has offered to carry you, Lady Heart.:* She turned to Kiera. *:Ready for your first ride, Kiera?:*

As Lady Moonbud began Kiera's riding lesson, Darkthorn glided over to Annalise then inclined his head, his powers tickling her mind. Powerful, but not near as much as his mate. He said in a private thought only she could hear, *:Lady Heart, it shall be an honor to bear the powerful soul healer who risked herself to save her family's ancient enemy.:*

Annalise met Darkthorn's midnight eyes and echoed his nod. His plain-speaking was little surprise given his logical white aura. "Thank you. It shall be an honor to ride the mate of the nightmara queen-heir. But, please, call me Annalise."

Chuckling, Darkthorn tossed his mane. *:A powerful soul healer, indeed, to read that. Very well, Annalise. Would you care to mount?:*

Her pulse leaping, she beamed. "Yes, but could I remove your saddle first? Inspired by the mara, I taught myself to ride without tack as a girl."

Darkthorn chuckled again and flicked his tail. *:Please do. Nightmara dislike saddles, but we assumed you'd need one.:* Once she removed his saddle and leapt on his back, the stallion began trotting around the paddock. *:While Moonbud is teaching Kiera, we must remain in the paddock in case they need us.:*

Her smile so wide it ached, Annalise almost laughed. Riding Darkthorn *was* smooth as silk, and his power surging beneath her was almost magical. Definitely like flying—or would be, if they were galloping. "I don't mind. Riding a nightmara is thrilling, no matter where we ride. Could we gallop for a bit?"

Darkthorn surged forward, and energy burst through her. The only thing that would make this ride better would be if Dare was galloping beside her. But at least she could tell him about it on their next morning walk.

CHAPTER 24

After finishing his correspondence around midmorning, Dare strode upstairs to his chambers to call Mother. He smiled as he activated his communication mirror. At this very moment, Annalise was doubtless galloping on a nightmara. Too bad he couldn't join her. Not that he minded calling Mother, but riding a nightmara would be exhilarating. And seeing Annalise's beams atop one would be even more so.

When Mother appeared in the mirror, she leaned forward with a frown between her brows. "Are you well? Any word about Lord Greysnowe's assassins?"

Dare almost winced. Clearly, Mother had spent the last week worrying about him. He should have contacted her earlier to reassure her. "Nothing new, and my servants haven't seen Lord Greysnowe at The Fox in over two weeks, so he's quit contacting assassins."

Mother paled. "He must have hired one then."

Dare shook his head. "None of the assassins Lord Greysnowe met at The Fox would talk to him." Dare flashed a wry smile. And Lord Greysnowe's last visit to The Fox had been the evening before Dare would have sent his weekly letter. "I suspect he quit contacting assassins because I quit sending letters seeking peace."

Her normal color returning, Mother frowned. "How typical of the Ravenstone-Greysnowe feud." After he snorted, she arched her brows. "Any *other* news involving the Greysnowes?"

He clenched his hands in his lap. His first dance with Annalise that had been so wonderfully romantic, and her radiant joy at riding a nightmara today. Not that he could share either with Mother. "Not really." To distract her from the Greysnowes, he added, "However, King Devon introduced his future queen, Lady Kiera, at his Harvestfete masquerade."

Mother's eyes widened. "What's she like?"

Dare smiled. "Loyal, warm, insightful. And she already possesses the air of a queen. So perfect for King Devon." Much more than Annalise had ever been. He leaned forward. "How was Harvestfete at home?"

Mother stilled then shrugged. "Much the same as ever, except without you."

He shifted in his seat. This was the first Harvestfete he'd not celebrated at home—Mother must have been lonesome. His heart squeezed. Yet he couldn't leave Ormas without Annalise, so Goddess knew when he'd return.

Tilting her head, Mother flashed a bright smile. "Did I tell you that Pearl learned how to remain aloft?" When he shook his head, she began to describe that. He and Mother talked about her angelkitten then said goodbye.

After he deactivated the communication mirror then set it on the windowsill to recharge, Dare sagged and rubbed his chest. Keeping Annalise a secret from Mother was becoming more and more distressing. Plus, she'd be hurt that he'd kept such a momentous secret for so long. But until Annalise agreed they should quit concealing their soulbond, he must remain silent.

. . .

Two mornings later, Dare met Annalise in the park for their walk. Warmth flooded him. She was still beaming. After she petted Raven and Bear, he tossed the hellhounds sticks then grinned and took her arm. "How was your nightmara ride?"

Yellow enthusiasm flaring about her, Annalise beamed brighter. "So thrilling. Lady Moonbud's mate Darkthorn carried me bareback, and we galloped around the nightmara paddock while Lady Moonbud began teaching Kiera to ride. 'Tis true what people say about riding nightmara—it feels like flying. Darkthorn was smooth as silk, and his power was almost magical."

Dare squeezed her arm, his pulse quickening. Goddess, if only he could kiss her to taste her joy. "Shall you get to ride him again?"

Annalise nodded, her hair shimmering in the dappled light. "Every three days when Kiera has her riding lessons." Her smile dimmed. "As you expected, the nightmara realized my powers and our soulbond at once. But they didn't reveal them to Kiera, so our secrets are safe."

He swallowed a sigh as he tossed another stick for Raven. 'Twould almost be better if the nightmara had shared their secrets. Then he and Annalise could quit lying to everyone. Although her parents would likely start contacting assassins again.

Annalise grinned and returned his squeeze. "I'm gone most of the morning for my nightmara rides, and Mother and Father don't know how often those rides are. I thought we could risk visiting natural areas near Ormas once a week or so. Mother and Father shall assume I'm on a nightmara ride."

Dare echoed her grin while tossing Bear's stick. He could finally show Annalise the sights like he'd imagined when he'd visited natural areas two months ago to distract himself. "Did you have any specific places you wanted to visit?"

Annalise hummed. "Not really. When at court, Mother and Father rarely allow me time to leave Ormas, so the only nearby natural areas I know about are the royal bay and the royal forest." She glanced at him beneath her lashes. "But I expect a nature witch like you knows many others."

Chuckling, he rubbed his beard. True, but which natural area should he choose? Not the royal bay since she'd been there before, nor the royal forest since that required permission from King Devon. But Blacke Woods, Column Caverns, and Glass Lake were also nearby, and equally lovely in different ways.

Annalise smiled and nudged him. "Wherever you pick shall be perfect. Just let me know which gate to meet at."

Dare stiffened. Then she'd be riding alone through the streets of Ormas. Granted, they'd not be crowded due to the early hour, but 'twasn't safe for her to ride so unprotected. "We'll meet here at our usual time."

Annalise blinked then frowned. "That risks someone from court seeing us together—like the Duke of Oakmoor or others visiting the park."

He leaned toward her. Her risking her safety was infinitely worse. "Perhaps, but you can't ride through Ormas unprotected. 'Tisn't like you can bring a footman with you on our secret rides. And most at court don't rouse until late morning. Although we should probably leave the angelcats and hellhounds behind to be less recognizable."

Annalise sighed but nodded. "Very well. Although I suspect Finn shall howl when I leave him behind—I only hope he doesn't rouse everyone."

Dare hummed. "So shall Lily. They've become accustomed to seeing their mate every other day." His heart fluttered. Just like he'd become accustomed to seeing Annalise. Their private meetings settled his soul better than nature did.

Her cerulean eyes flickering, Annalise inclined her head then asked about his next ride with Alex. They discussed that and several upcoming court events before they decided to return home.

After calling Finn, Annalise grinned at Dare. "I look forward to our adventure. Until then."

As Annalise glided from the park with her grumbling angelcat, Dare watched her with a soft smile. He looked forward to their adventure too. Blacke Woods, Column Caverns, or Glass Lake? He chuckled. Column Caverns would be like nothing she'd ever seen since Wildewall had no limestone caverns. They'd visit there first.

SHORTLY AFTER DAWN two days later, Dare rode to the park and met Annalise, who was covered in a black cloak. Not that anyone who'd seen her riding before would fail to recognize her —her massive, pale-gray stallion was unforgettable. He grinned at her. "Morning. Ready for our adventure?"

Annalise nodded, and they rode through Ormas and out the southern gate. However, out of sight of the gate, he waggled his brows at her and asked, "Care to gallop?"

Grinning back, Annalise giggled. "Always. Where are we headed?"

Dare shook his head. If he told her now, he'd miss her delight when she first saw Column Caverns. "'Tis a secret, but we'll ride this road until Merriltown, where we take the eastern road."

Her lips twitching, Annalise blew a sigh. "How about we gallop to Merriltown then you can lead me to our *secret* destination?"

He nodded, and they urged Ebony and Storm to a gallop then thundered down the road. Throughout their gallop, he kept glancing at Annalise, and every time his heart leapt. Yellow joy swirling around her, she was beaming like a child on Longnight. She enjoyed galloping as much as he did. Goddess, she was so perfect for him.

When Merriltown appeared in the distance, they bent over Ebony and Storm and urged their stallions even faster until halting them before the first cottage. Patting their stallions' damp withers, he and Annalise beamed at each other.

After a moment, Annalise tilted her head. "Shall you lead us to our secret destination, or are we going to stare at each other the rest of the morning?"

Dare quirked a wry grin as he kneed Ebony. He and Annalise *had* been staring at each other like sunflowers at the sun. "I could stare at you all morning, but 'twould be a shame to miss our destination."

Laughter curving her lips, Annalise tsked when they turned onto the eastern road. "Promises, promises."

They fell into a comfortable silence as they rode for a quarter of an hour then turned onto the winding path that led to Column Caverns and rode for another quarter of an hour.

Just before the caverns, he dismounted and tied Ebony in a copse of maples then extracted water and a collapsible bucket from his satchel. After galloping, their stallions needed water, but there wasn't any aboveground water nearby. "We can leave Ebony and Storm here. They shan't like where we're headed."

As he poured water into the bucket, Annalise leapt from her saddle and tied Storm beside Ebony. "That sounds ominous."

Dare chuckled at her teasing and returned the half-empty water back to his satchel. "I promise it isn't." He took her arm and led her to Column Caverns' ragged entrance. Before they entered, he muttered a basic light spell, and a fist-sized ball that glowed like the sun appeared above their heads. "Watch your step. Nature created the path through the caverns, so 'tisn't always smooth."

Peering into the shadowy entrance, Annalise smiled. "I'm certain you shan't let me fall. Where are we?"

The glowing ball lighting their way, he led her into the caverns and studied her face. He couldn't miss her radiant smile when she saw the wonder ahead. "Column Caverns, a system of limestone caverns created by an underground river many, many years ago."

Annalise gasped when they reached the center of the first cavern. Her lips parting, she pointed at the pale, almost translucent sheetlike stone formation along the wall. "What is that? 'Tis like a waterfall made of earth."

His heart quickening, Dare forced himself to not kiss Annalise's tempting lips. "A flowstone drapery. And look." He struck the drapery with his hand, and a bell-like toll rang through the cavern.

White awe pulsing around her, Annalise gasped again then fingered the drapery. "How magical."

Dare grinned, warmth suffusing his chest. She understood the glory of nature too. Another reason she was so perfect for him. "No magic, just nature."

Annalise slanted him a narrow glance. "You know what I mean, nature witch."

He kissed Annalise's palm. "I do, soul healer. Come, there's much more to see." Grinning, he led her into the next cavern. "Look up."

Annalise smiled at the milk-white clusters hanging from the cavern ceiling. "They're like stone chandeliers."

Dare nodded. Add some witchlights, and they would be. "Dripstones. These are particularly intricate and some of my favorite." He drew her into the third cavern. "But the dripstones in most of the caverns have grown into columns, hence the name."

Annalise grinned at the massive columns. "They're magnificent." She pointed to one at the far end. "Why is that one pink while the others are white?"

As they threaded through the sprawling caverns, he explained how different minerals made the columns white, pink, or amber, while Annalise beamed and caressed the many columns they passed.

At the final cavern, Dare paused before the entrance, breathless. He couldn't miss Annalise's reaction when they entered. "This is my favorite cavern."

When he led Annalise inside, she inhaled and gaped at the mirror-like lake reflecting the ceiling's many dripstones. "I can see why. How deep is it? I can't see the bottom."

He smiled. He'd reacted the same when he'd first visited two months ago. "Not deep. When I visited before, Bear leapt in, but the water only came to the middle of his chest."

Yellow delight glowing around her, Annalise leaned forward and threaded her fingers through the water, making the reflected dripstones dance. "So beautiful."

Breathless, Dare grasped her other hand and pulled her into his arms. What other lady would delight in caverns adorned with stone formations rather than jewels? "Not as beautiful as you."

Pushing against his chest, Annalise frowned at him. "So everyone says. My potent aura makes my physical beauty irresistible."

He sighed and lowered his head until their lips almost met. Tingling warmth flooded him. Annalise's deep kindness, serene strength, and clever mind made her beautiful. "I wasn't speaking of your physical beauty or potent magic."

Her arms relaxing, Annalise blinked up at him. "Oh."

Dare pulled Annalise closer then kissed her, and their souls meshed. As she slid her arms about his neck, her heady honeysuckle scent weaved about him, and he deepened their kiss. He could never get enough of her. Not because of her otherworldly beauty or their irresistible soulbond or her potent magic.

But because he loved her.

He loved her because she was always kind and considerate, even when others didn't deserve it. He loved her because she enjoyed outdoor pursuits, adored Wildewall, and understood nature's glory. And most of all, he loved her because she'd do anything to preserve the happiness of the ones she loved, like her new friends, devoted pets, hellion brother, and ambitious parents. Hopefully, one day she'd love him the way he loved her.

Dare broke their kiss. Even though she might not feel the

same yet, he must confess the love filling his heart. He gazed into her eyes, which had deepened to navy during their kiss. His pulse racing, he swallowed then began, "Annalise, I—"

CHAPTER 25

*B*efore Dare could finish, Annalise pressed her fingers against his mouth and separated their souls. From the indigo swirling about him and the glow in his amber eyes, he was about to confess something she couldn't bear to hear. Not when everything was so impossible. She forced a smile despite her tender lips. "If we don't leave soon, we shan't return to Ormas before luncheon."

Muddy-yellow hurt flaring about him, Dare nodded. "As you wish." He offered his arm.

She swallowed, her heart twisting. If she touched him, she'd be unable to resist kissing him again. She stepped back and shook her head. "I can manage." When muddy-yellow hurt flared about him anew, she winced, and tears pricked her eyes.

They didn't speak as they threaded through the stunning caverns with Dare's glowing ball of light above their heads, and she could barely glance at him as the tense silence throbbed between them.

Once they were mounted atop Storm and Ebony, Annalise glanced at Dare. Weight compressed her chest. His usual genial grin was gone, and muddy-white melancholy hung about him.

She coughed then said, "Dare, thanks for bringing me. The caverns were stunning."

His smile stiff, Dare inclined a nod. "I'm glad you enjoyed it." He shifted in his saddle. "Since you're concerned about being late, shall we gallop back?"

She echoed his nod, and they urged Storm and Ebony to a gallop down the winding path, which they continued the entire ride back to Ormas. Yet unlike before, or when she galloped with Alex, her pulse didn't quicken, and her chest remained tight. Especially whenever she glanced at Dare, whose brow was furrowed and lips pinched.

When Ormas appeared in the distance, Dare pulled Ebony to a halt, and Annalise halted Storm as well. His eyes fixed on the gate, he said, "All of court shall be about now, so I'll cast an invisibility spell on myself to prevent anyone from seeing us together. Give me a moment—'tisn't nature magic, so it takes more effort."

She lowered her gaze and patted Storm's damp withers. Even after she'd hurt him, Dare still looked out for her. Goddess, he was so wonderful. Why did their families have to be ancestral enemies who couldn't live in harmony? She swallowed then replied, "Of course."

Dare crooned a singsong chant and waved above his head then Ebony's. During his spell, the white glow of magic grew around him and his stallion, until it flared, and they vanished—except for the faint glow of magic around them, not that anyone but someone who could read auras would see that. Unlike most magic, invisibility spells or enchanted items turned their glow inward, so ordinary witches couldn't see them like they could other active magic.

Once he finished casting his spell, Dare said, "Lead the way. I'll ride on your left."

Annalise nodded then urged Storm to a trot, and Dare echoed her. Like when they'd left the cavern, the silence throbbed between them. If only she could think of something to say to ease his hurt. When they reached her family's townhouse, she paused and glanced at the faint glow beside her. "Just after dawn, two days from today in the park?"

Dare murmured, "Until then."

She stared after Dare as his invisibility spell drifted down the street. They needed a distraction during their next morning walk, but what? She sighed then rode to the stables.

After grooming Storm, Annalise slipped upstairs to her chambers. She rang for Grace then petted a yowling Finn and released Rain and Aria from their golden birdcage. She gave her magical pets a few dried treats hidden in her desk, jerked venison for Finn and dried berries for the faebirds, but she didn't feed them breakfast—she'd done that before she'd left since she'd known she'd be gone most of the morning.

As her magical pets devoured their treats, she blinked at Rain and Aria. Introducing them to Dare would be the perfect distraction. Besides, if she didn't bring them soon, he'd not get to meet them until next season—the mornings would soon become too cold for the fragile faebirds. She smiled. Doubtless Dare's kindness would instantly charm Rain and Aria. She could hardly wait to see them perch on his head.

Just after dawn two mornings later, Annalise placed Rain and Aria in their travel cage then headed to the park to meet Dare.

The entire walk, Finn meowed and darted past her then darted back to rub her skirt before starting the cycle over again. He was definitely excited to see his mate for the first time in four days. When they neared Lily, Finn bolted toward her without glancing back at Annalise. The two angelcats rubbed against each other then leapt into the oak trees, whose leaves were just starting to turn vermilion.

When Annalise reached him, Dare shook his head with a wry smile. "We may need to bring Lily and Finn on future rides, even if they make us recognizable. They missed each other too much."

She sighed but nodded, her chest squeezing. Understandable.

She and Dare would feel the same without their frequent private meetings.

Then Raven and Bear lunged toward her, so Dare chuckled and restrained them. "Behave. You'll scare the faebirds." The hellhounds sighed, and he released them. While they walked rather than ran over to her, he arched his brows. "Rain and Aria, I presume?"

Annalise nodded again as she bent to pat the hellhounds' heads, who both remained sedate after Dare's chiding—Bear only licked her hand, while Raven sat at her feet. Smiling at Dare, she straightened and opened the faebirds' cage. "I wanted you to meet them." She grasped Rain then handed him to Dare. The male faebird would attack if she gave Dare Aria first.

Yellow delight glowing about him, Dare cradled Rain in one hand then petted the faebird's sapphire chest with a finger. "Aren't you a pretty fellow."

Her heart fluttering, she smiled when Rain trilled and nuzzled Dare's finger. As expected, the chary faebird liked him. "If you release him, he'll perch on your head. Then I can introduce Aria."

Dare opened his hand, and Rain flitted to his head. Dare coughed a laugh as the faebird began preening him. "That tickles. Do they always do that?"

Annalise hummed while handing him Aria. "Yes, they're fascinated by hair." Although faebirds never acted so familiar with anyone they couldn't trust, and they rarely misjudged. As tiny creatures preyed upon by many others, they'd learned to sense another's true self within moments.

Grinning, Dare petted Aria's amethyst chest with a finger. "You're even prettier than your mate."

Annalise chuckled when Aria coyly tilted her head and trilled twice as loud as Rain had. The little flirt.

Chuckling as well, Dare set Aria on his head beside Rain, and she also began preening him. A rugged, bearded gentleman should have appeared ridiculous with two tiny, jewel-like faebirds preening his long, black hair, but he didn't.

Her throat thickening, Annalise swallowed, and tears burned her eyes. Instead, Dare appeared perfect—kindhearted, steady, and strong. No wonder she loved him.

She blinked and licked her lips. Wait, she loved him? Then she suppressed a snort. Of course she did—she'd just refused to admit it to herself because everything was so impossible. Which was why she'd halted his confession at Column Caverns. Loving him like she did, hearing him confess the same would hurt too much when they could never marry without destroying their families.

As Dare reached up to pet Rain and Aria, Annalise sighed, and warmth flooded her chest. When exactly had she fallen in love with him? He'd fascinated her since their secret encounter years ago, and she'd known she couldn't let him die when she'd soul-healed him, but neither of those were love. Then their irrevocable soulbond had strengthened his pull, but that was still mere attraction, not love. She tilted her head. No, she'd only fallen in love once she'd gotten to know him during their morning walks. And 'twasn't a shallow love either—'twas as lasting as the love between griffins, who remained devoted to their mates until death and rarely outlived each other.

Pain echoed through her. Despite their stifled soulbond becoming impossible to control, they never should have started their morning walks. Adding lasting love to their irresistible soulbond made resisting him and concealing their soulbond even more excruciating than it already had been. Goddess, what were they to do?

Suddenly, she inhaled and stiffened. Dare had been saying something, not that she'd heard him. "What?"

Dare frowned and leaned toward her, Rain and Aria whistling while fluttering their wings to remain balanced. "Are you all right?"

Annalise gritted a tremulous smile. How could she be all

right when their love was impossible? "Of course. Just thinking. What did you say?"

Dare hummed but straightened and waggled his brows at her. "I said that you should wear them to court one day. Set a new fashion—faebird hats."

Her heart squeezed. He was so wonderful to attempt to distract her from her obvious upset, especially after she'd hurt him when he'd attempted to confess his love. Shoving that aside, she shook her head and replied, "Faebird hats would be doomed to fail. Not only might they defecate on the wearer's head, but they'd likely sicken and die if exposed to foul weather." She sighed. "I'd better return Rain and Aria to their cage. I've my third nightmara ride today, and I mustn't be late."

Dare nodded and extracted the faebirds from his hair. "Shall you be at Lady Ducharme's fencing party this afternoon? Alex didn't think you would when he and I discussed it during our ride yesterday, but it *is* an event held by a councilor."

Annalise sighed as she placed Rain and Aria in their cage. Attending a fencing party and watching Dare exhibit his sword fighting would be thrilling—not that Mother would ever let her. "Mother says such events aren't ladylike, so unfortunately not. But my parents and I are attending the Farsons' rout party tonight."

Dare smiled at her. "I'll see you there then."

Her pulse quickening, she swallowed. "Yes, but we mustn't risk slipping outside to meet. If we continue disappearing at every court event we both attend, someone shall notice, most likely Mother and Father." Plus, she needed time to recover from realizing her love.

Dare grimaced but nodded. "True enough."

Annalise called Finn so they could leave, but the angelcat hissed and refused to untwine himself from Lily. She sighed. Although Finn loved her, his mate was more important to him now. Thank the Goddess Dare had cast that contraceptive spell three weeks ago—otherwise Lily would definitely be carrying angelkittens. "I think you should keep Finn until our next morning walk."

Eyeing the bristling Finn, Dare rubbed his beard. "'Twould be cruel to separate them, but shan't your parents notice?"

She almost snorted. Only that she'd less white fur on her gowns. "No, Mother insists Finn spend most of his time in my chambers when we live in Ormas."

Dare nodded, and they said goodbye before Annalise returned to her family's townhouse. She deposited Rain and Aria in her chambers then went to the kitchen to fetch their breakfast. Her throat clogged when she told Cook she'd not need Finn's.

After feeding Rain and Aria, she changed into her riding habit with Grace's help then headed downstairs for breakfast. She smiled at her family as she sat beside Alex then served herself.

Mother pursed her lips as Annalise began devouring her heaped plate. "Another nightmara ride, I see. At least today you're not skipping breakfast with us. Unlike last time."

Annalise sipped her tea to hide the faint blush warming her cheeks. Except last time had been her ride with Dare, not a nightmara ride like today.

Alex grinned over his beefsteak. "I'd skip any meal necessary if *I* was fortunate enough to ride a nightmara."

Father chuckled. "Me too."

Her blush having faded, Annalise lowered her tea and was about to reply when Mother sighed and said, "I just think that Kiera creature is demanding too much of your time, Annalise. If she *somehow* manages to marry King Devon, you must find another husband, so you should start approaching other suitable gentlemen now. Otherwise, you'll never have a family of your own."

As Father nodded, Annalise stiffened. No doubt soon they'd start shoving her at any unwed duke or duke's heir again. She stuffed her beefsteak in her roll then leapt to her feet. Less than she usually ate, so she'd be starving by midmorning, but 'twas better than discussing marrying someone besides Dare. "I must go, or I'll be late." She swept from the breakfast room before her parents could reply.

She rode Storm to the palace then left him in the palace stables to meet Kiera in the gardens. She frowned when she joined Kiera. Her friend appeared exhausted—gray fog tarnished her indigo aura, and shadows underscored her eyes. "Are you feeling well?"

Kiera lifted her chin. "I'm fine. I have to be."

Annalise studied Kiera. Hopefully so. Although if Kiera did collapse, she could soul-heal her. Kiera might not even notice if the healing was minor and didn't require much meshing of their souls.

Unlike on her previous nightmara rides, Annalise requested Darkthorn keep to a walk, so she could watch Kiera. As the stallion glided around the nightmara paddock, he asked her about Wildewall, and they discussed that the entire ride.

At the Farsons' rout party that evening, Annalise smiled when the young Duke of Golddell immediately joined her. The diffident duke clearly found her comforting after their long talk with the Farsons at his soiree two months ago. And his quiet company allowed her to escape her parents and continue watching Kiera, who appeared even more exhausted. Not that she could risk soul-healing Kiera before all of court.

She was so concerned for her friend that she only glanced at Dare once an hour, despite the sultry Lady Blaine standing beside him. When she and her parents left, she pursed her lips. She must get Kiera to talk at Lady Dabar's salon tomorrow afternoon. Since only ladies were invited, surely she could manage a private word with Kiera.

Yet the following day, Kiera wasn't at Lady Dabar's salon. Lady Dabar grinned as she told the other ladies that King Devon had said Kiera was visiting the orphans. Annalise concealed a frown at that. Kiera had planned to attend Lady Dabar's—why the sudden change?

So at the Islayes' concert that evening, Annalise swept straight to Kiera, despite Mother and Father grumbling behind her. "What happened today?"

Her aura bright once more, Kiera blushed then shrugged. "I collapsed after the rout and didn't wake until this afternoon. Traveling to and from the orphanage every day while also acting as queen was too much." She sighed, muddy-indigo grief pulsing around her. "I transferred my responsibilities at the orphanage to Wren and Hawke."

Annalise squeezed Kiera's hand. Surrendering the orphans must have been heartrending. "They love the orphans too and shall care for them well."

Kiera sighed again. "I know. Shall we find seats?"

Sitting beside Kiera and King Devon, Annalise glanced up and stilled. Dare was several rows ahead to her right with Lady Blaine beside him. Her heart surging, Annalise laced her hands in her lap. She could watch him the entire evening without anyone realizing, not even Mother and Father.

After the second song, Kiera murmured in her ear, "You must love ballads."

Annalise suppressed a blush. Was that what the bards were performing? She nodded without removing her gaze from Dare. She'd only the rest of the concert to watch her fill.

CHAPTER 26

When the Islayes' concert ended, Dare turned to face Annalise—her ardent stare had caressed him since the first ballad. Their eyes met across the room, and the indigo glow about her flared even brighter. His heart quickened. Given her expression and aura, she *must* share his love. As he'd suspected once he'd time to reflect, she'd not halted his confession of love at Column Caverns because she didn't love him, but because she believed their love impossible.

Suddenly, Lady Blaine grasped his arm and drawled, "Are you eyeing Lady Annalise?"

He stiffened and forced himself to break his locked stare with Annalise to face Lady Blaine. He'd forgotten the husband-hunting countess had captured the seat beside him. He arched his brows to feign cool surprise. "Of course not. I was watching King Devon and Lady Kiera beside her. They're truly perfect for each other."

Lady Blaine's eyes narrowed, but she nodded. "They are, despite Lady Kiera's humble upbringing." She quirked a smile. "Or perhaps because of it."

Dare blinked at Lady Blaine. Astonishing the fashionable countess could see that. She seemed preoccupied by wealth and status. He freed his arm. "Most likely. I must go. Good evening." Before Lady Blaine could reply, he strode over to say farewell to Lord and Lady Islaye. He flashed a genial grin. "The concert was lovely."

Lady Islaye echoed his grin. "I adore ballads." Her blue eyes gleaming, she squeezed her husband's arm. "They remind me of our courtship."

Lord Islaye blushed then coughed and leaned toward Dare. "Could we meet next week? Your mother says you're an even more powerful nature witch than she is, so I'd like your advice on a magical matter."

His brows rising, Dare hummed. Of course, Lord Islaye knew about his powers even though they'd never discussed it. As childhood friends, Mother and the studious count exchanged frequent letters—Father used to grumble about that to tease her. But since Lord Islaye served on the council as the Minister of Magic, whatever magical matter he had was doubtless serious. A chill prickling his neck, Dare inclined his head. "I'm at your disposal."

Lord Islaye relaxed with a sigh. "Excellent. I'll contact Lord Nolan, so the three of us can arrange a meeting."

His chill growing, Dare nodded again before taking his leave. Since Lord Islaye needed advice from a nature witch, the Minister of Natural Resources also being involved wasn't surprising. But that definitely hinted at a kingdom-wide matter.

During their morning walk the following morning, Dare mentioned his conversation with Lord Islaye to Annalise since she might have heard something as Lady Kiera's friend. Then he arched his brows and asked, "Any idea what the matter might be?"

Annalise frowned and shook her head. "Kiera hasn't mentioned anything, and I've heard no rumors about it at court either. I hope 'tisn't too serious."

He grimaced. "So do I." He slanted Annalise a sidelong glance. If only they could discuss their love, but since their visit to Column Caves, she'd ignored his attempts to take her arm. And if she considered touching him too dangerous, she'd surely flee if he mentioned love. He smiled at her. "Enough about that; could we risk visiting another natural area next time?"

Humming, Annalise licked her lips. "I think so. Where did you want to visit?"

Tingling suffusing him, Dare studied her lips. Goddess, he burned to kiss her. "Glass Lake, I think. However, 'tis the same distance as Column Caverns, so we must gallop there and back to ensure you return before luncheon."

As muddy-blue guilt pulsed about her, Annalise winced, and her eyes darkened.

He stepped closer with a soft smile to comfort her. "That wasn't meant as a barb, Annalise, just a statement." Capturing her hand, he pressed a kiss on her palm. When she shivered but didn't pull away, his pulse surged, and he threaded his arm through hers. "You'll like Glass Lake, I promise."

Annalise smiled and arched her brows. "As much as Doimhn Lake?"

Warmth flooding him, Dare grinned. He'd hung her embroidery of their favorite lake back home beside his bed and fell asleep imagining visiting it with her. Truly the perfect natalday gift. He squeezed her arm. "Probably not. Glass Lake is nowhere near as magical as Doimhn Lake."

Annalise chuckled. "Well, Doimhn Lake *is* in Wildewall." She returned his squeeze. "But I'm sure I'll enjoy visiting Glass Lake."

He and Annalise smiled at each other until Bear dropped his drool-covered stick at their feet. They both started at that, but Dare tossed the stick for the hellhound.

As they watched Bear course after his stick, Annalise blew a sigh. "I should probably go since I'll be gone most of the morning next time." She turned and called, "Come on, Finn."

Unlike when she'd called him at their previous morning walk, Finn leapt from the oak branches and rubbed against Annalise's skirt with a purring meow, like he had when he'd first seen her today. Lily soon echoed him, and as Annalise began to leave, both angelcats followed her.

When Annalise halted then glanced at him, Dare smiled and shrugged. "Finn and Lily must have decided not to separate anymore." Wise angelcats. "I suspect they'll alternate where they live."

Annalise pursed her lips. "Although Mother and Father mostly ignore Finn, I hope they don't notice I sometimes have two angelcats. But at least we don't have to worry about angelkittens thanks to your contraceptive spell." She sighed then waved and left.

Weight compressing his chest, he stared after her. Goddess, please let the angelcats stop needing to alternate soon. He grimaced then called Raven and Bear to return to Ravenstone House.

TWO MORNINGS LATER, Dare rode to the park and met Annalise, but the angelcats weren't with her. As they began riding from the park, Annalise said, "I left Finn and Lily in my chambers. Galloping with them perched behind us would be impossible."

He nodded but swallowed a sigh. Made sense, although he missed Lily. Raven and Bear did too, so they'd begun hunting for her throughout Ravenstone House. Shoving that aside, he smiled at Annalise. "I left Raven and Bear behind for the same reason."

Once they rode out the eastern gate, he and Annalise urged Ebony and Storm to a gallop. When they neared the royal forest, he slowed Ebony to a walk and nodded at the thick trees. "Have you ever ridden there?"

Annalise shook her head. "King Devon's escort only extended to court events. But I'd like to ride there one day to see Esme the Great's melissae hive. Have you?"

Dare smiled at her. Of course, a soul healer would desire that, especially one descended from Esme the Great. "A few times, but not this season. Perhaps I can request permission to ride there next week."

Annalise beamed back. "I'd enjoy that." Still beaming, she tilted her head. "How much further to Glass Lake?"

He chuckled. Her enthusiasm was adorable. "A half hour if we keep to a walk."

Annalise winked at him. "Why would we do that?" She urged Storm to a gallop.

Laughing, Dare kneed Ebony to join them, and they galloped together the rest of the way. Goddess, how he loved her.

When they reached Glass Lake, they halted Ebony and Storm, and white awe surrounding her, Annalise sighed at the sparkling lake reflecting the azure sky. "Oh, Dare, 'tis lovely."

He waggled his brows to tease her. "As lovely as Doimhn Lake?"

Annalise giggled. "Of course not, but 'tis a close second." She sidled Storm closer then caressed Dare's cheek. "Thank you for bringing me."

His pulse quickening, he kissed her palm. Too bad they were atop horses—he'd kiss more than her hand if they weren't. "'Tis a joy to visit natural areas with a lady who loves them as much as I do."

Annalise blushed. Then she lowered her hand and flashed a smile. "Shall we tie Storm and Ebony to those willows, so we can walk along the shore?"

Once their stallions were tied and drinking the clear lake water, he offered Annalise his arm, and they began walking along the lake. He grinned as his heart swelled. What a perfect outing with the lady he loved.

After a moment, Annalise bent and dipped her fingers in the water then jerked back. "'Tis freezing."

Dare chuckled. Well, 'twas autumn, and although sunny, the morning was cool. "Glass Lake is fed by underground springs and drains into Morwynne River. So the water is always fresh, clear, and often cold."

Annalise tilted her head, her white-blonde hair shimmering. "Must be refreshing during the summer. I'm surprised that I've not heard anyone at court mention visiting."

Aching to touch her radiant hair, he swallowed then shrugged. "They'd have to endure a long, hot ride to and fro, so I suspect most would visit the beach instead. Ormas is on the coast, after all."

Annalise hummed. "True, so this would be more private. I'd much prefer visiting here."

Dare squeezed her arm. So would he, especially with her. A movement on the shallows of the lake caught his eye. He pointed and said, "Look."

Yellow delight flaring about her, Annalise beamed and halted. "A heron! Fishing for bass, pike, or trout?"

His pulse surged at her exuberance. "Whichever he can catch, most likely." He drew her into his arms—he *had* to kiss her.

Her lips parting, Annalise stared up at him and whispered, "Dare, don't."

As her heady honeysuckle scent surrounded him, he shuddered but didn't release her or lower his head. "I'll stop if you ask me to."

Annalise sighed then slid her arms about his neck as their souls meshed. "I should ask that, but I can't."

Heat flooding him, Dare captured her lips in a ravenous kiss. Thank the Goddess she couldn't resist him either. When she threaded her fingers in his hair, he rumbled and pulled her tighter against him. They continued devouring each other's mouths until his body became painfully hard. Then he wrenched his head back. He'd make love to her if they continued, and she wasn't ready for that.

He swallowed and separated their souls. "We should go if you're to return before luncheon."

Annalise blinked then lowered her arms and stepped back. "Yes, of course."

He and Annalise galloped back to Ormas, and like after their visit to Column Caverns, he cast an invisibility spell at the gate, so he could ride with her through Ormas. At her family's townhouse, he murmured, "I'll see you tonight at the Duke of Osbourne's card party."

When Dare returned to Ravenstone House, a letter was waiting from Lord Islaye requesting a ride with him and Lord Nolan in a few days. His stomach tensing, Dare wrote his acceptance then wrote King Devon to request permission to ride in the royal forest next week.

At Osbourne House that evening, Lady Blaine attached herself to him as soon as he arrived. To ensure her suspicions weren't roused again, he made himself not watch Annalise. Thankfully, Lord Treyvan was Annalise's card partner, and she was safe with the happily married duke's heir, even though Miss Winston and her cad of a brother were playing against them. However, when Annalise left shortly after King Devon and Lady Kiera, Dare sighed and left as well.

He didn't see Annalise again until their next morning walk. She brought Finn and Lily, but she left soon after, claiming she couldn't be late for her nightmara ride. As Annalise swept from the park without the angelcats, he stared after her, his chest aching. The nightmara ride was a mere excuse—she didn't want to risk them kissing like at Glass Lake. He grimaced and trudged back to Ravenstone House.

The following morning, Alex eyed Dare as they rode along the royal bay after crossing swords. "You didn't ask about my family during our sword fight today. What about sharpening my mind?"

Dare gripped his reins. Now that he knew he loved Annalise, asking her perceptive brother about her was too dangerous. He forced his fingers to relax. "You've mastered conversing while crossing swords. Why, do you have news to share?"

Grinning, Alex leaned toward Dare. "Yes, apparently our family is growing."

Dare stiffened, his heart seizing. Oh, Goddess. He made

himself drawl, "Your parents have found a husband for your sister then?"

Alex snickered. "Hardly. But Annalise *does* have a second angelcat now. Not that Father and Mother have noticed yet." He raised his eyes skyward. "Mother shall doubtless shout when she does."

Swallowing a sigh, Dare managed to nod then asked Alex about his last sword fight at Lady Ducharme's fencing salon to distract the younger gentleman.

At their morning walk the following day, Dare told Annalise when she arrived, "Your brother noticed Lily."

Annalise paled. "I was worried he might have. Lily escaped my chambers on her first day staying with me. She's clearly not accustomed to being contained."

He snorted a laugh. No, Lily was accustomed to reigning over everyone. He patted Annalise's hand. "Fortunately, I've never mentioned Lily to Alex, so he shan't discover our soulbond through our angelcats."

Annalise relaxed with a sigh. "Thank the Goddess for that."

Dare and Annalise strolled around the park for another hour before separating. However, Finn and Lily remained with him rather than leaving with her. No doubt the angelcats enjoyed the greater freedom at Ravenstone House. He set his jaw as Annalise left with drooping shoulders. Regardless, he'd ensure Finn and Lily went with her next time.

Later that morning, he activated his communication mirror to call Mother, and she said once she appeared, "Is that handsome angelcat with Lily her mate?"

Suppressing a curse, he glanced behind him. Of course, the angelcats were curled together on the only table Mother could see. He turned around and managed a smile. "Yes, he is."

Mother beamed. "At last. I thought she'd never find one."

Dare shifted in his seat but nodded. To prevent her from asking more about Finn, he said, "Lord Islaye asked for my advice about a magical matter. Did he mention it to you?"

Mother frowned and smoothed back her windswept hair. "No, he's not mentioned anything to me. That likely means 'tis a council secret."

He winced. Wonderful, more secrets.

Mother added, "If you need my help, just let me know."

Dare nodded and asked about things at home. He and Mother talked for a while, although he never mentioned Pearl. He couldn't risk her asking about his new angelcat again. Then they said goodbye, and he deactivated the communication mirror and set it on the windowsill to recharge.

The following morning, he tensed as he rode to meet Lord Islaye and Lord Nolan on the path between the palace and the royal bay. Time to learn Lord Islaye's mysterious magical matter.

Once they began riding toward the palace, Lord Islaye swallowed then said, "A mysterious ore was recently unearthed in Magehaven. It disrupts any nearby magic, and 'tis unstable, but its influence is spreading and may soon reach the Walle. My magic marshals, Lord Nolan's land rangers, and Lady Juliet have all had no success identifying or counteracting it. We're attempting to locate an alchemist without magic to try, but I wondered if you had any ideas since you're a nature witch."

A prickle skittering across his skin, Dare stiffened. Lord Islaye's magical matter was as serious as he'd feared. Destroying the Walle could start a catastrophic war with magical creatures like the Stone Wars. No wonder 'twas a council secret. But locating an alchemist without magic would take ages since nearly all alchemists were witches—except Miss Winston. Should he tell Lord Islaye and Lord Nolan about her?

He swallowed a sigh. No, 'twasn't his secret to reveal, but when he saw Miss Winston at the Nolans' ball tonight, he'd mention the council was seeking a magicless alchemist to study an ore in Magehaven then encourage her to approach them despite the scandal of a lady working as an alchemist.

So he simply asked Lord Islaye, "Have you attempted a composition spell?"

Lord Islaye grimaced. "Yes, but the ore doesn't react predictably. Half the time, the composition spell yields no results. Then if it does work, the spell never yields the same minerals twice."

Rubbing his beard, Dare winced. "Unfortunately, my connection to nature is through magic, so I'm not sure what to do when even the simplest spells don't function. However, I'll check my spellbooks tonight and see what I can discover." 'Twas fortunate he'd performed that library spell two months ago.

Lord Islaye and Lord Nolan thanked him, then Lord Nolan's eyes widened, and he asked, "Is that Lady Kiera riding Lady Moonbud and Lady Annalise riding another nightmara?"

As Lord Islaye and Lord Nolan stared at Annalise and the others riding toward them, Dare let himself stare as well. He'd been right—her beams atop a nightmara were exhilarating. He swallowed then replied, "I believe so." Hopefully, his indifferent tone disguised his deep love for her.

CHAPTER 27

As Dare, Lord Islaye, and Lord Nolan stared while riding past, Annalise forced herself to smile at the two councilors but glance over Dare without acknowledging him. Yet when their eyes met for a moment, indigo flared about him, and her heart quickened. Goddess, she loved him like a firecat loved flame—she burned to curl against him and never leave.

Darkthorn chuckled and bobbed his black head. *:You're accomplished at concealing your true feelings. Only a nightmara or another creature that can read auras can see how you love Lord Ravenstone.:*

Her chest twisted. She had to be. If she revealed her true feelings, she'd destroy her family.

Darkthorn glanced toward Kiera and Moonbud. *:Your aura and mind are open, unlike your friend, who's remarkably skilled at shielding her mind for someone without magic.:*

Annalise hummed and eyed Kiera. Interesting. Yet Kiera's aura was open to *her*. Because Kiera was her friend or because she could read auras better than the nightmara? Burying that thought to avoid offending Darkthorn, she shrugged and murmured so Kiera and Leila couldn't overhear, "I could shield my mind if I wished, but I trust you and the other nightmara, so why bother? I save my energy for concealing my true feelings from those I need to."

Muddy-yellow disapproval pulsing about him, Darkthorn snorted. *:Like your parents.:*

She winced and shifted on the nightmara stallion's back. "Yes." If only she didn't have to.

Darkthorn studied Kiera again. *:So Kiera doesn't trust us? Not encouraging for the future queen that shall negotiate our treaty with Calatini.:*

Annalise froze. Had she just harmed the renewal of the essential Nightmara-Calatini Treaty? She swallowed. "'Tisn't that Kiera doesn't trust you. Doubtless she's just attempting to conceal her belief that her betrothal to King Devon is fake."

Darkthorn hummed and nodded. *:I should have realized that. King Devon **did** ask Moonbud for time to court Kiera.:*

Annalise exhaled and almost sagged. Thankfully, she'd not harmed the treaty.

Flicking his tail, Darkthorn followed Moonbud as she turned around on the well-tended path. *:Although Kiera's belief her betrothal is fake is ridiculous. She's King Devon's true mate that we called for him.:*

Annalise tilted her head. So *that* had been the nightmara magic glittering about Kiera and King Devon at the king's summer masquerade.

Darkthorn snorted. *:As ridiculous as you denying your love for Lord Ravenstone. From what I've read in your thoughts, your parents shall never surrender their precious feud. So you and Lord Ravenstone better elope if you ever want a chance to live.:*

She stiffened as her throat constricted. Mother and Father would be devastated if she eloped with anyone, let alone their ancestral enemy. "I can't."

Darkthorn blew a sigh. *:You humans can be so foolish.:*

Annalise glared at his inky mane. Nightmara could be too— like when they'd refused to negotiate with King Devon simply because he was male. Yet she swallowed her irritation and asked his thoughts on Kiera's education initiative that would make basic education mandatory for all children in Calatini. Arguing about which creature was more foolish would only upset them both.

THE FOLLOWING morning just after dawn, Annalise shivered as she rode Storm to the park to meet Dare. Icy wind from the north had swept through Ormas around midnight, and the air was still below freezing, so all the plants were white with frost—the first hard frost of the season. She pulled her cloak tighter about her. Hopefully, the air wouldn't be as frigid at Lady Blaine's fire ball tonight.

She managed to smile when she joined Dare, who was alone except for Ebony. A pang bolted through her. Even though galloping with angelcats would be impossible, she'd still hoped to see Finn. He'd slept on her bed every night until he'd stayed with Lily, and she missed him.

Dare leaned toward her. "Are you warm enough? I can perform a warming spell."

Tenderness suffused her at Dare considering her first like always. She flashed a true smile. "I'll be fine once we start galloping. Shall we go?" Once they began riding through Ormas, she arched her brows at him. "So what was Lord Islaye's magical matter?"

Grimacing, Dare sighed. "A mysterious ore in Magehaven that disrupts magic. No one has been able to identify or counteract it, and its disruption on magic is spreading and may soon reach the Walle."

Annalise inhaled. That *was* serious. Without the Walle, the magical wall raised by elves after the catastrophic Stone Wars, nothing would protect human kingdoms and magical creatures' kingdoms from each other.

Dare sighed again as they turned onto Center Street. "I checked my spellbooks and sent Lord Islaye my findings last night, but I doubt they'll help much. Then at the Nolans' ball, I told Miss Winston the council was seeking an alchemist without magic and encouraged her to approach them." He frowned. "Although I don't think I convinced her."

Blinking, Annalise stilled. Miss Winston was an alchemist? Possible—since Miss Winston wasn't a witch, she'd not have tin motes in her aura revealing she was an alchemist. And that explained Dare's intense conversation with her last night. Annalise almost snorted. She'd assumed it had been to escape Lady Blaine.

To hearten Dare, she smiled and replied, "Miss Winston shall approach the council when she's ready." The daughter of a baron working would be a scandal, so Miss Winston was wise to prepare herself. When Dare frowned harder, Annalise beamed and said to distract him, "I'm eager to see the royal forest and Esme the Great's melissae hive. Thanks for arranging today's ride."

His frown vanishing, Dare returned her grin. "Of course." Then he hummed and asked, "But shall the melissae be active in this cold weather? 'Twould be disappointing if you couldn't see them."

Annalise urged Storm a bit faster. "Unlike ordinary bees, melissae only retreat to their hive when 'tis below freezing. By the time we reach them, they should be active, although perhaps a bit sluggish. But we should still take care when approaching their hive. If we startle them, they'll attack before they recognize me as a soul healer." She could heal the melissae's fatal stings, but they'd still burn like fresh lava.

Dare quirked a teasing brow. "So we gallop *to* the royal forest, but not in it. Shall you be able to manage that?"

Swallowing her laughter, she tsked and shook her head. "We should be safe enough to gallop there as long as we can't hear the melissae's buzzing."

Once they rode out the eastern gate, she and Dare exchanged grins then urged Storm and Ebony to a gallop, and they thundered past the frost-covered fields. Her hood soon blew back, but warmed by riding, she left her head bare. And when they reached the royal forest, the frost had melted, and the air was merely cool.

Dare waggled his brows. "Although we can gallop in the royal forest, perhaps we should allow Ebony and Storm a break."

Annalise hummed and patted Storm's damp withers. "They'd appreciate that." As she and Dare rode into the royal forest, she glanced at the massive oak, birch, and maple trees ablaze with vermilion, gold, or scarlet leaves. Light filled her chest. "How wondrous to ride among such ancient trees. It reminds me of the forests back in Wildewall."

Indigo tenderness glowing about him, Dare patted the scaly bark of a massive birch tree. "I know. I'd ride here more often except King Devon prefers it, and I don't want to encroach. He gets little enough privacy at court."

She beamed and leaned toward Dare. He always thought of how his actions would impact everyone else. "'Tis kind of you to consider that."

A faint blush darkening his cheeks, Dare shrugged. "How could I not?"

Warmth flooded Annalise. And only he'd believe his kindness was nothing. To ease his blush, she asked, "How long until we reach Esme the Great's melissae hive?"

Dare rubbed his beard and eyed the meandering path through the royal forest. "Almost an hour at this pace."

She grimaced. An hour would consume her time with the melissae. She kneed Storm to a canter, and Dare urged Ebony to match them. As they rode, a buzzing soon began that grew with every step closer to the heart of the royal forest.

Once they reached the small clearing the royal forest had been created to protect, Annalise halted Storm then slid to the ground and tied him to a maple tree. The stallion might panic when surrounded by bee-like creatures as large as songbirds, which might upset the melissae. While Dare tied Ebony beside

Storm, she studied the many melissae buzzing between the ancient cottage in the center of the clearing and the still-flowering plants surrounding it. She grinned, her head whirling. She'd never seen so many melissae at once.

She glided into the clearing, and as she approached, a melissa twice as large as the rest emerged from the ancient cottage—the melissa queen. When they were a handbreadth apart, the melissa queen said, :*Welcome, sister.*:

The inside of her skull tickling at the melissa queen's buzzing thoughts, Annalise beamed at the melissa queen. Since the Goddess had bound the first soul healer Brigid to the melissae, they always called soul healers sisters. She pressed a hand to her heart. "Annalise, distant daughter of Esme the Great."

Her buzzing softening to a purr, the melissa queen swirled around Annalise. :*Heart-sister daughter.*: She hovered before Dare. :*Who this?*:

Before Annalise could reply, Dare bowed, and bronze motes in his lush green aura flared as he replied, "Dare, Annalise's... soulbond."

Annalise blinked at Dare. Although some nature witches could communicate with creatures, not many could communicate with the melissae since their thoughts were too alien. A powerful Rhiannon descendant indeed.

The melissa queen flew around Dare. :*Good mate.*: She circled both Annalise and Dare. :*Many larvae.*:

A blush burning her cheeks, Annalise shifted and couldn't glance at Dare as weight squeezed her chest. Babies between them couldn't happen while everything was so impossible.

The melissa queen hovered before them. :*Come. Eat ambrosia.*:

Annalise gasped then she and Dare exchanged a wide glance. The melissae only bestowed their life-giving ambrosia to bless those they truly trusted. Although most soul healers were gifted ambrosia at least once in their lives, never when first meeting a melissae hive, and their soulbonds weren't often similarly blessed. She swallowed and replied, "We can't."

Her buzzing growing strident, the melissae queen swirled around them. :*Can. Bless mating. Come.*: She swooped toward the ancient cottage. :*Ambrosia here.*:

Dare grasped Annalise's hand and murmured, "We mustn't anger the melissa queen by refusing."

Annalise sighed and allowed Dare to tug her toward the impatient melissa queen. An angry one might sting, and their stings were three times as fatal as an ordinary melissa's.

The melissa queen hovered before the cottage's door. :*Inside. Come.*:

Dare opened the weathered door then waved Annalise to enter. Gripping his hand and pulling him with her, she swallowed and glided into the buzzing melissae hive. The heady sweetness of ambrosia filling the air, massive ambrosia-combs hung from the entire ceiling, and countless melissae darted to and fro. She gasped. 'Twas breathtaking.

The melissa queen flew to a pale-yellow comb near the door. :*Fresh. No eggs. Break piece. Eat.*:

Annalise glanced at Dare, and he nodded, so she removed her gloves and broke off the bottom of the ambrosia-comb then split it in two and handed him half. Her stomach fluttering, she ate her piece while he ate his. Richer than honey and potent as spiritmead, the ambrosia's sweetness burst on her tongue. Then energy flared in her veins like wildfire, and she swayed as giddiness swept through her. She blinked and studied Dare, who swayed too. When their dazed eyes met, she giggled, and he chuckled.

Purring, the melissa queen circled them. :*No sick one moon.*:

Forcing herself to quit giggling, Annalise licked the last of the ambrosia from her lips, and the energy inside her flared again.

Before she could thank the melissa queen, Dare yanked her into his arms and seized her lips in a deep kiss.

Her pulse racing as their entire souls instantly meshed, she kissed him back and buried her sticky hands in his long hair. Oh, Goddess, she loved, loved, loved him. And the ambrosia on his tongue made his kisses even more irresistible. She whimpered and pressed against him, and they stumbled into the doorframe.

The melissa queen buzzed with laughter. *:No mating here. Make mess. Ambrosia everywhere.:*

A blush scorching her skin, Annalise wrenched herself apart from Dare and stumbled outside. If not for the melissa queen's laughter, they would have forgotten themselves and made love. That ambrosia was *dangerous*. She smiled at the melissa queen. "Thank you for the ambrosia."

The melissae queen hovered outside the ancient cottage as Dare closed the door. *:Welcome, heart-sister daughter and heart-sister daughter's mate.:*

Energy still coursing through her, Annalise bounced across the clearing to Storm then untied the stallion and leapt into her saddle. As Dare leapt onto Ebony, she slid her gloves onto her formerly sticky hands. She eyed Dare's disheveled black hair. "I got ambrosia in your hair."

Dare chuckled. "I always bathe after a ride anyway. Shall we gallop back?"

She nodded then kneed Storm, and they galloped down the meandering path. When a branch hit her, she giggled, and Dare soon began chuckling as well. Laughing and exchanging grins, they raced back to Ormas. Outside the eastern gate, he cast his invisibility spell then escorted her back to her family's townhouse. To avoid giggling, she kept her gaze averted from the faint glow around him and Ebony. She whispered as they separated, "See you at Lady Blaine's fire ball tonight."

When Annalise bounced from the stables after grooming Storm, Alex blinked at her as he handed his reins to a groom. "Annalise? What happened? You look like a pixie after devouring a bowl of faeberries."

She beamed at Alex. "Just had an exhilarating gallop." And the ambrosia was still burning in her veins.

Alex cocked his head. "I suppose so. You'd better not let

Mother see you like that. She'd harp about you galloping for ages."

Annalise bobbed a nod then darted upstairs to her chambers. She'd remain there until 'twas time to attend Lady Blaine's fire ball. Hopefully, the ambrosia would have subsided by then.

THE AMBROSIA DID SUBSIDE SLIGHTLY—ENOUGH that Annalise could contain her grins and glide rather than dart everywhere. Yet energy still vibrated her insides as she joined Mother and Father to leave. When Mother's brow furrowed, Annalise smoothed her silvery blue ballgown and forced herself to don Lady Snow's serene smile. That placated Mother since Mother quit frowning as they climbed into the carriage, although she began lecturing about gentlemen to pursue, including King Devon.

At the sprawling garden holding the fire ball, Annalise slipped away from Mother and Father when they began fawning over the Duke of Oakmoor. Disappearing into the shadows between the open braziers was easy, albeit cold. Since no one could see her face in the darkness, she let herself grin. Containing the ambrosia was onerous. Swaying to the wild music of the fire dancers, she glanced about the garden and almost giggled at King Devon's loving arm about Kiera. Pursuing him like Mother wanted would be impossible.

Then Dare strode into the garden, and tingling flooded her. Their eyes met, and he looked toward the area of the garden with the darkest shadows. She inclined a faint nod then glided across the garden, keeping away from the braziers, and slipped into the grotto along the wall.

Dare soon joined her and handed her a mug of spiced cider then gestured behind him. Once the ivy grew into an impenetrable tangle across the grotto's entrance, he muttered, and a hot ball of light appeared above their heads. As the grotto became balmy, they tossed aside their cloaks and gloves. He set his spiced cider on the stone bench along the wall then offered his hand. "Dance with me? No one shall see us through the ivy."

Her heart fluttering, Annalise flashed Dare a coy smile over her mug. "But then I can't drink my cider." She giggled. "Although I *suppose* I can drink that later."

She set her mug beside his then accepted his outstretched hand. When he pulled her close, she let herself stumble into him and twined her arms about his neck. Her pulse surging, she beamed up at him. Goddess, his hard body pressed against hers felt so right. "Oops."

Dare groaned and kissed her as if they hadn't kissed in years, not hours. Like before, their entire souls instantly meshed, and their combined hunger exploded like a forest fire after a summer of no rain.

Throbbing with emptiness as they devoured each other, Annalise yanked off his cravat and wrenched open his waistcoat. She needed his bare skin. She buried her hands beneath his shirt and splayed them across his chest, and her throbbing burgeoned at the crisp hair rubbing her palms.

Shuddering and kissing her harder, Dare unlaced her ball-gown and shift then tossed them aside along with his own clothes.

As their bare bodies pressed together, she purred and undulated against Dare. She needed him inside her. Now.

Rumbling, he tumbled her to the ground, and they came together like long-lost mated griffins. Their meshed souls fusing as their bodies joined, they cried each other's names in explosive release.

Her entire body glowing, Annalise sighed and kissed Dare's throat as he flipped her above him with their bodies and souls still one. She cuddled against him. Now they'd never be apart. Thank the Goddess they'd consummated their soulbond at last.

Suddenly, her breath froze, and her stomach roiled. They'd *consummated* their soulbond. Now their love and hunger would be even more impossible to deny or conceal. *And* she'd likely conceive. Dear Goddess, what had they *done*?

CHAPTER 28

$\mathcal{U}$tterly relaxed and his chest light as he remained entwined with Annalise and inhaled her heady honeysuckle scent, Dare stiffened when her sudden panic reverberated through him. Then she began separating their souls and bodies, so he tightened his arms and held her fast. He couldn't let her go. Not now. "What's wrong?"

Annalise stilled and quit separating their souls. "What's *wrong*?" She sagged against him, and her tears soaked his chest as her grief pierced him like a melissa's stinger.

His stomach clenched. Dear Goddess, for Annalise to be crying, he must have hurt her. She'd been a virgin until he'd made love to her on the ground in a near freezing garden, with her parents and the rest of court nearby. Not that anyone could find them with the impenetrable ivy he'd grown over the grotto entrance, but still. He'd treated her worse than a stag in rut.

Separating their bodies, Dare sat up with Annalise curled in his lap. He cupped her face and lifted her head to meet his gaze. "I'm sorry for hurting you. Please let me atone for that. As a nature witch, I can balance others' energy to promote healing. Not as effective as a true healing spell from a witch healer, but it shall help."

Tears glittering on her lashes, Annalise blinked at him as her confusion washed over him. "What?"

He wiped the tears from her cheeks. How could he have been so thoughtless when he loved her so? "From when I took your virginity. But I swear I'll do what I can to help."

Annalise blushed, and her embarrassment scorched him. "Oh. I wasn't crying because of that. At least, not exactly."

Dare gulped a shaky breath. He mustn't have been too rough then. Thank the Goddess. "Why *exactly* were you crying?"

Annalise blushed harder, her gaze skittering away as her embarrassment scorched him again. "Could we discuss this wearing clothes? Being naked is distracting."

His body stirred against hers. True. If he'd not been panicked that he'd hurt her, he would have been plotting how to make love to her again. He nodded and released her then tugged on his trousers and shirt.

Wearing her shift with her silvery blue ballgown undone, Annalise gave him her back. "Could you lace my ballgown?"

Aching to kiss her bare skin above her shift, Dare forced himself to do as she asked and don the rest of his clothes before his control vanished.

Annalise grasped her spiced cider then sank onto the stone bench with a deep sigh. As he placed his mug on the ground and sat beside her, she separated their souls. Yet instead of a thread connecting their souls like before, part of their souls remained entwined. She sighed again and glowered into her cider.

His heart twisting, he plucked her mug from her grasp then set it beside his, so he could take her hand. He kissed her palm then murmured, "Annalise, please, tell me why you were crying."

Annalise raised her gaze to meet his, her eyes dark as night. "We consummated our soulbond." When he frowned in confusion, she glared at him. "As I told you *before,* a consummated soulbond is much stronger. It shall be excruciating to conceal now."

Dare squeezed her hands as warmth suffused his chest. "Then perhaps we shouldn't try. We could elope tonight—your parents mightn't accept our marriage," he'd have them watched in case they hired assassins to murder their daughter's loathsome husband, "but at least Alex shall understand."

Annalise ripped her hands free and fisted them on her hips. "I *can't*. Although their ambition and obsession with the feud blind them, they love me, and betraying them like that would destroy them." Her grief flooded him through their entwined souls as she drooped on the stone bench.

To hearten her, he gathered her in his arms and kissed her brow. Burying his hunger to never let her go, he said, "Then we shan't elope tonight. Now, explain why a consummated soulbond is excruciating."

Annalise sighed against his throat. "Because its pull is even more irresistible, and we'll be incessantly hungry for each other."

When she extracted herself from his embrace, Dare took her hand again. Then he blinked at their interlaced fingers. Without thinking, he'd taken her hand because he couldn't bear not touching her. That *would* be excruciating to conceal. He swallowed. "I see what you mean. But why did making love strengthen our soulbond?"

Arching her brows, Annalise shook her head. "Joining our bodies while our souls were meshed fused our souls together. Can't you feel the difference?" She pressed her free hand over his heart. "Now we can more than read each other's emotions through our auras—we can feel them inside as well."

He blinked and nodded. So *that* was why he'd sensed part of their souls were still entwined. "Does it weaken with distance?"

Annalise lowered her hand then shrugged. "Somewhat, but how much depends on the strength of the soulbond, and I fear ours is likely very strong, given how powerful our magic is." She stilled then mentally added, :*We can also communicate with our thoughts now. Again, I don't know how far.*:

Smoothing his beard, Dare smiled. No more covert looks or

risky notes for them. :*That shall be useful, especially while we're concealing our soulbond*: He added aloud, "And if we continue our morning walks, I'm certain we can control our hunger."

Annalise grimaced and shook her head. "We should quit those now that we've made love. Succumbing to our passion again shall be too tempting if we're so alone. And we mustn't increase the chances of pregnancy, even though I'll likely conceive from tonight."

A pang darting through him, he extracted the gold contraceptive charm about his neck. "My strong-magic contraceptive charm shall have prevented that."

Wincing, Annalise nibbled her lip. "Those don't work on soul healers. Our high-energy auras neutralize them as well as make us incredibly fertile. And only another soul healer or a Rhiannon-descendant healer can create a contraceptive charm that works for a soul healer. But I don't know any, and even if I did, I couldn't risk them learning about my powers—they might tell Mother and Father."

His heart quickening, he clenched his free hand to not caress her stomach. Even now she could be carrying his child. He rasped, "When shall you know if you've conceived?"

Annalise tilted her head and hummed. "Probably three weeks when I miss my courses." She grimaced. "I could tell within a week for anyone else, but my potent aura shall likely mask the glow of pregnancy for three weeks at least."

Dare gaped at her, his chest hollow. She wanted to remain apart for that long? "I don't think I can last without seeing you alone for three weeks."

Annalise caressed his face and sighed. "Neither could I. But we can't be as alone as on our morning walks. We shall have to confine ourselves to slipping away from court events. At least we can communicate at them now without anyone realizing."

He swallowed his reply that they'd just made love at a court event. 'Twould only upset her. Instead, he forced a nod and said, "Very well."

Freeing her hand he'd been holding, Annalise rose then began smoothing her ballgown and tidying her hair. "We'd better return to the fire ball. Doubtless we've missed most of it. I hope Mother and Father haven't realized I'm missing."

Once they finished repairing their appearance and donned their cloaks and gloves, Dare extinguished his warming light spell then withdrew the ivy across the grotto's entrance.

However, when he began to follow her from the grotto, Annalise waved him away. "Remain here for a while. I'll be fine alone." She brushed a kiss against his lips. "With our consummated soulbond, you'll feel if I require help. And I promise to walk straight to Mother and Father."

He sighed but let Annalise leave alone, although he paced about the grotto until he sensed she'd joined her parents. When he strode from the grotto, he shook his head. She was right about their consummated soulbond being much stronger—unlike before, he still felt her presence as if she was beside him.

As soon as he rejoined the fire ball, the sultry Lady Blaine slid her arm through his and purred, "Lord Ravenstone, where have you been? We've not danced yet." She coyly leaned toward him, then her eyes narrowed. "And why do you smell like honeysuckle?"

Dare stilled as a blush burned his neck. Please let Lady Blaine not know Annalise's scent. Anyone who did would likely guess he'd been intimate with her. He forced a bland smile and freed his arm. "I imbibed too much honeyed spiritmead, so I was finding you to say farewell. Your fire ball was enchanting."

Lady Blaine moued. "Oh, very well. But you must swear to escort me to the Westons' musical evening later this week."

He stiffened. If he refused, he'd vex the husband-hunting countess, and she might reflect on the honeysuckle scent surrounding him. He inclined his head. "Of course. Until then."

He fled before Lady Blaine could invent further requests. Hopefully, escorting her to the Westons' musical evening wouldn't be too excruciating.

. . .

TWO MORNINGS later when he should have been meeting
Annalise for their morning walk, Dare forced himself to ride
Ebony to the royal bay instead. His chest burned as he flung his
powers wide to gather the natural energy pulsing around him.
'Twas no longer enough to settle his soul—he needed Annalise.
However, he galloped along the beach until both he and Ebony
were sweating then kept the tired stallion to a walk the entire
ride back to Ormas.

When his magical pets and Finn greeted him after he strode
into Ravenstone House, he frowned while petting them. He
must bring Finn and Lily to Annalise—she'd not seen Finn in
four days and surely missed him. Reaching toward her presence,
he said silently, :*Finn misses you. How can we exchange the
angelcats?*:

Annalise's longing darted through him. :*I'm on my nightmara
ride now. Wait outside the palace in an hour. Finn and Lily can ride
behind me back to my family's townhouse.*:

After casting an invisibility spell on himself and the angelcats, Dare followed her instructions. When they met outside the
palace, he clenched his hands behind his back to prevent himself
from pulling her off Storm and into his arms. Goddess, he
needed her like parched soil needed rain. Yet he managed to
release the invisibility spell on the angelcats and watch her ride
away with them.

But the following morning, he couldn't help asking Alex
about Annalise despite the risk of her perceptive brother discovering their secret involvement. Although he *did* make himself
wait until during their ride, since he'd told Alex that he'd
mastered conversing while crossing swords. As they rode along
the beach, he managed an insouciant smile. "How are things at
home?"

Alex snorted as he steered Biscuit around some driftwood.
"Turbulent. Father and Mother are furious about Annalise's

disappearance at Lady Blaine's fire ball. Apparently, she missed most of it and refuses to explain to their satisfaction." Alex arched his brows at Dare. "Did you attend and happen to see her?"

Dare gripped Ebony's reins. He'd more than seen Annalise; he'd made love to her. And even if they weren't concealing their soulbond, he couldn't tell her brother *that*. He forced his fingers to relax. "The light from the braziers didn't extend far."

His brows lowering, Alex hummed. "Well, Annalise must be in love to refuse to explain. She hates upsetting anyone, especially Father and Mother."

Stilling in the saddle, Dare swallowed. Yes, she was in love— he could feel it through their soulbond, although she'd never spoken the words. His throat clenched. But neither had he. Her upset after making love had distracted him. He set his jaw. He must remedy that when they were alone again.

Alex sighed. "But for Annalise to be so secretive means whomever she loves is someone Father and Mother shan't accept." He cocked his head. "Perhaps he's a groom—she does adore a good gallop."

Dare swallowed again, his chest aching at her radiant smiles and laughter whenever galloping. However, he murmured, "I hope not for your sister's sake." Then to deflect Alex, he asked the younger gentleman about his last visit to Lady Ducharme's fencing salon.

The following morning, he rode to the royal bay again instead of meeting Annalise for their morning walk. But like before, he found no peace there, even though he galloped until he and Ebony were sweating once more. He couldn't last not seeing her alone much longer. Please let her attend the Westons' musical evening tonight. He must convince her to slip away, so he could confess his love. He should create a faegift to show her how much.

So when he returned to Ormas, he visited Over the Walle, the witch shop serving magical creatures, to purchase a raw firegem.

The wood elf running the exotic witch shop blinked at him but sold him the gem useless to most witches. Then he visited Transmuted Metals, the alchemy witch shop, to purchase unworked silver and gold. The burly clerk there didn't blink at that.

After luncheon, Dare shut himself in his study with Raven and Bear to create Annalise's faegift. Since 'twas nature magic, he didn't require help from his magical pets, so the hellhounds just dozed beside his desk while he used his magic.

He gathered his will and directed it at the raw firegem. Slowly, sapphire filled the firegem until 'twas the precise shade of her cerulean eyes, and its shape became a perfect heart. Panting, he released his will and sagged in his chair. Typically, only dragons themselves could alter firegems or the hardened dragon flame inside them. However, his family had always been able to do so, and Mother had taught him years ago.

Once his breath had steadied, he gathered his will again and melded the silver and gold to create electrum that matched Annalise's white-blonde hair. Then he fashioned it into a delicate necklace and attached it to the now sapphire firegem. He sighed as he released his will. Creating the necklace had been *much* easier than altering the firegem.

Ravenous after all that spellwork, Dare devoured dinner then dressed for the Westons' musical evening, slipping Annalise's faegift into his pocket above his heart. Hopefully, she'd like it and see the sincere love behind it.

When he strode into Weston House, he forced himself not to glare at Winston pestering Annalise. He was about to rescue her despite the scandal when Lady Blaine captured his arm and drew him straight toward King Devon, Lady Kiera, Lord Beza Hawke, and young Miss Weston. Of course, the fashionable countess sought the king's notice. Yet instead, Lady Blaine addressed Lord Beza, who strode off with Miss Weston rather than speak to her. Understandable, given how she'd gossiped about his wife's scandalous pregnancy.

However, their kind future queen deflected everyone from

that clash by asking Lady Blaine, "Are you anticipating tonight's performance?"

Lady Blaine relaxed and smiled at Lady Kiera. "Oh, yes. The harpist is said to be the finest in Calatini."

As Annalise glided beside Lady Kiera, his soulbond burgeoned, and her faegift almost burned his chest, but Dare somehow kept his face blank and didn't pull her against him.

Annalise flashed Lady Snow's cool smile then replied to Lady Blaine, "She is. I heard her at a concert last year." She greeted everyone else then paused and nodded at him. "Lord Ravenstone."

His heart pounding in his throat, he stared back and clung to his blank expression. Goddess, Annalise was so close, yet she was as untouchable as the moon. They must slip away, so he could confess his love. :*We must talk. Alone.*:

CHAPTER 29

Her pulse rapid and body tingling, Annalise ignored
Kiera and the others to hold Dare's gaze with Lady
Snow's smile fixed on her lips. Goddess, she burned to curl
against him and proclaim he was hers, and she could feel his
matching love and hunger raging beneath his blank expression.
Yet they'd destroy her family if they succumbed. She set her jaw.
:*We can't talk alone here. There's too few people and no anterooms or
gardens nearby. Someone would notice if we slipped away.*:

Dare's hunger flared and echoed through their entwined
souls, but his face remained blank. :*Fine. Meet me in the park
tomorrow morning then.*:

She swallowed as her heart twisted. If only she could. But
without others from court around them, she'd shove him against
a tree and kiss him until they made love again. :*No. I've told you
we can't risk our morning walks now.*:

Dare stilled like a manticore about to pounce on a rainbow
unicorn, their favorite prey. :*When can we meet alone then?*:

Annalise almost licked her lips as a hungry shiver skittered
across her skin. :*The Duchess of Wildewall's autumn garden party in
a few days.*: She swallowed again. Goddess, how would either of
them last that long?

His amber eyes flickering, Dare purred silently, :*Until then.*: As she suppressed another hungry shiver, he bowed then drawled, "I suppose I should thank you for staunching my wound after your hellion brother stabbed me. Doubtless I owe you my life." His gaze bored into hers. :*Does **that** sound distant enough to conceal the truth?*:

Although her heart ached at his feigned indifference, she lifted her chin and deepened Lady Snow's smile. :*Perfectly.*: She replied aloud, "'Twas nothing. You owe your life to the Goddess and your healer."

Dare inclined his head, his gaze intent on her face. :*So I do, soul healer.*:

Her ribs clenched as he turned and began escorting Lady Blaine to a nearby chair for the performance. If only he was escorting her instead.

Gripping King Devon's arm, Kiera studied Annalise and asked, "Why didn't you wait to join us?"

Annalise concealed a wince. Because she'd *needed* to be near Dare after being apart four days. Their consummated soulbond had burned and goaded her like iron spurs did a kelpie. Concealing it was as excruciating as she'd feared.

King Devon frowned at her. "Yes, that could have gone very badly."

Annalise managed a grimace and seized a plausible excuse. "I know, but Mr. Winston began pestering me." She shuddered with genuine disgust. The cad *had* cornered and leered at her after she'd slipped away from Mother and Father. "Apparently, I've become prey again since you two announced your betrothal."

As Kiera glanced toward Mr. Winston, who was scowling at them like a vengeful basilisk, Annalise widened her eyes and leaned forward. "Do you mind if I join you?" 'Twould prevent Mr. Winston from leering. And keep her parents appeased, as long as she didn't stare at Dare the entire performance like she had at the Islayes' concert.

The indigo in her aura deepening, Kiera smiled and threaded her free arm through Annalise's. "Please do."

Warmth flooding her chest at her friend's caring, Annalise joined Kiera and King Devon in the front row for the harpist's performance, which made staring at Dare impossible. Swallowing her longing, she smiled at Kiera beside her. With her sincere kindness and wisdom, Kiera was truly the most wonderful friend. Too bad she couldn't share her true feelings about Dare without risking Mother and Father learning and doing something outrageous.

The following morning, Mother pursed her lips when Annalise swept into the breakfast room wearing a riding habit. "*Another* nightmara ride this morning? You've barely attended early court events the past few weeks."

Annalise hummed as she heaped her plate with beefsteak, eggs, and a flaky roll. She *did* have another nightmara ride today, although they were only every three days. On the other mornings since the fire ball, she'd gone on a punishing gallop alone to ensure she couldn't seek out Dare. But never out the northern gate since 'twould be too tempting to head to the royal bay to meet him.

Sitting beside Alex, she arched her brows at Mother. "As you've said, the Nightmara-Calatini Treaty is important since 'tis only renewed every twenty-five years, so missing early court events seems well worth it."

Mother sighed into her teacup. "I suppose. But you missing so many events makes finding a suitable husband impossible. You'll never be able to have your own family that way. Plus, missing events lessens your significance at court."

Annalise began her beefsteak to avoid replying. She and Dare had likely already started their family at Lady Blaine's fire ball. And she'd no interest in being significant at court. But admitting either to Mother and Father would only upset them. Besides, 'twas senseless to upset Mother and Father if she wasn't actually pregnant—which she *might* not be.

Finishing his eggs, Father glanced at Mother. "Except such dedication to Calatini affairs shall surely impress King Devon, so once he finally discards that Kiera creature, he'll know how perfect a queen Annalise shall be."

Alex smirked and leaned back in his chair. "But shall King Devon discard Lady Kiera after he was so determined to find her?"

When Mother and Father scowled at Alex, Annalise hid a wry smile behind her teacup. Like usual, Alex could see to the heart of another, and he couldn't resist provoking their parents with it. To restore peace, she murmured, "King Devon is too dutiful to not marry the perfect queen for Calatini." Which Kiera was.

Smiling now, Mother nodded. "True. So continue joining him like you did at the Westons' last night. No more disappearing like at Lady Blaine's fire ball."

Annalise swallowed a sigh, but she inclined her head as she began her eggs. She and Dare would need to keep their private meetings brief to avoid attracting her parents' notice.

Mother and Father began discussing the court events over the next few days, so Annalise quit listening to focus on finishing her breakfast. Once she did, she rose. "I must be off. I'll be back for luncheon."

Alex leapt up as well. "I'll join you. I need to head to Lady Ducharme's anyway." Once they were outside, he glanced around then leaned toward her. "So what's going on?"

She tensed, her stomach fluttering. Of course, he noticed her altered behavior since she and Dare had consummated their soulbond. Her perceptive brother knew her too well. However, she arched her brows to feign serenity. "Nothing is going on."

Alex snorted as they entered the stables. "Then why is Storm exhausted after many of your 'nightmara rides' but not after others?"

Annalise swallowed but strode to Storm's stall with Alex directly behind her. As the stallion nickered and nuzzled her, she muttered to Alex, "Because I've been using the nightmara rides as an excuse for a good gallop on the days I don't actually have one."

Alex frowned at her. "Alone? I'm not sure that's safe in Ormas."

She began saddling Storm. "I've been safe so far." And she needed privacy to let her true feelings show during her gallops. It made concealing them the rest of the time more bearable.

His brows still furrowed, Alex humphed and continued eyeing her. "Disregarding your gallops, you've been acting oddly with Father and Mother too. Disappearing at that fire ball then refusing to explain." He glanced about the stables then leaned closer. "Are you in love with someone Father and Mother shan't accept?"

Annalise froze, her pulse skittering. Oh, Goddess. Did he realize that someone was Dare? She forced herself to meet Alex's gaze. "They want me to become queen, so they shan't accept anyone other than King Devon."

Alex hummed. "Despite their ambitions, Father and Mother desire your happiness, so they'd accept another suitable lord if you truly loved him."

She swallowed a bitter laugh. Any lord except Dare. She turned back and checked Storm's saddle to conceal her expression.

Alex touched her shoulder. "Is he a groom, perhaps?"

Tears pricking her eyes, Annalise shifted away and blurted, "Does it matter? Mother and Father shall never accept him." At Alex's inhale, she whirled and gripped his arms. How could she have admitted that, even to Alex? "You mustn't tell your suspicions to anyone. *Please.*"

His eyes narrow, Alex scrutinized her but eventually nodded. "Very well." He grimaced. "Although I did discuss it with a friend the other day. But *he* shan't mention it to Father and Mother."

She sighed. Doubtless he'd told Lord Morwynne, but unlike his manipulative mother, the young count rarely attended court events and was too nice to gossip about his friend's sister. Mother and Father wouldn't discover her love for Dare from him. Releasing Alex's arms, she managed a weak smile. "Just don't discuss it with anyone else."

As Alex nodded, she leapt atop Storm then headed to the palace for her nightmara ride. Thankfully, the ride through Ormas would give her time to settle her upset before she faced Kiera and the nightmara. She'd revealed too much today already.

THE DAYS before the Duchess of Wildewall's autumn garden party passed much the same as the previous few days. Her hunger for Dare burning in her chest, Annalise galloped every morning to prevent herself from seeking him out. Then she spent as much time in her chambers as Mother would allow, so she could caress the enchanted heart carving from Dare while cuddling Finn and Lily with Rain and Aria perched in her hair. Mother and Father kept shoving her at King Devon and other suitable gentlemen at court events, while Alex continued scrutinizing her but never mentioned their discussion in the stables.

After the nightmara ride the morning of the duchess's party, Annalise galloped back to her family's townhouse then yanked on her lavender silk dress with Grace's help. Mother would hate being late to an event held by the head of their duchy. Fortunately, Wildewall House wasn't far.

When she and her parents arrived, almost everyone was already there, including Dare—with the sultry Lady Blaine clinging to his arm. His eyes met hers as she glanced past, and he asked, :*Where do you want to meet?*:

Annalise studied the duchess's garden, still vibrant despite last week's hard frost, although due to a frost-prevention spell rather than being pollinated by melissae. :*The wildflower garden tucked behind the weeping cherry tree. No one ventures there.*: 'Twas too common for most at court.

His exhilaration surging through her chest, Dare sipped his cider. :*You slip away first, and I'll follow.*:

Her heart quickening, she made herself turn and smile at the approaching Duke of Oakmoor, whose erratic magic was barely flickering this afternoon. When Mother and Father shoved her at the rakehell duke, she accepted his arm and allowed him to escort her to the refreshments table. He'd be much easier to slip away from than Mother and Father.

After they'd fetched spiced cider and filled their plates, the duke's ardent flirting made her stomach roil. Had he decided to seriously pursue her after Mother and Father's many attempts to match them? Great, just what she needed in addition to everything else. Leaving her plate untouched, she sipped her cider and watched for her chance to escape.

When the Duchess of Wildewall drew the Duke of Oakmoor aside to discuss a council matter, Annalise relaxed then glided to Kiera and King Devon beside a bed of yellow daisies halfway to the weeping cherry tree. "Afternoon."

Kiera grinned at her. "It's been *too* long since we've met. What, two hours?"

Annalise couldn't help a giggle at her friend's quip. Such a relief after the rakehell duke's flirting. "If that." Then she sobered and glanced around the garden. She'd better bolster her excuse from the Westons' musical evening. "Did either of you see Mr. Winston?"

Muddy-red anger flaring about him, King Devon scowled while devouring a stuffed mushroom. "I doubt the Duchess of Wildewall invited him. She never has to previous garden parties."

Annalise sighed to feign obvious relief. "Thank the Goddess. He's becoming vexing to avoid."

Kiera flashed a warm smile at Annalise before sighing and nodding toward Dare and Lady Blaine walking toward them. "Although the duchess *did* invite both the Greysnowes and Ravenstones."

Gripping her plate, Annalise forced herself to look away. *:Why are you approaching in public again?:*

His silent sigh echoed through her. *:Lady Blaine insisted on speaking to King Devon and Lady Kiera.:*

Annalise turned to Kiera. Hopefully, her hunger for Dare wasn't obvious. "As the head of our duchy, she must invite both. 'Twould inflame the feud if she didn't. But it always adds a dash of tension to her events."

Kiera grimaced. "Exciting."

Annalise sighed, her heart twisting. "Not particularly." She forced a brilliant smile. "I'd best go before Lord Ravenstone arrives." She couldn't risk meeting him in public again, especially with Kiera near. Her insightful friend might see too much.

She glided toward the weeping cherry tree then glanced behind her. No one was watching, not even Dare or her parents, so she slipped behind the weeping cherry's hanging branches adorned with brilliant orange leaves. Then she sank on the stone bench beside the wildflower garden to devour her heaped plate and finish her spiced cider while she waited for Dare to join her.

CHAPTER 30

Forcing himself not to stare after Annalise as she glided behind the vibrant weeping cherry tree, Dare managed polite conversation with King Devon and Lady Kiera. Somehow, he must escape Lady Blaine still clinging to his arm. Fortunately, the husband-hunting countess asked to speak with Lord Treyvan once he and his wife joined them.

After several moments, Dare excused himself then strode after Annalise. Although she'd slipped away unnoticed, he still glanced behind him when he reached the weeping cherry tree. No one was watching him either, so he hurried into the wild-flower garden. Then he gathered his will and gestured at the weeping cherry tree to cast a nature mimicry spell on the garden's entrance, so he and Annalise faded into the wildflowers and stone bench.

He faced Annalise, and warmth suffused his chest. Alone at last. He almost touched the pocket above his heart. Finally, he could confess his love and give her his faegift. He grinned at her. "The nature mimicry shall make the wildflower garden appear empty."

Her echoing love shimmering through their entwined souls, Annalise smiled back and set her empty plate and spiced cider on the ground beside the stone bench. "Hopefully, no one else decides to slip away here like we did."

Dare sat beside her then took her hand and kissed her palm. His heart surged as her heady honeysuckle scent wrapped around him. "I doubt they shall."

Shivering, Annalise caressed his face for a moment before tugging her hand free. "You know we can't risk touching."

He recaptured her hand and threaded his fingers through hers. Their starved soulbond burgeoned then eased. "After being apart for over a week, we can't not touch."

Annalise swallowed but didn't free her hand. "Fine, but I mustn't stay long. Mother and Father are watching me like suspicious gargoyles since my disappearance at Lady Blaine's fire ball."

Heat flared in his veins as their lovemaking that evening echoed through him. Suppressing his hunger, he said, "Alex mentioned that they were furious about that. I'm sorry."

Annalise sighed, and her pain bolted through him. "'Tis as much my fault as yours. Now, what did you want to discuss?"

To comfort her, Dare raised their joined hands then pressed a tender kiss on her hand. Too bad his love couldn't heal her strife with her parents. "Can't you tell through our consummated soulbond?"

Her breath quickening, Annalise swallowed. "Our consummated soulbond doesn't work like that. We can feel each other's emotions, but we can only hear thoughts the other sends deliberately."

He nodded. Good, surprises like his faegift were still possible. He inhaled then kissed her hand again and drew her closer, his heart pounding. "I wanted to tell you how much I love you."

Annalise lowered her gaze as her melancholy squeezed his chest. "I know you do. I can feel your love through our soulbond." She sighed. "And I love you too."

Dare stilled, his heart twisting. With his free hand, he tilted her chin until she met his gaze. "Why don't you sound or feel happy about that?"

Annalise blinked then sighed again. "Because our love is impossible and only makes concealing our soulbond more excruciating."

He almost grimaced. They should really quit concealing their soulbond, but she'd flee if he said that. Instead, he murmured, "We shan't need to conceal our soulbond forever." He leaned forward and brushed a featherlight kiss against her lips. "And no matter how excruciating, I'd never want to not have our love."

Annalise licked her lips, and his body hardened. Goddess, he burned to capture her lips in a true kiss. As he forced himself to remain still, she managed a tremulous smile then said, "Except without our soulbond you never would have fallen in love with me."

His throat tight, Dare brushed another kiss against her lips. "Our soulbond isn't why I love you. I was already half in love with you before then. You were the most intriguing lady I'd ever met, and no matter how I tried, I couldn't make myself forget you."

Swallowing, Annalise pulled her chin free as her ache echoed through him. "Because of my beauty, which my potent aura makes irresistible."

He kissed her hand holding his to hearten her. Doubtless her misconception was because her ambitious parents most valued her beauty. He waited until her dark gaze met his again. "I noticed your beauty, of course, but 'twas the glimpses of your true self that intrigued me. Your deep kindness, serene strength as well as your love of nature, Wildewall, and family. And with your powerful magic akin to mine, I never met a lady more like-minded and perfect for me."

Annalise inhaled a ragged breath.

Dare leaned toward her and sent all the love filling his heart through their entwined souls. Surely, 'twould convince her.

"Then once I actually got to know your true self during our morning walks, I went from halfway to completely in love."

Tears shimmering in her cerulean eyes, Annalise pressed her free hand against his face. "'Twas exactly the same for me. You'd fascinated me since our secret encounter—not only could I read in your aura that you were kindhearted, steady, strong, and a powerful nature witch who respected all living things, but you talked to me like a person and never ogled. And you always noticed details no one else did."

He shifted to kiss her palm while warmth flooded him. How could he not notice details about the most intriguing and lovable lady he'd ever met?

Annalise flashed her warm and radiant smile as her love reverberated through their entwined souls. "Then my fascination deepened to lasting love during our morning walks. So deep and lasting that remembering we must hide it because of our families' feud feels like a tygris devouring my still-beating heart."

His pulse surging, Dare pulled her against him and captured her tempting mouth in a deep kiss. Goddess, she was sweeter than the ambrosia they'd shared in the royal forest the day they'd made love.

When their entwined souls meshed, Annalise purred then pressed even closer and fisted her hands in his hair.

He shuddered as his body hardened at her equal hunger. Yet he forced himself to gentle their kiss. They couldn't risk making love at another court event. He raised his head then breathed, "I love you more than parched soil loves the rain."

Annalise brushed a kiss against his lips then replied in a tender voice containing none of her earlier melancholy, "And I love you more than a griffin loves her lifelong mate."

Their souls still meshed, he and Annalise smiled at each other for a timeless moment. Then he pulled back to extract her faegift from his pocket. He'd almost forgotten. He opened his hand to reveal the delicate, pale-electrum necklace. "I created a faegift as a token of my love."

Her delight and wonder swirling through their meshed souls, Annalise caressed the necklace's heart-shaped, sapphire firegem. "'Tis exquisite. And so perfect—it matches my coloring *and* alludes to my powers."

Dare smiled and attached her faegift about her neck. "But not so much that anyone who doesn't already know shall realize." Publicly acknowledged soul healers wore electrum torcs with heart terminals, not firegem necklaces. "I hope you like it."

Annalise fingered the firegem flickering like sapphire flame in the hollow of her throat. "I'll wear it with joy... starting tomorrow. Mother and Father shall wonder who gave it to me otherwise."

Light filling his chest, he grinned at Annalise and drawled to tease her, "You could always tell them that King Devon or the Duke of Oakmoor gave it to you."

Annalise shuddered then poked his arm. "I'm not claiming to wear another gentleman's token—not even to conceal our soul-bond and love."

Dare beamed and captured her hand then kissed her palm. His tenderhearted Annalise wouldn't. "I'm glad."

Annalise sighed and caressed her heart-shaped firegem again. "I wish I'd a token of my love to give you in return."

His heart warm, he feathered a kiss against her lips. She'd said the same after receiving his natalday gift. "You shall when we exchange wedding tokens during our wedding ceremony."

Stiffening, Annalise freed her hand and pulled away as her longing pierced him. "You know 'tis impossible for us to marry."

Dare stiffened as well, his throat aching. Why must Annalise keep denying their love? He leaned toward her. "Shall you still say that if you're carrying my child?"

Annalise paled then swallowed. "I don't wish to discuss that now."

He narrowed his eyes at Annalise. Refusing to discuss her likely pregnancy wouldn't make it disappear, and they needed a plan. "Shouldn't we discuss our future?"

Her grief swamping him, Annalise gripped her firegem at her throat. "We should, but I just can't bear it. In the future, I'll lose either you or my family."

Dare wrapped her in his arms to comfort her. Choosing between him and her family would devastate a lady who loved as deeply as Annalise did. He kissed her hair then said, "Then I shan't mention discussing our future again—as long as you promise to tell me once you know you're pregnant."

Annalise inhaled, her surprise darting through him like a minnow through a creek. "Of course, I'll tell you."

His chest easing, he was about to reply when Lord Greysnowe's voice came from the weeping cherry tree, "I believe Annalise is in the wildflower garden, your grace."

Still entwined, Dare and Annalise froze as Lady Greysnowe added, "Yes, Lady Blaine said she saw Annalise head here earlier. For some reason, our daughter has become fond of hidden corners lately."

Dare flung a nature mimicry spell about him and Annalise then dropped the one on the garden's entrance as her parents and the Duke of Oakmoor entered the wildflower garden. *:Hold still.:*

Annalise's hand fisted against his chest. *:I'll remain as still as a gnome taking a stone nap until they leave.:*

The Duke of Oakmoor flashed a suave smile. "Your exquisite daughter enjoys being elusive—'tis why many at court call her Lady Snow."

Dare swallowed his snort as Annalise tensed. She hid behind Lady Snow because she couldn't trust court with her secrets, not to be elusive.

Lady Greysnowe fluttered her lashes at the duke. "Annalise simply needs the right gentleman to warm her. Although she hides it well, she loves deeply and shall make an excellent wife."

As Annalise stiffened in his arms, Dare set his jaw. *:Not to him you shan't.:*

Annalise's lips curved against his throat. *:True.:*

The Duke of Oakmoor nodded at Annalise's parents. "Yes, Lady Annalise shall make an excellent wife and be the perfect hostess for the court events I must hold as the Minister of Foreign Relations."

Lord and Lady Greysnowe grinned at each other while Annalise shuddered in Dare's embrace and said, :*So the duke **has** decided to seriously pursue me. Goddess, I was afraid of that.*:

His stomach hardening, Dare risked kissing Annalise's hair. Although the rakehell duke always flirted with her, he'd never appeared serious about it. Not that he'd avoid seducing her if he could. :*Since when?*:

Annalise's silent sigh brushed his throat. :*Since today. Not what I need in addition to concealing our soulbond, love, and possible pregnancy.*:

The Duke of Oakmoor leaned toward Lord and Lady Greysnowe. "Now that I've decided to marry, I should be able to secure your daughter's agreement soon. We can announce our betrothal at my soiree in three weeks then marry before Longnight."

Her indignation flaring through Dare, Annalise stiffened against him again. :*How dare that arrogant rakehell assume he can win me so easily?*:

Dare smiled and squeezed his adorable Annalise. :*Do you know why the duke is so impatient?*:

Annalise relaxed. :*No. He needs an heir, but he's needed one since he became duke as a boy over forty years ago. Perhaps it involves the appearance of his erratic magic.*:

Dare frowned at the Duke of Oakmoor. But why would late-appearing magic make the duke impatient for a wife?

He was about to ask Annalise that when Lord Greysnowe grinned and clapped the duke's shoulder then said, "I imagine you're eager to hold your heir in your arms by this time next year."

Once the Duke of Oakmoor nodded, Lady Greysnowe took

his arm with a grin almost as radiant as her daughter's. "Come, let's check other hidden areas to find Annalise."

After the duke and Annalise's parents swept from the wildflower garden, Dare and Annalise sighed and relaxed, then he dropped his nature mimicry spell. Still nestled together, they stared at each other without speaking. Goddess, he ached for another kiss. He began bending his head.

But before their lips touched, Annalise whispered, "We'd better return to the others before someone else stumbles upon us."

He grimaced but forced himself to release her. She was right, and if he held her much longer, they might forget themselves and make love again. "When shall I see you again?"

Annalise hummed and tilted her head. "I'm not certain, but we should exchange the angelcats soon. Lily misses you—and her freedom."

Dare rubbed his beard as weight squeezed his chest. "I'll stop by Greysnowe House shortly after dawn tomorrow." No one should notice him then, and they might resist each other with her parents so close. He sighed then rose. "I'll return first. Until tomorrow."

He strode back to the others, heading to the refreshments table for a mug of spiced cider.

After his first sip, Lady Blaine sashayed over toward him. Her smoky eyes probing, she flashed a coy smile and captured his arm. "Lord Ravenstone, there you are. You disappeared ages ago." She leaned closer and sniffed. "And you smell like honeysuckle again."

Although his neck prickled, Dare made himself smile. Had Lady Blaine noticed he'd appeared from where she'd seen Annalise go? He turned Lady Blaine away from the weeping cherry tree to prevent her from seeing Annalise's return. Then to distract Lady Blaine, he asked, "How was your discussion with Lord Treyvan?"

CHAPTER 31

lone in the wildflower garden long after Dare had left, Annalise fingered his wonderful faegift at her throat while blankly staring at the riot of wildflowers before her. She should rejoin the others, but the peace of the quiet garden was so restful. And facing her parents and the Duke of Oakmoor would be anything but.

Eventually, Dare called, his mental voice worried, :*Annalise, are you well? Other guests have begun leaving.*:

She sighed and unclasped Dare's necklace then dropped it inside her gown between her breasts. Sending love through their entwined souls to reassure him, she replied, :*Just enjoying the peace of the garden.*:

Dare murmured, :*If you're avoiding the Duke of Oakmoor, he left shortly after King Devon and Lady Kiera.*:

Her chest easing slightly, Annalise rose. Good, she must only face Mother and Father. :*You should leave before I return.*:

Dare sighed, his longing echoing in their entwined souls. :*Very well. I'll see you tomorrow shortly after dawn to exchange Lily and Finn.*:

She collected her empty plate and mug then left the wildflower garden. After handing her dishes to a nearby servant, she glided over to Mother and Father.

Mother pursed her lips and eyed Annalise. "Where have you been? You disappeared like at Lady Blaine's fire ball. The Duke of Oakmoor wished to speak with you."

As Father nodded to echo Mother, Annalise gritted a serene smile. "His overpowering sandalwood scent made me nauseous." As did his arrogant assumption that she'd marry him.

Still eyeing her, Mother hummed then grasped her arm and drew her across the emptying garden toward the Duchess of Wildewall. Once they'd said farewell to their hostess, they climbed into their carriage with Annalise sitting in the backward seat across from her parents. Indigo concern pulsing about her, Mother frowned then asked, "Are you well? You've not been acting yourself lately."

Annalise laced her fingers in her lap to avoid touching her stomach possibly carrying Dare's child or his faegift nestled between her breasts. "Just pining for Wildewall. We've usually left Ormas by now."

Mother and Father exchanged a glance then Mother said, "The Duke of Oakmoor expressed interest in courting you and intends to take you riding tomorrow."

Lifting her chin, Annalise held their gaze. "I don't wish to be courted by a gentleman my parents' age whom I don't love. Please don't force me." Goddess, let their love for her overpower their ambitions.

Mother and Father traded another glance, then Father sighed and replied, "I'll explain your disinterest when the duke visits tomorrow."

Mother leaned forward. "But you *must* start allowing other suitable gentlemen to court you. Otherwise, you'll never have a family of your own, and you're too loving not to want that."

Annalise clenched her hands and turned to stare out the window. She *did* want a family, but only with Dare. To avoid further discussion, she leapt from the carriage as soon as it halted before her family's townhouse then darted upstairs to her chambers and locked the door.

After releasing Rain and Aria and letting them perch in her hair, she curled on her bed with Finn and Lily then extracted Dare's faegift. She sighed and caressed the exquisite, pale-electrum necklace. She could almost sense the love he'd poured into enchanting the faegift that sparkled with his bronze motes, especially around the sapphire firegem glimmering with residual magic. Openly wearing a token of his devotion, even though only they'd recognize that, would be comforting when Mother and Father shoved her at other gentlemen.

JUST AFTER DAWN the following morning, Annalise rose and donned Dare's faegift then herded Finn and Lily downstairs. The angelcats bounded along the banister beside her—both were excited to be released from her chambers. She sighed. If only she could allow them to roam freely through the townhouse like Dare did.

When she opened the front door, Dare was hidden between the same two townhouses he'd used the morning he'd visited to prevent her from enduring that tempest. Her pulse quickened as their gazes met.

Then Lily trilled a meow and darted across the empty street to Dare, and Finn rubbed Annalise's skirt before hurtling after his mate.

Gripping the doorframe to ensure she didn't join them, Annalise smiled at Dare. :*I've not fed them breakfast yet.*:

Dare inclined his head while bending to pet Lily, who was rubbing his ankles. :*Then I'd better return them to Ravenstone House and feed them before I ride to the royal bay. Otherwise, they might try to devour me when I return. Until later, my heart.*:

She warmed. Dare was her heart too. :*Until later, my love.*: Then she forced herself to shut the door. So she wasn't tempted to follow him to the royal bay, she darted back upstairs to her chambers then petted Rain and Aria. She'd visit Storm in the stables after breakfast.

When she joined everyone in the breakfast room several hours later, Mother tilted her head. "That's a lovely necklace. Where did you get it?"

Annalise swallowed and tensed. She *must* sound offhand, so Mother and Father wouldn't ask about Dare's faegift again. Sitting beside Alex, she murmured, "I'm not certain. I noticed it this morning and decided to wear it."

Although Alex eyed her, Mother merely hummed. "It matches your extraordinary beauty, and the craftsmanship is stunning."

Annalise nodded but suppressed a wild giggle. Mother wouldn't admit that if she knew a "treacherous" Ravenstone had created it.

As Annalise began her beefsteak, Father cleared his throat then asked, "Are you certain you wish to decline the Duke of Oakmoor's courtship?"

Alex's brows flew upward, but before he could speak, Annalise nodded again and replied, "Very." Then she kicked her brother's ankle beneath the table while slanting him a narrow glance. She couldn't risk him provoking Mother and Father into allowing the duke's courtship out of annoyance at their son's teasing.

Alex blinked then turned and told Father about yesterday's kelpie races.

When nothing more was mentioned about her necklace or the duke, Annalise relaxed and devoured her breakfast then excused herself to visit Storm.

After that, she began wearing Dare's faegift except when sleeping, although she did wear it beneath her gowns whenever possible. Yet Mother and Father never mentioned it again, although Alex kept eyeing it.

Two mornings later, Alex arched a brow as they headed outside—she for her nightmara ride and he for Lady Ducharme's. "Where's Finn and his mate? I've not seen them for a couple of days."

Annalise fingered the heart-shaped firegem at her throat. Hopefully, Alex would never see the angelcats with Dare. "They like to explore Ormas together."

His gaze intent on Dare's faegift again, Alex nodded as they strode into the stables. "I see. What's with that new necklace? You were much too casual when Mother asked about it the other day, and you used to only wear jewelry when she made you. 'Tis a gift from *him*, isn't it?"

She glanced around to check if any of the grooms had overheard. She exhaled when none were nearby. Then she leaned toward Alex and muttered, "I told you not to discuss him with anyone, and that includes me."

Alex hummed, certainty intensifying his orange aura. "With a gift like that, he can't possibly be a groom, so he must be a gentleman Father and Mother shan't accept."

Annalise glared at him as her pulse surged. "*Alex*."

Alex flashed an impish grin. "Don't fret; I'll not reveal your secret. And I shan't say any more—for now."

Exhaling, she mounted Storm and rode to the palace, where she met Kiera outside. When multiple people pestered Kiera about her momentous education initiative on their way to their nightmara ride, Annalise invited Kiera and Wren to luncheon, so her friend could enjoy a relaxing event with no queenly duties.

Around noon that day, Wren arrived from the orphanage with a brilliant grin. "Afternoon! Thanks for inviting me. 'Tis wonderful to have adult company for once."

Annalise blinked at the intensity of Wren's violet aura about her waist and the gray fog tarnishing it elsewhere. Her friend's aura was much brighter than it should be for a lady three months pregnant—even more than before. And that fog of ill health wasn't normal for most pregnancies. Swallowing her concern, she returned Wren's grin and asked, "What about Lord Beza Hawke?"

Wren chuckled and waved a hand. "Sometimes Hawke is worse than the orphans, so he doesn't count."

Escorting Wren to the family dining room, Annalise smiled and nodded at Wren's stomach. "I doubt a child was responsible for that."

Wren blushed but chuckled again as indigo love glowed about her. "Definitely not."

A pang darted through Annalise. Too bad she couldn't be as open about her own possible pregnancy. Shoving that aside, she gestured toward the table. "Sit and rest while I wait in the entrance hall for Kiera."

When she glided into the entrance hall, she tensed at Mother and Father ignoring Kiera with muddy-orange disdain flaring about them. She frowned at her parents. "Mother, Father, how could you act so churlish? Kiera is our future queen and my friend."

Mother sniffed and shook her head. "She shan't be *our* queen. The Ravenstones chose her."

Annalise tensed further as heat scorched her neck. Why must Mother and Father keep harping about that? "You know they did no such thing." She turned to Father. "Please don't allow the feud to delude you."

His eyes narrow, Father snorted. "We're not deluded. We simply know what treacherous ogres the Ravenstones are." He offered Mother his arm, and they swept outside without another word.

Suppressing a wince, Annalise covered her face. So embarrassing. "I apologize for their shocking manners."

Kiera sighed. "At least they behave honestly. A rare thing at court."

Annalise grimaced and lowered her hands, her blush cooling

at Kiera's wry smile. Thank the Goddess her friend didn't blame her for Mother and Father's rancor. "I should have informed them that I'd never marry King Devon when he first began escorting me. But 'twas such a relief that they ceased foisting gentlemen on me."

Kiera nodded, the devoted indigo of her aura deepening. However, she only asked, "Was Wren able to attend?"

Annalise relaxed and grinned. "Yes, she's waiting in the family dining room." When Kiera beamed back, she waved for Kiera to follow her.

As they entered the family dining room, Wren was dozing in her seat. Kiera immediately tsked and drawled, "Waiting, you said? Sleeping, more like."

Annalise almost frowned when Wren replied without moving, "I'm awake. Just resting my eyes until there's food." What a lie. Their exhausted, pregnant friend had clearly been sleeping.

While Kiera scolded Wren for lying, Annalise rang for luncheon. Food should help revive Wren.

As Annalise sat across from them, Wren embraced Kiera and said, "'Tis wonderful to see you finally. How has acting as queen been going?"

Kiera returned Wren's embrace then shrugged. "Well, I suppose. Still hectic, but now that I'm staying at the palace, I can get adequate sleep." She arched her brows at Wren. "Unlike you, clearly."

Annalise eyed the concerning gray fog about Wren as the servants brought luncheon then left. Then she frowned and leaned toward Wren. "You do appear tired."

Wren chuckled while she began her creamy tuber soup. "No doubt." She grinned then paused and patted her stomach. "Thanks to the twins."

Annalise froze with her spoon halfway to her mouth then she and Kiera chorused, "Twins?" That *did* explain Wren's aura being overly intense at her waist and likely the gray fog tarnishing it.

Wren bobbed a nod. "Yes, our healer confirmed the double heartbeats two weeks ago."

Beneath the table, Annalise touched her stomach as her breath stilled. Goddess, what if she was carrying twins too?

Kiera gaped at Wren. "But I saw Hawke at the Westons' last week, and he never said a word."

Her lips twitching, Wren began devouring her tuber soup again. "I threatened to wallop him if he divulged our news. I wanted to tell you myself. In fact, you two are the first besides us to know."

Annalise blinked as her chest twisted. She made herself begin eating as well. "Why the secrecy?" Doubtless Wren and Lord Beza's parents would be ecstatic—unlike her parents would be if she was carrying Dare's child.

While Kiera almost sputtered mid-swallow, Wren shrugged and finished her soup then began her grilled fish. "We wanted time to celebrate without enduring the fuss our families, particularly the duchess, shall make."

Fingering Dare's firegem at her throat, Annalise managed a wry smile. But at least the Duchess of Childes's fuss would be delighted instead of furious. "Understandable."

Her gaze fixed on Dare's faegift, Kiera leaned toward her. "Your new necklace is exquisite. That mixture of electrum perfectly matches your hair. But how did you find a firegem the precise shade of your eyes?"

Annalise stilled then lowered her hand. She must quit touching Dare's necklace to comfort herself. It drew too much attention. Yet she couldn't lie to her friends about his wonderful faegift. She swallowed then replied, "I believe a nature witch enchanted it."

When Kiera and Wren exchanged a wide glance, Annalise almost winced. Obviously they realized only a powerful Rhiannon descendant could enchant a firegem. But as long as neither knew Dare was a nature witch, her secret would be safe.

After a moment, Kiera murmured, "It suits you."

A blush burning her cheeks, Annalise inclined her head. "Thank you." To distract them from Dare's faegift, she smiled at Wren and asked, "So how are the orphans?"

CHAPTER 32

As they rode along the royal bay after crossing swords, Alex grinned at the sparkling ocean then leaned toward Dare. "The ocean is so blue today—the same color as Annalise's eyes."

His heart quickening, Dare swallowed. No, Annalise's eyes were more intense, like a winter's deep blue sky at twilight. He gripped Ebony's reins. Goddess, he missed her. After they'd finally confessed their love, seeing her across the street for a few moments while exchanging angelcats three days ago wasn't enough. But nothing would change until she was ready to tell her family or agreed to elope.

Still leaning toward Dare, Alex added, "And the same color as the new firegem necklace she's begun wearing constantly."

Dare froze. Why was Alex telling him about that? Had the younger gentleman somehow realized he'd given the necklace to Annalise? But how? Could Alex have recognized his magical signature on the faegift? Surely not—the only magic he'd performed before Alex had been gathering natural energy, and that shouldn't have revealed his magical signature since it wasn't a spell or enchantment. Yet Alex must have some reason for mentioning Annalise's sapphire firegem.

He forced himself to meet Alex's gaze with a nonchalant smile. "Is it? I wouldn't know."

His eyes gleaming, Alex hummed and leaned back in his saddle. "No, I suppose you wouldn't, since Greysnowes and Ravenstones rarely attend the same court events. Well, 'tis exquisite and is perfect for her. Whoever she received it from knows her well and clearly adores her."

Dare swallowed to ease his aching throat. So he did, not that he could admit that to Alex when Annalise was determined to remain silent about their involvement. He managed another smile. "I'm glad for your sister." He paused and arched a brow. "Now that we're not crossing swords, the wind is cold today. Shall we race to the cliffs to warm ourselves?" Hopefully, 'twould distract Alex too.

Alex nodded, and they thundered across the beach. They raced neck and neck until Alex pulled Biscuit ahead just before the cliffs. He smirked at Dare. "I win—again."

Dare laughed. His distraction appeared successful. Before Alex could recall the faegift, Dare said he must return, so they galloped back to Ormas. When he entered Ravenstone House, his magical pets and Finn bounded over to greet him and demanded petting and more food. Chuckling at them, he strode upstairs to his chambers to call Mother.

After the communication mirror glowed white and Mother appeared, she smoothed back her windswept hair. "How was the royal bay today?"

He shrugged. Lonely without Annalise, despite her brother. "Cold. Alex joined me today, and I won our sword fight, but he won our race."

A faint frown between her brows, Mother leaned forward. "So your friendship with him is still going well?"

Dare shrugged again. When Alex wasn't mentioning Annalise. "Of course."

Mother exhaled and sat back then smiled. "I'll be glad to meet him."

He blinked at Mother. She'd likely never meet Alex. When he returned to Wildewall with Annalise, Alex couldn't risk visiting them without provoking his parents' fury. He shook his head. "Alex would find it odd if I asked him to join our weekly mirror calls."

Mother stilled then waved a hand. "Never mind." She grinned over his shoulder. "I see Lily and her mate are back. Have you named him yet?"

Dare glanced behind him and sighed. Naturally, the angelcats were curled together on the table behind him again. "He's too well-fed not to have an owner, so I suspect he already has a name."

Then to distract Mother, he asked about Pearl, and they discussed her angelkitten's latest antics before they said goodbye.

Afterward, he rubbed his beard. Why had Mother mentioned meeting Alex? Perhaps she wanted to check their friendship was genuine? But why now? He grimaced. Mother and Alex meeting, even through a communication mirror, would be dangerous—they were both perceptive and knew too much, so together they might discover his and Annalise's involvement.

Two mornings later, Dare was about to enter his study when the front door burst open, and Mother bustled inside Ravenstone House with a gray angelkitten curled in her arms. He halted, his head whirling. What was *she* doing in *Ormas*?

Her worry bolting through their entwined souls, Annalise asked, :*Dare, what's wrong? I could sense your shock from the nightmara paddock.*:

He gaped as Mother beamed at Brown while praising the butler's son's splendid performance as acting butler back at Ravenstone Castle. :*Mother... Mother is **here**.*:

Annalise gasped. :*In Ormas? I thought she despised living in cities and always refused to attend court, no matter how your father begged her to join him.*:

Dare eyed Mother. That, having more children, and the feud were all Mother and Father had ever truly argued over. :*Yes, she always said nature witches didn't belong here.*:

Annalise whispered, :*Do you think she knows about us?*:

He tensed. Goddess, he hoped not. But Mother would know soon if he and Annalise weren't vigilant. Concealing the truth during weekly mirror calls was nothing compared to doing so when Mother was living with him. And if she discovered his secret involvement with Annalise, she might tell the Greysnowes in an attempt to heal the feud before he and Annalise could elope. He swallowed. :*I'll ask Mother— indirectly.*:

Forcing himself to smile, he strode into the entrance hall. "Mother, 'tis wonderful to see you. But what are you doing in Ormas?"

Handing Pearl to Brown despite the angelkitten's grumble, Mother turned toward Dare and grinned. "After hearing about your duel with young Lord Alexander, I was too worried not to visit. I left for Ormas the following morning." She shrugged. "I never guessed you two would become close friends since then. But I was already on my way, and you clearly need help finding a wife, so I decided to continue onward."

Although he no longer needed Mother's help finding a wife, Dare couldn't resist a wry chuckle. "I suppose that explains why you were always outside during our mirror calls. But why did you never say you were headed here?"

Mother smoothed back her hair and shrugged again. "I knew you'd tell me not to bother." She touched his chest. "But I wanted to reassure myself you were well in person."

Warmth flooding him at Mother's loving concern, he patted her hand. "I'm fine, Mother. I likely would have told you not to bother, but I'm glad you're here. I've missed you."

Mother flung her arms about him and squeezed. "Me too."

After a moment, she drew back then sighed. "I'll go upstairs and get settled then join you for luncheon in a few hours."

Dare grinned at her. "Of course. I'll be in my study answering correspondence until then."

He hurried to his study and dropped into his chair. Tapping the stack of letters on his desk, he grimaced and sent to Annalise, *:We shan't be able to slip away at court events when Mother accompanies me. She's too observant not to notice.:*

Annalise sighed, her pang piercing their entwined souls. *:And we can't risk meeting anywhere else. The temptation to make love would be too great. The coming weeks shall be* **excruciating**.*:*

Dare rubbed his forehead. No doubt it would. He already missed her like melissae missed flowers during the winter, and never seeing her alone would make that far worse. *:Well, at least we can still communicate mentally.:* He was about to suggest they talk every day when Annalise's gasp echoed through him. He stiffened. *:What is it?:*

Annalise muttered, *:King Devon just requested that Kiera return during our nightmara ride, so she and Moonbud galloped back. Something must have happened.:*

Dare swallowed, his neck prickling. Could one of the royal agents have informed King Devon about Mother's unexpected arrival? But would King Devon have summoned Lady Kiera back for *that*? He made himself begin opening his letters. *:Doubtless all of court shall know why by the sirenic play tonight.:*

Annalise snorted. *:True. I just hope it doesn't involve your mother's arrival.:* She paused then asked, *:Are you attending the sirenic play? Kiera invited me to accompany her and King Devon.:*

Dare's chest twisted. At least Annalise would be safe from other gentlemen with them. And he could see her wear his faegift at court, albeit across a crowded theater. *:Yes, and I'll ask Mother to join me, so we must be careful tonight. We can't have her noticing our ardent glances like Alex did.:*

Annalise blew a sigh. *:True enough. Until tonight then.:*

As her presence faded, he began answering his letters. He'd

just finished when Brown told him luncheon was ready. He headed to the family dining room and sat beside Mother with a warm smile. "All settled in?"

Mother nodded as he served her orange cucurbit soup. "Yes, although I'll retire early tonight. After four months of traveling, I could use rest in a decent bed."

Dare hummed. He should have realized. "There's a sirenic play opening tonight. That shouldn't be too late. Did you want to join me?"

Mother pursed her lips. "Although sirenic plays are always stunning, not tonight. I doubt I'll make it much past dinner."

He exhaled as he finished his soup. Thank the Goddess he could watch Annalise without Mother observing. Before he could reply to Mother, Brown strode into the family dining room and handed him a letter from Lord Islaye. Had the Minister of Magic somehow learned his childhood friend was in Ormas?

His stomach tensing, Dare tore open the letter then gasped when he read Lord Islaye's brief scrawl about the Magehaven ore.

As Annalise's worried presence surrounded him like earlier, Mother frowned and leaned toward him, her roll stuffed with cold venison and cheese halfway to her mouth. Annalise mentally asked, :*What's happened now?*: while Mother asked aloud, "What is it?"

He dropped the letter beside his plate to gulp some wine. Also sending Annalise his reply, he told Mother, "That mysterious ore Lord Islaye asked me about exploded, killing twelve and wounding thirty-eight."

While Annalise's horror swamped him, Mother paled and lowered her stuffed roll. "Dear Goddess."

Wincing, Dare set down his wine glass. So much worse than Mother's unexpected arrival or concealing the truth from her. When he next saw Miss Winston, he *must* convince her to approach the council. Surely, the catastrophic explosion would outweigh the scandal of her working as an alchemist.

After sending Annalise reassurance until she calmed and withdrew with a mental kiss, he said to Mother, "Lord Islaye requested I visit tomorrow to provide advice."

Mother nodded. "I'll join you. We should bring the angelcats and hellhounds to help provide magical energy in case we must cast spells not involving nature."

To distract him and Mother from the explosion in Magehaven, he mentioned the court events in the upcoming weeks. He and Mother discussed that as well as her journey to Ormas during the rest of luncheon. However, he was careful to never mention any of the Greysnowes, especially Annalise.

After luncheon, he and Mother retreated to his study and perused the book he'd enchanted with the library spell to find information about other explosions or mining and cave disasters. Then they shared dinner before Mother retired and he left for the sirenic play. Please let Miss Winston attend, so they could talk privately.

But not long after he arrived, Lady Blaine sashayed toward him with a coy smile. "Could I join you in your box tonight?"

Dare swallowed a sigh. If only he'd an excuse to refuse the husband-hunting countess. He made himself smile. "If you like. Although I'm greeting some friends first."

Lady Blaine captured his arm as he glanced about for Miss Winston. "Of course."

Spotting Miss Winston and her brother near the stairs, he strode through the crowd with Lady Blaine clinging to him. After everyone exchanged greetings, he leaned toward Miss Winston. "Did you hear about that explosion in Magehaven?"

Miss Winston frowned and shook her head as Winston returned his gaze to the crowd.

Her expression sincere and free of coquetry for once, Lady Blaine shuddered and replied, "An ore exploded and killed or wounded fifty people."

Miss Winston gasped and paled, although Winston merely hummed. She turned to Dare. "The ore that you mentioned before?" When he nodded, she swallowed then glanced at her brother and said, "I'm sure the council shall find the magicless alchemist they need soon."

Dare exhaled and returned Miss Winston's nod. Clearly, she meant to approach the council, but she didn't want her family to know. Thank the Goddess.

Once Lady Staghorn summoned Miss Winston and her brother, Lady Blaine hummed and shook her head. "I wonder how Miss Winston shall convince Lord and Lady Winston to allow her to work for the council. A baron's daughter working as an alchemist shall be a scandal."

He stiffened. Somehow, the fashionable countess knew Miss Winston's secret. Hopefully, she'd never discover his and Annalise's secret involvement as well.

Then the Campbells joined them, and Sir Ellis smiled at him and said, "Didn't realize you were attending tonight."

Dare shrugged. "I only decided this morning. Care to watch the play in my box?" 'Twould protect him from Lady Blaine.

Lady Campbell sipped her sparkling wine. "We would, but Lady Ducharme already invited us."

Sir Ellis clapped his shoulder. "Although we must discuss the flying sword fights after the performance. They're the best part of sirenic plays."

As Dare nodded, Lady Blaine tilted her head and squeezed his arm. "I prefer the bewitching duets and romance."

Lady Campbell chuckled. "Most ladies do."

Dare and Sir Ellis exchanged wry smiles as the two ladies grinned at each other. Then everyone headed to their respective boxes. As he sat beside Lady Blaine, Dare glanced about the theater. He'd an excellent view of the stage, but an even better one of the royal box containing Annalise. His heart surged as their eyes met. Keeping his face blank, he drawled, :*What a lovely necklace you're wearing.*:

Its flickering, sapphire light highlighting her faint smile,

Annalise caressed the heart-shaped firegem. *:'Twas a faegift from the gentleman I love who adores me.:*

His lips twitched as he suppressed a grin. *:He has excellent taste.:*

Annalise giggled. *:I think so.:*

Dare tensed when Lady Blaine touched his arm and purred, "Staring at Lady Kiera and King Devon again?"

He shifted away from the sultry countess. Although Lady Kiera and King Devon were cuddling beside Annalise, he'd not even noticed them. Fortunately, the sirenic play began and diverted Lady Blaine's attention.

Turning from the royal box, he forced himself to watch the stage. Yet King Devon leaving during the first song caught his eye. *:Something wrong?:*

Annalise hummed. *:The Duchess of Wildewall asked to talk with King Devon—I suspect about your mother's arrival.:*

Dare hid a grimace and returned his attention to the stage until Annalise's disgust flooded him a few moments later. He glanced at the royal box and stiffened. Winston was smirking at Annalise and Lady Kiera. His pulse flaring, he rose. "Winston is pestering Lady Kiera and her friend. Excuse me."

Lady Blaine's eyes narrowed as she rose as well. "How chivalrous of you. I'll join you."

They rushed to the royal box and arrived as Lady Kiera said, "The only passion I have for you, Mr. Winston, is *loathing*."

Dare almost growled and scrutinized Annalise, who paled. What had that cad done to make the warm Lady Kiera so scathing?

Before he could speak, Lady Blaine interjected, "But Mr. Winston has so little experience with passion, he often mistakes the two."

Dare gritted a cold smile and gripped Winston's shoulder. "And I believe we should discuss the difference between passion and loathing, Winston."

As he propelled Winston from the royal box, Annalise said, *:Dare, don't.:*

Dare clenched his jaw. *:The fortune-hunting cad must learn.:* He shoved Winston into a nearby closet. "Ladies don't appreciate when you pester them." When Winston smirked, Dare punched the cad's stomach to prevent whatever odious retort Winston was about to make.

Annalise's love and distress swamped him. *:Please stop. He's not worth it.:*

As Winston straightened with another smirk, fire flared through Dare, and he punched Winston again. *:I have to make sure he quits pestering you.:*

CHAPTER 33

nnalise shivered at Dare's protective fury flaring in their entwined souls. Somehow, she must convince him to stop before he seriously wounded Mr. Winston. She fisted her hands in her lap. :*If you get executed for murder, I'll never be able to marry you.*:

Dare's wry chuckle echoed through her. :*I don't intend to murder him—just a few punches to teach him to avoid you.*:

Absently replying to Lady Blaine's comment about deterring Mr. Winston, Annalise swallowed a sigh. Thank the Goddess Dare's fury had eased. :*Considering his greed, I doubt Mr. Winston shall learn that, especially since you can't mention me without starting rumors.*:

His love warming her, Dare murmured, :*I should have realized my tenderhearted soul healer couldn't bear even a few punches, no matter how the cad pestering her deserved them.*: When she sent him a grimace, he chuckled again. :*Very well, I'll stop and return to Ravenstone House. I've had enough drama for today.*:

Annalise was about to reply when Lady Blaine glanced at Kiera and said, "I was pleased to rescue you, but Lord Ravenstone was the one to observe Mr. Winston pestering you and insist we must remove him."

Annalise stilled as Lady Blaine's glance slid to her with a faint smirk. Oh, Goddess. Did Lady Blaine suspect Dare had been rescuing her, not Kiera? If the fashionable countess did, she'd spread gossip about them like she had about Wren's pregnancy.

Kiera smiled at Lady Blaine. "I'm grateful to you both."

Lady Blaine tossed her head. "If you weren't in love with King Devon, I'd be jealous of the attention Lord Ravenstone pays you, Lady Kiera."

Annalise tensed further as Lady Blaine's gaze slid to her once again. The sultry countess *must* suspect something. So she snorted and drawled, bitterness tainting her mouth at supporting the feud, "Lord Ravenstone is probably attempting to cozen up to you, so he can trick you into acting against the Greysnowes."

Kiera arched her brows then frowned. "I doubt that."

Lady Blaine's eyes narrowed, and muddy-green suspicion glowed about her. "Despite your families' centuries-long feud, Lord Ravenstone isn't the sort for such spite. Now Mr. Winston, however..."

Annalise grimaced with Kiera and Lady Blaine as her chest tightened. Her lies had only made Lady Blaine more suspicious. So without another word, she returned her attention to the sirenic play. She relaxed when King Devon soon returned and Lady Blaine left. Then she almost smiled as Kiera nestled against him like before. Despite her friend's belief their betrothal was fake, they were perfect for each other.

As soon as the sirenic play ended, Mother and Father burst into King Devon's box and strode past the royal guards along the wall.

Annalise winced at the muddy-orange upset swirling about them. What outrageous insult were they going to hurl at Kiera now?

She blinked when Mother merely grasped her arm and

pursed a tight smile at King Devon and Kiera, saying, "Excuse us, we must get Annalise home."

After saying farewell to Kiera and King Devon, Annalise allowed Mother to pull her from the royal box and into the carriage. She eyed Mother and Father while settling across from them. What had upset them so much that they'd forgotten their ambitions?

As Father draped a comforting arm about her, Mother laced her fingers in her lap then said, "Lady Morwynne just told us Lady Ravenstone has arrived in Ormas."

Annalise suppressed a snort. Of course the devious Lady Morwynne had. She adored provoking and manipulating others. But why were Mother and Father upset about Dare's mother rather than derisive? She inclined her head. "I see."

Mother frowned at her. "You must promise to avoid that vile woman, no matter how she beguiles you."

Annalise blinked. What?

Father drew Mother closer against him. "Yes, she's cruel and deceitful—the perfect wife for a treacherous Ravenstone. She'd destroy a loving girl like you."

Annalise gaped at her parents. Dare's mother couldn't be like that. She'd raised *him*, after all. And why were Mother and Father so vehement? Had they met Dare's mother? If so, they'd never mentioned that. Why? She forced a serene smile. "I promise to be careful, like I always am."

Once they returned to her family's townhouse, she darted to her chambers then reached out to Dare as Grace helped her into her nightgown, :*Has your mother met my parents?*:

His confusion prickling her skin, Dare replied, :*Not that I know of. Why?*:

Sighing, Annalise unclasped his faegift from her neck and set it on her bedside table. :*Because Mother and Father's rancor for her seems more personal than with other Ravenstones.*:

Dare hummed. :*Odd.*: He paused then said, :*You and Alex*

should ride to the royal bay tomorrow. I know you've not ridden there since before Summerday.:

Her brows rising, Annalise slid into bed. What did riding to the royal bay have to do with his mother? *:Is that a devious way to arrange a meeting without your mother knowing?*:

Dare snorted a laugh. *:Not a good one, since your brother would know, and he suspects us more than she does.*: He sighed. *:No, I mentioned riding to the royal bay because I shan't have time to go tomorrow and you could use an enjoyable outing with Alex.*:

She smiled at his usual tender care and sent her love through their entwined souls. *:What are you doing tomorrow instead of your ride to the royal bay?*:

After sending his love back, Dare sighed again. *:Mother and I are meeting with Lord Islaye to offer advice about the explosion in Magehaven. I'm not sure how much help we'll be, but at least I convinced Miss Winston to approach the council when we spoke before the sirenic play.*:

Warmth flooded her chest. Of course he had. Dare was always generous and helped bring people together. *:I'll gladly ride to the royal bay for you. Good night, my love.*:

She smiled into her pillow as Dare whispered back, *:Good night, my heart.*:

So the following morning shortly after dawn, Annalise dressed in her favorite sapphire riding habit then knocked on Alex's door. She grinned when he blinked at her. "Care to ride to the royal bay this morning? We've not visited in ages."

His eyes narrowing, Alex hummed. "I suppose I could miss Lady Ducharme's fencing salon today. I'll meet you in the stables in a bit."

Annalise gathered some rolls and cheese from the kitchen before heading out to the stables. She'd just started saddling Storm when Alex joined her and saddled Biscuit. Soon they were riding through the empty streets of Ormas, and she handed Alex some rolls and cheese. "In case we miss breakfast later."

Alex chuckled, and they devoured their food before they rode out the northern gate. Then they encouraged Storm and Biscuit to a trot until they reached the royal bay.

As they rode on the winding path down the cliffs, she smiled at the frothy ocean. Its autumn wildness made it even more lovely. Dare was so wonderful to have suggested she visit. If only he was with her. She sighed and touched her stomach. But that was much too dangerous until she knew if she was pregnant. Which she would in a week.

Shoving that aside, she grinned at Alex. "Shall we gallop along the beach?"

Alex grinned back, and they raced across the beach toward the cliffs. As they reined in Storm and Biscuit, Alex glanced over his shoulder, obviously expecting someone.

Annalise caressed Dare's firegem at her throat as a pang darted through her. Doubtless Alex was expecting Dare. Fortunately, without success. Although encountering Dare wouldn't cause a nearly fatal duel like last time, Alex would surely discover their involvement if he saw her and Dare together. To distract Alex, she flashed a brilliant smile and said, "Let's ride back on the edge of the surf."

His brows rising, Alex studied her. "You wish to return to Ormas already? We've not been here above half an hour."

She grimaced while steering Storm toward the wet sand. "Mother and Father were upset last night, and us remaining gone all morning shall upset them further." She should have considered that before asking Alex to join her, but visiting the royal bay had been too tempting.

Indigo concern pulsing around him, Alex urged Biscuit between her and the surf. "Upset about what?"

Annalise shrugged then forced herself to drawl, "Lady Ravenstone arriving in Ormas."

Alex gaped at her. "But everyone says she despises court."

Touching Dare's faegift again, Annalise hummed then gazed at the turbulent waves past Alex to feign disinterest. "Perhaps Lord Ravenstone remaining in Ormas so long convinced her to attend."

Wincing, Alex shifted in his saddle. "Or perhaps word of our duel did." He frowned at Biscuit's neck for several moments then arched his brows at her. "How do *you* feel about Lady Ravenstone's unexpected arrival?"

Annalise lowered her hand then made herself meet Alex's gaze with a wry smile. She must convince him that the arrival of Dare's mother meant nothing to her. "Me? I only care that Lady Ravenstone's arrival may prompt Mother and Father to be even more outrageous about our families' feud."

Alex snorted. "It might. Should I attend court events again to help you restrain them?"

She swallowed and gripped her reins. Then during the few court events they both attended, she and Dare would have to conceal the truth from not only court and Dare's mother but Alex as well. She shook her head. "I can manage. No need for both of us to suffer court events."

Alex eyed her then exhaled. "I'm glad my sacrifice shan't be necessary."

Annalise chuckled at his obvious relief. "Did you only offer because you knew I'd refuse?"

Alex grinned and waggled his brows. "Maybe..."

She pretended to throw something at him, then they rode back to Ormas.

OVER THE NEXT TWO DAYS, Annalise attended court events with Mother and Father, who hunted for Lady Ravenstone at every event. However, Dare and his mother never appeared, and Dare never mentally contacted her—no doubt because they were engrossed with the Magehaven ore.

But as she was saddling Storm to ride to the palace for her

next nightmara ride, Dare suddenly said, :*We should meet to exchange the angelcats.*:

Her heart quickening at seeing him for the first time in three days, she leapt atop Storm. :*Shall your mother notice if you meet me after today's nightmara ride?*:

Dare sent her a shrug. :*I told Mother and Lord Islaye I'd purchase supplies for our tests regarding the Magehaven ore, so she shan't suspect my absence. Although I'll need to explain why I allowed the angelcats to slip away when we're using their energy for spells not involving nature.*:

Annalise frowned as she began riding to the palace. His mental voice sounded weary. :*How's studying the Magehaven ore going?*:

Dare sighed. :*We're not making much progress, and I've not visited a natural area since Mother arrived, so my magic is drained, and I'm hungry for nature—almost as hungry as I am for you.*:

Warming, she echoed his sigh. She was hungry for him too, but they couldn't risk truly meeting right now. So she only said, :*You and your mother should ride to the royal bay tomorrow. You can't help anyone if you cripple yourselves and your magic.*:

Dare's wry acknowledgement darted through her. :*I'll suggest it to Mother tonight. I'll see you soon.*:

Annalise leapt from her saddle at the palace stables. Not soon enough.

She met Kiera outside the palace, and while they walked to the nightmara stables, Kiera described consulting a wood elf and a veiled witch about the Magehaven ore. From what Kiera said, her veiled witch must be the powerful Rhiannon-descendant seer who had created Kiera's and Wren's spells for the king's summer masquerade.

Darkthorn confirmed that as they galloped beside Kiera and Moonbud. Then he showed her directions to the veiled witch's shop, Rhiannon's Veils, and said, :*You should visit her. Meeting another powerful witch would make you feel less isolated. And the veiled witch is quite obliging. She's even agreed to help Moonbud to develop traps to protect the plains from poachers.:*

Her skin prickling, Annalise suppressed a shiver. The veiled witch might be obliging, but a seer would immediately recognize her as a soul healer and see her soulbond with Dare. Much too risky.

Darkthorn snorted. :*Although from your thoughts, I see you won't. Foolish human.*:

She pursed her lips. As a stallion with few secrets, Darkthorn couldn't understand. But saying that wouldn't help, so she asked about Moonbud's traps to distract him.

After her nightmara ride, her pulse surged as she rode Storm from the palace. Like before, Dare was wearing an invisibility spell, and she hungrily eyed the faint glow concealing him while caressing his faegift at her throat. Goddess, if only she could ride across the street and leap into his arms. However, she managed to restrain herself when he released the spell on the angelcats and they appeared. Once Finn and Lily leapt behind her, she rode back to her family's townhouse despite the ache filling her chest.

Early on the morning after he'd exchanged angelcats with Annalise, Dare grinned at Mother when he met her in the entrance hall with Raven and Bear beside him. "Ready to visit the royal bay in person?"

Petting Pearl curled in her arms, Mother flashed a vibrant grin despite the exhaustion creasing her face. "Definitely." She glanced around the entrance hall. "Where are Lily and her mate? I've not seen them since yesterday morning."

He stilled. Not surprising Mother had noticed the angelcats' disappearance. 'Twas part of why he'd asked to exchange them with Annalise—he wanted Mother to accept their disappearances as ordinary. Smiling at Mother, he opened the front door. "Exploring Ormas together, probably."

Their breaths misting in the chilly autumn air, Mother followed him outside and into the stables. "Or maybe they're visiting Finn's owner. Have you attempted to follow them?"

To feign indifference, Dare shrugged as he saddled Ebony and Mother saddled Willow. "Following angelcats is almost impossible, and they've not come to harm on any of their jaunts, so I've not bothered."

Mother hummed as they mounted, her eyes narrowing. "I see."

With Raven and Bear loping beside them and Pearl perched behind Mother, they rode through the empty streets of Ormas and out the northern gate. They kept to a trot the hellhounds could match as they rode to the royal bay. When they arrived, they halted Ebony and Willow at the edge of the cliffs above the bay. Although chilly, the royal bay was beautiful today—turbulent waves crashed against the golden sand, the sun blazed in the clear azure sky, and gulls swooped in the fierce breeze.

He grinned at Mother, whose face glowed as she stared at the royal bay. "What do you think?"

Mother beamed as they rode on the winding path down the cliffs. "'Tis even more stunning in person. Definitely the perfect retreat for a nature witch to settle their soul and revive their magical and physical energy."

Dare smiled, warmth filling his chest. "A retreat we sorely need after draining ourselves attempting to neutralize the Mage-haven ore." Thank the Goddess Annalise had urged him and Mother to visit.

Mother inhaled the salty breeze buffeting them. "So we do. 'Tis much wilder than I expected from our mirror call."

He chuckled at her delight. The royal bay's wildness made it an even better retreat for nature witches. "The waves seem more turbulent during autumn, probably because the winds are coming from both the north and the south."

Mother grinned. "Most likely. Let's ride over to the waves then gather natural energy to replenish ourselves."

Dare nodded, and they rode across the beach with Raven and Bear trotting beside them. When they reached the ocean, the hellhounds began chasing each other along the surf, spattering seawater and wet sand everywhere.

Mother giggled. "I can see why you brought Raven and Bear. They're bursting with energy. Shall they catch some fish for us?"

He flashed a wry grin. "If they catch any, I suspect they'll devour them."

Mother giggled again. "Such gluttons." She shooed Pearl into the sand. "Go play, you hellion."

Dare and Mother both laughed when the angelkitten stepped on the wet sand along the surf and disdainfully shook her paw. They laughed harder when a wave swamped her, and Pearl leapt back and hissed. After glowering at Mother, the angelkitten attacked her wet fur with her tongue.

Still laughing, Mother slid from the saddle. "Poor Pearl doesn't appreciate our outing." She tilted her head. "Although feeling the waves seems wonderful to me."

As Mother removed her riding boots and stockings, he leapt down and did likewise then rolled up his trousers. He beamed. Most mothers would disdain playing in the surf, but not his. Tenderness flooded him. Annalise probably would play in the surf too if she wasn't worried about her parents realizing. Mother would love her once they could finally meet.

Holding her riding habit above the ocean, Mother yelped when a wave broke against her legs. "Goddess, 'tis freezing. Perhaps Pearl wasn't so missish, after all."

Dare gasped as he waded into the icy water. But to tease Mother, he waggled his brows and asked, "What did you expect? Longnight is less than two months away."

Mother tsked with a playfully beleaguered sigh. "How did I raise such a disrespectful son?" When he shrugged, she laughed before continuing, "Shall we replenish our magic now? I'll gather the natural energy toward the south, while you can gather toward the north."

He nodded then flung out his powers. His drained magic soaked up the natural energy like parched soil soaked the rain. As he continued gathering natural energy for his magic, the restless hunger for nature writhing beneath his skin gradually faded as well.

Once his magic would hold no more, he retracted his powers

then turned to Mother, whose face was no longer creased with exhaustion. "All finished?"

Mother beamed and smoothed back her windswept hair. "Some time ago. Since your magic is more powerful than mine, it took longer to replenish." She bounded from the waves. "Shall we ride along the beach before returning to Ormas?" As she muttered a drying spell then donned her stockings and boots, he nodded and did the same. Once they were both mounted, she arched her brows with a grin. "Race you to the cliffs."

He laughed and urged Ebony after Mother and Willow. They thundered across the sand side by side, but he pulled ahead just before the cliffs. He grinned at her. "I won."

Mother tsked and shook her head. "So disrespectful." She sighed. "We should return now since Lord Islaye is expecting us midmorning. Too bad your angelcats are missing. Not that our spells worked better when they were providing us magical energy along with your hellhounds and Lord Islaye's Bailey."

Dare almost grimaced. True, he and Mother had been little help so far since magic didn't behave normally around the ore. Hopefully, Miss Winston would have better success—when she finally approached the council. Lord Islaye hadn't mentioned her, so she mustn't have yet. Please let her do so soon. He echoed Mother's sigh then replied, "I suppose we must return."

He whistled for Raven and Bear while Mother collected Pearl, then they rode back to the winding path on the cliffs.

Once they ascended the cliffs, Mother frowned and said, "I've decided I should attend Lady Morwynne's ball tonight. As a councilor, she'll surely invite both the Ravenstones and Greysnowes, and I'd prefer facing them at my first court event rather than waiting."

Dare eyed Mother's furrowed brow. She rarely appeared so troubled. Annalise might be right about Mother meeting her parents before. Perhaps Mother would tell him if he asked. "You appear worried. Why?"

Mother stilled. "Meetings are always complicated between

Ravenstones and Greysnowes." She flashed a smile. "Come, we mustn't dawdle."

As Mother urged Willow faster, Dare rubbed his beard then kneed Ebony and sent Raven and Bear energy so they could match Mother and Willow's pace. Yes, Mother and the Greysnowes definitely shared a secret history. But what? And would it make her more or less likely to tell the Greysnowes about his secret involvement with Annalise if she discovered that?

After another frustrating day analyzing the Magehaven ore with Lord Islaye, Dare and Mother once again ate dinner with Lord and Lady Islaye before returning to Ravenstone House with Raven, Bear, and Pearl. However, tonight he and Mother changed for Lady Morwynne's ball rather than spending a quiet evening with their magical pets.

As they greeted the superior Lady Morwynne, he gritted a genial grin despite the hunger for Annalise burning in his chest. Soon he'd see her again. And somehow he mustn't betray his reaction to Mother. He swallowed as he and Mother began circulating the ballroom so he could introduce her to everyone.

They'd only met King Devon and Lady Kiera when his soulbond burgeoned at Annalise's arrival with her parents. Although he shouldn't, he couldn't help turning toward her. His heart quickened. As always, she appeared radiant, and his faegift still flickered at her throat. Their eyes met, and love surged through their entwined souls.

Beside him, Mother stiffened.

Dare wrenched his gaze from Annalise to scrutinize Mother. Had she noticed him staring at Annalise? She'd soon suspect their secret involvement if she had.

Her amber eyes dark and skin pale, Mother was watching the Greysnowes like a moonrabbit watched basilisks. From her reaction to Annalise's parents, she probably wouldn't tell them about his involvement with Annalise if she discovered it. Which wasn't like her—she always said the first step to resolving problems with others was being open.

Then Mother paled further when Lady Greysnowe glanced at her then whirled away. Mother appeared about to faint, and she never fainted.

He squeezed Mother's arm, his chest tight. "Are you all right?"

Mother swallowed and lifted her chin. "I'm fine. Come, you must introduce me to everyone before the dancing starts."

As they began circulating again, Dare continued monitoring Annalise's parents. Would they approach and hurl insults that would attract unwelcome attention? Yet no matter where he and Mother were, the Greysnowes remained across the ballroom and never turned toward Mother. Lady Greysnowe also kept Annalise close to her side rather than shoving her at unwed lords. Most peculiar.

Then the first dance began, and he led Mother out onto the floor since he couldn't dance with Annalise and Lady Blaine thankfully hadn't attended tonight. Perhaps gossip about Mother's arrival had dissuaded the husband-hunting countess.

He smiled at that—until Mother winced when they twirled past Annalise and her parents, who were all standing on the outskirts of the ballroom rather than dancing like usual. Her secret history with the Greysnowes was definitely distressing her.

Eyeing Mother, Dare reached out to Annalise, :*Have your parents said what happened between them and Mother?*:

Annalise hummed. :*No, but something definitely did. From their auras, I can read Mother is upset, Father furious, and your mother regretful. And those feelings flare when our parents glance at each other.*:

He almost frowned. Mother was always kind and sought to resolve others' problems, so what could have happened between her and Annalise's parents? He attempted asking again, but Mother kept ignoring or deflecting him.

Midway through Lady Morwynne's ball, Mother turned to him with a tight smile. "Do you mind leaving now? I'm unaccustomed to such late hours and ache for my bed."

His throat clenching, Dare took her untouched flute of sparkling wine then handed their flutes to a nearby servant. Mother was never so weary—her request must be an excuse. "Of course not. I'm riding to the royal bay at dawn tomorrow and could use the rest too."

Mother brightened as he escorted her from the ballroom. "Another ride to the royal bay? I'll join you."

He tensed and smoothed his beard. Except then Mother and Alex would meet. "Not tomorrow. I'm meeting Alex to practice sword fighting. Perhaps the day after instead?"

Mother sighed while climbing into the carriage. "Very well."

Dare studied Mother as he settled in the backward seat. If only she would confess the trouble between her and Annalise's parents. He suppressed a grimace. If only *he* could confess the truth about him and Annalise to Mother. Such secrets between them were painful.

THE FOLLOWING morning after they'd cleaned and sheathed their swords, Alex frowned at Dare and sighed. "I hope Father and Mother weren't too outrageous at Lady Morwynne's ball yesterday. They ranted about your mother's effrontery to attend for upward of an hour last night."

Dare winced while they mounted Ebony and Biscuit. Despite the feud, he'd never dreamt Mother meeting the Greysnowes would be so rancorous. How much worse would it be when he and Annalise eloped? He swallowed. "They simply stayed as far away from Mother as possible. No confrontations, thank the Goddess."

Alex relaxed as they rode down the cliff to the beach. "Good.

I would have asked Annalise, but she'd already retired when I returned to the townhouse—probably to escape Father and Mother's ranting."

His chest squeezing, Dare winced again. Not surprising. Such rancor would distress his tenderhearted soul healer. He managed a tight smile. "Wise of your sister."

Alex chuckled, his lips twitching. "Very." He arched a brow. "Did you happen to notice if Annalise was still wearing that sapphire firegem necklace last night?"

Dare tensed. Why was Alex asking about the faegift he'd given Annalise again? He forced himself to shrug. "I believe so."

Alex hummed and leaned back in his saddle. "She *must* adore whoever gave it to her to wear it so often. Fitting, given how he obviously adores her. I wonder why Annalise hasn't mentioned him to Father and Mother yet. They're impatient for her to marry."

Dare clenched Ebony's reins. Except not to him. "No doubt your sister has reasons for remaining silent."

Alex nodded. "I suppose so. And the gentleman she loves would say nothing if she desires secrecy."

His mouth drying, Dare shifted in his saddle and struggled to devise a reply that wouldn't betray their soulbond and love.

After a moment, Alex shook his head then asked, "Shall we race to the cliffs?"

Dare relaxed and nodded. Thank the Goddess Alex had stopped mentioning Annalise. Before long, the younger gentleman would discover their involvement, which would upset her.

CHAPTER 35

Two days after Lady Morwynne's ball, Annalise hurried to the palace after luncheon to meet Kiera for their nightmara ride. She'd not seen her friend since that evening, and court was gossiping about King Devon and Kiera's mysterious absence yesterday. She touched her stomach. Tomorrow she'd know if court would have something more scandalous to gossip about.

Shoving that aside, she forced herself to consider King Devon and Kiera's absence again. She swallowed. Hopefully, nothing was wrong, even though Kiera had moved their nightmara ride to the afternoon rather than the morning like usual.

However, when they met outside the palace, Kiera appeared fine, although somewhat strained. Understandable given the explosion of the Magehaven ore. Yet as they strode to the nightmara stables, Kiera revealed Mr. Winston had planned to kidnap her, so King Devon had banished the future baron from Ormas.

Annalise gaped at Kiera. Was Mr. Winston mad? Although his kidnapping attempt and banishment did explain Kiera's strain as well as her and King Devon's absence at court events yesterday. But at least Kiera had today's nightmara ride to relax her before the Landrys' rout party or the Campbells' card party tonight.

Since Moonbud wanted a longer ride, they galloped to the royal forest. Soon everyone, including Kiera, was beaming and laughing, even though the royal guards had fallen behind. Moonbud asked Leila and Nightrose to wait for the guards then tossed Darkthorn a coy glance and darted off the path.

Annalise giggled as Darkthorn dashed after his mate with a whinny. Nightmara flirting was adorable as well as exhilarating.

But then, Moonbud and Kiera burst into the clearing with Esme the Great's melissae hive.

Her pulse surging and bile burning her throat, Annalise stiffened as the strident melissae swarmed Kiera and Moonbud. Dear Goddess, the melissae's stings would kill them within moments. She leapt from Darkthorn's back and screamed at the melissa queen, "No!" She mentally added, :*'Twas an accident! Please stop attacking my friends.*:

As the melissae quieted, the melissa queen swirled to face Annalise. :*Accident? Friends?*: When Annalise nodded, the melissa queen turned back to her hive. :*Stop. Friends. Go home.*: Once the melissae hurtled back to their cottage, the melissa queen faced Annalise again. :*Sorry, heart-sister daughter.*:

While the melissa queen whisked inside the cottage too, Annalise raced across the clearing to Kiera and Moonbud to soul-heal them. From the black staining their entire auras, they hadn't long. She knelt beside Kiera first. Kiera was closer to death since she was smaller than the nightmara queen-heir but with nearly as many melissae stings.

She cupped Kiera's face and drew energy from her soul until it matched Kiera's indigo. Then she enveloped Kiera's soul with hers, tingling swamping her as their souls meshed. She whimpered when her blood boiled as she absorbed the melissae stings. Goddess, 'twas almost as excruciating as when she'd soul-healed Dare. But at least because of their soulbond, she couldn't form another with Kiera. Once the agony from the melissae stings faded, she wove energy back into Kiera's aura where the pain had been to finish healing her. Then she separated their souls, tingling flooding her again. Her head swirled when her soul burst back to its usual form.

As Annalise staggered upright to soul-heal Moonbud, Dare's panic swamped their entwined souls, and he mentally shouted, *:Annalise! Your power just exploded in our soulbond. Are you all right?:*

She sighed and sent him a smile. *:I'm fine. I just soul-healed Kiera from melissae stings.:*

Dare grunted. *:I didn't realize soul-healing required so much energy. Even here at Lord Islaye's, I almost fainted, and I wasn't the one performing the soul-healing.:*

Annalise grimaced as she knelt beside Moonbud. Although soul-healing only took a heartbeat, soul-healing fatal wounds *did* require copious energy. *:Sorry, I didn't know you'd sense that through our soulbond so strongly. But I couldn't delay—Kiera was dying.:* She pressed her palms against the nightmara queen-heir. *:Brace yourself. I'm about to soul-heal Moonbud.:*

His concern flooding their entwined souls, Dare whispered, *:Be careful, Annalise.:*

She sent him another smile then drew energy from her soul until it matched Moonbud's red with blazing silver motes. The boiling agony while she soul-healed the nightmara queen-heir was even more excruciating than with Kiera. When she finished, she was icy yet panting and trembling, too drained to even rise. *:Goddess, no wonder Esme the Great's primer for soul healers warned never to soul-heal more than three fatal wounds in succession.:*

As Moonbud lurched to her feet, energy from Dare surged through Annalise. He said, *:That should sustain you until you can eat and rest to recover. Head home, and I'll check on you later.:*

While Darkthorn bounded to Moonbud and began nuzzling her, Annalise replied to Dare, *:Thanks. Until then.:*

Once Dare's presence faded, she gulped a shuddering breath then rose. Even with his energy, she felt as weak as a newborn angelkitten. She stared into the forest and fingered his faegift at her throat. Not that she'd risk his life by requesting more energy, especially when the best recovery food for soul healers, ambrosia, was just steps away.

She was about to mentally ask the melissa queen for ambrosia when Kiera approached and murmured, "What just happened?"

Annalise tensed. Perhaps a half-truth would satisfy Kiera. Not facing but still watching her friend, she made herself shrug. "The melissae were startled when you burst into their clearing and attacked to defend their hive. I explained 'twas an accident to the melissa queen and asked her to halt the attack."

Kiera nibbled her lip. "But how did you heal our melissae stings?"

Swallowing, Annalise clutched Dare's heart-shaped firegem. Of course, her half-truth hadn't satisfied Kiera. So somehow she must tell her friend about her powers without revealing her soulbond with Dare. "I'm a soul healer, a very powerful one."

Kiera frowned, muddy-white confusion swirling about her.

Before Kiera could speak, Annalise suppressed a shiver then leaned toward her. "Swear you shan't tell King Devon I'm a soul healer." Since he'd been at the duel, he'd surely realize she'd soul-healed Dare and formed a soulbond. When Kiera blinked, Annalise gripped her friend's hands. She *must* convince Kiera to remain silent. "*Please.* 'Tisn't a state matter, and 'tis vital no one knows."

Kiera scrutinized her for a moment then squeezed her hands. "I shan't tell him unless absolutely necessary."

Her chill easing, Annalise beamed and embraced Kiera. "Thank you."

Then she and Kiera whirled to face Nightrose, Leila, and the royal guards thundering into the clearing.

Annalise swallowed, her stomach clenching. She couldn't risk asking the melissa queen for ambrosia now. 'Twould be tanta-mount to telling everyone she was a soul healer.

Kiera smoothed her riding habit then turned to Moonbud. "Shall we ride back to the palace?"

Moonbud separated from Darkthorn and inclined her head at Annalise. :*Thank you for soul-healing me, Lady Heart. The nightmara owe you a great debt.*:

Gulping a breath, Annalise met the nightmara queen-heir's taupe eyes and mentally replied so the others couldn't overhear, :*I was glad to help. All I ask is that you remain silent about my powers and soulbond like you have been.*:

Moonbud blinked. :*Of course.*:

While Kiera swung into the saddle atop Moonbud, Darkthorn knelt beside Annalise and said, :*You're too exhausted to mount like normal.*: Once she climbed on his back, he rose as if lifted by the smoothest levitation spell. :*My deepest thanks for saving my mate, Lady Heart. I couldn't bear a world without her in it.*:

Annalise patted his withers. She understood that. She murmured, "You're welcome."

As everyone rode back to Ormas, she sagged against Darkthorn and dozed. The energy Dare had sent her was fading fast. After the nightmara left them at the palace, she dragged herself atop Storm and rode back to the family townhouse. Goddess, she was exhausted.

So she asked the grooms to tend to Storm for once before plodding inside to the kitchen to request poached pears smothered in honey and cream. Not as restorative as ambrosia, but enough to help. After devouring the rich dessert, she trudged upstairs to take a nap.

Midway up the stairs, Alex grasped her elbow, indigo concern pulsing about him. "Annalise, what happened? You look terrible."

She sighed but leaned on his supporting arm. Without him, the stairs seemed almost insurmountable. "What are you doing back at this hour?"

Alex frowned and eyed her. "I'm here to bathe and change

after my ride with Arthur to Blacke Woods before attending the Campbells' card party."

Her head whirling, Annalise blinked at him and managed the next step. "I see."

Alex leaned toward her, and his frown deepened to a scowl. "So what happened?"

She swallowed a hysterical giggle. She'd saved their future queen as well as the nightmara's from death and was drained from doing so. Not that she could reveal that.

Alex's jaw clenched. "You can trust me with your secrets, you know. I swear I shan't tell anyone."

As they reached the upper floor, Annalise patted his arm with a deep sigh. He was such a wonderful brother to offer, but she still couldn't burden him with her secrets and risk their parents discovering them. So she only said, "During our night-mara ride, Kiera and I visited the royal forest, and the melissae frightened us when they defended their hive."

Alex gaped at her. "Goddess."

She patted his arm again. "So I'm exhausted and require a nap before dinner. See you later."

Before Alex could reply, she slipped into her chambers. She removed her riding boots then sank into bed with Finn and Lily curled against her and purring. She collapsed into a dreamless slumber until Grace shook her awake some time later.

Grace frowned at her. "My lady, should I tell Lord and Lady Greysnowe you're too ill to join them for dinner and the Landrys' rout party tonight?"

Annalise hauled herself from bed, dislodging Finn and Lily, who grumbled then stalked to the edge of the bed and began grooming each other. Mother and Father knew she was rarely ill and would ponder why. Besides, she'd feel better once she ate a proper meal. She smiled at her maid. "No, just help me dress for tonight."

As Grace helped her dress, Dare mentally said, his love warming her, :*How are you feeling?*:

Sending her love back, Annalise smoothed her icy-blue gown that hopefully disguised her faint pallor. :*Better, albeit still tired.*:

Dare sighed. :*Can you convince your parents to let you skip whatever court event you're attending tonight?*:

She thanked Grace then headed downstairs. :*I wish, but I can't risk Mother and Father thinking about my unusual fatigue. They might discover my powers.*:

His concern flaring in their entwined souls, Dare almost growled. :*You must take better care of yourself. Especially since, according to you, you're likely pregnant.*:

Annalise swallowed, her chest squeezing. She forced herself to not touch her stomach as she entered the family dining room. Mother and Father might notice and wonder why. :*I should know for certain tomorrow.*:

Dare's mental voice softened, :*Tell me as soon as you do.*:

Her heart warming at his tenderness, she greeted Mother and Father then sat across from them with a serene smile. :*I promised I would, didn't I?*:

Dare sighed. :*I remember.*:

As Dare's presence faded, Annalise sipped her tuber leek soup and absently nodded in response to Mother's grumbling about his mother. She glanced at her stomach and focused her powers. Perhaps now she could see if she was pregnant, despite her potent aura. But after a moment, her head swirled, and she almost dropped her spoon, so she released her powers. Her aura was still too bright to see any glow of pregnancy with such a short attempt, and she was too exhausted tonight to try longer. She'd just have to wait until tomorrow when her courses either began or not.

CHAPTER 36

*A*s Dare settled in the carriage across from Mother, he clenched his hands and forced himself not to check on Annalise again. After soul-healing two creatures from fatal melissae stings while likely carrying his child, she should be resting rather than attending some court event. She was so exhausted she might faint, or an unscrupulous gentleman could harm her. Too bad she wasn't attending the Campbells' card party. Then he could at least watch over her in person.

Eyeing him, Mother leaned toward him. "How are you feeling? Has your headache receded?"

Shoving Annalise from his mind, he smiled at Mother. A sudden headache had been his excuse for almost fainting at Lord Islaye's when Annalise had soul-healed Lady Kiera and Lady Moonbud. "I'm fine."

Mother hummed, her eyes still narrow.

Dare made himself blandly return her gaze. Until Annalise was ready to reveal their involvement, he couldn't let Mother realize the truth. Although Mother probably wouldn't tell Annalise's parents, she might attempt to push Annalise into acting before she was ready.

After a moment, Mother sighed and reclined against her seat.

"Sir Ellis and Lady Campbell are some of your friends who attend Lady Ducharme's fencing salon, aren't they?"

He blinked at Mother's shifted interest. "Yes, why do you ask?"

Mother shrugged. "I was wondering if they'd invite others from Lady Ducharme's fencing salon... like Lord Alexander."

Dare stiffened. Clearly, Mother still wanted to meet Alex—much too dangerous, especially after this afternoon. "You can't approach him tonight. Only our friends from Lady Ducharme's fencing salon know about our friendship, and more than our friends shall attend the Campbells' card party tonight."

Mother pursed her lips. "I suppose so. But at least I can see him."

He sighed as the carriage halted at Campbell House. Mother likely wouldn't be satisfied with just seeing Alex. He offered Mother his arm and escorted her inside.

Sir Ellis and Lady Campbell grinned when they approached, and Lady Campbell said, "I'm pleased you could attend tonight."

Mother grinned back. "Your card party is perfect for me to meet people in a more intimate setting than a stuffy ball."

Sir Ellis guffawed. "'Tis the first time I've heard a lady call a ball stuffy. What a wonderful mother you have, Lord Ravenstone."

Smiling, Dare squeezed Mother's arm. "I'm most fortunate."

Lady Campbell grinned and gestured toward the half-filled card tables. "Go find a seat."

As Dare escorted Mother to the nearest empty table, Alex glanced at them from across the room then inclined a faint nod that most wouldn't notice.

While Dare returned Alex's discreet nod, Mother hummed then murmured, "Lord Alexander greatly resembles his parents, doesn't he?"

Dare sat beside Mother with a wry grin. "Except for his attitude."

Mother stilled then began shuffling while they waited for

another couple to join them. "He resembles Lady Annalise as well, although he doesn't possess her otherworldly radiance. I can see why court calls her the most beautiful lady in Calatini."

Dare swallowed. Why was Mother mentioning Annalise? Could she already suspect the truth? She'd only seen them at the same court event once, and they'd carefully avoided each other. He managed to nod but remained silent to avoid betraying his feelings for Annalise.

Mother had opened her mouth to say more when Lady Ducharme and young Lord Morwynne strode to their table and sat. Thank the Goddess.

After everyone exchanged greetings, Lady Ducharme leaned toward him and Mother. "Any success regarding the Magehaven ore? Lord Islaye mentioned you were helping him."

Dare and Mother exchanged a glance. Not surprising Lord Islaye had mentioned that to his fellow councilor. Hopefully, he and Mother being nature witches wouldn't become court gossip.

Mother pursed a rueful smile. "Unfortunately not. Using magic, even nature magic, on that unpredictable ore does nothing."

Dare sighed. Although now, Lord Islaye finally had the help he needed—Miss Winston had recently approached King Devon and Lady Kiera. But because word of that hadn't spread at court yet, Dare only said, "And since King Devon sent word to Lord Islaye that they'd found an alchemist without magic, Lord Islaye decided we'd quit studying the Magehaven ore after today. At least until the alchemist examines it."

As Lady Ducharme and Lord Morwynne nodded, Mother dealt everyone cards. They played several hands before Mother glanced at Dare and asked, "Shall we circulate?"

He nodded, and they visited all the other card tables except Alex's. Then they played several hands with the Campbells, discussing their favorite pastimes in Ormas, from Lady Ducharme's fencing salon to kelpie races. After that, they circulated again before playing cards with the Duke and Duchess of Childes.

The duchess leaned toward Mother during their first hand. "I hope you'll attend my art gala tomorrow. My daughter-in-law Selena adores art, so she's ensured 'tis the best."

Mother smiled and ordered her cards. "I look forward to it."

Dare's heart quickened. Doubtless Annalise and her parents would attend as well, so he'd see her for the first time in two days. Plus, she should know if she was pregnant by then.

The Duchess of Childes beamed at Mother. "Excellent. As new to Ormas, you may not know that Selena, Lady Treyvan, is pregnant with our first grandchild, and our other daughter-in-law Wren, Lady Beza Hawke, is pregnant as well."

Dare blinked at her. Odd that the duchess began discussing her pregnant daughters-in-law when he was just thinking about Annalise being pregnant.

The Duke of Childes flashed a crooked grin as he played a card. "Caro is ecstatic that we'll have two grandchildren in the same year—although she secretly wishes for a third."

As the duchess tsked at her husband, Mother smiled at Dare and drawled, "You're most fortunate. I've no inkling when my son shall provide me with grandchildren."

The back of his neck heating, Dare shifted in his chair. Mother might have a grandchild much sooner than she expected. He played his final card to win the game. "But at least I can provide a winning hand."

Mother and the Duke and Duchess of Childes chuckled as he shuffled to play another hand. After several more hands, the duke and duchess left for the evening.

While Dare gathered the cards from the table, Alex dropped into the chair beside Mother. Dare tensed then glanced about the room. Nearly everyone had left—only their friends from Lady Ducharme's fencing salon remained. He exhaled and relaxed somewhat.

His eyes gleaming, Alex smirked at Mother. "Mother has

been ranting about you the past week, Lady Ravenstone. Are you as wicked as she says?"

Mother paled and winced. "No, but I can understand why she believes that."

Dare frowned at her. She appeared almost guilty. *What* had happened between her and Annalise's parents?

Alex hummed and leaned toward her. "Is that fur on your gown?"

Mother glanced down and brushed her bodice. "Yes, from my angelkitten Pearl."

Dare froze. He must distract them before Mother mentioned Finn and Lily—Alex would surely recognize them. "Shall we play three arcana?"

Once Dare dealt, Alex fanned his cards before him and smiled at Mother. "Has Dare taken you to the royal bay yet?"

Mother grinned back. "Yes, 'tis stunning. And I loved galloping across the sand."

Alex chuckled. "Who doesn't? What else have you seen in Ormas so far?"

Dare tensed as Mother and Alex talked during their interminable hand of cards. Yet he managed to divert them from Annalise or other topics that might reveal too much. He sighed when Mother played the winning hand. "'Tis late. We should go."

Alex extended a hand toward Mother. "Before you do, I must say something, since I doubt we'll meet again soon." He inhaled. "Lady Ravenstone, I apologize for nearly killing your son in that duel. I was mad to challenge Dare—not only is he renowned as a skilled swordsman, but he's the most decent gentleman I've ever met. And since he accepted my apology four months ago, he's become a brother to me."

As Dare blushed at the younger gentleman's praise, Mother leaned forward and embraced Alex. Once she released him, she beamed and said, "Then you two must end the Ravenstone-Greysnowe feud one day."

Dare met Alex's gaze and replied, "We intend to." As long as

Alex didn't despise him after discovering his secret involvement with Annalise. Nodding at Alex, Dare took Mother's arm, and they said farewell to the Campbells before returning to Ravenstone House.

Despite their late evening, Dare rose even earlier than normal the following morning. Today, Annalise would know if she was pregnant. Unable to remain still while waiting for her to contact him, he rode Ebony around Ormas until he returned to eat breakfast with Mother.

Then to distract himself, he took Mother to Column Caverns, and they ate luncheon there. If only he could have done the same with Annalise. Yet despite Mother's delight at the limestone caverns, he could barely smile. Why hadn't Annalise contacted him yet?

By the time he and Mother strode into Childes House, Dare burned to speak with Annalise. Their hunger surged in their entwined souls when their gazes met across the drawing room. He fisted his hands to avoid approaching her. :*Annalise, we must talk.*:

Annalise wrenched her gaze free. Then fingering his heart-shaped firegem, she studied the dancing sculpture between her and her mother. :*Not here. Meet me at the park at dawn tomorrow.*:

His pulse surged. For her to request a private meeting must mean she was pregnant.

Annalise continued, :*I'll bring the angelcats, so we can exchange them.*:

Dare swallowed, his chest clenching. :*Don't you have anything else to tell me?*:

Annalise gestured toward the sculpture and murmured something to her parents. :*Not yet.*:

Mother leaned toward him. "Dare, are you well? You appear tense."

He gritted a genial smile. Of course Mother had noticed. "I'm fine. Shall we view the moving paintings?" Those were farthest from Annalise and her parents.

Her eyes flicking toward the Greysnowes, Mother nodded, but before they could view the art, the sultry Lady Blaine sashayed toward them.

Dare almost sighed. He'd been mistaken about Mother's arrival having dissuaded the husband-hunting countess. Too bad.

Stopping beside him, Lady Blaine flashed a coy smile. "Lord Ravenstone, 'tis been an age. Introduce me to your mother."

After the introductions, Lady Blaine leaned toward Mother. "I wish we could have met sooner, but I missed Lady Morwynne's ball. For some—" She halted, her gaze focused across the drawing room. "Excuse me. The Duchess of Childes is beckoning me." She fluttered her lashes at Dare. "Until later."

As Lady Blaine swept away, Mother arched her brows at him and asked, "What was that about?"

Suppressing a grimace, he smoothed his beard. "Lady Blaine is hunting a husband. Not that we'd suit—she adores Ormas. Shall we return to the moving paintings?"

He and Mother began viewing the Duchess of Childes's superb art collection. As at Lady Morwynne's ball, they remained across the room from Annalise and her parents.

While they were studying the dancing sculptures, King Devon and Lady Kiera strode into the drawing room, and gossip flared through the guests. 'Twas the first they'd appeared at a court event since Lady Morwynne's ball. Not surprising they'd chosen the Duchess of Childes's event—the duchess's family were the king's closest relatives, and her son, Lord Treyvan, was his best friend. As King Devon and Lady Kiera spoke with Lord Treyvan and his pregnant wife, Annalise slipped away from her parents and joined them.

Mother squeezed Dare's arm. "We've looked at these dancing sculptures enough. We should greet King Devon and Lady Kiera."

His shoulders tensed. But then Mother would meet Annalise. Why was Mother so determined to meet the Greysnowes' children when she watched the Greysnowes as if they were basilisks? Yet protesting would only make Mother suspect his involvement with Annalise, so he nodded then escorted Mother across the room. He sent to Annalise, :*Beware, Mother and I are approaching.*:

Once they halted beside King Devon and Lady Kiera, Mother beamed at them. "Good evening, your majesties. Isn't the art displayed tonight wonderful?"

A loving arm about Lady Kiera, King Devon shrugged then replied, "I believe so, although we've not seen most of it yet."

Mother smiled at Lady Treyvan. "The Duchess of Childes said you ensured 'tis the best."

Leaning against Lord Treyvan, Lady Treyvan dimpled and rubbed her rounded stomach. "The duchess exaggerates. She chose the art; I merely offered my opinion when she asked."

Dare froze when Mother turned to Annalise. Why was Mother addressing Annalise in public? She'd only spoken to Alex in private because she'd known he and Alex were friends. Had she already guessed his secret involvement with Annalise?

Mother leaned toward Annalise with a vibrant grin. "Yet your radiance outshines the art tonight."

He exhaled. Mother wouldn't have said something so banal if she'd guessed his involvement with Annalise. Her interest in Annalise must be because of her history with Annalise's parents.

Her gaze carefully averted from him, Annalise flashed Lady Snow's cool smile. "Thank you."

But before Annalise could say more, Lord and Lady Greysnowe stormed over, and Lady Greysnowe grasped Annalise's arm while glowering at Mother. "Stay away from my daughter, you treacherous harpy."

As they yanked Annalise toward the moving paintings, Mother paled, and Annalise's embarrassment surged through

Dare. Annalise mentally whispered, *:Sorry, Dare. See you tomorrow.:*

Still pale, Mother tsked. "So melodramatic. But then, encounters between Ravenstones and Greysnowes usually are."

Lady Kiera leaned toward her with a soft smile. "Devon and I can't stay long, but we must view all the art first. Would you care to join us?"

Dare's chest eased. Their future queen was always so kind. Almost as much as Annalise.

Mother returned Lady Kiera's smile. "Thank you, your majesty, but I don't wish to intrude. Besides, Dare and I have already seen everything."

Once King Devon, Lady Kiera, and the Treyvans left to view the art, Dare arched his brows at Mother. "Since we've seen everything, would you care to leave?"

Mother hummed. "No, then all of court shall gossip that Lady Greysnowe routed me. Let's go greet other guests first."

Dare nodded and escorted Mother to the Campbells. His friends were tactful enough to avoid mentioning her confrontation with Lady Greysnowe. Yet while he and Mother circulated, he kept glancing at Annalise, and his heart twisted. Thank the Goddess he'd finally see her alone tomorrow.

CHAPTER 37

The following morning at dawn, Annalise sighed then slid from bed. She must head to the park to meet Dare —doubtless he was already pacing amidst the trees. Like she had every day since soul-healing Kiera, she pressed a hand against her stomach then focused her powers, but her potent aura still masked any glow of pregnancy. Frowning, she released her powers. Her courses hadn't begun yesterday, and they'd never been late before, so she could be carrying Dare's child. Yet since her powers hadn't confirmed that, she might not be. She swallowed. Please let her not be pregnant—'twould complicate everything.

Sighing again, she yanked on a heavy walking dress and her warmest cloak and gloves—with Longnight fast approaching, mornings were frigid, and the ground always covered with frost. She called Finn and Lily then hurried to the park with the angelcats prowling beside her.

When she reached the half-bare trees, Dare was pacing, just as she'd expected. Finn and Lily darted over and rubbed his legs. Once he bent and petted them, they bounded into the branches to explore.

Annalise smiled after the angelcats. Then Dare straightened, and as their gazes met, their love flared in their entwined souls. Truly alone since making love at Lady Blaine's fire ball, they flew into each other's arms like two lodestones. Then they shuddered as one when their mouths fused in a ravenous kiss and their souls meshed.

But when she fisted her gloved hands in his long hair, Dare groaned and wrenched his lips free. His chest heaving, he buried his face in her neck. "We must stop before we make love outside again. You were right about our private meetings being too tempting—especially after remaining apart for three weeks."

Although her body throbbed, Annalise sighed and lowered her arms, yet she couldn't bear to step back or separate their meshed souls. "We probably shouldn't have risked a private meeting today, but we had to talk."

His arms tightening about her, Dare lifted his head as his joy reverberated through their meshed souls. "You're pregnant?"

She blushed but shrugged. She must temper his excitement. "Perhaps. I missed my courses yesterday, which isn't normal, but my powers still can't detect any glow of pregnancy, and I should be able to by now, even with my potent aura."

Dare hummed. "Yet you're likely pregnant if soul healers are as incredibly fertile as you said. We must discuss our future."

Annalise almost grimaced. Such discussions were senseless until they knew for certain if she was pregnant or not. She stepped back and separated their meshed souls. "Must we?"

Dare narrowed his eyes at her. "We should marry in a private ceremony at once. Lady Kiera and Lady Beza Hawke can be your witnesses, while Mother and Alex can be mine."

She swallowed, her heart twisting. That sounded wonderful, except it might not even be necessary, and Mother and Father would never forgive her. "We can't."

Sighing, Dare took her hands and squeezed them. "We must. If we delay, our child's early birth shall engender gossip."

Annalise tugged her hands free. He was worried about *that*?

"Any marriage between a Greysnowe and a Ravenstone would engender gossip."

Dare frowned. "Yes, but not about our child."

She pursed her lips at his delusion. "If we elope because I'm pregnant, all of court shall realize why we did once our child is born—unless I have a year-long pregnancy like an elf."

His brow still furrowed, Dare rubbed his beard. "Fine. Then we can wait to marry. Although we must marry before our child is born."

Annalise snorted. "We're not certain I'm pregnant, remember?" Weight compressed her chest. "Besides, you know 'tis impossible for us to marry, thanks to Mother and Father's obsession with the feud."

Dare leaned toward her, his frown deepening. "We're old enough they can't legally prevent us from marrying."

She clutched his faegift at her throat. "Yes, but they'll never forgive me for marrying a Ravenstone." They'd consider that the ultimate betrayal.

His anger flaring across her skin, Dare gripped her shoulders. "So you'll let our child be born a bastard? Or do you intend to marry another to give our child a false name?"

Annalise shuddered as a chill swept through her at marrying anyone other than Dare. "Of course not."

Dare drew her closer, his amber eyes gleaming. "Then you must marry me before your pregnancy becomes obvious."

She glared at him and shoved his chest. Why couldn't he understand? "Except, as I said before, I might not even *be* pregnant." When he frowned, she glared harder. "And unlike *you*, I'll lose my parents if we marry. Mother and Father shall likely never speak to me again and cast an erase spell to remove my name from all the family histories." At that, she began to sob.

Dare pulled her against him then kissed her hair. "I know choosing feels impossible, but everything shall work itself out. After our marriage, we'll return to Wildewall and build the wonderful life full of abiding love and family that we've always wanted. Once our child is born, we can mend your relationship with your parents. Surely they'd want to meet their first grandchild."

Her face pressed against his chest, Annalise sobbed harder. Except Mother and Father would feel so betrayed that they'd likely hate any children she had with Dare and consider those grandchildren nothing more than treacherous Ravenstones.

Dare rubbed soothing circles on her back beneath her cloak. "Please, Annalise, don't sob so. We'll find a way to heal the feud. I promise."

She swallowed a wild laugh at his conviction. Burying her grief at losing her parents if they married, she inhaled his scent to settle herself then swallowed her tears. Lifting her head, she wiped her face. "I should return before I'm missed."

Brushing kisses beneath her damp eyes, Dare nodded then released her to take her arm. "I'll escort you." Before she could protest, he added, "I'll cast an invisibility spell over myself and the angelcats so no one sees us together."

Annalise nodded as her throat tightened at his typical solicitude. Goddess, why must she have to choose between him and her parents? Damn that ridiculous feud.

After calling Finn and Lily, Dare crooned his invisibility spell and vanished but for a faint glow. He asked as they left the park, "When can we meet again? We must settle our plans."

Her heart clenching, she swallowed. Except nothing could be settled until she knew if she was truly pregnant. "Perhaps we can manage to slip away for a few moments at the Landcastles' ball two days from now."

Dare sighed. "I suppose we can't risk another private meeting. 'Tis impossible to control our hunger for each other. We'll likely make love rather than talk." When they reached her family's townhouse, he bent and kissed her cheek beside her mouth. "Until then, my heart."

Fingering his heart-shaped firegem at her throat, Annalise

headed to the stables to visit Storm. The stallion's love should hearten her enough to face her parents over breakfast.

Storm's nickers and nuzzles did help, but when she sat beside him, Alex still frowned at her and asked, "Annalise, are you feeling well? You appear... muted."

Indigo concern flaring about them as well, Mother and Father stilled and eyed her. Mother leaned forward, saying, "Yes, you do appear pale."

Annalise nibbled on a roll and sipped her tea. "I'm fine. My sleep was restless last night." Not exactly a lie.

Mother and Father exchanged a glance then Mother said, "We'll skip Mrs. Reid's salon this afternoon and leave the Nolans' card party early tonight, so you can get additional rest."

Tears pricking her eyes, Annalise nodded and began her heaped plate. Despite their ambitions, Mother and Father genuinely loved her. If only they would accept her marrying Dare.

Alex flashed an impish grin. "Shall we go riding after breakfast? That should energize you."

Father frowned at Alex. "Riding is the opposite of resting, Alexander."

As Alex shrugged in response, Annalise couldn't help a smile. He was a wonderful brother to ask, but she couldn't withstand his questions right now. "Perhaps another time. Enjoy Lady Ducharme's fencing salon."

After breakfast, she retreated to her chambers then released Rain and Aria from their golden birdcage. While the faebirds sang in her hair, she extracted Dare's enchanted heart carving from her bedside table then curled on her bed. Caressing that and fingering his firegem necklace about her neck, she let her mind drift to a delightful fantasy where she and Dare raised their boisterous family in Wildewall and her parents visited often to enjoy their grandchildren. If only her parents would abandon the feud, so that fantasy could become reality.

. . .

WHEN ANNALISE ROSE the following morning, she checked again for the glow of pregnancy, but she could still read nothing. So she sighed then headed downstairs for breakfast.

Midway through, Mother eyed Annalise and said, "You still look pale. You'd better remain home today."

Annalise sipped her tea to conceal her surprise. Mother was letting her skip court events? "I can't. I've a nightmara ride with Kiera this morning."

Mother pursed her lips. "I suppose you can't skip that. But afterward, remain home and rest. None of the court events before the Duke and Duchess of Landcastle's ball tomorrow are important, and you must be well enough to attend that."

Her chest lightening, Annalise smiled at Mother. Not having to endure court events for the next day would be a relief. Too bad Mother and Father would never be as understanding about Dare.

After breakfast, she rode Storm to the palace. She sighed when she met Kiera outside. Her friend was glowing, and the indigo in her aura was brighter than usual. Clearly, King Devon's courtship was progressing well. Doubtless Kiera would agree to marry him in truth soon.

Annalise fingered Dare's faegift at her throat. Although her friend's joy was wonderful, 'twas painful to see when her own life was so impossible. Yet she forced a serene smile and murmured, "You look radiant today."

Kiera blushed and twisted her betrothal ring. "Not as radiant as you."

Annalise almost grimaced. Only thanks to her potent aura as a soul healer, which masked her turmoil. Fortunately, their arrival at the nightmara stables saved her from needing to reply.

While Kiera mounted Moonbud, Darkthorn eyed Annalise and snorted. :*Pregnant, hmm? Not surprising.*:

Annalise touched her stomach, her pulse skittering. How could the nightmara stallion see that when she couldn't? So no one could overhear, she mentally asked, :*You can tell I'm pregnant? How? Through my unborn child's aura?*:

Darkthorn tossed his mane. :*No, nightmara can only read unborn creatures' auras once they can dream. I read your pregnancy from your thoughts.*:

Exhaling, she leapt onto Darkthorn's back. So he didn't know for certain either. Like Dare, he assumed she must be pregnant because of her missed courses. :*If I was truly three weeks pregnant, my powers should have confirmed that, but they haven't.*:

Darkthorn snorted as they followed Moonbud and Kiera from the nightmara paddock. :*Now that you're pregnant, you and Lord Ravenstone can't delay eloping. You humans care greatly that children are born within marriage.*:

Her jaw tightening, Annalise swallowed an annoyed retort. Darkthorn wasn't wrong about bastards being unwelcome, but she'd not requested his advice, and he'd ignored that her pregnancy wasn't certain yet. Despite being able to read her thoughts, the stallion clearly couldn't understand her predicament. She inhaled a steadying breath then asked him about the progress on Moonbud's traps for the plains.

After her nightmara ride, Annalise returned to Greysnowe House and spent the rest of the day ensconced in her chambers with Rain and Aria, resting like Mother had suggested. However, the following morning at dawn, she slipped out for a brisk walk in the park. She couldn't risk a ride because Mother might decide she could attend afternoon court events. After spending time with Storm and breakfast, she returned to her chambers until she and her parents left for the Landcastles' ball.

When they entered Landcastle House, Dare and his mother were already standing near the musicians' balcony. Their matching green auras with bronze motes were almost a beacon in the crowded ballroom. Annalise met Dare's gaze, and their love surged through their entwined souls.

His hunger heating her blood, Dare asked, :*When can we meet?*:

Annalise clung to her serene smile as she greeted the Duke and Duchess of Landcastle. :*I'll slip away as soon as Mother and Father are distracted by gossip or dancing. You'd better distract your mother as well.*:

Dare hummed. :*If she and Lord Islaye or Lady Ducharme start talking, she'll not note my absence. You leave first and find an empty anteroom, then I'll follow.*:

Once she and her parents finished greeting their hosts, Lady Morwynne swept over, and the superior countess began gossiping with her parents, so Annalise left to find Kiera. If Mother and Father didn't notice, then she could slip away from the ball.

She blinked when she greeted Kiera. Unlike yesterday, muddy-yellow despair flared about Kiera, and her overly bright smile was fake. What had happened? Yet a crowded ballroom was no place to ask, so Annalise asked about their next nightmara ride instead.

When King Devon led Kiera out for the first dance, Annalise glanced at Mother and Father, who were still gossiping with Lady Morwynne. Her chest easing, she exhaled and slipped into the closest anteroom. As she waited for Dare to join her, she smoothed her ice-lavender satin ballgown. Goddess, please let this discussion be less turbulent than the last.

CHAPTER 38

When Annalise glided into an anteroom during the first dance, Dare inhaled and set his jaw. He must escape the sultry Lady Blaine, who'd been clinging to his arm since Mother had drifted away with Lord and Lady Islaye. The husband-hunting countess had even remained *after* he'd said he didn't mean to dance tonight. Why did she persist in pursuing him when he clearly wasn't interested?

He wrested his arm free and nodded at Lady Blaine. "Excuse me, I need some air." Then he strode out into the Landcastles' frigid garden. No matter how desperate, a court lady like Lady Blaine wouldn't follow him there.

Running to keep warm, he crossed the garden and returned inside through the drawing room. Then forcing a genial grin, he slipped back into the ballroom and sauntered through the crowd toward the anteroom, but he didn't pause to greet anyone. Annalise was waiting. When he reached the anteroom, he glanced behind him at Mother and Annalise's parents, but Mother was still with Lord and Lady Islaye, and the Greysnowes were speaking to Lady Morwynne. He exhaled. Thankfully, their parents were all too engrossed to notice their absence.

As the music for the second dance began, Dare entered the anteroom and met Annalise's gaze, hunger flaring in their entwined souls. They flew together, and their souls meshed as they devoured each other's mouths. But after a moment, he groaned and lifted his head. "We must stop. Anyone glancing inside the anteroom could see us."

Her eyes navy with passion, Annalise blinked at him, but she lowered her arms and separated their meshed souls. "There's a sofa along the wall beside the door that's out of direct sight."

He made himself release Annalise and step back. Touching her was too dangerous. He burned to make love to her until they collapsed, despite their parents and all of court being in the next room as well as them needing to settle their plans. While they sat on opposite ends of the sofa with him between her and the door, he said, "If anyone enters the anteroom, I'll cast an invisibility spell to ensure we aren't seen together. We can't risk gossip before we elope—your parents might manage to thwart us."

Swallowing, Annalise licked her lips, and he shuddered as his body hardened further. Goddess, how could he concentrate on talking? Yet they must, so he suppressed his hunger as she replied, "I told you we can't elope. My parents shall never forgive such a betrayal. Eloping would destroy any hope of healing the feud."

Dare arched his brows and glanced at her stomach where their child grew. "Surely they'll forgive us when they realize why we did."

Annalise shook her head. "Except that why isn't certain yet. But if 'twas, knowing why would only infuriate them further." She grimaced. "Consider how you'd feel if *I* was your daughter."

He almost winced as that doused his hunger quicker than an icy bath. He'd want to murder his daughter's seducer. "Maybe explaining the irresistible pull of our soulbond would help?"

Annalise twisted his flickering faegift about her neck. "My ancestress explaining that to her former betrothed is what began the feud between our families."

His heart squeezing, Dare risked taking her other hand. "No, my ancestor refusing to forgive her did."

Annalise slid her hand free, her sorrow piercing him. "I suppose. Yet how can I admit our soulbond to Mother and Father? Not only am I soulbound to a Ravenstone, but they'll be hurt when they realize I never shared I was a soul healer with them. And learning I used my secret powers to save their ancestral enemy would only exacerbate that."

He recaptured her hand and kissed her palm to hearten her. "But everyone knows that healers can't help healing any more than the sun can't help shining. Besides, saving me saved your brother from being executed."

Annalise sighed. "Mother and Father were so gleeful that Alex nearly killed you, I doubt they'll agree." She stilled as the music from the ballroom faded. "The second dance just ended. We'd better return before we're missed."

He grimaced but nodded. They couldn't chance their parents hunting the anterooms and discovering them together. "When can we meet next? We didn't settle anything tonight."

Annalise pursed her lips. "The Duke of Oakmoor's soiree, I think. Although Mother and Father refused his offer of courtship like I asked, he didn't rescind his invitation, so we should still attend—he's a wealthy councilor, after all."

Dare rubbed his beard. The duke's soiree was nearly a week away. Not seeing Annalise until then would be excruciating. And their hunger would be even harder to control when they finally met again. Yet if they risked a private meeting, they'd doubtless make love within moments, so they must wait. He sighed and rose. "Very well. I'll return now, and you remain here until after the third dance at least."

His chest aching, he strode back to the ballroom.

After a few steps, Lady Blaine grasped his arm with a coy smile. "Lord Ravenstone, you're back. How was your *air*? And however did you get to that anteroom from the garden?"

He froze, his skin prickling. Why did Lady Blaine sound so mocking?

Lady Blaine fluttered her lashes at him. "I know you said you didn't mean to dance tonight, but surely you can't object to a turn about the ballroom?"

Dare swallowed but nodded. He must distract Lady Blaine from him being in the anteroom until after Annalise emerged.

Purring a laugh, Lady Blaine tugged him toward the refreshments table. "Excellent. Let's fetch some sparkling wine." Once they did, she sipped her drink then smirked at him. "Precisely what I needed after watching a gentleman I was pursuing kiss another lady. 'Tis the second time this season."

He stiffened, his pulse stuttering. Dear Goddess, Lady Blaine *knew*. Why hadn't he checked for her before entering the anteroom like he had Mother and Annalise's parents?

Her presence surrounding him, Annalise asked, :*Dare, what's wrong?*:

Eyeing the smirking countess as she sipped her sparkling wine again, Dare replied, :*Lady Blaine saw us together in the anteroom.*:

Annalise gasped. :*Oh, Goddess. She'll tell all of court before the end of the ball—just like with Wren. What are we going to do?*:

He sent Annalise reassurance through their entwined souls. :*I'll manage something.*:

Lady Blaine finished her drink. "Yes, the sparkling wine definitely helps. I should have asked Wren and Hawke for some last time." She twirled her empty flute before her lips. "So you and Lady Annalise, hmm? I suppose it *would* take a rugged gentleman like you to thaw Lady Snow."

Dare glared at Lady Blaine. From her smug drawl, she'd love telling court about Annalise's scandalous involvement, just like Annalise feared. "What do you intend to do?"

Arching a brow, Lady Blaine waved her empty flute. "Stop pursuing you, of course, and find another wealthy gentleman." She hummed. "Since the Duke of Oakmoor sought to court Lady

Annalise, the aging rakehell must finally be ready to marry. I think I'll start with him. I'd enjoy being wife to the Minister of Foreign Relations."

His jaw twitching, Dare leaned toward Lady Blaine and growled, "I don't care what gentlemen you pursue as long 'tisn't me. Who do you intend to tell about what you saw tonight?"

Lady Blaine moued. "Not very genial when your love is threatened, are you?" She tsked then added, "I shan't tell anyone." She paled, and her lips twisted. "I learned not to meddle after interfering with Wren and Hawke's relationship so disastrously."

He scrutinized the fashionable countess, his chest easing. Could she truly mean that? Gossip about him and Annalise would certainly enhance her prestige at court.

Lady Blaine tossed her head. "I'm being sincere, Lord Raven-stone. I wish you and Lady Annalise the best." She chuckled. "And I can't *wait* to see the Greysnowes' reaction to their perfect, beautiful daughter being a soul healer and marrying their ances-tral enemy instead of King Devon." As the music quieted, she tugged his arm. "Escort me to the Duke of Oakmoor, so he can ask for my next dance."

Relaxing, Dare took Lady Blaine's arm and handed her empty flute to a nearby servant. She evidently preferred finding a new husband to gossip. "Thank you for your discretion."

He escorted Lady Blaine across the ballroom to the Duke of Oakmoor then escaped with a sigh. As the fourth dance began, he retreated to the garden door and glanced about for Mother and Annalise's parents. All three were still engrossed with their companions from earlier.

When Annalise emerged midway through the dance, she hovered outside the anteroom without glancing at him. :*Well?*:

Sipping his sparkling wine, he made himself watch the dancers rather than stare at Annalise. :*Lady Blaine swears that she shan't gossip about us, and I believe her.*:

Annalise sighed, her unease surging through him. :*We'll see.*:

As Annalise rejoined King Devon and Lady Kiera, Dare sent her his love through their entwined souls. Hopefully, 'twould reassure her. :*Whatever happens, we'll manage.*:

When the next dance began, Lord and Lady Islaye glided onto the floor, so Mother bustled back to Dare. She flashed a wry smile then said, "I see Lady Blaine is still hunting you."

He nodded at Lady Blaine and the Duke of Oakmoor, who were dancing their second dance in a row. "Not after learning the Duke of Oakmoor wants to marry. He's much better game."

Mother hummed and tilted her head. "Now that you've escaped the fashionable countess, you should go dance with a lady you wish to court. Since I arrived in Ormas, I've not seen you dance with or approach any available ladies. How can you expect to find a wife like that?"

Dare gripped his flute of sparkling wine. Not surprising that Mother had noticed, but since consummating his soulbond with Annalise, he couldn't feign courting anyone else, even if they were uninterested like Miss Winston or Miss Hawke. He made himself smile at Mother. "You forget that I've been at court for over half a year, so I'm well acquainted with all the ladies here."

Her eyes narrowing, Mother hummed again. "Yet you court none of them. If you find ladies in Ormas so uninteresting, why haven't you returned to Wildewall?"

He swallowed and handed his half-empty flute to a nearby servant. He'd break it soon otherwise. His throat clenching at deceiving Mother, he replied, "Because the likelihood of a new lady arriving is much higher in Ormas than back home, and I must find a wife."

Mother pursed her lips. "I suppose that's true." She sighed. "Since you don't intend to dance, shall we return to Ravenstone House?"

Dare nodded, his throat easing. Spending the rest of the evening not staring at Annalise and feigning indifference while Mother watched him would be torturous. He smiled and escorted Mother from the crowded ballroom.

. . .

DARE TOOK Mother to Blacke Woods the following day and made sure they returned too late to attend the Escanas' rout party that evening. He didn't want Mother noticing him still not courting anyone. So he'd continue avoiding court events until the Duke of Oakmoor's soiree when he could meet Annalise. Mother would notice, but she'd assume 'twas because he needed more time to visit natural areas and revive his powers.

Then early the following morning, Dare met Alex above the royal bay for their sword fight and ride. As Alex lunged forward with his sword outstretched, he frowned and said, "I'm concerned about Annalise. She's been upset the past few days, but she refuses to tell me why."

His chest tight, Dare flicked aside Alex's sword. Her pregnancy forcing her to choose between him and her family was why she was upset, even though she kept insisting she might not be pregnant. But he couldn't tell her brother about her pregnancy. "If 'twas truly important, I'm certain she'd tell you."

Alex hummed, his eyes narrowing. "I don't think she would. Although she loves me, she's extremely private." He feinted. "Why, she's not even told me the name of the gentleman she loves, although she wears his faegift every day."

Dare stiffened as he parried then riposted. If only she would tell Alex, then Alex likely wouldn't be angry to learn about their involvement, and they'd have one ally. "Perhaps she doesn't wish to burden you."

Alex snorted and lunged forward. "That *does* sound like Annalise. I'll simply need to pester her until she confesses the truth." He grinned. "Starting as soon as I return to Greysnowe House."

Suppressing a wince, Dare danced beyond Alex's reach. Her brother's pestering would upset Annalise even more, which she didn't need while carrying his child. "Don't pester her. She'll confess when she's ready."

Alex attacked again, his sword glinting. "She'll never confess unless I pester her."

Dare grimaced and slipped past Alex's guard to win their sword fight. Alex was obviously determined. Too bad he couldn't warn Annalise, but unless she reacted naturally, Alex would suspect the truth, and she wasn't ready to tell him yet.

CHAPTER 39

When Annalise returned from her nightmara ride two days after the Landcastles' ball, Alex was leaning against Storm's stall door. Grinning, he said, "Finally. I've been waiting for ages."

She blinked at Alex as she slid from the saddle. Waiting? Why? She arched her brows. "Oh?"

Alex opened the stall and waved for her and Storm to enter. Once they did, he shut the stall door and leaned over it toward them. "I wanted to speak with you about why you've been upset the past few days."

Annalise froze. Oh, Goddess. What could she say? She forced her fingers to resume unbuckling Storm's girth. As she hung his saddle on the stall door, she replied, "I'm not upset."

Snorting, Alex handed her a hoof pick. "I mentioned your silence to a friend during our visit to the royal bay this morning, and he said you might be remaining silent to not burden me with your secrets."

She froze again while cleaning Storm's hooves. Alex was discussing her with *Dare*? Why? And why hadn't Dare warned her?

Alex leaned closer. "He's right, isn't he?"

Annalise swallowed and made herself clean Storm's last hoof. Then she rose and accepted the curry comb from Alex. "I don't wish to discuss it."

Muddy-yellow hurt swirling about him, Alex frowned at her. "You can trust me with your secrets, I promise."

She winced then finished grooming Storm. She'd not meant to hurt her brother with her secrecy. Sighing, she patted Storm, who nickered and nuzzled her, then left his stall. "I do trust you. But if I told you, we'd be unable to resist speaking about it again, and someone might overhear us." Like Lady Blaine had at the Landcastles' ball. She shuddered. "And whoever overheard us might tell Mother and Father."

Alex scowled while they strode from the stables and into the townhouse. "We could keep our conversations to when we're completely alone."

Pursing her lips, Annalise nodded at Wilson beside the front door. Their family's servants were everywhere in the townhouse, and most's first loyalty was to Mother and Father. "Like we are right now?"

Alex scowled harder. "No, I thought during our rides."

She sighed as they began up the stairs. They'd be completely alone then, but if Alex knew about her soulbond with Dare and her possible pregnancy, he'd doubtless treat her differently. And that would make Mother and Father suspicious. "I'm sorry, Alex, but I can't risk telling you."

His jaw clenching, Alex grunted. "Since you won't tell me, perhaps I should have Jack ask Grace what she knows."

A chill skittering across her skin, Annalise gripped Dare's heart-shaped firegem. Although she and her maid hadn't discussed her possible pregnancy, Grace had brought her mentha tea and dry toast first thing every morning since she'd missed her courses, likely to help ease the nausea common with early pregnancy. Yet Grace was too loyal to tell anyone her mistress might be pregnant, but if her favorite cousin asked often enough, she might inadvertently reveal something. When they reached upstairs, Annalise whirled to glare at Alex. "Don't make your valet pester my maid."

Glaring back, Alex leaned toward her. "Fine. I won't. But I *am* going to keep pestering you to tell me." He tapped her fingers gripping Dare's faegift. "Concealing the truth from everyone isn't healthy."

She jerked back and dropped Dare's firegem like the hardened dragon flame inside had burned her. As a rare and coveted soul healer soulbound to her family's ancestral enemy and possibly carrying his child, she'd no choice *but* to conceal the truth. "You pestering me shall simply make it worse."

Alex tsked and shook his head. "Only until you tell me the truth. Then you'll feel relieved someone else knows."

Annalise glowered at Alex's back as he strolled to his chambers. Little brothers could be so vexing. She sighed, her shoulders sagging. Although he wasn't wrong. Alex knowing everything would be a relief. But she just couldn't risk it.

AFTER THAT, Annalise avoided being alone with Alex by remaining close to Mother. She couldn't bear Alex pestering her about Dare again. She'd either begin crying or confess everything—or both. But remaining close to Mother meant she had to endure Mother's endless gripes about Dare's mother and the feud.

By the time she and Mother attended Lady Treyvan's salon two afternoons later, she'd had enough of Mother's griping. Fortunately, she could escape by initiating a close conversation with another lady. She glanced about the drawing room. Too bad Wren and Kiera weren't here—she'd enjoy talking with them.

Annalise stilled at Lady Blaine sitting on a sofa with space for only one other lady. The perfect escape from Mother, and she must talk to Lady Blaine to verify Dare's belief the fashionable countess wouldn't gossip. So she glided across the drawing room and settled beside Lady Blaine on the sofa.

Her smoky eyes gleaming, Lady Blaine purred a laugh. "Lady Annalise, *what* a surprise you've joined me."

Scrutinizing Lady Blaine's driven red aura to detect any lies, Annalise leaned toward her and murmured too quiet for anyone else to hear, "He said you shan't gossip about us."

Lady Blaine smiled and murmured back, "And I shan't." Muddy-blue anguish flared about her. "Gossiping about Wren and Hawke was senseless and cost me dearly, so I swore never to do so again."

Annalise blinked at Lady Blaine. Cost her how? Lady Blaine was as fashionable as ever, and she was still invited to events hosted by Wren's husband's family, like his sister-in-law's salon today. Yet Dare was right—Lady Blaine was sincere about not gossiping about them.

Lady Blaine held her gaze. "Agree to marry him soon. You're fortunate to have someone who adores you so." She inhaled, her aura clearing. "Although you should wait to start a family, so court doesn't assume 'tis why you eloped."

Her stomach fluttering, Annalise stared at Lady Blaine. Was the sultry countess mocking her? She reviewed what Lady Blaine had overheard. Although she and Dare had discussed her powers and their soulbond, they'd only hinted at her possible pregnancy. She exhaled. So perhaps Lady Blaine didn't know everything.

Her gaze flicking about the drawing room, Lady Blaine chuckled. "We'd better quit whispering. All the other ladies shall gossip since we've never been close."

Annalise straightened. True, so she must provide an excuse for their private conversation. But what? She and Lady Blaine had little in common other than both being attractive. The last they'd spoken had been two weeks ago when Dare and Lady Blaine had rescued her and Kiera from Mr. Winston at the sirenic play. She hummed. Perhaps Mr. Winston's banishment last week would do. Most at court didn't seem aware of it yet.

She flashed a serene smile and raised her voice enough the

ladies beside them could hear, "And then King Devon banished Mr. Winston from Ormas, so you needn't worry about him pestering you again."

Lady Blaine's eyes widened briefly, then she smirked. "Me and all the other ladies in Ormas."

Annalise rose then greeted their hostess, Lady Treyvan, who appeared tired as she rubbed her rounded stomach and discussed art with her friends. Annalise fingered Dare's firegem necklace to avoid touching her own stomach. If she was pregnant, she'd be the same as Lady Treyvan in just half a year. She swallowed. Please let either her tardy courses start soon or her powers read the glow of pregnancy, so she'd know for certain.

ALTHOUGH SHE USUALLY ROSE EARLY, Annalise slept well past dawn the following morning, and Grace had to shake her awake to attend her nightmara ride. Her worry over her possible pregnancy must be upsetting her sleep. Nibbling on her breakfast of dry toast, much less than she usually ate, as she rode Storm through Ormas, Annalise focused her powers on her stomach, but she *still* couldn't read the glow of pregnancy. Goddess, why?

When she and Kiera arrived in the nightmara paddock, Darkthorn eyed her. :*Do you need help mounting? You appear weary.*:

She sighed. She *was* weary, but Kiera would notice if she mounted differently than usual. She murmured, "I'll manage."

Darkthorn hummed as she hauled herself atop his back. :*I'll keep to a walk today.*: Once they followed Kiera and Moonbud from the nightmara paddock, he added, :*You should visit the veiled witch. Although she's a seer not a healer, she might know something that can help you or know a Rhiannon-descendant witch healer who could.*:

Annalise swallowed, her skin prickling. The veiled witch might be able to read if she was pregnant or not, but the seer would also see all her other secrets as well. Too dangerous. "I'll be fine. I just need some restful sleep."

So after she returned from her exhausting nightmara ride, she devoured an early luncheon then collapsed into slumber and slept until Grace woke her shortly before dinner to help her into a simple navy gown for tonight.

Then during dinner, Mother leaned forward with a frown. "At the Duke of Oakmoor's soiree tonight, remember to watch for Lord Ravenstone and his vile mother. Who knows what wicked scheme they're plotting. They'd love to best or humiliate us at such a significant court event."

Annalise almost raised her eyes skyward. Not more griping about Dare's mother and the feud. "I promise I'll watch for them." Because she and Dare must slip away to talk. Hopefully, without anyone seeing them this time.

When she and her parents arrived at Oakmoor House, Annalise hid a grimace as Lady Morwynne joined them before they'd greeted their host. Wonderful, the devious countess would surely provoke Mother and Father, so they'd act even more outrageously tonight.

To avoid that, she left them behind to join Kiera and King Devon greeting the Duke of Oakmoor and Lady Blaine, who was acting as his hostess. From the smoldering glances between the duke and Lady Blaine, the two must be courting. Annalise nearly chuckled. A *much* better match than her and the duke or Dare and Lady Blaine.

Her gaze bright with laughter, Lady Blaine smiled at Annalise as she approached. "Evening, Lady Annalise. Where are your parents?"

Suppressing another grimace at the reminder, Annalise smiled back and halted beside Kiera. "They're in the hall conversing with Lady Morwynne."

Once she and the Duke of Oakmoor had exchanged polite greetings, she, Kiera, and King Devon continued into the drawing room. She tensed when her parents and Lady Morwynne joined them while King Devon was handing her and Kiera flutes of sparkling wine. The smirk curving Lady

Morwynne's lips was much too smug.

Without glancing at Kiera beside her, Father frowned at Annalise. "You squander entirely too much time with this Ravenstone pawn."

As Mother nodded, Annalise almost flushed, and her temples tightened. Lady Morwynne had definitely provoked Mother and Father for them to be so churlish to their future queen in public.

Before she could reply, Kiera beamed at Mother and Father then said, "I'd not call enjoying time with a friend squandering."

When Mother's eyes narrowed, Annalise lifted her chin and blurted to forestall Mother, "Neither would I."

Muddy-red frustration flickering about her, Mother pursed her lips. "You should be dancing. 'Tis unfortunate Lady Blaine landed the elusive Duke of Oakmoor. He's eminently suitable, even if he invited the treacherous Ravenstones to his soiree."

Annalise stilled. *What* had Lady Morwynne said to make Mother mention the Duke of Oakmoor like that after they'd refused him for her? Thank the Goddess Dare and his mother hadn't arrived yet—in her current mood, Mother likely would have stormed across the drawing room and hurled a flute of sparkling wine in Lady Ravenstone's face.

Her temples now throbbing, Annalise exhaled. "I don't want to *land* an *eminently suitable* gentleman."

Mother and Father blinked at her as muddy-orange shock flared about them. Then Mother turned to Father and asked, "Why did the Goddess curse us with such an obstinate child?"

The indigo in her aura deepening, Kiera frowned at Mother and took Annalise's arm. "Good fortune, perhaps? Come, Annalise." She drew Annalise away with King Devon striding behind them. Once they were out of earshot, she muttered to Annalise, "Sorry to be brusque to your parents. But they should value you as more than a means to further their ambitions."

Annalise squeezed Kiera's arm, warmth suffusing her chest. Kiera was truly the most devoted friend. "They do, despite allowing their ambition to blind them at times. Plus, I've never expressed that opinion so bluntly before to avoid upsetting them, so they were disconcerted."

Kiera hummed and began to reply, until a beaming Lord and Lady Weston waylaid them, and Lady Weston flung her arms about Kiera.

When Lady Weston drew Kiera away to discuss her granddaughters, who'd briefly lived under Kiera's care at her former orphanage, Annalise inhaled as her soulbond flared at Dare's arrival. Not allowing herself to turn around, she mentally said, *:We should meet somewhere no one shall see us tonight.:*

As King Devon halted beside her rather than joining Kiera with the Westons, Dare replied, *:How about the garden? 'Tis too frigid for most of court, but I can cast a warming spell. I'll slip outside as soon as Mother and I finish greeting the Duke of Oakmoor and Lady Blaine. Then you can follow me.:*

She smiled. Dare was so solicitous. *:Sounds good.:*

While Dare headed outside, King Devon, who was watching Kiera with a loving smile, leaned toward Annalise and murmured, "Have you noticed a secret weighing on Kiera recently?"

Her neck prickling, Annalise swallowed. Kiera had been distressed the past few days, but the only secret she'd discussed with Kiera had been her being a soul healer. She fingered Dare's faegift at her throat. But why would that secret weigh on Kiera? "I don't believe so."

As King Devon sighed and kept watching Kiera, Annalise excused herself then handed her untouched flute of sparkling wine to a servant before entering the garden to meet Dare.

CHAPTER 40

As soon as Annalise glided into the Duke of Oakmoor's garden, Dare's heart quickened, and burning hunger flared in their entwined souls. It had been so long since they'd been alone in such a romantically dark and secluded garden—Lady Blaine's fire ball. He captured Annalise's hand and drew her into the alcove he'd warmed by calling heat from deep inside the earth. As they sank onto the stone bench, he whispered a faint light spell that allowed them to see each other then grew ivy across the alcove to conceal the light.

Staring into each other's eyes, he pulled her into his lap while she wrapped her arms about his neck. As he seized her mouth in a ravenous kiss, their souls meshed, and her heady honeysuckle scent swamped him. His body hardened when she purred and buried her fingers in his hair. Goddess, he needed her. He slid his hand beneath her navy skirt and up her legs.

Annalise shuddered before suddenly stiffening and wrenching their mouths and souls apart. :*Your mother just entered the garden.*:

Dare doused his light and warming spells because, as powerful Rhiannon descendants, he and Mother could always sense nature magic. And having often performed magic together, they easily recognized each other's magical signature. Even so, after releasing his other spells, he cast a nature mimicry spell about him and Annalise. Although they were both wearing dark clothes, her white-blonde hair was too radiant to miss, even at night and behind a curtain of ivy. To prevent Mother from locating them, he infused his nature magic throughout the garden.

As the air in the alcove froze, he drew Annalise closer to warm her. :*Remember, don't move.*:

Annalise shivered against him. :*I'll try, but 'tis freezing without your warming spell.*:

His chest squeezing, he risked warming the air about Annalise's skin. Goddess, let his nature magic throughout the garden be enough to mask that warming spell as well as his nature mimicry spell.

No longer shivering, Annalise kissed his throat without moving. :*Thanks, my love.*:

Then through the ivy covering the alcove, he and Annalise watched Mother bustle through the dark garden and peer into every hidden corner and alcove. They quit breathing when her gaze stilled on their alcove and she strode closer.

After several agonizing moments, Mother blinked and shook her head then rushed past them to check the rest of the garden.

Dare met Annalise's darkened eyes as they relaxed and silently gulped a breath. They should be safe as long as Mother didn't return to their alcove.

Soon Mother finished checking the garden and hurried back inside.

He and Annalise sagged against each other. He released his nature mimicry spell then recast his light and warming spells. "That was close."

Annalise shuddered, her chagrin bolting through him. "Too close. We were so engrossed kissing that I almost didn't notice her entering the garden."

Dare echoed her shudder. If Annalise hadn't noticed Mother's aura, Mother would have stumbled on them. *Not* how he wanted Mother to discover their involvement.

As her chagrin turned rueful, Annalise pursed her lips. "We should avoid meeting in gardens during court events. We forget ourselves too easily. The pull of our consummated soulbond is becoming too irresistible to fight."

He swallowed. Except she was carrying his child and deserved nothing less than tenderness from him. He should have been more gentle. He rubbed soothing circles on her back. "Annalise, I'm sorry."

Annalise blinked, her confusion darting through him. "For what?"

He forced himself to set her on the stone bench. His ears burning as he repaired his disheveled clothes, he muttered, "For almost ravishing you."

Smoothing her rumpled gown, Annalise blushed. "I was just as eager as you were. In truth, we almost ravished each other."

Dare sighed. True, but still. "I was too rough with you—after all, you're pregnant."

Annalise glowered at him. "*Possibly* pregnant—my powers still can't read any glow of pregnancy. But even if I am carrying your child, being pregnant wouldn't make me delicate."

He eyed Annalise. Her courses were over a week late, so she *must* be pregnant. Clearly, she was clinging to her powers not confirming her pregnancy to avoid having to choose between him and her parents. Yet they couldn't wait forever to elope. He hummed. "*If* you're pregnant, how soon until you begin to show?"

Annalise tilted her head. "Around three months—unless I'm carrying twins."

Dare nodded, his heart swelling as energy surged through him. So a month before Plantfete, and they'd be parents a month after Summerday. "We must elope before you show, preferably soon. Not only shall others realize you're pregnant, but our child should be born in Wildewall, and traveling shall be difficult for you if we wait too long. Perhaps we should purchase a flying carpet to hasten the long journey home."

Annalise stiffened then pulled away. "You make everything sound *so* simple. As if our families weren't ancestral enemies, and my parents shan't disown me for marrying you."

Leaning toward her, he grasped her hands and kissed her palms. Somehow, he must convince her this time. "Not simple, but necessary. Our child deserves a name, and we deserve to be happy."

Tears shimmered in Annalise's cerulean eyes. "How can I be happy after destroying my own family?"

Dare enfolded her in his arms and kissed her hair to comfort her. "That *shall* hurt, but we'll build a new family together. I love you enough to try, and I know you feel the same."

Annalise sighed against his throat. "Dare, I love you too, but I also love my family and can't bear upsetting them."

He squeezed her tighter. "I know, but consider what I said." He lowered his arms. "We'd better return to the soiree." Mother would doubtless check the garden again soon.

Nodding, Annalise leapt upright then swayed.

His pulse racing, Dare surged to his feet and pulled Annalise against him. Damnation, he'd *definitely* been too rough with her earlier. "Are you all right?"

Annalise hummed with a wry smile then patted his chest. "Just a bit lightheaded. I'll rise slower in the future."

He relaxed then stepped back and took Annalise's arm. Withdrawing the ivy from across the alcove, he escorted her through the garden, but not toward the drawing room. "So our parents, or anyone else, don't connect our disappearances, we'll return inside through the ballroom. Then you can rejoin the soiree from the hall while I head back to the garden and enter that way."

Annalise frowned as they swept into the dark and still ballroom. "But then your mother shall realize you were in the garden when she checked."

Releasing his warming spell, Dare shrugged then escorted

Annalise to the hall. "She already knows. I had to infuse the garden with my magic to disguise the spells about us. So she'd be more suspicious if I returned from elsewhere." He brushed a kiss against Annalise's lips then made himself release her. "Until later, my heart."

Her love flooding him, Annalise caressed his face then turned and glided into the hall.

He strode back through the empty ballroom and frigid garden to the drawing room. Just before the door, he released his light spell and inhaled a bracing breath. Time to face Mother.

The moment he entered, Mother bustled over and grasped his arm. "Finally. Where were you?"

Dare met her gaze and gritted a faint smile. "Concealed in one of the garden alcoves." Not precisely a lie.

Mother hummed then leaned closer and inhaled. "I see. Why?"

His neck prickling, he managed to shrug. Had Mother noticed Annalise's honeysuckle scent on him like Lady Blaine had? He swallowed then lied, "I didn't gather enough natural energy during our ride this morning."

Humming again, Mother squeezed his arm. "Then we must remain at the royal bay twice as long tomorrow. We can bring a picnic, so we needn't return for luncheon."

Dare sighed as his prickling faded. Thank the Goddess Mother had accepted his lie. "Sounds good."

Mother flashed a vibrant grin. "Shall we leave? King Devon and Lady Kiera left ages ago."

He nodded and escorted Mother across the drawing room to say farewell to the Duke of Oakmoor and Lady Blaine. However, after Mother's questions, he kept his eyes averted from Annalise, who was standing with her parents near the refreshments table. Mother would surely notice any intimate glances between them.

· · ·

THE FOLLOWING MORNING, Dare jerked awake when Thom shook his shoulder and asked, "Aren't you riding with Lady Ravenstone soon?"

Rubbing the sleep from his eyes, Dare slid from bed as Lily and Finn stretched on the covers while Raven and Bear stirred before the glowing fireplace. "I am. Thanks for waking me."

After yanking on his riding clothes and greatcoat with Thom's help, Dare herded his magical pets to the kitchen and fed them before he snatched some rolls stuffed with meat and cheese to eat in the saddle.

Mother eyed his full hands when he joined her in the entrance hall. "Overslept, I see. Unusual for you, even during late autumn. You *must* be short on natural energy."

He nodded but stifled a grimace. Except he wasn't. Unlike most nature witches, his and Mother's powers weren't tied to the seasons. And although he'd cast multiple spells in the garden with Annalise last night, his powers weren't drained. Perhaps the stress of lying to Mother had marred his rest and made him oversleep.

While he and Mother rode through the empty streets of Ormas, Dare devoured his stuffed rolls. Then they trotted to the royal bay and flung out their powers to gather the natural energy around them. As Mother had promised, they kept gathering twice as long as yesterday, so when they finally stopped, he was ravenous, and his magic was overflowing. He and Mother were debating where to lay out their blanket to eat luncheon when approaching hoofbeats interrupted them.

Galloping across the sand toward them, Alex called, "Hey, Dare."

Dare rubbed his beard as he eyed Annalise's brother. Why was Alex here? Their ride wasn't for another three days.

His usual grin missing, Alex halted Biscuit before them. "Thank the Goddess you're still here. Sorry to intrude, but I must speak with you."

As Mother's brows rose, Dare swallowed and clenched

Ebony's reins, and his chest tightened. Had something happened to Annalise? He'd not sensed anything through their soulbond. He waved for Alex to continue.

Frowning, Alex leaned forward in the saddle. "I'm worried about Annalise. She's been avoiding me since I asked her why she's upset recently."

Dare sighed. Not surprising since Annalise was determined not to tell Alex about their involvement.

Alex's frown deepened. "And this morning, I learned she's not been rising early for her morning walks or rides the past few days. 'Tisn't like her at all—she told me that she *needs* those daily outings to survive her seasons in Ormas. I think she may be ill."

Suppressing a wince, Dare shifted on Ebony. Annalise was pregnant not ill, although he couldn't tell her brother that. As Mother's gaze darted between him and Alex, Dare shrugged and replied, "Perhaps the mornings have become too cold for her. It *is* just over a month before Longnight."

Alex grunted. "I *suppose* that could be the reason." He drooped atop Biscuit. "I wish Annalise would simply talk to me. She's so alone right now—even Finn and his mate have abandoned her. I've not seen the angelcats for at least a week."

Tensing, Dare forced himself to smile. Please let Mother not realize that Annalise's angelcats were Lily and her mate. "Annalise shall talk to you when she's ready."

His eyes narrow, Alex scrutinized Dare's face. "If you say so." He sighed. "I should go. I'm meeting Arthur for luncheon at The Gold Griffin. Thanks for the advice."

After Alex left, Mother arched her brows at Dare. "Does Lord Alexander ask you about his sister often?"

He managed a shrug. "Alex asks my thoughts on many things. We're close friends."

Mother hummed. Then she gestured toward the cliffs. "Let's eat luncheon up there. No sand, and the view is stunning."

Dare nodded, and they rode up the cliffs. After luncheon

while trotting back to Ormas, he reached out to Annalise, :*We should exchange the angelcats. Alex has noticed their absence.*:

Annalise sighed then replied, :*Of course he has. How about we meet at the park after your ride to the royal bay tomorrow? Although we can't risk touching—we forget ourselves in parks as well as gardens.*:

He swallowed a chuckle. So they did. He sent her his love through their entwined souls. :*Sounds good. See you tomorrow.*:

When he met Annalise in the park midmorning the following day with the angelcats, he stiffened as his chest clenched. Perhaps Alex was right about her being ill. She was paler than usual with faint smudges beneath her eyes, and her radiance was almost muted with a wispy gray fog about her transparent aura with electrum motes. "Annalise, are you well?"

CHAPTER 41

Aching to fly into Dare's arms and kiss him, Annalise clenched her hands by her sides to remain still. Kisses would only lead to them making love against a tree. And unlike their usual dawn meetings, most of court was about now, so someone would likely see them. Besides, she must return to her family's townhouse before she was missed.

She smiled at Dare then answered his question about her health, "I'm fine. A bit more tired than usual thanks to worrying about my possible pregnancy."

Dare leaned toward her, his concern bleeding into their entwined souls. "Are you certain that's all? You appear exhausted."

She almost grimaced. Not surprising. Although she'd begun sleeping far later than she used to, she never felt as if she'd had enough rest. But 'twas simply because her sleep was restless, and admitting her fatigue would just worry Dare further. So she sent him reassurance through their entwined souls and said, "Nothing a long nap shan't fix."

Dare hummed and smoothed his beard. "Well, I suppose you'll be better in about eight months or so." He narrowed his eyes at her. "And you'll be my wife well before then."

Her chest squeezing, Annalise lifted her chin. Why must Dare keep insisting she must be pregnant when her powers still hadn't confirmed it? "I've no time to debate that again. I must return before I'm missed."

She called for Finn and Lily, and they bounded from the trees to rub her skirt and purr. Waving at Dare, she hurried from the park with the angelcats prowling beside her.

As soon as she returned to her family's townhouse, Alex grasped her arm, muddy-yellow worry swirling about him. "Where have you been?"

Annalise sighed. So much for not being missed. She waved toward Finn and Lily. "Walking with the angelcats in the park."

Alex grunted then pulled her into the empty morning room and shut the door behind them and the angelcats. "You should have been resting rather than walking alone in the park."

Sighing again, she sank onto the sofa then scratched Finn's chin when he leapt into her lap. "I wasn't alone—Finn and his mate were with me." And so was Dare, not that she could tell Alex that.

As Lily also leapt into her lap to demand petting, Alex scowled and flung himself beside her on the sofa. "Even so, you shouldn't have been walking without another person. You appear tired. What if you had collapsed?"

Annalise stopped petting the angelcats to squeeze Alex's shoulder. He was such a wonderful brother to worry so. "That's hardly likely. I swear I'm fine."

Alex sighed and leaned toward her. "I wish you'd confide in me."

She rose, dumping Finn and Lily from her lap, who grumbled meows. She must get Alex to quit pestering her about that. "I told you I can't."

Then she hurried from the morning room and began upstairs with the still grumbling angelcats following her.

She was halfway up the steps when Mother called, "Annalise,

there you are. We must leave for the Blakeley's autumn garden party."

Gripping the banister, Annalise shifted to conceal Lily as she turned to face Mother and Father, who were frowning up at her. She couldn't risk them asking questions about her second angel-cat. "Do you mind if I remain here to rest instead?"

Indigo concern flaring about them, Mother and Father exchanged a glance. Then Mother sighed and said, "Very well. You appear like you need it."

Annalise managed to smile at her parents. "Thanks." Then walking behind Finn and Lily to conceal them, she headed upstairs to her chambers before collapsing into slumber.

THE FOLLOWING MORNING, Annalise groaned when Grace woke her for her nightmara ride. Goddess, she needed more sleep. Even sleeping all afternoon yesterday then convincing her parents to leave the Osteens' musical evening early last night hadn't helped. Yet she couldn't skip her nightmara ride—Kiera expected her support.

She hauled herself from bed and focused her powers on her stomach like she had every morning for the past two weeks. Then she gasped, her pulse quickening. Her potent aura *finally* no longer masked the glow of pregnancy.

A surge of tenderness suffusing her, she smiled and pressed a hand against her stomach. Her and Dare's child was growing there. For the first time, she didn't tense at that possibility, but instead light filled her chest.

Annalise started when Grace coughed then handed her mentha tea and dry toast. Blushing, Annalise ate her snack then let Grace help her into a riding habit. She'd no time to sit around musing.

While she rode Storm across Ormas, she devoured several rolls stuffed with meat and cheese. However, the entire time, her mind was whirling and focused on her and Dare's unborn child.

Would they be a girl or a boy? Would they be a soul healer or nature witch or neither? Would they resemble her or Dare? What if she was carrying *twins* like Wren?

Yet her reverie halted when she met Kiera outside the palace. Muddy-yellow despair glowed about her friend like it had the past week. What could be distressing Kiera? A secret like King Devon suggested? Annalise's throat tightened. Goddess, *could* it be her being a soul healer? She coughed then said, "At the Duke of Oakmoor's soiree, King Devon asked if I'd noticed a secret weighing on you."

Kiera tensed and eyed her. "What did you tell him?"

Annalise fingered Dare's heart-shaped firegem at her throat. From Kiera's pained expression, it *must* be about her being a soul healer. She made herself shrug. "What could I tell him? I knew 'twas my secret weighing on you." She grimaced. "I feel so guilty for coming between you and the king."

Kiera twisted her betrothal ring then pursed a wry smile. "You didn't. If you'd not healed me, I never could have made love to him that night."

Annalise gaped at her friend. *That* must be why Kiera had glowed at their nightmara ride after her soul-healing. But why had her joy turned to despair the following day? "You? Oh..."

Kiera blushed. "I know our betrothal is only temporary, but I couldn't resist him any longer."

Annalise swallowed. Just like she couldn't resist Dare. Almost blushing to match Kiera as making love to Dare echoed through her, she forced herself to release his faegift with a sigh. "Because you love him."

The indigo in her aura flaring, Kiera blushed darker and nodded. Despite not admitting her love aloud, she clearly adored King Devon as much as he adored her. They were so perfect for each other.

When Kiera turned away and studied the nearing nightmara stables, Annalise couldn't help caressing Dare's necklace again. Like her friend and King Devon, she and Dare adored each other and were perfect together—if not for their families' feud. She touched her stomach with her free hand. And they were about to have a child together. A child she already adored as much as she did Dare and would do anything to protect.

She set her jaw. Dare was right—they couldn't allow the ancestral strife between their families and her parents' blind rancor to prevent them from ensuring their child's happiness as well as their own. And waiting for Mother and Father to forgive the past and live in harmony with the Ravenstones was futile.

She swallowed as tears pricked her eyes. Although Mother and Father would never forgive her for such a betrayal, she must elope with Dare. And soon, before Alex or Mother and Father realized she was pregnant.

As she and Kiera reached the nightmara stables, Annalise lowered her hands and fisted them by her sides. After her nightmara ride, she must contact Dare to meet. Planning their elopement would be easier in person.

Darkthorn snorted and flicked his tail when she and Kiera entered the nightmara paddock. :*I see you've decided to be sensible at last.*:

While Moonbud told Kiera how their first lesson about jumping would proceed, Annalise climbed atop Darkthorn and barely resisted yanking the stallion's mane. Must he be so smug? "I have. When are you nightmara going to be sensible and renew the treaty with Kiera?"

Darkthorn's ears darted back. :*Unfair. We'd have renewed the treaty as soon as Kiera arrived, except King Devon requested time to court her and earn her trust.*:

She blinked. Well, that explained Kiera's riding lessons. She smiled at her friend trotting over poles atop Moonbud. Considering how Kiera adored King Devon, his plan was close to succeeding. She chuckled. Yet she and Dare would be wed far sooner than Kiera and King Devon—royal weddings required months of preparation.

She patted Darkthorn's back. Despite his smugness, she

shouldn't have lashed out and upset him. "Sorry, that **was** unfair. How's the creation of Moonbud's traps going?" They discussed that for the rest of the ride.

When Annalise dismounted after Moonbud declared today's lesson finished, black spots flickered before her eyes, and her knees wobbled. She gripped Darkthorn's mane to remain upright. Goddess, she was exhausted. She touched her stomach again. No doubt her recent fatigue had been due to her early pregnancy, not restless sleep. She must make sure to get more rest—starting with a nap when she returned to her family's townhouse.

Kiera eyed her as they began back to the palace. "Are you attending the Merrileas' shokolat party this afternoon?"

Sighing, Annalise nodded. She'd rather nap instead, except she and Dare could arrange to meet there. "Mother refuses to miss court events held by councilors or dukes and duchesses, no matter how trivial."

Kiera tsked. "Devon and I shan't be there. I'll be visiting the orphanage, and he has an important meeting. The Duke and Duchess of Merrilea are so easygoing that they shan't mind us missing their party. However, we'll be attending the Magehavens' ball tomorrow evening, so I'll see you then."

Annalise hid a grimace. Mother had already demanded she wear her new rose satin ballgown and most recent natalday diamonds for the Duke and Duchess of Magehaven's ball. Not that she'd replace Dare's perfect necklace with the elaborate set of jewelry from Mother and Father. Hopefully, Mother would be satisfied with just the ballgown. She sighed again. "I'll definitely be there."

Kiera beamed at her as they reached the palace. Then they said their goodbyes, and Annalise headed to the stables to fetch Storm.

As she rode across Ormas, she gathered her waning energy and reached out to Dare, :*Shall you be at the Merrileas' shokolat party this afternoon?*:

His loving presence warming her more than her riding cloak, Dare hummed then replied, :*Yes, Mother and I shall both attend.*:

Annalise forced herself to conceal her thoughts and exhaustion. Dare deserved to hear in person that she was definitely pregnant and wanted to elope, and he'd worry too much about her exhaustion. :*Can we meet in the ballroom? It should be empty, and we must talk.*:

Dare's eagerness darted through her. :*Of course.*: Then he sighed. :*Although I must find a way to distract Mother. She'll be scrutinizing me after my suspicious disappearance at the Duke of Oakmoor's soiree.*:

Annalise pursed her lips as she turned Storm onto the street leading to Greysnowe House. They couldn't have Dare's mother interrupt them again. They'd too much to discuss. :*Perhaps arrange a conversation between her and the Islayes **and** Lady Ducharme this time.*:

Dare chuckled. :*That should be enough to engross her. I'll see you soon.*:

She sent her love through their entwined souls. :*Until then.*:

She retracted her mind and sagged in the saddle as weight crushed her and her head whirled. She needed that nap more than ever. Please let the short one she could manage before luncheon and the Merrileas' shokolat party be enough.

At her family's stables, Annalise staggered from Storm then asked the grooms to take care of him. She sighed and patted her stallion's shoulder before trudging inside. If only she'd the energy to unsaddle or groom him herself like normal. Poor Storm would miss the attention.

Somehow, she managed to drag herself upstairs to her chambers without Mother and Father or Alex spotting her. She couldn't risk them seeing her exhaustion. They, Mother especially, might begin to suspect she was pregnant.

She petted Finn and Lily once each then whistled a greeting at Rain and Aria before removing her riding clothes and boots

with trembling hands. Then she collapsed on her bed and sank
into slumber like a golden ball in a frog prince's pool.

CHAPTER 42

*A*fter he and Mother swept into Merrilea House, Dare glanced about the drawing room for Annalise then tensed once he found her. Sitting near the refreshments table with a cup of shokolat before her lips, she was even paler than she'd been at the park when exchanging angelcats yesterday. The smudges beneath her eyes were darker too, and her radiance was definitely muted with the gray fog about her aura no longer wispy. Goddess, could it be mere pregnancy that made her appear so ill?

He reached out to Annalise while he and Mother greeted the easygoing Duke and Duchess of Merrilea, :*Are you feeling well?*:

Annalise lowered her cup of shokolat without tasting it. :*Just tired. If we weren't able to meet here, I'd have begged Mother and Father to let me stay behind to rest.*: She sighed. :*Although getting them to agree would be difficult—this is an event held by a duke and duchess, after all.*:

As he and Mother joined Lord and Lady Islaye, Dare suppressed a grimace. Why must Annalise's parents be such ambitious fools? They should have made her stay behind as soon as they saw how ill she looked. :*Perhaps you should leave to rest. We can meet another time when you're better.*:

Her determination surging through him, Annalise lifted her chin. :*No, I don't want to wait to speak with you.*: She slowly rose then handed her cup of shokolat to a nearby servant. :*I'll tell Mother and Father I require a moment to rest and slip into the ballroom. Meet me once you distract your mother.*:

He sighed. He must distract Mother at once then keep his meeting with Annalise brief, so she could return to Greysnowe House and rest. :*Very well. But if the ballroom hasn't any chairs, head to one of its anterooms, so you can sit and rest.*:

Annalise's love surged in their entwined souls as she spoke to her mother. :*Of course. See you soon.*:

Once Annalise drifted from the drawing room, Dare asked the Islayes how Lady Kiera's education initiative was progressing. Then like Annalise had suggested, he beckoned Lady Ducharme to join them. Soon Mother, the Islayes, and Lady Ducharme were all engrossed in discussing the education initiative, so he murmured an excuse then slipped away.

To appear casual, he talked with several groups of people on his way to the door. Then after he left the drawing room, he strode to the dark ballroom and followed Annalise's aura into the anteroom near the front.

When he joined her, Annalise was asleep, sitting upright on the anteroom's sofa with her chin pillowed on her chest. Goddess, 'twas a shame to wake her, but she'd insisted on speaking with him. So he sat beside her and rubbed her arm. "Annalise, wake up."

Annalise blinked at him then a beam suffused her face, almost hiding her exhaustion. She leaned forward and brushed a kiss against his lips. "I love awakening beside you. I'm eager to do it every morning."

Dare stilled, his pulse quickening. Could she mean... "Oh?"

Her cerulean eyes bright, she hummed and caressed his cheek. "I've decided that you're right, my love. We must elope as soon as possible."

Energy surging through him, he grinned at Annalise. At last!

He drew her against him and kissed her. Yet he kept his kiss gentle—she wasn't up to anything strenuous right now. He raised his head after a too-brief moment. "What made you finally agree?"

Annalise sighed, her tenderness and joy bathing him. "I saw the glow of pregnancy for the first time this morning, and I *knew* I must ensure our child's happiness as well as our own, even though 'twould cost me my parents."

His heart fluttering, Dare feathered another kiss against her lips. "I swear we'll enjoy a wonderful life full of abiding love and family in Wildewall until we breathe our last. I love you so, Annalise."

Annalise smiled at him, her echoing love flaring in their entwined souls. "I love you just as much and can't wait to begin that wonderful life together. How soon can we elope?"

Dare hummed and eyed her. He'd love to elope now, but Annalise needed decent sleep first. Yet she'd deny that if he mentioned it, so he must devise an excuse. "Tomorrow, perhaps? I must visit the Great Temple and find a priest willing to marry us without your parents' approval. We're of age, but such irregularity shall deter most priests."

Annalise grimaced. "True enough. Hopefully, explaining our families' feud shall help. Then at least they'll know you're not marrying me for my dowry." Her lips twisted in a wry smile. "Which is fortunate since Mother and Father shall refuse to pay it after we marry."

As her grief pierced him, he waggled his brows then said to cheer her, "No, I'm marrying you because I can't resist ravishing you." When she giggled, he relaxed. "What about witnesses?"

Tilting her head, Annalise sighed. "Both Kiera and Wren are too busy to be available so suddenly, and explaining to Alex and your mother shall take too long. Could we simply have a couple of priests as witnesses?"

A pang darted through Dare. Annalise deserved so much more than a clandestine wedding ceremony with no family or friends as witnesses. Yet because of the feud and their need to marry at once, they could do nothing else. Swallowing a sigh, he nodded. "I'll visit the Great Temple this afternoon." He narrowed his eyes at her. "You return to Greysnowe House and rest. And *don't* attend any court events tonight."

Annalise chuckled. "I should be able to manage that. The best court event tonight is a concert at The Nightingale, so Mother and Father shan't mind too much if I miss it. When shall we meet tomorrow?"

He studied her. She must rest her fill before their elopement. "How about midmorning in the park? Bring Lily and Finn with you, but leave Rain and Aria behind. The faebirds are too delicate to survive traveling about Ormas in the cold. We can have Alex bring them once we're married, along with anything else you want but couldn't carry."

Beaming, Annalise gently kissed him. "Everything is settled then." Then she sighed. "Must we return to the shokolat party now? I don't want to go back and don Lady Snow's icy mask."

His heart squeezing, Dare leaned back in the sofa, pulling Annalise with him so they were nestled together with her head resting on his chest. He kissed her hair. "We can remain here awhile."

Annalise sighed and nuzzled him. "Good."

As they sat together, warmth flooded him. After a moment, he rested a hand against her stomach. "So when you saw the glow of pregnancy, could you see if our child was a girl or a boy?"

Smiling against him, Annalise laid her hand atop his. "No, I can only read pregnancy through auras, which reveal personality, emotions, health, and magic, but not gender. Besides, our child's aura shan't appear separate from mine until much further in my pregnancy." She squeezed his hand. "Can you invoke healing sight like a witch healer? You'd see what we're having then."

Dare chuckled and kissed her hair again. "Although nature

witches are similar enough to healers that I can balance energy to promote healing and cast contraceptive spells, invoking their healing sight is far beyond me. I was merely curious, anyway. I don't care if we have a girl or boy or both."

Annalise hummed. "Me either. Although I'd prefer not both at once. Our children shall likely inherit our magical strength and develop their powers similarly, and raising twins with precocious magic shall be exhausting."

He grinned and squeezed her shoulders. Raising twins couldn't be that bad. "When did your powers develop?"

Annalise shrugged. "I've always been able to read auras, but I performed my first soul-healing at seven, and my powers finished developing by fifteen. Most soul healers develop their powers when their courses begin, although more powerful ones develop earlier."

Dare inhaled a sharp breath. Annalise must be very powerful then—perhaps the most powerful since the Spring Queen or Esme the Great. "If you developed your powers so young, how did your parents never discover them?"

Smiling, Annalise hummed. "My nursemaid Alice, remember? After warning me never to reveal my powers, she covered any slips I made until I was accustomed to concealing them." She kissed his chest. "Alice shall be so glad I'm marrying for love at long last. She'll be delighted to meet you."

Although her kiss warmed him, he blinked at Annalise. Her former nursemaid surely wasn't another soul healer, so she'd never had instruction on using her powers. Amazing. "You learned to soul-heal without *anyone* instructing you?"

Annalise shifted against him. "My powers are largely instinctual, although when I was ten, I did discover a primer Esme the Great wrote for her soul healer descendants. With the help of the water elves, she'd cleverly enchanted it so it only appeared to those with soul healer powers. Reading that helped refine my control immensely." She poked his stomach. "Enough about me. What about your powers?"

Dare smoothed his beard. The development of his powers was unremarkable compared to hers. "Similarly to you, I could always sense natural energy and do small nature magic. However, Mother began instructing me at five, so she ensured I never got into trouble I couldn't handle. When I was seventeen, my powers finished developing, and Mother completed my instruction."

Grinning against him, Annalise hummed. "Your powers appeared as early as mine. Not surprising considering you're a powerful Rhiannon descendant." She shook her head. "Since we both had such precocious magic, 'tis likely our children shall be the same. I *definitely* don't want twins like Wren."

His brows rose. Lady Beza Hawke was having twins? Surprising the Duchess of Childes hadn't thrown a fete to celebrate that like she had for her first grandchild.

Annalise sighed then extracted herself from his arms. "We should return to the shokolat party. I'll go first since I'll doubtless fall asleep again if I don't."

Dare rose, pulling Annalise upright. He pressed a gentle kiss against her lips. "Remember, convince your parents to leave so you can rest."

Annalise smiled. "I'll attempt to convince them before you return." She tenderly returned his kiss. "See you tomorrow, Dare."

Weight compressing his chest, he sighed as Annalise drifted from the anteroom. Thank the Goddess she was finally going to be his wife tomorrow, so they could quit feigning indifference.

AFTER RETURNING FROM THE MERRILEAS' shokolat party, Dare hurried to the Great Temple and asked the first priest he encountered, "Excuse me, could you direct me to a priest free to officiate a wedding ceremony tomorrow morning?"

The rabbity priest blinked at him. "You're a lord, aren't you?"

When Dare nodded, the priest sighed. "Follow me." Then the priest scurried from the nave.

Dare strode after the rabbity priest through the north cloister into the Center of Learning. He stiffened when his escort entered a study full of novice priests being taught by Priest Melchior Hawke. Damnation, a priest unconnected to court would be much safer. And Priest Melchior was the middle son of the Duke and Duchess of Childes as well as King Devon's cousin.

After the rabbity priest muttered in Priest Melchior's ear and darted away, Priest Melchior excused himself to his students then stepped into the hall beside Dare, shutting the door behind him. He turned to Dare with a kind smile. "You wish to marry tomorrow morning, Lord Ravenstone? Why such haste?"

Dare swallowed but managed to return the priest's smile. "Because her parents shall attempt to obstruct our marriage if they learn of it beforehand."

Priest Melchior hummed, his eyes narrowing. "And the lady's name?"

Dare inhaled then leaned forward and muttered, "Lady Annalise Greysnowe."

Priest Melchior nodded. "I suspected as much when you explained your haste. Very well, meet me in the Harvest Garden tomorrow. The chapels shall likely be occupied."

His chest easing, Dare swept a bow. "My deepest thanks, Priest Melchior. We'll be here tomorrow around midmorning."

When he returned to Ravenstone House, he headed to his study and wrote to Alex canceling their sword fight and ride tomorrow at the royal bay. Then he handled the rest of his correspondence, so he could spend all his time with Annalise after their marriage. After that, he joined Mother for dinner.

While he served her leek and mushroom soup, Mother arched her brows and asked, "How did your errand this afternoon go?"

Dare managed to shrug with a faint smile. Thank the Goddess he could quit lying to Mother after he and Annalise married tomorrow. "It went well, but I've more errands tomorrow, so I'll be gone most of the day."

After dinner, he and Mother attended the concert at The Nightingale. He exhaled when Annalise's parents arrived alone —she'd convinced them to let her rest. Then he turned his gaze to the stage, although he barely heard a note of the music.

Dare retired as soon as they returned from the concert, but he took ages to drift into slumber. Yet he still leapt from bed at dawn then yanked on his clothes. Although he and Annalise were meeting at midmorning, leaving now would do no harm, and the tame bit of nature in the park would settle him. He grabbed some rolls stuffed with meat and cheese from the kitchen and devoured them while he strode to the park. As he reached the bare yet well-tended trees, he blew a sigh and gathered the natural energy around him. Unable to remain still, he paced while he waited for Annalise.

He'd only been in the park for half an hour when Annalise's panic and anguish burst through their entwined souls. He froze then reached out to her, :*Annalise, what's wrong?*:

Her mental voice faint and trembling, Annalise replied, :*Our unborn child.*: She broke off with a gasp that turned into a moan. :*Oh, Goddess, it hurts.*:

His chest clenching and pulse surging, Dare bolted through the trees toward Greysnowe House, casting an invisibility spell about himself while he ran. :*Hold on; I'll be there soon.*:

CHAPTER 43

When Dare said he was headed over, Annalise curled in a tighter ball and tears scalded her cheeks at the excruciating cramp wracking her. With Finn and Lily purring reassurance against her back, she inhaled a shuddering breath then replied, :*No, stay away. What if someone sees you?*:

Dare's love and concern surrounded her. :*I've cast an invisibility spell, so don't fret about that.*:

She sighed as the excruciating cramp eased. :*You still shouldn't risk it. There's nothing you can do.*: Muffling a sob, she laid a hand on her stomach. There was nothing anyone could do —not even the best witch healer or another soul healer could stop a miscarriage once it started.

She swallowed. Unless she was wrong. Please, Goddess, let her be wrong. Like she had when the first wrenching cramp had woken her moments ago, she focused her powers on her stomach. Yet the glow of pregnancy was still gone. She strained and flung every speck of her powers at her stomach. But still nothing.

Releasing her powers, Annalise buried her face in her pillow and sobbed while Finn and Lily nuzzled her and Rain and Aria trilled soothing melodies from their golden birdcage. No, she'd not been wrong. Her and Dare's unborn child was dead. Then another agonizing cramp seized her, and she whimpered.

Soon after that cramp abated, Dare wrapped his arms about her and pulled her into his lap. His worry flared in their entwined souls. "Annalise, you're bleeding."

Sobbing harder, she clung to Dare and pressed her face against his chest then inhaled his scent to calm herself.

Dare began to rise. His voice ragged, he said, "I'll take you to a witch healer."

Forcing herself to quit sobbing so she could speak, Annalise shook her head then replied against his chest, "No need. I'll be fine in a few days. I'm just bleeding because," another sob burst free, "because I lost our child."

His anguish surging through her, Dare dropped back onto the bed and squeezed her tighter against him. "Oh, Goddess."

While she sobbed again, Dare rested his chin on her head then rocked her and rubbed her back. As they nestled together, Finn and Lily curled beside them and purred while Rain and Aria resumed their dulcet singing.

After several more cramps gripped her, each one slightly weaker than the last, her tears finally slowed, although the ache in her chest remained. She pulled back enough to lift her head and meet Dare's gaze.

His eyes dark and face damp from tears like hers, Dare studied her and wiped away her tears. "Are you certain I shouldn't take you to a witch healer?"

Annalise's aching heart warmed at his solicitude, and she pressed a palm against his damp cheek. "I'm certain." Unless she was fatally ill, visiting a witch healer was too risky because they'd recognize her as a soul healer. After he tenderly kissed her palm, she sighed and lowered her hand. "You should leave before Grace enters to wake me."

Dare frowned and pulled her closer. "No. We must remain together right now. Sharing our grief makes it easier to bear."

She inhaled his scent to soothe herself then sighed again. Even so, Dare remaining was impossible. "We can't risk anyone seeing you in my chambers."

Dare kissed her hair. "Whenever we hear the door open, I'll recast my invisibility spell and stand along the wall."

Annalise began to reply, but another cramp bolted through her. Dare rubbed her back and murmured reassurance until it passed. Then she exhaled and pulled back. "Shan't your mother notice your absence?"

Dare shook his head. "At dinner last night, I told her I'd errands most of the day."

Relaxing against him, Annalise nodded. Even though she should send Dare away, having him near comforted her too much. So they cuddled together through several bouts of scalding tears and dwindling cramps until her door opened some time later.

Dare immediately muttered his invisibility spell then burst upright, tumbling Annalise into the bed and startling Finn and Lily.

Grace entered with a tray of mentha tea and dry toast. "Already awake, I see." She halted and gaped at the bed. "Dear Goddess."

Petting the angelcats until they curled against her like before, Annalise managed a tremulous smile. "My courses," she swallowed as tears burned her eyes again, "came this morning."

Wincing as indigo sympathy pulsed about her, Grace handed Annalise the mentha tea and dry toast. "So I see. I'll prepare a hot bath at once then have an upper housemaid replace your bedding."

Dare's faint glow along the wall shifted. :*I'll turn away during your bath so you've some privacy.*:

Annalise sent her thanks through their entwined souls then sipped her mentha tea and nibbled her dry toast. She'd just finished when a faint cramp coursed through her. Then Grace helped her into her hot bath and let her soak while her bedding was replaced. By the time she was clean, dressed in a fresh night-gown, and tucked back in bed with Finn and Lily purring against her and Rain and Aria perched on her bed singing, her cramps were done, although her courses continued.

Grace eyed her. "I'll let Lady Greysnowe know you're too ill to leave bed today."

As soon as Grace left, Dare's faint glow strode back to the bed. Then without dislodging the angelcats, he sat beside Annalise and took her hand. "I shan't remove my invisibility spell since I expect your mother shall be here soon."

Her aching chest squeezing more, she sighed and threaded her fingers through his. "Yes, and be careful when she visits. She shouldn't sense you, but we can't risk her becoming suspicious."

Dare's lips brushed against her temple. "Of course."

Then the door swung open, and Dare bounded back to the wall as Mother swept inside.

Ignoring the angelcats despite seeing Lily for the first time, Mother sat in the spot Dare had just left and placed a hand on Annalise's forehead as muddy-yellow worry flared about her. "Grace was right. You look wretched—whiter than a banshee."

Annalise shrugged with a tight smile. "My courses were more brutal than normal." So much more.

Mother hummed and pursed her lips. "Except your courses never trouble you, and you haven't been well the past few days. You must have contracted an illness."

Annalise swallowed. No, she'd conceived Dare's child—a child who'd never be born now. Glancing down to hide the tears pricking her eyes, she petted Finn and Lily to hearten herself.

Mother sighed. "Until you recover, you must remain in bed and only consume tea, soup, and bread."

As Dare's surprise darted through her, Annalise lifted her gaze and quit petting the angelcats. She'd starve on invalid fare within a week. "I need more substantial food than that."

Grimacing, Mother tsked. "Nonsense. Overeating rich food shall only upset your stomach and make your illness worse." She narrowed her eyes at Grace. "And I'll be checking Annalise's trays, so no smuggling her richer food."

While Grace bobbed her head, Annalise suppressed a sigh and resumed petting Finn and Lily. Even her loyal maid couldn't risk disobeying a command like that.

Mother rose and pressed a gentle kiss on Annalise's forehead. "Rest now. Your father and I shall make your excuses at court events until you're better. Too bad most of the upcoming events are held by councilors or dukes and duchesses." She sighed. "But I suppose that can't be helped. Your father and I shall check on you before we leave for the Duke and Duchess of Blackham's luncheon."

After Mother strode out, Grace nodded at Annalise. "I'll bring you a breakfast tray."

Without removing his invisibility spell, Dare sat beside Annalise again once Grace left. "Why is your mother restricting your food?"

Annalise shrugged as she took Dare's hand. "She's never approved of how much I eat to fuel my high-energy aura. I've always told her 'tis because I'm constantly active, so Mother assumes I shan't need to eat as much if I'm resting." When his annoyance flooded her, she squeezed his hand. "But I'll survive being hungry for a few days."

Before Dare could reply, Grace returned with a laden breakfast tray, and he hurried back to the wall. As Grace set the tray on Annalise's lap, she winked and murmured, "I convinced Cook plain eggs weren't richer than soup and bread."

Annalise smiled at her maid. Eggs would definitely add nourishment to the invalid fare. Grace was the best. "Thanks, Grace." As she devoured the eggs, dry toast, and egg soup, she asked Dare, :*Should I save you something? I can send Grace away, so you can eat.*:

Dare's love surged through their entwined souls. :*No, I ate breakfast earlier.*:

After Annalise finished eating, Grace scooped up the empty

tray. "I'll be back in an hour or two with more food. Try to sleep, my lady." Clearly, her maid intended to circumvent Mother's restrictions by bringing invalid fare often.

Once they were alone again, Dare removed his invisibility spell then shifted Finn and Lily to lie on the covers beside Annalise. He wrapped an arm about her shoulders. "Yes, sleep now. I'll remain right here, but I'll take care no one sees me."

Although she should convince Dare to leave, she nestled against him and laid her head on his chest. She needed his comfort right now. As Rain and Aria sang sweet lullabies, she drifted into slumber in his embrace and slept the rest of the morning, except when Grace brought another laden tray of food. Yet still drained from her cramps earlier, once her maid left, Annalise soon fell back asleep in Dare's arms.

She only fully woke when Mother and Father strode into her chambers just before luncheon. Indigo concern glowing about them, they halted beside the bed as Dare, wearing his invisibility spell, returned to the wall.

Mother leaned forward and smoothed Annalise's disheveled hair from her face and asked, "How are you feeling?"

Warmed by their concern, Annalise lifted a shoulder. "Somewhat better after sleeping all morning."

Mother and Father smiled then Mother said, "Good. Keep resting then. We'll check on you again later."

Father bent and kissed Annalise's brow. "Rest well, Annalise."

Once Mother and Father left for luncheon at Blackham House, Dare removed his invisibility spell and reclined beside Annalise again. He wrapped an arm about her. "Watching your mother and father act like loving parents is amazing. They're always bent on furthering their ambitions at court events. Or scowling when they spot me or Mother."

Absently scratching Finn's chin, Annalise sighed. And doubtless Mother and Father would do worse than scowl if they realized Dare was here. She should really ask him to leave, but his embrace was too wonderful. "Now you can fathom why I struggled deciding to elope."

Dare stilled then swallowed, his disquiet swamping her. "Yes. I—"

Then her door slammed open, and Alex burst inside, his gaze fixed on the overfull tray of food he was carrying.

As Dare flung his invisibility spell about himself and hurtled toward the wall, Annalise inhaled and smoothed her covers with trembling hands. Goddess, if Alex had glanced up, he would have *seen* her and Dare nestled together like mated griffins.

Alex plunked his tray on her bedside table then pulled a chair beside her bed. Dropping into the chair, he smirked at her. "I heard Mother ordered you to rest and restricted you to soup and bread." Frowning, he leaned forward and indigo concern flared about him. "You do look pallid."

She grimaced as she petted Lily. She wasn't explaining her courses to her brother. "I'll be fine in a few days."

Alex snorted. "Not if you only eat soup and bread like Mother ordered. She never has understood your prodigious appetite. Since she forbade Grace from doing so, I brought you a proper meal."

Annalise eyed the tray Alex had brought. It had enough real food for at least three ravenous soul healers, including the beefsteak that she desperately needed during her courses. And she could share the tray with Dare if Alex didn't take it when he left. She smiled at him. "Thanks, Alex. Although you know when Mother hears about this, she'll scold and forbid you to bring me any more."

Widening his eyes, Alex blinked at her. "Except if she asks, I requested the tray for me—I'm particularly sharp-set for some reason today."

Despite her grief, her lips twitched at Alex's feigned innocence. She waved toward the overfull tray. "Then you must join me." There'd still be plenty left for Dare.

Alex hummed and rose. "I can't. I'm meeting friends at The

Gold Griffin for luncheon and cards." He gripped her shoulder. "I'll see you later. Feel better."

After Alex strode out, Dare sighed and dropped his invisibility spell. "Thank the Goddess that Alex didn't see me."

Gesturing for Dare to sit in Alex's chair, Annalise tsked and shook her head. "Yes. After we eat, you'd better return to Ravenstone House."

Dare blew another sigh as he sat beside her. "I don't want to leave you."

She touched his knee, her heart twisting. "And I don't want you to leave, my love, but you must, and you can't return. We'd slip eventually, and someone shall discover us together in my chambers. Even without the feud, 'twould be a scandal."

Dare grimaced and smoothed his beard. "I suppose."

Annalise squeezed Dare's knee to reassure him. "I promise I'll reach out if I need you. And we can meet once I'm fully recovered to discuss matters." She flashed a grin. "Now set that overfull tray on the bed, so we can share it."

She and Dare devoured the entire tray with Finn and Lily begging and attempting to steal food like they'd not eaten for days. Then Dare sighed and rose. He brushed a tender kiss against her lips before recasting his invisibility spell and striding from her chambers.

Her chest aching, Annalise lay down as Finn and Lily curled against her and Rain and Aria sang her to sleep once again. If only she and Dare could remain together always. Her eyes drifted shut. And once they'd eloped, they would. She just needed to recover first.

CHAPTER 44

While striding back to Ravenstone House, Dare kept his invisibility spell wrapped about himself. He could have stepped into an alley to remove it once he was a few townhouses away from Greysnowe House, but wearing it meant he didn't have to control his expression. And he needed that after Annalise's miscarriage. He also needed time alone with nature to settle himself before Mother saw him.

So instead of going inside, he headed to the stables. He gritted a faint smile then dropped his invisibility spell to avoid startling the grooms—he couldn't have them quitting because a ghost was saddling Ebony. Once he finished that, he mounted then trotted through the crowded streets of Ormas, keeping his fake smile on his face.

However, as soon as he and Ebony rode through the northern gate, he quit guarding his expression and prodded his stallion to a gallop. Strenuous exertion would help settle him too. Ebony was sweating and winded when they reached the royal bay. Dare winced then patted Ebony's damp withers. "Sorry for the grueling ride. I'll make sure you get plenty of sweet oats when we return to Ormas."

To bolster his stallion until then, Dare sent Ebony energy as they rode on the winding path down the cliffs. Then he kneed Ebony, and they galloped on the wet sand before the turbulent surf. As the icy seawater sprayed them and the raging wind lashed his face, he gulped a deep breath and flung his anguish into the sea, earth, and sky. Spurred by his magic, the turbulent waves grew wilder, the wet sand quaked, and the raging wind howled as the clouds darkened.

He kept flinging his anguish into the surrounding nature until his powers were drained like cracked soil during a drought. Then he slowed Ebony to a walk, his chest heaving and tears freezing his face. Why, Goddess? Why had this happened to him and Annalise? And just when they were about to begin their wonderful life together too. 'Twas almost as if the world had cursed them for daring to love their ancestral enemy.

His heart aching, Dare clenched Ebony's reins. Plus, after having lost their unborn child, Annalise would surely refuse to elope—they no longer had a child to protect, and doubtless she couldn't bear to lose any more family. That must be what she wanted to discuss once she was fully recovered. And although they'd be stronger together, he couldn't pressure her to elope while they grieved their unborn child. He'd be too desperate, and she'd be too fragile, so he'd likely devastate her.

He shuddered a breath. No, for now he must accept her refusal then wait until their grief eased to beg her to marry him. Yet doing that would require fortitude he didn't have so soon after losing their child, so he must avoid discussing their future with Annalise until he did.

Dare sighed then opened his drained powers to gather the natural energy around him before he and Ebony rode back to Ormas. Like water into a dry sponge, energy wicked into his magic, and he continued until 'twas overflowing. However, after using his powers so heavily, he was freezing, trembling, and starving. Hopefully, he could manage a gallop—he needed some rich food soon to recover, despite eating luncheon with Annalise two hours ago.

As he and Ebony began back, he stiffened at the thunder of approaching hoofbeats. The Farsons, the Duke of Golddell, Lady Farson's brother Lord Blaine, and Miss Hawke were galloping across the sand toward him—doubtless a courtship outing for Lord Blaine and Miss Hawke amid family.

Halting Ebony, Dare gritted a genial smile to conceal his grief and exhaustion. Gossip spreading about either would engender questions that might reveal his involvement with Annalise. His face aching with his feigned cheer, he exchanged greetings with everyone then wished them a pleasant ride before he continued back to Ormas.

Once he and Ebony climbed the cliffs, he sent Ebony energy then urged the stallion to a gallop. Despite his exhaustion, he managed to cling to Ebony's back until they reached the stables of Ravenstone House. Cooling Ebony with his magic, he slid to the ground before unsaddling and grooming his stallion like always. He left Ebony with water and hay before asking Roberts to give Ebony sweet oats an hour later.

Then he patted Ebony's shoulder. As Ebony nuzzled him, he murmured in his stallion's ear, "There, sweet oats, just like I promised."

Trembling and lightheaded, Dare headed straight to the kitchen. He collapsed on a wooden chair then asked, "Could you make me shokolat nut oatmeal balls, please?"

As soon as Cook handed him a laden plate, he devoured twenty shokolat nut oatmeal balls, energy trickling back with each one. Then he thanked Cook and went upstairs to his study. He'd some letters to write after today's unsuccessful elopement. He wrote Priest Melchior explaining that he and Annalise hadn't gone to the Great Temple because she'd fallen ill, that they'd marry another time, and begged the priest to remain silent. Then he wrote Alex accepting Alex's offer to meet for their sword fight and ride tomorrow morning instead of today. Since he and Annalise hadn't eloped, he'd no reason not to meet Alex. His letters finished, he rang for Brown.

The butler was striding out with his letters when Mother bustled into the study with a vibrant grin. "Dare, there you are. How did your errands go?" She halted and frowned at him. "You look weary."

His chest clenching, Dare smoothed his beard. Despite his hopes yesterday, he must continue lying to Mother for Goddess knew how long. And he must conceal his grief over his and Annalise's lost child. Not only would Mother worry, but she might discover his involvement with Annalise. He made himself shrug. "My errands were fine, albeit more tiring," and devastating, "than I'd expected."

Mother hummed and tilted her head. "Do you intend to skip the Magehavens' ball tonight then?"

He sighed. He'd much rather remain here, but both him and Annalise missing an important court event might make people suspect their involvement. And Annalise's parents realizing that right now would destroy her. Besides, perhaps a crowded court event might distract him from his grief. He forced a smile. "No, I'll still attend. I'd like to hear if the Magehavens have any updates about the Magehaven ore."

Her brows rising, Mother tsked. "Lord Islaye would have told me if there were. You *should* be hoping the Magehavens invited a new lady or two who'll interest you. Then you might actually find a wife."

Dare closed his eyes and swallowed as his heart twisted. Discussing marriage after today felt like flaying already bleeding skin. Opening his eyes, he gritted another smile. "That seems unlikely."

Mother pursed her lips. "Perhaps. And even *if* a new lady attends, you'll doubtless have slipped away to the garden again before you've a chance to meet her."

He almost winced. Although she'd not asked about his lengthy absence at the Merrileas' shokolat party yesterday, she was clearly suspicious. Not that he could explain until he and

Annalise were safely married. He met Mother's narrowed gaze. "I promise I shan't slip away tonight."

Mother hummed and continued eyeing him. "But shall you dance with anyone?"

Dare suppressed a shudder at holding any lady other than Annalise in his arms. Especially a lady interested in marriage. Dancing with such a lady would be cruel. "Likely not. I'm too tired to dance after my errands today."

Humming again, Mother slowly nodded. "I see."

As Mother bustled from his study, he sighed and sagged back in his chair. What could he do to allay Mother's suspicions? He couldn't court anyone but Annalise, and they'd continue slipping away whenever they attended the same court events. Plus, somehow he must keep concealing his grief from Mother. Tonight she'd accept his excuse of tiring errands, but what about tomorrow? Perhaps always smiling, remaining active, and circulating at court events would be enough.

So after an afternoon spent hiding in his chambers then bolting dinner there, Dare smiled at Mother when he met her in the entrance hall. "Ready to head to Magehaven House?"

On their carriage ride, he asked Mother about her day and kept her discussing that until they greeted their hosts. As Mother had said, the Duke and Duchess of Magehaven had no updates about the Magehaven ore. And they fortunately hadn't invited any new ladies to their ball, so he needn't approach those ladies to allay Mother.

Once Mother and the Islayes were engrossed in debating the best weather charms, Dare murmured an excuse and began circulating. Like a melissa busy pollinating bee balm during summer, he strode about the ballroom, pausing at groups containing both gentlemen and ladies for several moments before continuing to the next group. And he kept a genial grin on his face the entire time.

However, when he passed the Greysnowes gossiping with Lady Morwynne midway through the ball, his chest spasmed at their rancorous glares. If only Annalise's parents knew he'd almost become their son-in-law today. Her parents would have done more than glare if she'd not lost their unborn child and they'd eloped as planned. Yet nothing, not even Lord Greysnowe challenging him to a duel, would have separated him and Annalise once they'd married.

His throat clenching, Dare swallowed and fisted his hands by his sides. Although he'd promised Mother he'd not slip away, he needed some time alone to settle himself. He escaped into the Magehavens' garden and allowed his feigned grin to fade. Entering a shadowy alcove, he knelt and pressed his palms against the frozen earth then sent his mind into the garden. The calm of the sleeping plants awaiting the warmth of spring seeped into his soul. Everything had its season, and although some might die, their sacrifice was never wasted. Even death served a purpose in life.

He retracted his powers then rose with a sigh. His anguish over his and Annalise's lost child had made him forget that, and he'd probably forget again while he grieved in the coming days. When gathering natural energy, he must remember to commune with nature as well. Perhaps he could use their soulbond to help Annalise see nature's wisdom too. He'd attempt that when they met next.

Dare returned to the ballroom, and as soon as he stepped inside, Mother waylaid him. Arching a brow, she said, "I thought you weren't going to slip away to the garden tonight."

He shrugged and flashed a wry smile. Not surprising Mother had noticed and confronted him on it. "I simply needed some air."

Mother sipped her sparkling wine. "It *is* dreadfully hot in such a crowded ballroom."

Dare offered Mother his arm. Thank the Goddess she'd not probed further. "Shall we rejoin Lord and Lady Islaye?"

• • •

THE REST OF THE MAGEHAVENS' ball passed smoothly, but Dare and Mother left well before midnight. Then after a night full of restless dreams, Thom shook him awake for his sword fight and ride with Alex at the royal bay the following morning.

When Dare met Alex, he made himself smile and act normal. Like Mother, Alex mustn't realize his grief. They began crossing swords, and Dare soon won with a feint Alex usually would have parried. Was Alex simply upset over Annalise's illness, or did he realize the truth?

To find out, Dare arched his brows at Alex while they cleaned their swords and asked, "Are you feeling well today?"

Alex sighed and sheathed his sword. "I feel fine—I'm just worried about Annalise."

Dare froze, his pulse surging. Had something else happened to Annalise? So she could rest, he'd not checked on her yesterday nor before he'd left this morning. Please let her not be worse. He swallowed then gritted a light tone as he mounted Ebony, "Oh?"

Grunting, Alex swung atop Biscuit. "She was so pallid when I saw her at luncheon yesterday, and she was asleep when I visited her before dinner. Her maid said 'tis just women's issues, but Annalise has never been ill like this before."

Pain piercing his chest, Dare clenched Ebony's reins. Except Annalise had never suffered a miscarriage before. Not that he could tell Alex that. He managed to smile at Alex. "I'm certain her maid would tell you or your parents if 'twas something more serious."

Alex eyed him for a long moment. "Do you think so?" At his nod, Alex relaxed. "Oh, good."

To distract Alex, Dare proposed a race to the cliffs. However, on the ride back to Ormas, he reached out to Annalise, :*How are you feeling this morning?*:

Her mental voice drowsy as if he'd woken her, Annalise replied, :*Still exhausted, even though all I've done is sleep and eat since...*: her anguish flooded him, :*....my courses started.*:

He frowned, his stomach tensing. Was Annalise's exhaustion

normal after a miscarriage? Too bad he couldn't risk asking Mother or a healer. He set his jaw. :*I could send you energy through our soulbond to help you recover.*:

Annalise sighed. :*Perhaps later. I'll continue sleeping and eating for now. I do hope Alex brings me more beefsteak for luncheon today.*:

Dare eyed Alex riding beside him, blithely unaware of his silent conversation with Annalise. :*Should I suggest that to him? We're riding back from the royal bay now, and he mentioned your illness earlier.*:

Her love surrounding him, Annalise hummed. :*Not unless you're still discussing me. Otherwise, your interest shall make Alex suspicious.*:

He grimaced. True. He sent her his love through their entwined souls. :*Very well. Go back to sleep. I'll check on you tonight. Love you, my heart.*:

Annalise whispered back, :*Love you too, Dare.*:

As her presence faded, Dare sighed. Goddess, let Annalise recover soon.

CHAPTER 45

Two mornings after her and Dare's loss, Annalise groaned when Grace shook her awake several hours after dawn, well later than she usually woke. All she wanted to do right now was sleep. Not only was she exhausted, but in sleep she could forget their child was gone. She buried her face in her pillow. "Let me sleep."

Grace shook her shoulder again. "I would, my lady, but a letter from the palace arrived for you overnight. The night porter just gave it to me."

Annalise sighed and sat up, dislodging Finn and Lily curled against her. The letter must be from Kiera, and whatever had made her friend send a letter in the middle of the night must be important. She'd better read it at once.

She blinked then frowned when she read Kiera's brief invitation to breakfast. She glanced at the clock on the mantel—she'd be late, but she should be able to make breakfast if she rushed. Except she'd no energy to rush. She reached out to Dare, :*Would you mind sending me energy through our soulbond? Kiera invited me to breakfast, and I doubt I'll manage it otherwise.*:

Dare's loving presence surrounded her. :*Of course, but shouldn't you stay in bed resting?*:

Annalise sighed. If only she could. *:I can't. Kiera wrote 'twas urgent, and although we're friends, I can't ignore an urgent summons from our future queen.:*

Dare echoed her sigh. *:True.:* Then a rush of energy surged through their entwined souls. *:Is that enough, my heart?:*

Annalise inhaled and straightened, exhaustion not weighing her down for the first time since her miscarriage. *:Yes, thanks.:*

His love warming her, Dare said, *:Have fun at breakfast. We'll talk later.:*

Annalise sent her love back in reply. As his presence faded, she slid from bed and said to Grace, "I must dress at once. Kiera invited me to breakfast at the palace."

Grace frowned but helped Annalise dress without a word. After donning her warmest cloak, Annalise asked Grace to feed the angelcats and faebirds, who all should have eaten breakfast hours ago but had let her rest instead. Then she headed downstairs.

Despite the energy Dare had sent her, the short walk to the carriage drained her, so she slept the entire carriage ride to the palace. When the outrider roused her, she made herself trudge upstairs to the royal wing. Then she asked a maid for directions to the private dining room where Kiera had written they'd eat breakfast.

When Annalise joined Kiera and King Devon, muddy-yellow worry flared about Kiera as she helped Annalise to the table, yet muddy-green suspicion swirled about King Devon as he narrowly eyed her. What had happened to make King Devon eye her so? However, Kiera insisted they eat before discussing anything.

After finishing her beefsteak, Annalise eyed Kiera and King Devon but continued eating. Amazing that Kiera had kept the king silent when he was clearly desperate to talk. So Annalise took pity on him and asked about their urgent matter.

She almost dropped her fork when Kiera and King Devon

explained that someone had sent Kiera a poisoned bottle of sparkling wine with a note supposedly from *her* to apologize for being ill. A chill surging through her, she scanned their auras for any trace of gray or black indicating illness. She relaxed when she spotted none. Yet she still asked, her head whirling from using her powers, "Poisoned? Are you two well?"

Kiera smiled and nodded at King Devon. "Yes, thanks to Devon's protection charm."

Annalise exhaled then leaned back into her chair. "Praise the Goddess."

King Devon hummed, still narrowly eyeing her. "Any idea who sent that bottle?"

Stiffening, Annalise lifted her chin. Despite that letter, she'd never hurt Kiera nor anyone else—she was a healer, after all. "Do you suspect me, your majesty?"

Green trust glowing about her, Kiera grasped Annalise's hand across the table. "No, but you might know who could impersonate you."

Holding King Devon's suspicious gaze, Annalise leaned forward. "Given my parents' ambitions, I comprehend why you might suspect me, but I swear I'd never poison anyone, much less Kiera."

His lips wry, King Devon inclined his head. "I suspect everyone right now."

Annalise's chest squeezed. Of course he did. Dare would likely be the same if someone had attempted to poison her. "Understandable." She studied her supposed note. "The writing appears an imitation of mine, and few outside my family knew I was ill. But despite their faults, my family wouldn't poison our future queen."

Kiera sighed and waved toward the platter of beefsteak that she and King Devon rarely ate for breakfast. "The servants knew you were ill. The poisoner must have heard you were ill through them."

Annalise frowned but hummed. "I suppose. Are you protected from future attempts?" When Kiera nodded, Annalise squeezed her friend's hand. "Good. Let me know if you ever need me." She'd soul-heal Kiera and King Devon even if she must reveal her secret powers.

Although King Devon blinked, Kiera nodded and returned her squeeze, clearly understanding her meaning. "Of course."

Releasing Kiera's hand, Annalise rose and almost swayed. She probably shouldn't have used her powers earlier. If only she could request more energy from Dare without worrying him. "I must return to bed. Unfortunately, I'm not well enough for our nightmara ride today. Perhaps next time."

Once Kiera embraced her and told her to rest, Annalise swept a deep curtsy for King Devon then trudged back to her carriage. Like earlier, she fell asleep on the ride back to Greysnowe House. Then she staggered inside and somehow made it to her bed before succumbing to slumber once more.

OVER THE NEXT FEW DAYS, Annalise spent most of her time sleeping. She only roused when Grace woke her to eat or Dare reached out to check on her. However, each day she felt a bit better, and her courses ended the evening before her next nightmara ride. So that morning, she woke several hours after dawn —later than she used to, but still before breakfast—and felt well enough to head downstairs.

When she glided into the breakfast room, Mother, Father, and Alex all beamed at her. Warmed by their loving welcome, she took her seat beside Alex. Too bad Mother and Father's love would end once she eloped with Dare. A pang darting through her, she smiled back and began heaping her plate with food. "Morning, everyone."

Alex smirked then tsked at her. "Well, finally. I thought you'd become one of those spoiled ladies who never rise before noon."

Mother and Father frowned at Alex, then Mother said, "Don't

tease your sister, Alexander. She's been ill." She turned to Annalise with a smile. "Although you appear recovered now. Do you think you can manage the Duchess of Wildewall's ball tonight? She *is* the head of our duchy."

Her heart quickening, Annalise nodded and caressed Dare's faegift at her throat. If she attended, she and Dare could meet for the first time in five days and discuss their elopement. She smiled at Mother as she began her beefsteak. "I'll take a nap after my nightmara ride to ensure I can attend."

Mother grinned over her teacup. "Wonderful. Make sure to circulate tonight to offset missing court events recently. And dance with as many suitable gentlemen as possible."

As Father nodded and Alex snorted, Annalise suppressed a shudder. She couldn't bear an entire evening dancing with everyone but Dare. "I'll circulate, but I doubt I'll have enough energy to dance."

Mother pursed her lips. "I suppose 'tis better to not attempt too much your first evening back. We can't have you fainting mid-dance."

Alex snorted again. "Yes, 'twould frighten all those suitable gentlemen."

Mother and Father glowered at Alex, but to prevent their scold, Annalise touched his arm and asked, "Would you mind acting as my escort tonight? I might need help repelling overeager suitors." As well as Mother and Father's matchmaking.

Alex hummed and studied her. "If you like. Arthur mentioned he's attending, so I can talk with him when you don't need my escort."

Annalise smiled as she sipped her tea. Good, she could distract Alex with Lord Morwynne before slipping out to meet Dare. "Thanks, Alex."

Father grinned at Alex. "The duchess shall be gratified you're attending her ball when you avoid other court events."

Annalise and Alex exchanged a wry glance. The duchess

would more likely be worried he'd attended to challenge Dare to another duel.

Yet Mother grinned at Father then said, "How true." She turned to Annalise. "While you've been ill, not much has happened at court, despite all the events held by councilors or dukes and duchesses. And we told everyone you remained home to tend to a sick faebird."

Father chuckled. "Yes, the young Duke of Golddell was devastated at his musical evening last night. Clearly, he's smitten."

Annalise almost laughed when Alex smirked and drawled, "How *unfortunate* he's much too young to marry."

Mother glowered at Alex again then turned back to Annalise. "Fortunately, most at court were more interested in the absences of King Devon and his fake betrothed rather than yours." Her lips twisted. "There are rumors that Kiera creature might be pregnant."

Tears burning her eyes, Annalise froze and stared at her half-eaten plate. Why must Mother mention pregnancy rumors after she'd suffered a miscarriage five days ago?

Mother continued, "In addition to missing most court events, she's not drunk any sparkling wine when she and King Devon have attended." Tilting her head, she hummed. "Is that why she invited you to breakfast a few days ago? To tell you she was with child?"

Annalise gulped a bracing breath. If Mother knew the truth behind her illness, she'd not ask such a cruel question. Yet she didn't, and sobbing would only make Mother and Father suspicious. So Annalise blinked back her tears and lifted her gaze. "No, Kiera invited me to discuss another matter." Forcing a serene smile, she rose. "Excuse me, I must head to the palace for my nightmara ride."

Before anyone could reply, she fled the breakfast room. After having the grooms saddle Storm for once, she rode to the palace. She pulled up her cloak hood to cover her face then released the tears she'd curbed at breakfast. However, she made herself quit crying when she neared the palace. Her tears would worry Kiera.

When they met outside the palace, Kiera scrutinized her, and yellow relief swirled about Kiera. "You look much better today."

Her chest clenching, Annalise managed a smile as she gripped Dare's heart-shaped firegem. "Yes, my illness is over."

Kiera nodded as they began toward the nightmara stables. "If you need to leave early to rest, please do so."

Annalise smiled at her friend. Kiera was always so kind. "I shall, thanks."

Once they joined Moonbud and Darkthorn in the nightmara paddock, the nightmara queen-heir craned her head toward Annalise and said, :*We grieve for your loss, Annalise.*:

Annalise glanced at Kiera, who wasn't frowning at her in confusion, so Moonbud must have sent that thought only to her. To keep their conversation private, she mentally replied, :*Thank you, Moonbud.*:

Darkthorn strode over and nuzzled Annalise's hair. :*I'll kneel to make mounting easier, and we'll keep to a walk today.*:

Her nightmara ride went smoothly, although her bones ached afterward. She'd *definitely* need a nap this afternoon to attend tonight's ball.

When she and Kiera neared the palace, Annalise nibbled her lip and eyed her friend. She should tell Kiera about those pregnancy rumors. Hopefully, she'd not start crying. She coughed. "Mother asked me if you were with child at breakfast this morning."

Muddy-orange shock flaring about her, Kiera gaped at Annalise. "*What?*"

Annalise swiftly explained the rumors then said, "I'll see you at the Duchess of Wildewall's ball tonight. Until then." She turned and began toward the palace stables before her grief overwhelmed her.

As soon as she returned to Greysnowe House, she headed

upstairs to her chambers then collapsed on her bed and immediately succumbed to slumber. However, when Grace woke her with a dinner tray, Annalise felt almost normal. She devoured her meal before changing into her sapphire ballgown the exact shade of Dare's firegem. Then she headed downstairs, and she and her family left for the Duchess of Wildewall's ball.

While Annalise and her family greeted the duchess, she met Dare's gaze, and love surged in their entwined souls. Goddess, it had been so long since they'd met.

As Dare turned and spoke to his mother, he asked Annalise, :*When can we meet?*:

She forced her attention to drift across the ballroom. Alex was already eyeing her. :*Not until later. My parents and Alex shall be watching me too closely at first.*:

Dare sighed. :*I'll watch for you to slip into an anteroom then meet you.*:

Alex remained by Annalise's side throughout the beginning of the ball and discouraged potential suitors, especially the ones sent by Mother and Father, using his perceptive quips.

After Alex had routed Lord Meade, Annalise grinned at him. "You make a better guard than a hellhound."

Alex arched a brow then smirked. "I assume 'tis why you begged me to attend."

She squeezed Alex's arm. He was the best brother. "Yes." She tugged him toward Kiera and King Devon. "Come, you must meet our future queen. You'll like her as much as I do." Once they reached Kiera and King Devon, she beamed at her friend. "Evening. Kiera, allow me to introduce my brother, Lord Alexander Greysnowe."

Her navy eyes gleaming, Kiera smiled at Alex. "A pleasure finally to meet the imp who dared dip Annalise's hair in ink growing up. I'm surprised tonight is the first we've met."

Alex shrugged. "Much to Mother and Father's dismay, I've decided most court events are too dull to attend." He smirked at

Annalise again. "I only attended tonight because Annalise begged me. She didn't want to be saddled with a bounder on her first evening out since her illness."

Annalise stiffened and elbowed Alex. He wasn't the best brother—he was the most embarrassing. "Alex! If you attended more often, you'd remember to leash your tongue."

Alex arched his brows and smirked again. "Why? Their majesties are your friends, aren't they?"

She leaned forward and lowered her voice, "Yes, but those who might overhear are not." When Alex simply shrugged, she glared at her annoyingly unrepentant brother.

She was about to scold him further when Mother and Father swept over. And once again, they nodded at King Devon while ignoring Kiera. Why must they always let their ambitions provoke them into being so churlish toward Kiera?

Father glowered at Annalise. "Why aren't you circulating? You've been missing from court for five days."

Her jaw tightening, Annalise lifted her chin. She and Alex had been circulating the entire ball. Mother and Father were just upset Alex had foiled their matchmaking. She gestured toward Kiera and King Devon. "What do you call conversing with the king and his betrothed?"

Mother sniffed. "While King Devon is taken, you must pursue other opportunities."

As King Devon glowered at Mother and Father, Annalise almost winced, but before she could speak, Alex snickered and said, "Yes, the Duke of Osbourne is free. Who cares that he's ancient and hasn't noticed any lady since his wife died eight years ago?"

Ignoring Alex, Father sneered at Kiera. "I'd thank you to cease poisoning our children with your common opinions."

Annalise froze. Goddess, *why* had Father mentioned poisoning after someone had attempted to poison Kiera? King Devon was already suspicious of them.

King Devon stiffened then gritted, "What do you mean by that?"

As Mother and Father gawked at the king's harsh tone, Annalise did wince this time. Yes, King Devon clearly believed Mother and Father were Kiera's poisoners.

Fortunately, Kiera pulled King Devon away before he could punch Father or accuse Mother and Father of treason.

Once Kiera and King Devon left, Alex tsked and shook his head. "Are you *trying* to make King Devon despise us? What a triumph for the Ravenstones."

While her parents and Alex began arguing, Annalise took advantage of their distraction to slip into a nearby anteroom to meet Dare. Because Lady Blaine had seen them at their last meeting during a ball, Annalise sat on the sofa out of direct sight from the door.

Two dances later, Dare strode into the anteroom. Sitting beside her, he took her hands and kissed her palms. "How are you feeling?"

As tingling darted up her arms at his kiss, she caressed his bearded face, and warmth suffused her chest. "Much better. Especially now that we're together, my love."

His amber eyes darkening with hunger, Dare pulled her against him. "Goddess, I need you."

Annalise wrapped her arms about his neck then buried her fingers in his long, black hair, and heat flared in her veins. "Me too."

They shifted and captured each other's mouths, their souls meshing at once. Groaning, they pressed closer together and deepened their ravenous kiss.

Then Alex drawled, "If Father and Mother caught you two like this, they'd have an apoplexy."

A chill bolting through their meshed souls, she and Dare wrenched their bodies and souls apart then swung to face Alex, who smirked at them with yellow laughter dancing about him.

Annalise swallowed, her pulse surging and chest tight. Of

course, Alex had discovered them as soon as they all attended the same court event. Despite needing his help discouraging suitors, she never should have asked him to attend tonight. Now that he'd discovered them, they'd no choice but to confess their soulbond and love. Yet how would Alex react when he realized they'd been lying to him for months?

CHAPTER 46

*D*are tensed as Alex sauntered across the anteroom and dropped into the chair beside the sofa. The younger gentleman didn't appear upset to discover them kissing, but would he be angry when they confessed the depth of their involvement? After all, they'd made love without being married, and until recently, Annalise had been carrying his child.

Continuing to smirk, Alex shook his head. "Although if you two always meet to kiss at court events, 'tis astounding that Father and Mother haven't discovered your love yet. I suppose their ambition to have Annalise marry King Devon or another influential lord has been blinding them."

Annalise sighed. She was still pale with faint shadows beneath her eyes and gray fog about her aura, although she looked better than during her miscarriage five days ago. "In their defense, my recent illness," her grief surged through Dare, "has distracted them as well."

To comfort her, Dare threaded his fingers through hers and sent his love through their entwined souls. Soon they must meet outside, so he could use their soulbond to share the solace nature had given him about their lost child.

Alex snorted a laugh. "I know. When Father and Mother realized you'd left, I used your illness as an excuse. Then I told them I'd sit with you until you felt well enough to return to the ball. So they probably shan't hunt for you."

Dare smiled at Alex. Of course, he'd devised the perfect excuse. "Thanks, Alex. Your parents discovering us would be distressing, especially during a court event where others could overhear. Hopefully, my mother shan't hunt for me either. Or at least check the garden rather than the anterooms."

Alex frowned and eyed him and Annalise. "Why do you two risk meeting at court events? Surely, private meetings would be less likely to be discovered."

Dare and Annalise traded a wry glance. Private meetings were more dangerous than court events. Then Annalise sighed as she turned back to Alex and said, "If we don't meet, our soulbond becomes ravenous and excruciating to resist. We met privately for a while, but our passion became impossible to control, so we had to stop."

Blinking, Alex leaned toward them. "Soulbond?" He arched his brows at Annalise. "But you have no powers—Father and Mother always said so."

Annalise shifted beside Dare then swallowed, her regret darting through him. "No, I'm a soul healer, but I concealed my powers, so no one could exploit them."

Alex stilled, his mouth agape. "Like our ancestress Esme the Great and our distant aunt who caused the Greysnowe-Ravenstone feud?"

Releasing Annalise's hand, Dare wrapped his arm about her to hearten her. "Yes. And your sister and I are soulbound because she healed my fatal wound after our duel."

Alex inhaled a sharp breath and blinked at Annalise. "No wonder you sent everyone to fetch a witch healer. You needed time alone with Dare to heal him." As Annalise nodded, Alex turned to Dare. "And no wonder you were so understanding about our distant aunt's impossible situation. You're experiencing the same with Annalise."

Dare shook his head. "I've always felt that about the tragic situation that started the feud between our families." He pursed a wry smile. "Although my soulbond with Annalise certainly reinforced my conviction."

Alex hummed. "I imagine so."

Inhaling, Dare pulled Annalise against him. He must convince Alex their love was genuine. "But Annalise and I aren't in love because of our irresistible soulbond. Since we met during our first season, we were always drawn to one another, and our soulbond simply allowed us to truly get to know each other and fall in love."

Her love warming his chest, Annalise turned and silently caressed his face.

Snickering, Alex raised his eyes skyward. "Yes, I remember those ardent glances you and Annalise exchanged whenever you two met. They're why I assumed you were a cad and challenged you to that mad duel where I nearly killed you." He snorted. "Although I suppose some good came out of that since it led to you two forming a soulbond and falling in love."

Annalise sighed as she lowered her hand and turned to Alex with a pleading smile. "I'm sorry that I never told you about my powers and that we've lied about our soulbond and love for months."

Alex tsked and grinned. "You may not have told me, but I realized your love a while ago, although I never suspected your powers."

Dare and Annalise shared rueful smiles. Not surprising her perceptive brother had realized their involvement. Dare arched his brows at Alex then asked, "What betrayed us?"

His lips twitching, Alex chuckled. "'Twas obvious to anyone who truly knew you—especially if they knew you both. First, there were those ardent glances of yours. Plus, you two wanted the same life back in Wildewall. And you both often asked, ever so casually and obliquely, about the other." He arched a brow at Dare. "Then your description of your perfect wife matched

Annalise." He turned to Annalise. "So when you admitted being in love with someone our parents would never accept, I suspected 'twas Dare." He nodded at Dare's faegift. "And once you began wearing that necklace every day, I *knew* it must be."

Dare and Annalise glanced at each other. So Alex had known the truth for a month and suspected it even longer.

Annalise shook her head. "That explains why you kept asking me to share my secrets as well as discussing me with Dare." She sighed and leaned toward Alex. "'Tisn't that I didn't trust you, but I didn't wish to burden you, and more people knowing secrets makes them harder to keep." She shrugged. "Besides, I was accustomed to concealing my powers—I've done so since before you could talk—and our soulbond and love involved my powers."

Alex hummed. "I can understand that, I suppose." He turned to Dare. "And I assume you remained silent because Annalise didn't wish to tell me." When Dare ruefully nodded, Alex arched his brows at them. "But now that I know the truth, what do you two intend to do?"

Annalise lifted her chin and laid a hand on Dare's knee. "The same as we were intending to do before—elope. We were meeting tonight to discuss details."

Dare blinked at her, a jolt coursing through him. Even without their unborn child to protect, she still wished to elope? His heart surged. Thank the Goddess.

Alex chuckled and shook his head. "I'm not surprised you two plan to elope. Only sensible course given the feud between our families. I'm just surprised you've not eloped already."

Dare shifted and tightened his arm about Annalise. Did Alex doubt the depth of their love because they'd not eloped yet?

Before he could reply, Annalise grimaced then told Alex, "'Tis my fault. Dare spoke of marriage as soon as we were soulbound, but I was worried about upsetting Mother and Father." She sighed. "You know they'll hate me forever when I betray them by eloping with a Ravenstone."

Alex echoed Annalise's sigh. "I know. They're too obsessed with the feud not to. And that you chose to marry their ancestral enemy over King Devon shall infuriate them further." He leaned forward. "If you two require any help, please let me know."

Dare relaxed as Annalise beamed at her brother and said, "Thanks, Alex. Your support means more than I can say."

Alex winked at her. "'Tis nothing." He turned to Dare with a grin. "I'll be glad to have you as a brother in truth."

Dare grinned back, his chest lightening. With their shared interests and his understanding heart, Alex would make a wonderful brother. "Me too."

His grin turning impish, Alex leaned back in his chair. "Now that we've no more secrets, Annalise should join our rides to the royal bay."

Dare straightened and grinned harder. Then he and Annalise could spend time together outside of court events, and they'd not go too far with her brother along. "I agree, although we should leave our swords behind."

Her breath quickening, Annalise squeezed his knee. "No, don't. Watching you exhibit your sword fighting shall be thrilling."

As Annalise's desire coursed through their entwined souls, his pulse surged, and tingling warmth flooded him. He met her gaze. "Truly?"

At her nod, he began bending his head to kiss her but halted when Alex snickered and drawled, "Did you two forget I was here?"

Dare and Annalise jerked back then turned to face Alex. As Dare's neck heated, Annalise blushed and nodded.

Alex tsked, his eyes gleaming. "No wonder you two can't meet privately. I think I should ride between you at the royal bay."

Dare sighed. Doubtless prudent considering their hunger for each other. Perhaps once they married, they'd have better restraint around others.

Annalise smoothed her sapphire ballgown. "When's your next ride?"

Alex grinned. "The day after tomorrow." He waggled his brows at Dare. "Unless Dare is too impatient to wait that long."

Sighing again, Dare shook his head. "Mother is expecting the two of us to ride tomorrow, and I can't cancel without raising her suspicions." She was already too suspicious.

Annalise fingered his firegem flickering at her throat. "I'll bring Finn and Lily along, so we can exchange them again. The poor angelcats have been confined in my chambers for over a week."

Alex blinked. "You've been exchanging angelcats?"

Dare shrugged and rubbed his beard. "After Lily and Finn met, they soon became mates and refused to be parted, so we've been exchanging them."

Alex chuckled. "Well, that explains Finn's disappearances. How appropriate your angelcats are mates."

As Annalise hummed in reply, Dare glanced at the clock on the mantel. They'd left the ballroom some time ago, so Mother was likely hunting for him. And he and Annalise hadn't discussed details about their elopement yet. He smiled at Alex. "Could Annalise and I speak privately for a moment?"

Flashing a grin, Alex rose. "Of course. But no kissing. I'll sit across the anteroom and watch the door."

Once Alex sprawled in a chair near the door, Dare removed his arm from Annalise's shoulders so he could turn and take her hands. To prevent Alex from overhearing, he mentally said, :*You still wish to elope like you told Alex?*:

Her surprise darting through him like salmon in a river, Annalise blinked then squeezed his hands. :*Of course. Why wouldn't I?*:

He swallowed as his throat constricted. He mustn't pressure her while they grieved. :*Because you just lost our child and can't bear to lose your parents too.*:

Tears shimmering in her eyes, Annalise sighed and shook her

head. :*Our unborn child wasn't the only reason I decided to elope. I finally realized you were right—we couldn't allow our families' ancestral strife and my parents' blind rancor to prevent us from building a wonderful life full of abiding love and family.*:

His heart swelling, Dare grinned and kissed her palms. Surely such kisses weren't what Alex meant. :*I love you, Annalise.*:

Annalise leaned forward and brushed her lips against his, her heady honeysuckle scent weaving about him. :*I love you too.*:

He shuddered as his body hardened at Annalise's featherlight kiss. Yet he forced himself to remain still and not yank her into his arms for a true kiss. Her brother was just across the anteroom.

Licking her lips, Annalise sat back with a sigh. :*We'd better avoid kissing as much as possible until we elope. I'd rather not become pregnant again until after we're married.*:

Dare echoed her sigh. Such restraint would be sensible, but Goddess, he burned to kiss her and make love to her. :*Hopefully, we can elope soon then.*:

Annalise swallowed and eyed him through her lashes. :*Would you mind if we waited until after the Longnight season?*: Her sorrow pierced him. :*I'd like one last Longnight with Mother and Father before they disown me.*:

His chest squeezing, he kissed her palms again. He'd waited five months for her to agree to marry him, so what was one and a half more? Especially when she needed that time to create memories with her parents that must last the rest of her life. :*Of course we can wait until then. Although we should try to only meet when Alex can chaperone us. I'm not sure we can trust our restraint otherwise.*:

Annalise hummed. :*How true.*: She tugged her hands free. :*We'd better return to the ball.*: She rose and turned toward her brother. "Alex, are you ready to escort me back now?"

Alex rose from his chair across the anteroom. "Certainly, but how did you two discuss details without speaking?"

Blushing, Annalise took Alex's arm. "We can communicate with our thoughts because of our soulbond."

His eyes widening, Alex glanced between Annalise and Dare. "Advantageous."

Dare and Annalise smiled at each other. Not only did speaking mentally make arranging meetings easier, 'twas what had let them withstand remaining apart during her recovery. He murmured, "Very."

As Alex shook his head and led Annalise back into the ballroom, Dare forced himself to remain on the sofa. So no one would connect their reappearances, he waited several dances before returning to the ballroom.

Not long after his return, Mother bustled over to him. "Dare, where have you been? You slipped away once again, and I couldn't find you in the duchess's garden."

He managed a shrug. Thank the Goddess she'd not thought to check the anterooms. "I'm sorry for worrying you. I needed some time away from the ballroom."

Mother sighed as she took his arm. "I can't understand why you insist on remaining in Ormas when you never approach any ladies and disappear from most court events."

Dare almost winced. If only he could explain to Mother about Annalise. "I've decided to return to Wildewall after the Longnight season. If I can't find a wife in Ormas by then, I never shall."

Humming, Mother leaned closer and inhaled. "I see."

He stiffened, his neck prickling. Mother had done the same at the Duke of Oakmoor's soiree after he'd returned from being in the garden with Annalise. She *must* have noticed Annalise's honeysuckle scent on him that evening to be checking tonight. Yet why hadn't she said anything?

He made himself smile. "Shall we say farewell to the Duchess of Wildewall then return to Ravenstone House?"

Mother nodded, and they left the duchess's ball. And

although Mother eyed him on the carriage ride, she didn't ask again about his disappearance tonight.

CHAPTER 47

When Kiera and King Devon strode into the breakfast room the following morning, a chill darted through Annalise, but she continued sipping her tea. After Mother and Father's churlish behavior at the duchess's ball yesterday, doubtless Kiera and King Devon had come to accuse Mother and Father of attempting to poison Kiera. Not that they had.

However, the rest of her family didn't remain so calm at their king and future queen's unexpected and early visit. Father choked on his bacon and eggs, Mother dropped her toast, and Alex froze with his laden fork halfway to his mouth.

While Kiera sat beside Annalise and squeezed her hand, King Devon sat beside Kiera and glared at Mother and Father, who both paled. Flashing a cold smile, King Devon said, "We're here to finish the discussion we began last night."

As Alex blinked and their parents swallowed then glanced at each other, Annalise suppressed a sigh and set down her teacup. Unfortunately, she'd been right about Kiera and King Devon's visit.

His smile stiff, Father thrust out his chin. "I'm not certain what you mean."

Muddy-red anger flaring about him, King Devon began to retort until Kiera laid her hand on his and said, "You claimed I was poisoning your children with my opinions. Did you repay that by sending me a poisoned bottle of sparkling wine supposedly from Annalise?"

Tense silence echoed through the breakfast room as Mother and Father jerked back and gaped at Kiera.

Annalise exhaled. As she'd thought, Mother and Father clearly knew nothing about the attempt to poison Kiera.

Pale but his jaw tight, Alex leaned toward King Devon and Kiera then said, "Father and Mother have acted almost treasonously toward Lady Kiera, but they'd never poison anyone."

King Devon extracted some papers from his satchel and tossed them before Alex. "Then why was your father seen with assassins in recent months?"

The back of her throat burning, Annalise recoiled from Mother and Father as Alex began reading and paled further. Assassins? Father had contacted assassins? How could he have done something so evil? "What?!"

Muddy-yellow unease swirling about him, Father stiffened and muttered to his plate, "I've not met with any assassins in the last two months."

Annalise pressed her free hand against her churning stomach. Not meeting with assassins for months didn't atone for meeting them in the first place.

King Devon glared at Father. "Which is why I never pursued the matter, other than having my guards neutralize those assassins. But they could have sold you a poison at your first meeting."

Her nausea surging, Annalise almost winced. Father's meetings with assassins explained why King Devon immediately suspected Mother and Father of poisoning Kiera.

Mother stiff beside him, Father swallowed but waved a hand and told King Devon, "Not hardly. They were all incensed that I approached them in public and refused to offer their services, which suited me fine."

Annalise gaped at Mother and Father as Alex frowned at them and asked, "Why would you approach assassins if you didn't wish to hire them?"

Mother and Father traded a glance then shrugged. Despite their auras betraying their unease, they appeared unrepentant about contacting assassins.

Eyeing them, Annalise shuddered. Dear Goddess, maybe Mother and Father were behind poisoning Kiera like King Devon believed. She fingered Dare's faegift to comfort herself. "You *must* explain why—poisoning Kiera is treason as well as evil."

Muddy-yellow anxiety pulsing about her, Mother lifted her chin and blurted, "'Tis all that whelp Ravenstone's fault."

A chill dousing her, Annalise froze. Mother and Father were truly behind Kiera's poisoning? And they blamed *Dare* for their treason? Had their blind obsession with the feud driven them mad?

Dare's presence suddenly surrounded her. :*Annalise, what's wrong? Your distress has been reverberating through our entwined souls.*:

She shivered and gripped his faegift. :*King Devon told us Father had contacted assassins, and Mother just admitted to attempting to poison Kiera.*:

His shock bolting through her, Dare whispered, :*They what? When your father quit contacting assassins as soon as I quit sending letters seeking peace, I assumed 'twas a mere ploy to end my letters.*:

Annalise almost gasped. Dare knew about Father's assassins? She swallowed a hysterical giggle. They must have been the escalating schemes Dare had blamed for quitting his letters. :*Why didn't you tell me about Father's assassins?*:

Dare sighed. :*Because I knew learning your father sought to hire assassins would devastate you. And since I had informed King Devon, I figured he'd handle matters, so nothing would come of it.*:

Her chest clenching, Annalise shivered again. Except something *had* come of it. Mother and Father had sent her friend a poisoned bottle of sparkling wine.

But before she could tell Dare that, King Devon glared at Father and gritted, "Explain."

Muddy-yellow anxiety intensifying about him, Father swallowed then exhaled. "After his duel with Alexander on Summerday, Ravenstone sent us letters requesting we meet to end the feud. Claimed almost dying made him want peace. As if we'd believe *anything* a treacherous Ravenstone claimed." He croaked a laugh. "Well, those public meetings with assassins were my answer."

Whimpering as her chest loosened but bitterness flooded her mouth, Annalise covered her face with her hands then murmured, "Oh, Father." As Kiera squeezed her shoulder, she reached out to Dare, :*Well, you were right—Father just admitted contacting assassins was a ploy to end your letters. I doubt they attempted to poison Kiera.*:

Dare sighed, his love enfolding her like a heartening embrace. :*I'm glad.*:

Then Mother added after Father, "He was quite clever about it. He made sure to meet when Ravenstone's people were watching. But he had to pretend not to notice them."

At Mother's boast, Annalise lowered her hands and eyed her parents. Although muddy-yellow anxiety still swirled about Mother and Father, a hint of muddy-orange pride glowed about them as well. Her stomach roiled. Just like when they'd gloated about Alex nearly killing Dare.

After exchanging a glance with Kiera, King Devon sighed and shook his head. "I expect you to write to Lord Ravenstone and explain at once. I don't want your feud escalating any further."

Their anxiety swamping the hint of pride in their auras, Mother and Father grimaced then nodded.

Annalise swallowed and almost winced. The feud would definitely escalate when she and Dare eloped after the Longnight season. Please, Goddess, let them not truly hire assassins then. She reached out to Dare again, :*King Devon ordered Mother and Father to write you an explanation about the assassins, so don't assume they're ending the feud when you receive it.*:

Dare sighed. :*If only they would.*: He paused. :*Mother is calling me. I'll reach out tonight.*:

Alex smirked at Mother and Father over a forkful of eggs. "Don't fret, Father. Lord Ravenstone shall remain gracious, like when I apologized for almost killing him. He seems a decent sort."

Annalise sighed as Mother and Father glared back, which only made Alex smirk harder. Dare *was* a decent sort, but were Mother and Father? Decent people didn't even *pretend* to hire assassins.

King Devon rose. "We must go." He narrowed his eyes at Mother and Father. "Mention the poisoning attempt to no one."

Muddy-yellow anxiety flaring about them again, Mother and Father jerked nods while Kiera embraced Annalise and rose.

Kiera took King Devon's hand then studied Mother and Father. "Who knew Annalise was ill?"

Her blue eyes shaded, Mother sniffed and replied, "We knew, and our servants, of course. But we kept her illness quiet. We don't want any suitable gentlemen believing Annalise can't bear them strong sons."

Annalise drooped and fisted her hands to not touch her stomach. Goddess knew if she could bear strong sons. She'd lost her and Dare's unborn child. Shoving her grief aside, she made herself straighten and return her gaze to her parents.

Once Kiera and King Devon strode from the breakfast room, Mother and Father sagged and exchanged wide glances. Then Mother shuddered and asked, "Did we just escape getting arrested for treason?"

While Annalise sighed at their astonishment, Alex snorted then replied, "Barely. How could you have been mad enough to contact assassins?"

Father bristled. "We had to make Ravenstone quit sending those deceitful letters."

Alex snorted again. "Lord Ravenstone's letters *weren't* deceitful. He truly seeks peace."

Not letting herself nod since 'twould hint at her involvement with Dare, Annalise leaned forward with a frown instead. Somehow she must make Mother and Father see how ruinous their ploy had been. "And to make Lord Ravenstone quit his letters by contacting assassins? King Devon could have arrested Father for conspiracy to commit murder."

Mother shifted in her chair but lifted her chin. "Your father never meant to hire any of those assassins."

Alex sighed. "Mother, people don't usually contact assassins unless they mean to hire them."

Nodding, Annalise pursed her lips and suppressed a shiver. "And since your explanation made you sound guilty of poisoning Kiera at first, we're fortunate that Kiera wasn't hurt and was here to restrain King Devon."

Mother frowning beside him, Father scowled at her then asked, "What do you mean by that?"

Annalise tsked. Why must their ambitions always blind them? She shook her head. "Without Kiera, King Devon would have had the royal guards arrest you as soon as you sounded like you were admitting your guilt. He adores Kiera and is probably frantic to find her poisoner before they attempt to assassinate her again."

Alex leaned toward Mother and Father. "Father, consider how *you'd* act if Mother was almost poisoned."

Mother and Father swallowed while trading a glance, muddy-yellow unease flickering about them. Then Mother muttered, "But Lady Morwynne said King Devon's betrothal was a sham to appease the nightmara."

Resisting the urge to raise her eyes skyward, Annalise sighed and sipped her tea. "With their power over dreams and the mind, the nightmara would recognize a fake betrothed at once and would refuse to negotiate with her. Yet Moonbud and the other nightmara accepted Kiera straightaway, and Moonbud even offered to teach her to ride. The nightmara queen-heir would never do that unless she regarded Kiera as an equal."

Mother and Father blinked then tensed before Father said, "But due to Kiera's common birth, Lady Morwynne was so certain the betrothal must be a sham."

Finishing his eggs, Alex snorted. "After King Devon spent two months hunting for her? Even without attending court events, I heard about the king's determined hunt."

Annalise hummed. "Yes, King Devon even requested my help hunting for her. 'Tis why he escorted me to court events after they'd met." When Mother and Father gaped at her, she shook her head. "You really shouldn't trust anything Lady Morwynne tells you. She's devious, grasping, and manipulative."

Mother sniffed and poured herself more tea. "Lady Morwynne has always been kind to us."

Sighing, Annalise shook her head again. Meaning the superior countess had flattered Mother and Father's ambitions and inflamed their obsession with the feud. She arched her brows at Mother and Father. "Doubtless Lady Morwynne was only kind so she could manipulate you."

Alex nodded, his face grave for once. "Most likely. What Arthur has mentioned about his mother is... troubling."

Father stiffened and gritted a tight smile. "If Lady Morwynne is so villainous, why has King Devon allowed her to serve on the council for eight years?"

Grimacing, Annalise leaned forward. Please let this convince Mother and Father of Lady Morwynne's treachery. "Because Lady Morwynne is careful never to be caught doing anything wicked herself. She provokes others into doing so. Recall how she provoked you with lies about Kiera, so you were always churlish to our future queen in public. Yet did Lady Morwynne ever once do the same?"

Mother and Father paled as they glanced at each other. Then Mother replied, "No, she didn't."

Her chest easing, Annalise relaxed in her chair. Thank the Goddess that had finally convinced them. "You should avoid Lady Morwynne in the future as well as apologize to Kiera for behaving so churlishly toward her."

Alex narrowed his eyes at Mother and Father. "*And* quit shoving Annalise at King Devon or other suitable lords. Let Annalise find her husband her own way."

Mother and Father winced then exchanged another glance. Father swallowed and said, "We'll apologize once Lady Kiera unearths her poisoner. She and King Devon shan't believe us until then."

Annalise frowned. Delaying would only make their apology more uncomfortable. And Goddess knew when Kiera and King Devon would unearth her poisoner.

But before she could say that, Mother added, "Although we'll quit matchmaking at once." Muddy-blue regret pulsing about her, she grimaced. "Since we've been so blind about our friends, we'll likely botch that too."

Annalise eyed Mother and Father. They were too upset to listen about apologizing to Kiera. So instead, she smiled and said, "As you've mentioned before, I do wish to marry and start a family. But my husband must see me as a person, not just the most beautiful lady in Calatini." Her smile faded. Although Mother and Father would loathe her forever when they learned her choice of husband.

As Alex squeezed her hand beneath the table, Mother and Father nodded, then Mother said, "Understandable. Please let us know if you require any help or advice finding that gentleman."

· · ·

So that evening, Mother and Father let Annalise skip the Islayes' ball, despite being held by a councilor and his wife. Instead, after mentally updating Dare, Annalise followed his advice and headed to bed early so she could rest after her distressing morning. Yet despite her extra sleep, she was too exhausted to join Alex on his ride to the royal bay with Dare the next morning. She made Alex take Finn and Lily then collapsed back in her bed and slept until breakfast.

The following day, Annalise managed to rise for her nightmara ride with Kiera, but after luncheon, she napped for several hours to ensure she could attend the Dabars' ball that evening. Kiera had said she would attend, so 'twould be the first time Mother and Father would see Kiera since the poisoner confrontation, and she must encourage them to apologize.

When they arrived, she glanced about for Kiera and King Devon then smiled when she spotted them. They both appeared much more relaxed than they'd been the past week. King Devon probably because Kiera now had a matching glow about her left wrist—a powerful protection charm like his that would defend her from poisons or enchantments. Kiera also must be relieved she could drink sparkling wine and disprove the pregnancy rumors at court. They'd both be happy to hear Mother and Father's apology.

She smiled at Mother and Father then nodded toward Kiera and King Devon. "Perhaps instead of waiting, you should apologize to Kiera now. They appear in a pleasant mood."

Mother and Father eyed Kiera and King Devon, then Father grimaced and said, "True, but they shan't believe us until they know for certain we're not responsible."

Mother nodded then shooed Annalise toward Kiera and King Devon. "However, you should go spend time with Lady Kiera."

Annalise sighed but glided across the ballroom. From the red determination glowing about them, Mother and Father wouldn't budge about apologizing tonight.

To prevent herself from seeking out Dare, she spent the entire ball with Kiera and King Devon even though her friends danced every dance while she danced none. Throughout the ball, she glanced at Mother and Father, but they never once shoved her at suitable gentlemen. They were serious about their promise to quit matchmaking. Hopefully, 'twould last.

CHAPTER 48

A week after their previous ride, Dare made himself smile as he met Alex on the cliffs above the royal bay. Like before, Annalise wasn't with her brother, but not because she needed more sleep. She'd mentioned during their mental conversation before bed yesterday that she'd a nightmara ride this morning.

He sighed. He ached to speak to Annalise in person, despite their mental conversations every night. During the past week, they'd seen each other at the Dabars' ball and the Valcrests' reception, although they'd not slipped away to meet to avoid fueling Mother's suspicions. So he and Annalise had last met at the Duchess of Wildewall's ball when Alex discovered them. Much too long to remain apart. Thank the Goddess 'twould be over after the Longnight season ended.

Alex grinned as he leapt from Biscuit's saddle. "What, no hellhounds today?"

Shrugging, Dare patted Ebony then dismounted as well. "I only brought Raven and Bear last week to see Annalise. They've not seen her in almost two months, and they miss her." Although not as much as he did.

Alex frowned and tapped his pommel. "Speaking of Annalise, I'm worried about her again. She's still not recovered from her illness. She hasn't resumed rising early for her morning walks or rides yet, and she naps most afternoons, which isn't like her at all. Before her illness, Annalise was always full of energy."

His chest tightening, Dare rubbed his beard. Alex was right that Annalise hadn't recovered from her miscarriage. Although she no longer looked ill, her mental presence wasn't as radiant thanks to grief for their lost child. He'd been encouraging her to rest more to give her time alone to heal, but that had done little so far. If only he could hold her in his arms to comfort her or had a chance to share the solace nature had given him.

Yet since he couldn't explain her miscarriage to her brother, he simply said, "'Tis harder to rise early with the dawn coming so late now. I've had some trouble rising early as well."

Still frowning, Alex shook his head. "Even in the dead of winter, Annalise has always risen early—until now."

Dare swallowed, his heart clenching. She'd never suffered a miscarriage until now either. "Except before, we were all back in Wildewall by this time of year. And the natural energy there is purer and wilder than in Ormas. 'Tis why most nature witches settle in Wildewall."

Alex hummed and tapped his pommel again. "But Annalise is a soul healer not a nature witch."

Dare shrugged. "True, but her powers impact nature."

Alex tsked then chuckled. "Only a nature witch would say that."

Flashing a wry smile, Dare shrugged. "I know. But since Annalise's powers impact nature, they might be tied to the seasons like those of most nature witches. But she may never have noticed before because the natural energy back home was strong enough no matter the season." He grimaced. "I've been having the same trouble recently." Ever since he'd drained his powers after her miscarriage, he'd seemed to need more natural energy.

Alex cocked his head. "I suppose natural energy fueling her powers makes sense." He sighed then arched a brow. "Shall we cross swords now?"

Dare nodded, and they began sword fighting. After four months of practice, Alex had become excellent, so their sword fight was lengthy and strenuous, although Dare eventually won with a twisting riposte that slipped past Alex's guard.

After their sword fight, they galloped along the beach, and Dare gathered the natural energy around him until his magic overflowed, although it took most of their gallop. He frowned when he finally retracted his powers. Yes, he definitely needed more natural energy now. Perhaps Mother was wrong about their powers not being tied to the seasons.

Over the following days, he spent as much time as possible outside despite the cold, so he could gather more natural energy. Yet even so, he still tended to sleep later than usual. The shorter days *must* be draining him. How was Annalise faring? Since he'd been skipping court events to spend time outside, he'd not seen her since the Valcrests' reception. And when they mentally spoke at night, all she admitted to was being a bit tired.

So during their mental conversation three days before the start of the Longnight season, he mentioned Finn had been moping for her recently then arranged to meet her at the park around midmorning the following day to exchange the angel-cats. Neither of them could manage dawn right now.

EAGER TO SEE ANNALISE AGAIN, Dare rose at his usual time the following morning for the first time in weeks. He even managed to ride Ebony to the royal bay to gather natural energy before their walk, although without Mother. He couldn't risk being late meeting Annalise or Mother discovering his visit to a park near Greysnowe House.

After his ride, he tended to Ebony then bolted inside to gather the hellhounds and angelcats. Clearly sensing his excitement, Raven and Bear bayed as their eyes burst into flame, while Lily and Finn darted and leapt about him. Fortunately, he managed to herd the magical pets outside without Mother waylaying them.

He hurried to the park with the hellhounds and angelcats bounding beside him. As he entered, he inhaled the icy air and unfurled his powers. He'd gather more natural energy until Annalise arrived. He strode through the leafless oak, chestnut, and plane trees until he reached the clearing near the heart of the park where he and Alex had dueled. While Lily and Finn chased each other among the bare branches, he tossed sticks for Raven and Bear.

When Annalise arrived with Alex, Dare met her gaze, and their love flared in their entwined souls. She dropped her brother's arm, and they flew together. Their souls meshed as their mouths fused in a ravenous kiss.

Yet after that one kiss, he wrenched their mouths apart. They'd an audience and important matters to discuss.

Smirking at them across the clearing, Alex tsked and shook his head. "Must you two kiss in front of me? I'll never be able to unsee that."

As Dare released her, Annalise blushed and separated their meshed souls then said, "Sorry. Remaining apart so long makes our soulbond ravenous."

Alex snickered. "So I noticed."

Dare was about to reply when Finn yowled then hurtled from the branches into Annalise's arms.

Her joy warming Dare's chest, Annalise cuddled the angelcat and scratched his chin. "Missed me too, did you, Finn?"

Dare chuckled as Raven and Bear thundered over and pressed against her, their eyes flaming and tails thumping the ground. Then Lily leapt from the branches with a purring meow and hovered above Annalise to nuzzle her hair. He grinned at Annalise. "We all did."

Annalise smiled and bent to pet and scratch the excited magical pets mobbing her. "Apparently."

Once the hellhounds and angelcats finally had enough petting, Lily and Finn leapt back into the branches, while Raven and Bear coursed after the sticks Dare threw for them.

Annalise straightened then swayed as her lightheadedness swamped Dare.

Tensing, he grasped her elbow and scrutinized her. Although she looked better, she was slightly pale with barely noticeable shadows beneath her eyes. And that gray fog still tarnished her transparent aura with electrum motes. Could her exhaustion just be due to grief? He leaned toward her. "Are you all right?"

Annalise flashed a wry smile. "Our magical pets' excitement simply overwhelmed me for a moment."

His brow furrowed, Alex snorted. "Such excitement never overwhelmed you before."

As Annalise bristled, Dare shook his head to end Alex's reproof. 'Twasn't helping. "Could I speak privately to Annalise for a moment?"

Alex hummed then nodded at the returning hellhounds. "Very well. I'll toss sticks for Raven and Bear."

Once her brother had turned away, Dare pulled Annalise closer, and like always, his heart quickened at their embrace. :*Are you truly feeling well?*:

Annalise leaned against him with a sigh, her heady honeysuckle scent surrounding him. Then she murmured, "I've just felt a bit tired since I," her voice quavered, "lost our child. And using my powers, even mentally speaking with you, makes it worse."

His throat tightening, he swallowed. He'd better speak aloud then. "Do you think your powers might be tied to the seasons? I've been wondering the same about mine recently. Although Mother always said our powers aren't tied to the seasons, that may only be true in Wildewall where the power is purer and wilder."

Annalise blinked. "I never considered the shorter days. But the calm auras of plants and creatures do settle my soul, so that, along with recovering, could explain my recent tiredness."

Dare brushed a kiss against her brow and sent his love through their entwined souls. "You must make sure to rest and use your powers as little as possible. Plus, I can send you energy whenever you need it."

Annalise smiled, her echoing love washing over him. "Thanks, Dare." She sighed. "I suppose we'd better stop our mental conversations every night. I'll miss them."

He swallowed his own sigh. "To sate our soulbond, we'll just need to ask Alex to chaperone us more often at private meetings like this one." As she nodded, he eyed her. He must share the wisdom nature had given him to comfort her. "Do you think you could risk meshing our souls again? I want to show you through our soulbond something nature recently reminded me."

Once Annalise nodded again and meshed their souls, Dare sent their minds into the frozen park around them. Soon, the calm of the sleeping plants awaiting their season filled them. He retracted his powers then sent her energy before separating their souls. He squeezed her. "Do you see how even death serves a purpose in life?"

Tears shimmering in her eyes, Annalise managed a tremulous smile. "Yes, but remembering that is almost impossible after losing a child."

He kissed her brow, his chest aching. "I know. And we'll always be sad about losing them, but we should remember the joy and help they brought us." He sighed. "And perhaps their loss shall make us love our future children even more."

Annalise brushed away her tears. "I'll try, my love." She grimaced then feathered a kiss against his lips. "Alex and I should go before someone from court spots us together."

After Annalise called Finn and Lily from the trees then left with Alex, Dare remained in the park and tossed sticks for Raven and Bear to ensure no one connected their visits to the park.

Eventually, he called the hellhounds, and they returned to Ravenstone House.

When he strode inside with Raven and Bear, Mother bustled into the entrance hall. Inspecting him, she said, "You're back. Where are Lily and her mate?"

Dare almost winced. Not surprising Mother had immediately noticed the angelcats' disappearance. He forced a shrug then repeated his earlier excuse, "Exploring Ormas again, I expect."

Mother hummed, her eyes narrowing.

To distract her, he asked, "Have you needed more natural energy to fill your powers recently?"

Frowning, Mother blinked then squinted at him. "No, why?"

Dare grimaced, his stomach tightening. Could he have been wrong about his powers being tied to the seasons? "Because I've needed to gather more natural energy in recent weeks. I thought perhaps the energy here during late autumn wasn't enough."

Mother tilted her head. "Well, your powers *are* stronger than mine, and you've been here much longer than I have. So you might need more natural energy even though I don't yet."

He exhaled a sigh. That made sense. He studied her walking dress. "Are you headed somewhere?"

Mother grinned. "The Islayes' again. Miss Winston reached the Magehaven ore yesterday, and they've news. You should join me."

Dare nodded, and they headed to Islaye House. As soon as they arrived, Lord Islaye told them Miss Winston and an itinerant priest were testing different methods to stabilize the ore, and some appeared promising.

Because of the Magehaven ore, he and Mother spent most of the following two days with the Islayes, although they made sure to ride to the royal bay first. Considering how much natural energy he needed now, he'd never survive without those rides, not even for a couple of days.

Yet since they were often at the Islayes', Dare never managed to arrange another private meeting with Annalise, so his soulbond was ravenous by the first day of the Longnight season. His pulse swift, he grinned as Thom helped him change into evening clothes for the Duchess of Childes's Longnight ball. Thank the Goddess he'd see Annalise tonight. Although Mother would notice, they must slip away to meet. Hopefully, they'd not go too far after not meeting or mentally talking for days.

CHAPTER 49

*D*rained even after her afternoon nap, Annalise sighed as she rapped on the door to Alex's chambers. Hopefully, he'd not left to meet his friends. After not having met or mentally spoken to Dare for days, they must meet at the Duchess of Childes's Longnight ball. And they still needed Alex's chaperone to ensure they didn't make love once they were alone—despite her lingering fatigue. So as soon as Alex opened his door, she asked, "Could you accompany me to tonight's ball? I'll need your escort when I slip away."

Alex grinned. "Of course. Just let me change."

As Alex shut his door, Annalise leaned against the doorframe. Goddess, she was exhausted. The drain due to the shorter days was worsening, so remaining awake once the sun set was becoming impossible.

Soon Alex returned dressed in his evening clothes, and they met Mother and Father in the entrance hall.

Yellow excitement dancing about her, Mother grinned at them as they left Greysnowe House. "Ready for the first ball of the Longnight season? I can't wait to see what festivities the Duchess of Childes has arranged."

Annalise sighed as she and Alex settled in the backward seat across from Mother and Father. She was too tired for Mother's excitement. "I'm sure the ball shall be delightful."

Mother and Father exchanged a frown, and indigo concern pulsed about them. Then Mother asked, "Are you feeling well? You look pale again."

Managing a smile to allay their concern, Annalise sighed again and shrugged. "Merely tired. These late court events when the sun has been set for hours exhaust me since my illness." Her chest squeezed at referring to her miscarriage, but she clung to her smile.

Father hummed. "You should leave tonight's ball early then."

His mouth twitching, Alex gasped. "And risk angering the Duchess of Childes? Who are you, and what have you done with my parents?"

As Mother and Father glared at Alex, Annalise kicked his ankle. Must he provoke them when they were being sincere?

Alex sobered then studied her, his eyes narrowing. "I was just teasing. I'll escort Annalise back to Greysnowe House whenever she wants, so you two can stay and enjoy the ball."

Mother and Father quit glaring, then Mother replied, "Thanks, Alexander." She smiled at Annalise. "Even if you don't stay long, I'm sure you'll enjoy the ball too. 'Tis the first Long-night ball held at court in decades."

Annalise inclined her head. The season had continued months longer than usual this year—it typically ended when the council adjourned at Harvestfete, which hadn't happened because the nightmara hadn't renewed their treaty. And since the council hadn't adjourned, the season continued, with most at court seeming giddy to celebrate Longnight in Ormas for once. Yet she'd only enjoy the first Longnight ball held at court in decades because she'd finally see Dare again.

As Mother described all the upcoming Longnight court events, Annalise swallowed and fingered Dare's faegift at her throat. Goddess, 'twere even more than usual. Most at court were *definitely* giddy. How could she ever manage so many court events?

After they arrived at the ball and greeted the Duke and Duchess of Childes, Alex led Annalise straight to the refreshments table and handed her a mug of spiced cider and Longnight desserts. He murmured, "Eat before Dare arrives. You look like you'll faint otherwise."

She devoured the festive sweet biscuits and cakes, and some of her energy returned. Perhaps like a forest bear, eating more would help her survive the winter. She beamed at Alex as she sipped her cider. "Thanks. That helped."

Grinning, Alex filled their plates with Longnight desserts again. "Good. We'll remain here until you must slip away."

Soon after, Dare and his mother arrived, and he met Annalise's gaze across the ballroom. She swayed and her head swirled as their hunger surged in their entwined souls.

Alex gripped her arm, muddy-yellow worry flaring about him. "Are you all right?"

Annalise nodded and ate another orenge nut sweet biscuit. "I shall be once we slip away. But we'd better wait until Mother and Father are dancing and shan't notice."

So midway through the first Longnight reel, Alex led Annalise to the nearest anteroom. As he sat in a chair by the door, she sank into the sofa in the corner with a heavy sigh.

Dare strode into the anteroom two dances later. As Alex turned away to watch the door, Dare sat beside her and took her hands. His concern bathing her, he murmured, "You look tired."

She grimaced but squeezed Dare's hands to reassure him. "The shorter the days become, the harder 'tis for me to stay up late. I think I should quit attending evening court events."

Dare nodded then kissed her palms as he sent her some energy. "You should also leave once we're done meeting tonight, so you can rest."

Slipping her hands free, Annalise nestled against Dare's side. As he wrapped an arm about her shoulders to pull her closer, their ravenous soulbond eased slightly. She inhaled his scent and nuzzled his chest. "Leaving early sounds good, but we must sate our soulbond first."

Dare kissed her hair. "Of course, my heart."

His love warming her, she smiled against him. Thank the Goddess they'd only four more weeks of remaining apart. They could soon cuddle like this as much as they wanted. After a moment, she said, "I'm trying to decide what Longnight gifts to give everyone. Mother's and Father's must be perfect since these gifts shall be the last they'll accept from me."

Dare hummed, and they discussed Longnight gifts, although she still couldn't decide the perfect gifts for Mother and Father. Then she and Dare discussed their magical pets and arranged to meet in the park in a few days to exchange the angelcats. She was about to ask what court events he planned to attend when a huge yawn halted her.

Chuckling, Dare kissed her forehead. "You should leave before you fall asleep."

Annalise sighed but made herself straighten then caressed Dare's face, her palm tingling at his beard. If only she could remain longer, but sleeping on his chest at a crowded court event wasn't prudent. She leaned forward to brush a kiss against his lips. "'Tis your fault for being so comfortable." Once Dare helped her rise, she turned to Alex. "Time to return to Greysnowe House."

Alex leapt from his chair and took her arm then turned to Dare. "Instead of meeting at the royal bay tomorrow, we should meet at Lady Ducharme's fencing salon, so I can best you before everyone."

Dare arched a teasing brow. "Optimistic, considering the only time you bested me was when your sister distracted me. But we can meet at Lady Ducharme's if you like."

As she tsked at their male ribbing, Alex smirked at Dare. "Excellent. See you tomorrow." He escorted her from the anteroom with Dare staring after her like a lonely griffin.

Once they'd settled in the carriage, Alex grinned and shook his head. "When are you two finally eloping? Everyone at court shall discover your love if you keep looking at each other like that."

Annalise sighed and leaned back in her seat. "Soon, although I can't tell you exactly when. You must show true surprise when Mother and Father find out." Otherwise, they'd realize Alex knew and might disown him as well.

Alex grimaced but nodded then asked her what he could give Mother and Father for Longnight.

THE FOLLOWING MORNING AT BREAKFAST, Annalise told Mother and Father that she'd no longer attend evening court events. They accepted her decision without protest, although they exchanged concerned frowns. After Alex left to meet Dare at Lady Ducharme's fencing salon, Annalise retreated to her chambers. She released Rain and Aria from their golden birdcage then reclined on her bed with Finn and Lily.

Caressing Dare's enchanted heart carving and inhaling its honeysuckle scent while the faebirds sang and the angelcats purred, she finally decided the perfect Longnight gifts for everyone: a friendship stone they could create together for Kiera and Wren, an embroidery representing her parents' love for Mother, new horse tack decorated with enchanted paint for Father, the promise of an angelkitten from Finn and Lily's first litter for Alex, and wedding tokens for Dare.

Although she ached for a nap, Annalise made herself rise, so she could purchase everyone's Longnight gifts. On her way out, she encountered Alex, who was entering their family's townhouse with a frown.

Alex eyed her. "Where are you headed?"

She shrugged. "Broad Street to purchase Longnight gifts."

Taking her arm, Alex escorted her to the carriage. "I'll accompany you. I must purchase gifts as well, and you appear too tired to shop alone."

As the carriage rumbled toward Broad Street, Annalise arched her brows at Alex, who was frowning again, but not at her. "What's troubling you?"

Alex sighed. "While Dare and I were crossing swords at Lady Ducharme's, royal guards fetched Arthur. I hope he's not in trouble."

She squeezed Alex's hand. His friend was too affable and genuine for that. "I'm sure Kiera and King Devon just needed Lord Morwynne's help with a council matter."

Before Alex could reply, the carriage halted at Broad Street. Annalise shuddered when Alex helped her alight. The fashionable shops were even more crowded than usual—she and Alex weren't the only ones shopping for Longnight gifts. Yet she managed to order her and Dare's wedding tokens at Goldsmith's Gems then purchased the materials she needed to create the others' Longnight gifts at nearby shops. Alex purchased gifts as well, although they were both careful to not show their purchases to each other.

After their shopping, Alex escorted her to Layne's Tea Room, where they devoured a hearty luncheon. Drained from battling the crowds even with Alex's escort, she dozed on the carriage ride back to Greysnowe House. Once there, she headed up to her chambers for a proper nap until dinner, which she ate with Alex and their parents. But once Mother and Father left for the Nolans' Longnight charity auction, she returned to her chambers and went to bed again.

Annalise remained behind the following day, mostly sleeping with Finn and Lily curled beside her while Rain and Aria sang sweet lullabies. After all that extra rest, she began feeling more like herself that evening, although she was relieved to receive Kiera's note canceling their next nightmara ride. Riding would likely exhaust her again, and she should spend her morning creating her Longnight gifts rather than sleeping.

Since she didn't have her nightmara ride, Annalise joined Mother at Lady Islaye's salon the following afternoon. When they entered the drawing room decorated with garlands, snow-strings, and starlights, Mother glared at Lady Ravenstone like a baleful basilisk then dragged Annalise to a sofa across the room.

Once all the ladies had spiced cider and Longnight sweet biscuits, Lady Islaye led them in several Longnight games filled with cheer. After a dizzying game of blind seer's chase, Annalise murmured her excuses then slipped into an anteroom to rest. Who would have guessed that a ladies' salon would be almost as exhausting as riding?

She was dozing curled against the sofa's arm when the click of the door opening started her awake. Sitting upright, she blinked sleep from her eyes then gawked at Lady Ravenstone closing the door. Why had Dare's mother joined her? From the indigo concern swirling in Lady Ravenstone's healing green aura with many bronze motes, 'twasn't for villainous reasons like Mother would assume.

Dare's mother bustled across the anteroom and sat on the other end of the sofa. Humming, she eyed Annalise. "Are you all right? You look pale."

Annalise swallowed a sigh. If her pallor was enough for Lady Ravenstone to seek her out, doubtless the other ladies had noticed too. Soon all of court would be gossiping about Lady Snow's ill looks. Just what she needed before she eloped with Dare. She made herself smile. "I've simply had trouble with sleep in recent weeks."

Lady Ravenstone leaned toward her. "Is that all? You've not attended many court events lately, and your mother appeared worried when you left. I expect she'd have followed you, except the Duchess of Wildewall was telling her about how ill the Duke of Wildewall and their daughter were after using a travel spell to visit Ormas for the Longnight season."

Annalise resisted the urge to fidget, her heart twisting. She couldn't outright lie to her future mother-in-law, but she couldn't tell her the truth either. She fingered Dare's faegift at her throat. "We're usually back home in Wildewall at this time of year. 'Tis impossible to maintain such hectic social rounds when 'tis dark so early."

Lady Ravenstone's amber eyes, so like her son's, dropped to his faegift. "You sound as if you miss living in Wildewall."

Lowering her hand, Annalise exhaled a silent sigh. A topic she needn't lie about. She beamed at Dare's mother. "Very much. I can't wait until I'm back among Wildewall's wild forests, magical glens, and enchanted lakes."

Lady Ravenstone smiled back. "You enjoy outdoor pursuits then."

Annalise nodded. "I love walking in forests or other natural areas." A blush warming her cheeks, she lowered her gaze as kissing Dare at Column Caverns, Glass Lake, and the royal forest echoed through her. Shoving that aside, she lifted her gaze. "And I adore riding my stallion Storm—especially at a gallop."

Her lips twitching, Lady Ravenstone chuckled. "Your mother adored galloping too. We used to gallop together for hours."

Annalise gaped at Dare's mother. She and Mother had *galloped* together? Could they have been friends before they'd married two ancestral enemies? "But Mother says galloping is unladylike."

Lady Ravenstone winced, muddy-blue regret flaring about her. "I see." She swallowed then asked, "Do you like animals besides horses?"

Annalise smiled. Naturally a nature witch would ask that. "I love animals and have several pets—two faebirds and an angelcat."

Her aura clearing, Lady Ravenstone tilted her head. "Not surprising that your mother gave you an angelcat. She was forever bringing treats for mine."

Blinking, Annalise stared at Lady Ravenstone again. She and Mother *must* have been friends once. Was their shattered friendship why Mother never wanted to see Finn or Lily and often ignored them when she did?

Before she'd devised a reply, Lady Ravenstone leaned forward and inhaled then said, "Your honeysuckle scent is heavenly. It reminds me of summers in Wildewall."

Her neck prickling, Annalise caressed Dare's heart-shaped firegem again. Why was his mother mentioning her scent? "'Tis why I wear it."

Lady Ravenstone hummed as her gaze returned to her son's faegift. "That faegift is exquisite and perfectly matches your striking hair and eyes. Where did you get it?"

Annalise tensed as her stomach lurched. How had Lady Ravenstone recognized her necklace as a faegift? She must leave before Dare's mother probed further. She forced a brilliant smile. "I'm not certain. I should return to reassure Mother."

She leapt upright then swayed as her head whirled and black spots danced before her eyes.

Leaping up as well, Lady Ravenstone gripped Annalise's elbow. "You're not well."

Annalise leaned on Lady Ravenstone and gulped a breath. She never should have leapt upright while exhausted. "I'll be fine."

Lady Ravenstone hummed then crooned a singsong chant. Dare's mother gasped as the white glow of magic flared about her.

Annalise stiffened. What spell had Lady Ravenstone just cast?

She was about to circumspectly ask when Mother burst into the anteroom then hurtled toward them and wrenched Annalise from Lady Ravenstone. Glaring, Mother spat, "Stay away from my daughter, you treacherous harpy."

As Annalise wobbled and gaped at Mother, Lady Ravenstone winced then raised her hands. "Emmeline, please. I was simply talking to her."

Still glaring, Mother wrapped her arm about Annalise. "We

both know what your *talking* leads to." She steered Annalise toward the door. "Come, Annalise, we'd better return home, so you can rest."

Annalise nodded and leaned on Mother's arm as Mother led her to the carriage. Once they'd dropped into their seats, she closed her eyes and rested her whirling head on the seat then murmured, "Mother, Lady Ravenstone *was* simply talking to me."

Mother humphed. "That may have been what it *seemed* like, but I assure 'twas nothing so innocent. That vile woman is as trustworthy as a deceitful djinn."

Annalise sighed. Unlikely, considering Lady Ravenstone's aura hadn't shown any deception. Not that she could tell Mother that. Although even if she could, Mother doubtless wouldn't listen—she despised Lady Ravenstone too much.

CHAPTER 50

Three evenings after the Duchess of Childes's Longnight ball, Dare sighed as he sat in the carriage on the backward seat across from Mother. The Westons' caroling party tonight would be merry—too bad Annalise wouldn't be there. The festive music would cheer her, and they could see each other, even if they couldn't slip away to meet at the Westons'. After three days apart, their soulbond was ravenous again. At least they'd planned to exchange the angelcats in the park tomorrow morning.

Once she tucked her heavy cloak around her, Mother smiled at him. "I didn't have a chance to tell you at dinner, but I spoke with Lady Annalise at Lady Islaye's salon this afternoon."

He stilled. Why was Mother telling him that? Did she suspect his secret involvement with Annalise? She couldn't know—she would have told him if she knew. Mother was always direct about resolving problems.

Mother tilted her head. "Lady Annalise was sweeter and more intriguing than I'd expected given her icy nickname. Plus, her lack of rancor toward her family's ancestral enemy reminded me of her brother. Are she and Lord Alexander close?"

Dare swallowed then gritted a faint smile to feign indiffer-ence. "I believe so."

Mother hummed. "Interesting since Lady Annalise is six years older. Why are they so close, do you think?"

Clinging to his smile, he shrugged. Maybe if he appeared bored, Mother would quit mentioning Annalise. He murmured, "Perhaps because Alex is perceptive and is one of the few people who sees her as more than Lady Snow."

Humming again, Mother nodded slowly. "Yes, of course." She leaned forward. "Considering how close Lady Annalise and her brother are, I can't believe she didn't attempt to stop him from dueling with you, one of the most skilled swordsmen in Calatini."

Dare shifted in his seat. Why was Mother *still* mentioning Annalise? Yet he couldn't have her thinking ill of her future daughter-in-law, so he must reveal some of the truth. "She did. She brought King Devon to stop us."

Her brows rising, Mother eyed him. "You never mentioned she was at your duel."

The back of his neck prickling, he shrugged again. Please let this satisfy Mother's curiosity. "Her parents wouldn't be pleased that she stopped her brother from killing me."

Mother sighed. "I suppose they wouldn't." She straightened and pursed her lips. "Do you think Lady Annalise shall attend the Westons' caroling party tonight? I must thank her for saving your life."

Dare swallowed as his throat constricted. If only Mother knew how true her statement was. "I'm not certain. Lady Annalise has attended the Westons' musical evenings before, although she doesn't always."

Fortunately, the carriage halted at Weston House before Mother could mention Annalise again. Once they greeted the Westons, he led Mother to the refreshments table for mugs of spiced cider before escorting her to a seat near the back.

Mother beamed and glanced about the room as more guests

arrived. After King Devon and Lady Kiera arrived, she sighed but continued smiling. "It doesn't seem as if Lady Annalise is attending tonight."

Suppressing a frown as his chest squeezed, Dare stared into his spiced cider. "I'm sure you'll be able to thank her another time." Most likely once he brought her back to Ravenstone House as his bride in a few weeks.

Then Miss Weston announced her sister was about to open the caroling. The little girl, who was likely a decade younger than her teenage sister, bounced to the keyharp and began to play and sing. As her celestial voice rose in a dulcet carol, everyone around him began to smile.

Yet he merely sighed. Hopefully, tonight's caroling wouldn't last long. He must get to bed, so he'd not sleep too late tomorrow. He couldn't miss meeting Annalise.

THE FOLLOWING MORNING, Dare woke when Thom shook him awake for breakfast. After eating, he handled correspondence in his study for several hours. Then with Raven and Bear, he strode to the clearing in the park where he'd dueled Alex, gathering natural energy while he waited for Annalise.

He tensed when Annalise trudged into the clearing with Alex and the angelcats prowling in the trees above them. Although she still looked better than during her miscarriage, she was paler than when they'd met four days ago, and the gray fog tarnishing her transparent aura was darker too. So despite the hunger flaring in their entwined souls, he merely drew her into his arms then brushed a gentle kiss against her lips and sent her energy until his vision dimmed and pulse pounded. He raised his head and smiled down at her. "How are you feeling?"

As Alex nodded at Dare then turned away to toss sticks for the hellhounds, Annalise sighed and shook her head with a shrug. "Tired, although much less so now that you sent me energy until you almost fainted. You really shouldn't have sent so much."

Setting his jaw, Dare frowned at Annalise. He'd drain himself dry to keep her well. "You looked as if you needed it. Are your parents making you do too much?"

Annalise sighed again. "No, Mother and Father have been wonderful since almost getting arrested for treason. They've been encouraging me to rest and not attend court events, and they've stopped matchmaking like they promised." She grimaced. "The drain due to the shorter days is simply stronger now."

He nodded, his chest tight. Hopefully, 'twould begin to ease when the days began lengthening after Longnight in ten days. He rubbed her back. "I'll begin sending you energy when I gather natural energy every day. That should help."

Her love warming him, Annalise caressed his face. "Thanks, Dare. Just don't drain yourself or your powers."

Dare kissed Annalise's palm then sent back his love through their entwined souls. "Only if you promise the same. Perhaps you should quit any strenuous activities and rest more."

Annalise pursed her lips. "I already have. I quit my morning walks as well as most court events. And the only riding I'm doing now is my nightmara rides every three days, but Darkthorn has been keeping to a walk, and I suspect those rides shall end soon anyway."

He frowned as a chill darted through him. If she was exhausted after such limited activities, her drain from the shorter days was *much* worse than his. Yet as a nature witch, he should have been more drained than her by that.

Her white-blonde hair shimmering in the dappled sunlight, Annalise shook her head and sighed. "Practically all I've been doing lately is sleeping and working on my Longnight gifts."

Dare hummed. He'd yet to decide his gifts. He should make himself go shopping tomorrow. He arched his brows at Annalise. "What are you giving everyone?"

Annalise tsked and poked his chest. "Are you attempting to find out your gift? I can't reveal that, but I'm giving Kiera and Wren a friendship stone for us to create together, Mother an embroidery, Father a painted saddle, and—" she glanced at Alex then mentally added, :*Alex an angelkitten.*:

He swallowed a laugh. No doubt Annalise meant an angelkitten from Lily and Finn's first litter—they must ensure her brother received the greatest hellion. He grinned at her. "Those gifts sound perfect for everyone. I hope my gift to you equals the one you give me."

Caressing his heart-shaped firegem, Annalise glanced at him beneath her lashes with a coy smile. "I'm certain it shall be. You give the best gifts, my love."

His heart quickening, Dare captured her tempting lips in a deep kiss, and their souls meshed. He kissed her harder when she wrapped her arms about his neck and fisted her hands in his hair. He shuddered as her heady honeysuckle scent flooded him. Goddess, he needed her. He began steering her toward the closest tree.

Then a volley of twigs hit his back, and Alex drawled, "I hope you two plan to elope soon." As Dare and Annalise leapt apart, Alex tsked and shook his head. "Chaperoning you together is demanding... and traumatic."

As Annalise blushed while separating their souls, Dare met Alex's gaze and shrugged. He'd not apologize for kissing her. "I expect you'll be the same when you find a lady you wish to marry."

Alex chuckled. "Most likely." He pointed a twig at them. "I'm going to turn around again now and toss sticks for Raven and Bear again. But stop almost coupling in my presence. I'll throw more than twigs next time."

Once Alex turned away, Dare and Annalise exchanged a wry smile. Then she threaded her fingers through his and said, "He's serious about throwing more. We'd best not risk another embrace."

He squeezed her hand and sighed. "We should probably separate soon anyway. Someone from court could stumble across us at any moment." And his control would surely vanish soon.

Annalise grimaced. "True. But before we do—your mother sought me out at Lady Islaye's salon yesterday. She was cordial and solicitous, but she asked about my scent and your faegift then cast some kind of a spell before Mother burst in and whisked me away."

Dare winced and rubbed his beard. No wonder Mother had probed yesterday evening. "Mother mentioned your conversation and got me to admit you were at the duel. If we attend any court events with her there, I don't think we can risk meeting again. She's too suspicious now."

Fingering his necklace at her throat, Annalise sighed and lifted a shoulder. "Fortunately, it shan't be long until we can quit our deception." She glanced at her brother then added silently, *:Please don't tell Alex about when we plan to elope. He must be surprised, or Mother and Father might disown him too.:*

Dare nodded then Annalise released his hand and tapped Alex's shoulder. He stared after her as she and her brother left the clearing. The end of the Longnight season couldn't come soon enough. Once Annalise and Alex were gone, he called the hellhounds and angelcats, and they returned to Ravenstone House.

AFTER RIDING to the royal bay with Mother to gather natural energy the following morning and sending half of it to Annalise, Dare devoured luncheon then visited several witch shops to find the perfect Longnight gifts for everyone. At The Arte of Spells, the magical art gallery, he purchased an exquisite moving painting for Mother. Then at Bewitching Raiments, the apparel and equipment witch shop, he purchased an enchanted sword for Alex. Finally, at Mirage, the illusion witch shop, he purchased six unenchanted mirrors to create linked communication mirrors for Annalise. 'Twould take at least a week to enchant so many, but then she could speak to everyone even when they returned to Wildewall.

As soon as he returned to Ravenstone House, he locked himself in his study with Lily, Finn, Raven, and Bear to enchant Annalise's linked communication mirrors. He gathered his spell ingredients and set a massive clear quartz bowl on the edge of his desk before calling the angelcats and hellhounds. Finn and Lily leapt atop his desk beside the clear quartz bowl, while Raven and Bear flanked him.

Gathering magical energy from the four pets, he crooned a singsong chant and focused his will. Then he poured unicorn water into the bowl then stirred in lavender oil, clary oil, and faedust. The magical liquid began glowing and bubbling as its sweet yet herbaceous scent perfumed the air. Panting, he slid the mirrors into the massive, glowing bowl one at a time then covered the bowl with heavy white linen. Once the mirrors absorbed all of the magical liquid, they'd be linked communication mirrors, and to renew the spell, he must simply repeat it on one of the mirrors once a year.

His head whirling, Dare staggered to his chair and collapsed. Goddess, performing spells not involving nature was exhausting thanks to the drain from the shorter days—even with the magical pets acting as familiars. After his breath slowed, he forced himself to the kitchen and requested shokolat nut oatmeal balls. Yet although the food helped him recover, he was too tired to join Mother at the Osteens' Longnight rout party that evening.

So as they rode to the royal bay the following morning, Mother eyed him with a frown between her brows. "Feeling better? You still appear a bit pale."

He grinned with a faint shrug to reassure her. "I'll be fine once we gather natural energy at the royal bay."

Mother hummed but urged Willow to a trot. "We should hurry then." After he'd kneed Ebony to match her and her mare, she slanted him a narrow glance. "I looked for Lady Annalise at

Osteen House yesterday to thank her, but she wasn't there again.
I don't think she's attended any court events since I spoke to her
at Lady Islaye's salon." Mother sighed. "That afternoon, she
appeared exhausted and almost fainted when she rose. I hope
she's not feeling worse—or that her mother confined her for
speaking to me."

Dare shifted in Ebony's saddle and gritted a calm smile.
Mother's suspicions would blossom if he appeared concerned.
"I'm certain Alex would have mentioned if his sister was ill or
confined when I saw him the other day. So doubtless Lady
Annalise is fine. Perhaps she'll attend the Dabars' Longnight
pastry feast tonight."

Mother pursed her lips. "I'll look for her again since I really
must thank her for saving your life, although I doubt she'll be
there."

He swallowed. No, Annalise wouldn't be, thank the Goddess.
Mother would definitely realize their soulbond and love if she
and Annalise spoke again. Gripping Ebony's reins, he smiled at
Mother. "Shall we gallop to the royal bay? I'm eager to gather
natural energy."

Mother nodded, and they thundered down the winding road
toward the royal bay.

CHAPTER 51

Two mornings after exchanging the angelcats, Annalise was leaning against Darkthorn with her arm across his back as Kiera and Moonbud sailed over every jump. Kiera's riding lessons were doubtless almost done, so their nightmara rides would end soon. Fortunate, considering Annalise had been too exhausted today to ride Darkthorn about the paddock, even at a walk.

As Kiera dismounted and began speaking with Moonbud, energy from Dare flooded Annalise, and she straightened with a sharp inhale. He must be gathering natural energy at the royal bay with his mother. The energy he'd sent every day the past three days had been vital. Because of it, she'd managed to spend most of those days awake rather than napping, although she was still too tired to attend evening court events.

Darkthorn snorted and tossed his mane. :*Your exhaustion doesn't seem normal. You should visit a witch healer—or the veiled witch.*:

Annalise swallowed as a prickle skittered across her skin. Not that suggestion again. Removing her arm from Darkthorn's back, she lifted her chin. "'Tis simply the drain due to shorter days. I'll be better soon." She strode toward Kiera, disregarding Darkthorn's second snort behind her.

After she and Kiera left the nightmara paddock with the royal guards, Kiera leaned toward her and murmured, "Since we've not seen each other for nearly a week, I've not been able to tell you—Devon and I unearthed my poisoner."

Annalise arched her brows then exhaled. Finally. "Who was it?"

Kiera grimaced. "Lady Morwynne—she wanted to prevent a commoner from becoming queen as well as my education initiative. We held her trial at the council meeting two days ago, and the councilors unanimously convicted her of treason. She'll be magically bound to their country estate, and her son shall assume her position on the council. I believe he intends to tell everyone she went mad."

Humming, Annalise slowly nodded. Lady Morwynne being Kiera's poisoner wasn't terribly surprising, given that the devious countess had provoked Mother and Father into always being churlish toward Kiera. "Lord Morwynne shall make an excellent councilor. He's nothing like his mother. Otherwise, he and Alex wouldn't be friends."

Kiera smiled. "True." Her smile became blinding as they reached the palace. "I must go. Devon and I are visiting the orphanage after luncheon, and I can't be late. See you at my riding test in three days."

Annalise sighed then headed toward her family's carriage beside the palace stables. Once she returned to Greysnowe House, she must continue working on her Longnight gifts. She'd only eight days left, and Father's horse tack was only three-quarters painted, while Mother's embroidery was barely begun.

THE FOLLOWING MORNING AT BREAKFAST, Annalise had just heaped her plate with food when Mother leaned toward her and Alex then said, "'Tis unfortunate you two couldn't attend the Dabars'

Longnight pastry feast yesterday evening. The food was delectable, and we heard the most unexpected rumors about Lady Morwynne. She's been magically confined to their country estate, and young Lord Morwynne has assumed her position as the Minister of Health and Community."

Annalise and Alex exchanged a glance, but Alex didn't appear surprised either. Lord Morwynne had likely told him. She turned back to Mother and Father. She must share the truth with them, so they'd finally apologize to Kiera for being so churlish toward their future queen. "Yes, Kiera said 'twas for attempting to poison her."

As Mother and Father gaped, Alex nodded and added, "Arthur said his mother is fortunate that King Devon and Lady Kiera didn't insist on executing her."

Annalise frowned at Mother and Father as she began her beefsteak. They mustn't gossip about this at court. "But don't tell anyone that Lady Morwynne attempted to poison Kiera. I suspect Kiera and King Devon intend to keep that quiet."

Their mouths closing, Mother and Father glanced at each other, then Father said, "Yes, of course. Gossip about a councilor attempting to poison our future queen would only incite unrest."

Mother gulped her tea and turned to Annalise. "You were definitely right about Lady Morwynne. We *never* should have listened to that treasonous harpy."

While Alex simply snorted, Annalise swallowed another sigh. If only Mother and Father would be as reasonable about Dare and Lady Ravenstone.

Mother and Father traded another glance, then Mother added, "Now that King Devon and Lady Kiera have unearthed her poisoner, we'll apologize to her at the next court event we encounter her."

Eyeing the muddy-yellow unease pulsing about Mother and Father, Annalise hummed as she finished her beefsteak. "Don't fret about apologizing to Kiera. She's kindhearted, so she'll forgive you at once."

Alex leaned toward Mother and Father. "Plus, King Devon shall no doubt quit glowering at you once you do."

Mother and Father nodded then began describing the delectable food at the Dabars' Longnight pastry feast. As they talked, Annalise devoured the rest of her breakfast before returning to her chambers to work on their Longnight gifts.

OVER THE NEXT TWO DAYS, Annalise spent most of her time in her chambers working on her Longnight gifts, so she completed Father's horse tack then half of Mother's embroidery. Despite focusing on her Longnight gifts, every morning at breakfast she asked Mother and Father how their apology to Kiera had gone. Yet they kept saying Kiera had been too busy to approach.

Her body sluggish and heavy, Annalise sighed while she finished breakfast before her last nightmara ride. Mother and Father might be right about Kiera being too busy. Doubtless Kiera was preparing for her riding test this morning then negotiating the Nightmara-Calatini Treaty soon after. Plus, the Longnight season was more hectic than the usual season.

When she headed to the carriage, Wilson handed her a note from Goldsmith's Gems. She opened it after she settled in the carriage, grinning as she read that the wedding tokens were ready. Excellent. She was eager to see them—hopefully, Dare would like them too. Plus, she could collect them on the return ride.

Still grinning, she leaned back in her seat and soon drifted into slumber. She jerked awake when the carriage halted. Rubbing sleep from her eyes, she stumbled to the ground then headed toward the palace to meet Kiera. Like last time, she was too exhausted to ride Darkthorn today.

When she joined Kiera, Kiera eyed her, and the indigo in Kiera's aura deepened. She asked, "Are you feeling well?"

Annalise almost winced as they began toward the nightmara stables with the royal guards. She must look wretched for Kiera to ask about that right before her crucial riding test. To reassure her friend, she shrugged and replied, "A bit tired, thanks to the shorter days."

Kiera frowned. "Is that why you've not attended the evening Longnight festivities?"

Annalise sighed and nodded. Of course, Kiera had noticed despite being busy with her poisoner, the nightmara, and Longnight events. "After only lasting an hour at the Duchess of Childes's Longnight ball, I decided it best. Fortunately, chastened by King Devon's accusations of treason, my parents have let me, although Goddess knows how long their forbearance shall last."

Sighing as well, Kiera pursed her lips. "Perhaps you should visit a healer."

As they reached the nightmara stables, Annalise grimaced and shook her head. "I would, but a magicless healer probably couldn't help, and a witch healer would realize I was a soul healer. I can't risk my parents discovering that."

Kiera winced, but before she could reply, Leila and her nightmara partner Nightrose escorted them to Moonbud and Darkthorn, and Kiera's riding test began.

When Annalise joined Darkthorn, the stallion murmured, :*No riding for us today—Moonbud wants me to observe Kiera with her. Opportune since you seem even more exhausted than before.*:

Annalise suppressed a grimace. She definitely must look wretched. Sighing, she turned to watch Kiera's riding test. Like she'd expected, Kiera controlled her restive stallion as if she'd been born in the saddle and sailed over every jump.

While Moonbud congratulated Kiera for passing her riding test, energy from Dare swamped Annalise, and her body lightened. Thank the Goddess. As she and Kiera strode back to the palace with the royal guards, she frowned and scrutinized her friend. Muddy-white melancholy swirled about Kiera despite her triumph. "Are you worried about negotiating the treaty in three days?"

Kiera sighed. "Not really. Moonbud and I know each other

well, so negotiating shouldn't be an issue. I just need to decide on my advisor besides Devon. A councilor, I think." She glanced at Annalise. "I hope you're not angry to be excluded."

Annalise grimaced and suppressed a snort. "Not hardly. Despite Mother and Father's ambitions, I've less interest in politics than Alex." She grinned then embraced Kiera. "But I wish you luck—not that you'll need it."

Squeezing her back, Kiera murmured, "Thanks, Annalise."

She and Kiera said goodbye, then she returned to her carriage and asked the driver to stop by Goldsmith's Gems on Broad Street.

At the jeweler's, she beamed when the clerk showed her the two wedding tokens. They were even better than she'd imagined when ordering them. To avoid attracting unwelcome attention, she made herself murmur, "These are perfect, Flora. Thank you so much."

Annalise paid Flora, including a generous tip, then returned to Greysnowe House with the wedding tokens in a cloak pocket. After wrapping the wedding tokens in festive green and gold paper, she slid Dare's Longnight gift in the drawer of her bedside table next to the enchanted heart carving he'd given her. She caressed his faegift flickering at her throat. Dare would surely like their wedding tokens.

Beaming, she hummed Longnight carols and began embroidering Mother's gift again. She didn't even mind the painstaking embroidery.

ANNALISE CONTINUED EMBROIDERING Mother's gift, even skipping Lady Farson's ladies' luncheon the following day celebrating Kiera's upcoming nightmara negotiations, so she was three-quarters completed when Grace brought her a note from King Devon shortly before dinner. She opened King Devon's note then smiled at him inviting Kiera's friends to the traditional Longnight play tomorrow evening as a surprise. How sweet. She hummed and tilted her head. She should be able to attend—if she took a nap in the afternoon and Dare sent her extra energy before dinner. She'd ask him tomorrow. She accepted King Devon's invitation then returned to Mother's embroidery.

So once energy from Dare flooded her the following morning, Annalise reached out to him for the first time in two weeks, *:Dare, could you send me more energy around dinner tonight?:*

Dare's presence surrounded her like a warm embrace. *:Of course, but why? And should you risk a mental conversation when you're so drained?:*

She smiled. Solicitous like always. She sent her love through their entwined souls. *:I had to speak with you. I'll be fine if we don't talk long. I need extra energy because King Devon invited Kiera's friends to tonight's Longnight play as a surprise.:*

Dare hummed. *:I see. Mother and I are attending that as well.:*

Her heart quickening at seeing him again, Annalise gripped her embroidery frame. Goddess, not staring at him tonight during the entire play would be excruciating. *:If only we could meet. I miss you, my love.:*

As Dare sighed, his love wrapped around her. *:Me too, my heart. Why don't we exchange angelcats midmorning the day after tomorrow in the park?:*

She beamed and fingered his heart-shaped firegem. *:We should exchange Longnight gifts too.:* She couldn't wait to see his face when he opened his.

Dare chuckled. *:Good idea considering 'tis Longnight Eve. I'll bring Alex's too. Now go rest. See you tonight.:*

Annalise embroidered Mother's gift the rest of the morning then took a long nap after luncheon. When she finally woke, she began embroidering again. If she kept at it, she should complete Mother's gift tomorrow afternoon—a day early.

When energy from Dare bathed her before dinner, she sent him silent thanks then rang for Grace. Her maid blinked at her request for help changing into her spruce satin gown with gold trim. She almost chuckled. Her request *was* surprising since she'd not attended any evening court events since the start of the Longnight season.

As she glided into the family dining room, Mother's brows rose. "You look dashing tonight."

Annalise smiled as she sat beside Alex. Until they'd quit matchmaking, Mother would have been surprised if she'd *not* donned an evening gown. "I'm attending the Longnight play with Kiera and King Devon."

As Alex frowned, Mother and Father traded a glance. Then Mother asked, "Are you certain you should? You've been retiring straight after dinner for almost two weeks."

Warmed by her family's obvious concern, Annalise sipped her beetroot soup then flashed a bright smile to reassure them. "I napped this afternoon to ensure I could. I promise I shan't stay long past the Longnight play."

Mother and Father sighed, but Mother began telling her the latest court gossip.

Then after dinner spent discussing court, Alex gripped her elbow and murmured, "I can give King Devon and Lady Kiera your excuses if you need to rest."

Annalise patted Alex's arm. "I told you; I'll be fine." She checked Mother and Father couldn't overhear then leaned toward him. "Could you escort me to the park midmorning on Longnight Eve? We're exchanging angelcats and Longnight gifts."

Alex nodded as they began toward the carriage. "I'll bring mine for him then."

After a carriage ride where Mother continued sharing court gossip, Alex escorted Annalise upstairs to the royal box. Before he left, he smiled at her and said, "Find me in Father and Mother's box if you need to leave early."

Smiling back, she nodded then sat between the heavily pregnant Lady Treyvan and Priest Melchior since the two free seats beside Wren must be for Kiera and King Devon. Smoothing her skirt, she glanced about the theater, and her eyes soon met

Dare's. Her heart surged, and love flared in their entwined souls, but she wrenched her gaze free and turned to Lord and Lady Treyvan. Despite her chest aching at her and Dare's lost child, she asked them, "Are you eager to hold your child in your arms?"

CHAPTER 52

As Annalise turned to Lord and Lady Treyvan, Dare smoothed his beard and forced himself to glance about the theater instead of staring at her. Mother was right beside him, and even though she was studying the crowd, she was doubtless watching him too. And he mustn't do anything that would fuel her suspicions. Yet not staring at Annalise was excruciating—after all, they'd not met since exchanging angelcats last week. Thank the Goddess they were meeting the day after tomorrow.

He was turned toward the curtained stage when Mother hummed then said, "I see Lady Annalise is actually here. She didn't even attend Lady Farson's ladies' luncheon yesterday celebrating Lady Kiera's upcoming negotiations with the nightmara, although her mother did." Mother shook her head. "Poor Lady Annalise looks worse than when I saw her last week. No wonder she's not been attending court events."

Allowing himself to follow Mother's gaze, he eyed Annalise like a thirsty wolf eyed water as she chuckled with Lady Kiera and Lady Beza Hawke. Despite the energy he'd sent her every day and the extra he'd sent tonight, she appeared even paler than before with shadows beneath her eyes and the gray fog tarnishing her transparent aura dark as thunderclouds. His chest clenched. She looked almost as ill as during her miscarriage.

Mother tsked. "Someone should tell her to leave and get some rest."

When Mother began to rise, Dare whirled and gripped her arm to stop her. "You can't approach her here."

Scrutinizing him, Mother pursed her lips. "Why not? I need to thank her for saving your life anyway."

He released Mother's arm but leaned toward her. "Because her parents—along with the rest of court—are watching. Not only would you incite gossip, but Lord and Lady Greysnowe would erupt like crazed chimeras if you approached her." And he and Annalise didn't need either just before they eloped.

Her shoulders sagging, Mother sighed. "True enough. Damn that feud. I hope Lady Annalise doesn't almost faint again tonight."

Once Mother returned to studying the rest of the crowd, Dare blew a silent sigh and covertly monitored Annalise as she shuffled back to her seat between Priest Melchior and Lady Treyvan. He'd make sure Annalise didn't faint.

So as the curtains opened and the Longnight play began, he sent Annalise a trickle of energy through their entwined souls. And he maintained that trickle throughout the traditional play about a tenderhearted arctic elf becoming the Goddess's Winter Queen.

After the play ended and the curtains closed, Mother frowned and leaned toward him. "Dare, are you feeling well? You're almost as pale as Lady Annalise."

As Annalise glided from the royal box, he ceased sending her energy. Please let her return to Greysnowe House without fainting. He flashed a grin at Mother. "I'm fine. The dim light just makes me appear pale." He offered her his arm. "Shall we go?"

Pursing her lips, Mother nodded then took his arm, and they strode through the crowd back to their carriage.

. . .

After riding with Mother to the royal bay to gather natural energy two mornings later, Dare closed himself in his study to wrap his Longnight gifts. He wrapped Mother's moving painting in white paper decorated with fir boughs and Alex's sword in festive gold paper with green flecks. Then he flipped back the white linen over the massive clear quartz bowl containing Annalise's linked communication mirrors. Good. Overnight, the mirrors had absorbed the last of the magical liquid. He slid her six mirrors into a beech wood box he'd infused with nature magic to smell like honeysuckle then wrapped the box in green paper with gold starbursts. He tucked Annalise's and Alex's wrapped gifts beneath his arms then strode from the study with the hellhounds and angelcats close behind.

In the entrance hall, Mother bustled toward him then halted. She arched her brows. "Where are you off to with gifts and all of your magical pets? Attending a Longnight court event I've not heard about?"

Dare swallowed and glanced down at the gifts beneath his arms. Despite the wrapping, Alex's was obviously a sword. So he told Mother, "Since 'tis Longnight Eve, I'm meeting Alex in a nearby park to exchange Longnight gifts."

Mother's lips quirked. "You're giving him *two* Longnight gifts? How excessive."

Tensing, he swallowed again. How could he explain without outright lying to Mother? "No, the box isn't for Alex."

Mother hummed. "I see." Her amber eyes gleaming, she grinned at him. "Well, have fun. I'll see you at dinner."

Before Mother could probe further, Dare strode outside with Raven and Bear coursing beside him while Lily and Finn leapt and darted around him and the hellhounds. Once they reached the clearing in the park, the angelcats began chasing each other in the trees, and he leaned his Longnight gifts against an oak tree. He tossed sticks for Raven and Bear then began further replenishing his natural energy. He must have enough to share more with Annalise before they parted.

Moments later, Annalise arrived, still pale and leaning on Alex's arm. Yet her warm and radiant smile lit her face as their love flared in their entwined souls. Stepping away from her brother, she wrapped her arms about Dare's neck then brushed a kiss against his lips. "Happy Longnight Eve, my love."

Ignoring Alex's teasing retch behind Annalise, Dare returned her kiss before lifting his head. "Happy Longnight Eve, my heart. How are you feeling?"

Her excitement washing over him, Annalise beamed and tilted her head. "Eager to exchange Longnight gifts." She lowered her arms then stepped back, and the angelcats and hellhounds mobbed her. Bending to pet them, she chuckled. "You and Alex should go first."

Dare and Alex grinned at each other, then Dare grasped Alex's gold-wrapped gift and offered it to him. "I hope you like it."

Alex snickered as he accepted his gift with one hand. "I wonder *what* it could be."

Glowering up at her brother, Annalise continued scratching the magical pets pressing against her. "Don't gibe."

Dare shrugged and flashed a wry smile. "In his defense, 'tis obvious what his gift is. Perhaps I should have purchased a box before wrapping it, but I figured Alex wouldn't care."

Alex chuckled and swished his still wrapped gift. "I don't."

Annalise rose, and Finn and Lily leapt back into the trees while Raven and Bear coursed after the sticks she tossed. She arched a brow at Alex. "Then why haven't you opened it yet?"

Alex winked. "Because I've only one hand free." He crooned a singsong chant, and a covered cage appeared in his left hand. He handed the cage to Dare. "I cast an invisibility spell on your gift rather than wrapping it." He waggled his brows at Annalise. "Although truthfully, 'tis your gift as well."

Dare and Annalise exchanged a glance, then he lifted the ivory canvas covering the cage. As Annalise inhaled, he grinned at the pair of dragon-shaped creatures the size of doves—draklizards.

Smiling, Alex leaned toward them. "Two mated draklizards to complete your menagerie. You mentioned that you wanted one soon, and I knew Annalise would adore them as well. The tan one is female, while the green is male. You two can decide who gets which one."

Dare grinned at Alex. Of course, the perceptive younger gentleman had chosen the ideal gift for him and Annalise. "Thanks, Alex. They're perfect."

He opened the brass cage then removed the draklizards and cuddled them against his chest while Annalise scratched their scaly heads. Within several heartbeats, the mottled-green male had climbed onto his shoulder and wrapped a tail around his neck, and the mottled-tan female had done the same to Annalise.

Glancing up from his now unwrapped sword, Alex snickered and shook his head. "Annalise, can you imagine Mother's horror if you arrived at some ball wearing such a necklace?"

Annalise hummed as she scratched her draklizard just above the draklizard's iridescent eyes. "You forget that draklizards can change their scales and eyes to match their surroundings. Mother would never see her."

Scratching his draklizard's head as well, Dare chuckled and waggled his brows to tease Annalise. "Although she might notice when your partners yowled and recoiled every time they attempted to dance with you."

Annalise slanted him a coy glance beneath her lashes. "Then I'd simply have to find a partner my draklizard wouldn't bite. Like a nature witch."

Before Dare could reply, Alex coughed then asked, "So what are you going to name them?"

Dare eyed his draklizard's mottled-green scales. The little fellow resembled ivy leaves. "Leaf."

As Raven and Bear dropped their sticks at her feet, Annalise ran a finger along her draklizard's mottled-tan back. "Sand."

While Annalise tossed sticks for the hellhounds, Alex chuckled and nodded. "How apt." He glanced at Dare. "I can sense my new sword is enchanted, so what does it do? Does it make me invincible?"

Dare chuckled. Such a hellion. "You wish. No, your sword is unbreakable and cleans itself when you say 'mundar.' And if you bind it to yourself using a drop of blood while saying 'ligar', it shall burn anyone else who touches it. But you can transfer ownership if you unbind it from yourself using another drop of blood while saying 'solvit' then repeating the binding ritual with the new owner. However, you must store the sword in the sun one day every two weeks to recharge the spell, and you must renew the spell once a season. There are instructions for renewing the spell in the pouch attached to the scabbard."

Alex grinned as he studied his sword again. "Very nice." He smirked at Dare and Annalise. "Aren't you two going to exchange gifts? Or did you decide your love was enough?"

Annalise grimaced at her brother. "Oh, hush." She turned to Dare and beamed as she extracted a small package in festive green and gold paper then handed it to him. "Open yours first."

Dare chuckled while he accepted his gift. Annalise was almost bouncing with excitement. Adorable. He tore off the wrapping then opened the small box. Two hair spirals, one bronze and one electrum, were nestled inside. He blinked and arched his brows at her.

Annalise beamed brighter. "They're our wedding tokens. I chose hair spirals so everyone could see our bond and devotion no matter what we wore."

Alex snickered. "Except for hats."

Frowning at Alex, Annalise sniffed. "Dare and I rarely wear those." She turned back to Dare, her beam returning. "Mine is bronze to match your magic, while yours is electrum to match my magic."

His heart fluttering, Dare caressed the delicate hair spirals. Annalise had chosen their wedding tokens with care—proving how much she wanted their marriage. Sending her his love through their entwined souls, he leaned forward and brushed a kiss against her lips. "They're lovely, my heart. The best Longnight gift I've ever received." He closed the box and slid their wedding tokens into the pocket above his heart. Then he bent and handed her the box wrapped in green paper with gold starbursts. "Now open yours."

As Raven and Bear dropped their sticks before Annalise, she tore open her gift. Sniffing, she hummed. "Honeysuckle, my favorite."

Dare chuckled and tossed the hellhounds' sticks since Annalise was occupied. "The box isn't your gift."

Humming again, Annalise tilted her head then opened the wood box. She inhaled. "Are these communication mirrors?"

While Alex craned to eye Annalise's mirrors, Dare nodded then added, "Linked ones. They must all be recharged in the sunlight after each use, but I can renew the spell on all of them by repeating the communication mirror creation spell on one once a year."

Annalise fingered the edge of one of the mirrors. "Why six? Most only have paired communication mirrors."

Dare grinned at Annalise. Paired communications mirrors weren't enough for her. "So you have enough to speak to everyone, even when we return to Wildewall. Plus, you and your friends can easily have group mirror calls with these."

Blinking, Annalise glanced up at him. "But shouldn't I need only four? One for me, one for Alex, one for Wren, and one for Kiera."

Dare shrugged. Not surprising Annalise would think that. "The fifth is for me, in case we're ever far enough apart that we can't communicate through our soulbond." He paused then said, "And the sixth is for your parents. Alex can hold it for them until they forgive you for eloping with me."

Tears shimmering in her cerulean eyes, Annalise swallowed then whispered, "Oh, Dare." Her love swamping him, she blinked back her tears. "Thank you so much. They're wonderful." She handed him a mirror. "Here, take yours."

Alex clapped Dare's shoulder. "Excellent gifts, my soon-to-be brother. An exacting standard to meet on future Longnights." He smirked when Annalise poked his arm with a frown. "Unfortunately, we should probably go."

Dare and Annalise sighed while they exchanged a yearning glance. Then they extracted their new draklizards from their necks and returned the grumbling pets to their brass cage.

Annalise called Finn and Lily then took Alex's arm while still gazing at Dare. "Have a happy Longnight."

Dare stepped forward and touched her arm. He'd almost forgotten. "Wait." He sent her energy through their soulbond until his head whirled. He gulped a breath. "Now you can go. Have a happy Longnight, Annalise."

She managed a tremulous smile. "I'll call you tomorrow afternoon with one of your communication mirrors. Until then, my love."

As Annalise and Alex left the clearing with Finn and Lily prowling the trees above them, Dare stared after her and sighed. If only he could wake on Longnight morning with her wrapped in his arms. 'Twould be even better than the lovely wedding tokens she'd given him. His chest squeezed. But such intimacies would have to wait until next Longnight.

CHAPTER 53

*D*espite retiring early on Longnight Eve, Annalise groaned and buried her face in her pillow when Grace shook her awake late on Longnight morning. Goddess, she was almost as exhausted as when she'd lost her and Dare's child—despite the energy Dare had sent her earlier.

Tsking, Grace yanked back her covers. "Your parents and brother are waiting. You already missed the first-foot, and they want to open gifts before your Longnight feast."

Annalise sighed. Her family usually opened their gifts before the first-foot, the first Longnight visitor who brought traditional gifts to bring good fortune for the year, arrived around midmorning. She really should rise. Spending Longnight with her family was why she'd not eloped with Dare yet. She forced herself from bed, displacing Finn and Lily curled against her. As the disgruntled angelcats groomed each other, she let Grace help her into her warmest dress. Then smoothing her deep-blue wool skirt, she said to her maid, "I assume you've already fed the angelcats and faebirds."

Grace nodded. "Otherwise Finn and his lady never would have let you sleep so long."

Grimacing, Annalise extracted an envelope from her desk.

How true. She turned back to Grace with a warm smile. "You always take such good care of me. Here, happy Longnight."

Grace grinned back as she accepted the Longnight missive containing ten gold, nearly half of what the maid earned during the rest of the year. "You're a pleasure to serve, my lady. I hope I can continue to do so—no matter where you live."

Annalise squeezed Grace's hand. "I'd like that."

Inhaling a steadying breath, she plodded downstairs to the drawing room. Doubtless her parents and Alex were waiting there beside the winter palace, an enchanted ice sculpture that held Longnight gifts. Before entering, she paused to gulp another breath then managed a brilliant smile and glided inside. "Happy Longnight. Sorry I slept so late."

Muddy-yellow worry flaring about everyone, Father and Alex stiffened with muttered curses while Mother leapt upright. She swept toward Annalise and said, "Dear Goddess. You look wretched, Annalise—almost as bad as during your illness last month. Come sit before you collapse."

Her chest squeezing, Annalise leaned on Mother's arm as they crossed the drawing room. Then she sank onto the sofa beside the winter palace with a sigh. "I'm fine, I promise. Just a bit tired. I'll feel better after the Longnight feast."

Mother and Father exchanged a worried glance while Alex snorted. Then Mother patted her hand and replied, "Let's quickly open gifts so we can eat. Alistair, why don't you give everyone their gifts?"

Father nodded then collected the gifts from the winter palace and distributed them. Like always, everyone had three gifts, one from each family member. He arched his brows as he returned to his seat on the other side of the winter palace. "How shall we open them this year?"

Alex flashed a grin from his seat beside Father. "Since Annalise is in such a hurry to eat, let's open the gifts she gave us all together."

Mother and Father glanced at each other, then they nodded, and Mother said, "Very well."

Tears pricking her eyes, Annalise smiled at her family as they removed the festive wrapping from their gifts and opened their boxes. 'Twas the last time they'd all enjoy a Longnight like this. Please let them like the gifts she'd chosen. Hopefully, Mother and Father wouldn't discard theirs once they discovered she'd eloped with Dare.

Alex snickered as he read his card. "The promise of an angel-cat. How fitting. I assume one of Finn's. When can I expect my gift?"

Annalise lifted a shoulder. The contraceptive spell Dare had placed on Lily should end soon. "In two months or so, most likely."

As Alex nodded, Father grinned at her. "I love my new horse tack. Blue and gold are my favorites. I sense the paint is enchanted?"

She grinned back. Father definitely liked his gift. "Yes, so it never wears off or fades as long as you renew the spell."

While Father studied his tack again, Mother touched Annalise's knee with tears shimmering in her blue eyes. "Your embroidery of entwined griffin feathers spelling my name and your father's is exquisite. Thank you."

Her throat clogging, Annalise beamed at Mother then squeezed the hand touching her knee. Mother had more than liked her gift. "I'm pleased you like it." She arched her brows. "Shall we all open Alex's gifts next?"

Everyone nodded, so she and her parents opened their gifts from Alex. Surely whatever he'd given her today would be small since his true gift had been Sand. She opened her box then blinked at the heavy, white leather gloves that glowed with Alex's magic.

Her box still unopened, Mother peered at the heavy gloves. "Alexander, did you get your sister *hawking* gloves?"

Arching a brow, Alex shrugged. "You told me gloves were suitable gifts for gentlemen to give ladies."

As Father coughed to disguise his laugh, Mother pursed her lips at Alex. "Ordinary gloves, not hawking gloves. They're unladylike."

Annalise almost laughed. Trust Alex to give her something appropriate yet not.

Alex widened his eyes with feigned innocence. "But Annalise has plenty of ordinary gloves." He winked at her. "Besides, I thought she might find these useful. I even enchanted them, so they'd not stain as long as the spell is renewed every year."

While Mother sighed beside her, Annalise grinned at Alex. Hawking gloves would be useful against her new draklizard's sharp talons. "I love them. Thanks, Alex." She turned to Mother. "Finish opening your box."

Mother hummed and narrowed her eyes at Alex. "My gift better be more appropriate than hawking gloves." She opened her box then exhaled as she extracted a delicate statue of a waltzing couple. Smiling, she pressed the button at the base, and the couple began dancing as a lush waltz played by a string quartet echoed through the drawing room. She beamed at Alex. "My favorite song—the first one your father and I danced to all those years ago. 'Tis lovely, thank you."

Annalise smiled and shook her head. Not surprising Alex had found the perfect gift to make Mother forgive him for his "unladylike" gift to her.

Alex waggled his brows. "Just wait until the ending. 'Tis when I knew I must purchase it for you."

As the lush waltz continued, Mother hummed again then glanced at Father. "What did Alexander get you?"

Father eyed the jug in his lap. "Spiritmead, I think."

Alex grinned at Father. "Not just any spiritmead. Some distilled by Old Man Ewan back home. After you mentioned missing it, I ordered some then fetched it with a transportation spell."

Father brightened then opened his jug and took a deep draft. "As rich as ever."

Annalise and Alex traded an amused glance, and she swallowed her laughter. Father certainly adored good spiritmead to risk provoking Mother by drinking directly from the jug.

Unsurprisingly, Mother tsked and chided, "Don't behave so uncouth before the children."

Father closed his jug. "Sorry, Emmeline."

Before he could continue, the lush waltz ended, and the gentleman in the dancing statue pulled the lady against him and passionately kissed her.

As Alex chuckled and Mother stared, Annalise began to laugh. No wonder Alex had said he must purchase it for Mother.

Father winked at Mother. "As I recall, our first dance ended the same."

Mother blushed then giggled. "So it did." She arched a brow at Alex. "Cheeky boy." She turned back to Father and said, "Let's open your gifts now."

Annalise, Mother, and Alex opened their gifts from Father. Annalise smiled and her chest warmed when she uncovered the plush nesting bed that glowed with Father's magic. Just what Lily would need when carrying angelkittens. "This nesting bed is wonderful. Thanks, Father."

Father smiled back. "Figured Finn's mate would need it soon. And I added a levitation charm since angelcats adore heights. Whenever the charm fades, bring it to me to renew."

Annalise nodded as the warmth in her chest chilled. Except by then, Father would despise her for eloping with a Ravenstone.

His head bent over his new book, Alex snickered. "Wherever did you find out about this book? 'Tis hilarious but not your style."

Father chuckled. "The Duke of Oakmoor mentioned it, and I could imagine you penning such irreverent yet incisive tales, so I had to purchase it for you."

Alex grinned as he closed his book. "I can't wait to read the rest. Thanks."

Shoving aside her sorrow at soon losing Mother and Father, Annalise turned to Mother, who'd been oddly silent since opening her gift. "What did Father get you?"

Mother beamed then showed everyone the elaborate set of jewelry nestled inside her box. "Black opals."

Annalise smiled. The rare, dark gems that shimmered with a fiery rainbow were Mother's favorite, and the elaborate necklace, bracelets, and earrings were precisely the kind Mother preferred. Father had chosen well.

Leaning forward, Mother gestured for them to continue. "Now open my gifts."

So Annalise, Alex, and Father tore open their last gift. Annalise gasped at the still clear, arachne silk shawl embroidered with electrum hearts. Goldwork was even more painstaking than ordinary embroidery—the delicate hearts must have taken Mother ages. She beamed at Mother. "This shawl is exquisite. Thank you."

Mother grinned. "I wanted you to have a shawl that matched that electrum heart necklace you're so fond of wearing."

Her throat constricting, Annalise caressed Dare's faegift at her throat. She'd treasure Mother's shawl when Mother no longer spoke to her for eloping with him.

Eyeing Annalise with a frown, Alex swung his new fob watch that glowed with magic. "Mother, why is this fob watch enchanted?"

Chuckling, Mother smiled at him. "'Tisn't a fob watch—'tis a journey charm. It adjusts its time to match your location. And if you tap it and ask directions, it shall guide you to your destination and tell you when you'll arrive. You can also tap it and ask for the weather of your location or your destination."

Annalise couldn't help a smile despite her melancholy. An ideal gift for her active brother.

Alex swung his journey charm again. "Very nice. How do I recharge and renew the spell?"

Mother flicked her fingers. "Store it in the sun one day a week to recharge. Then renew it using the instructions inside the box once a year."

As Alex nodded, Father arched his brows at Mother and held up his card with "Wind" written on it. "What does this mean?"

Mother chuckled, her eyes gleaming. "'Tis the name of your gift—a Tsarkan mare who arrived from Aherne's this morning."

Annalise and Alex laughed when Father leapt upright and began bolting from the drawing room. He'd been hunting for the perfect Tsarkan mare to breed with his Tsarkan stallion Desert for years.

Mother called after Father, "No visiting the stables until after the Longnight feast." Once Father sighed and halted, she turned to Annalise. "Do you require help getting to the family dining room?"

Setting her wonderful Longnight gifts on the sofa, Annalise managed to rise, although her head swirled and vision darkened. She flashed a brilliant smile. "Just Alex's arm."

Annalise leaned heavily on her brother as they walked to the family dining room. However, some of her energy returned after she devoured the traditional Longnight feast of venison, wild boar, roasted root vegetables, fresh orenges, and Longnight cake.

She and her family had returned to the drawing room and were playing a Longnight riddle game when a royal guard arrived and handed her a note from Kiera.

Mother arched her brows at Annalise. "What did Lady Kiera write? She and King Devon haven't attended court events since she renewed the Nightmara-Calatini Treaty."

Annalise stilled as she read Kiera's note inviting her to Kiera and King Devon's secret wedding at Waterstreet Orphanage. Keeping her face serene, she replied, "Kiera was simply wishing us a happy Longnight." Since she couldn't reveal the truth and needed an excuse to leave, she sighed and said, "I'm going to nap for a few hours."

Although Alex and her parents frowned at each other, she slipped upstairs before they could protest. Yet climbing the stairs consumed her energy from the Longnight feast.

She was donning her warmest cloak with trembling fingers when Moonbud mentally said, :*I sense Kiera invited you to her wedding too. I'll carry you to the orphanage.*:

Annalise exhaled. Then Father wouldn't notice Storm's absence when he visited Wind. :*Thanks, Moonbud.*:

Once Moonbud arrived outside the stables, the nightmara queen-heir knelt so Annalise could mount—she wasn't wearing a riding habit, so she must ride aside. Plus, she was still too drained to mount properly.

On the ride across Ormas, Annalise sagged against Moonbud and dozed until they reached the orphanage. She slid to the ground then leaned against Moonbud and trudged into the dining hall to join Kiera's other guests.

The indigo in her aura deepening, Kiera darted over and grasped Annalise's arm. "Are you ill again?"

Annalise managed a weak smile to reassure her friend. "The shorter days, remember? Don't fret about me—'tis your wedding day."

Kiera sighed then nodded, but before she could reply, King Devon strode over and led her away to start their wedding ceremony.

Following Kiera and King Devon, Annalise and the other guests of family and close friends crowded into the orphanage's tiny library, even Moonbud. Her body heavy, Annalise rested against the sole bookcase as Priest Melchior officiated their wedding ceremony. She shut her eyes when he performed their bloodbinding since the flare of Kiera's and King Devon's life forces joining was too bright for her right now.

After that, everyone returned to the dining hall. As King Devon entertained the rowdy orphans with the story of his pursuit of Kiera, Annalise sank onto a trestle table along the back wall. By the time he finished, she could barely keep her eyes open. She must return to Greysnowe House before she fell asleep. Gulping a breath, she staggered upright then began toward Moonbud. Yet before she'd taken two steps, her head whirled, and stygian blackness consumed her.

CHAPTER 54

After sleeping until the first-foot arrived midmorning, a lengthy ride to the royal bay to gather natural energy, then eating their Longnight feast, Dare and Mother headed to the drawing room with the hellhounds bounding beside them and the draklizards swooping above their heads. As they sat on the sofa beside the winter palace holding their gifts, Raven and Bear flopped at their feet while Leaf and Sand perched on the back of the sofa between them.

Mother chuckled and scratched Leaf's chest then Sand's. "I can't believe Lord Alexander gave you two draklizards as a Longnight gift."

Forcing himself not to shift in his seat, Dare smoothed his beard. Too bad he couldn't reveal that only Leaf was his. Instead, he shrugged and replied, "Alex is perceptive and knows me well." To distract Mother from the Greysnowes, he handed her his gift for her from the winter palace. "Happy Longnight, Mother."

Mother tore off the festive white paper then gasped at her gift. "A moving painting of Beillahd Mountain back home." She sighed as tears brightened her amber eyes. "Your father proposed to me on its vision summit. The painting is exquisite; thank you."

He grinned at her, warmth filling his chest. No wonder Beillahd Mountain was Mother's favorite area in Wildewall. "I'd hoped you'd like it."

Mother beamed back. "I do. How do I recharge and renew the spell?"

Dare hummed and gestured toward her moving painting. "The clerk at The Arte of Spells said instructions are written on the back. But I doubt 'tis complicated since they sell mostly to people without magic of their own."

Flipping over her painting, Mother hummed as she read. "Yes, I must simply detach then recharge the crystal on the back, either through sunlight or with natural energy, once a month. And the spell must be renewed yearly." She set her painting aside then handed him his gift from the winter palace. "For you."

He removed the festive green wrapping and opened the small box. He gaped at the two rings etched with hearts nestled inside. They appeared remarkably like Father's and Mother's wedding tokens, except the smaller ring was electrum rather than bronze. He glanced at Mother's middle finger on her left hand to check the similarity then froze. Her finger was bare. What?

Mother leaned toward him with a vibrant grin. "Henry's been gone over three years now, so 'twas time to hand down our wedding tokens." She smiled brighter. "And I suspect you'll need them soon."

Dare stiffened and stared at Mother, his neck prickling. Why was Mother saying that? She should believe he'd not found a wife yet.

Still beaming, Mother tilted her head. "As a nature witch, you can easily resize the rings if they don't fit. However, I already transformed mine to electrum to suit your future wife."

His stomach clenching, he continued staring at Mother. Dear Goddess, had she realized his secret involvement with Annalise?

Mother patted his knee. "And even though Henry wouldn't have approved of your future wife thanks to the feud, I most certainly do. Not only did she save your life, but when I spoke to her, she seemed perfect for you."

Dare swallowed as his stomach clenched further. Yes, Mother definitely knew. But when had she realized the truth? And why hadn't she said anything then?

Mother sighed. "Although I do wish you'd trusted me enough to tell me about your involvement with Lady Annalise. Surely you knew I wouldn't care about her being a Greysnowe. I raised you not to support feuds or vengeance, but instead to seek healing and peace."

He winced. As he'd feared, his silence about Annalise had hurt Mother. He began to reply but halted at a sudden commotion in the hall.

As footsteps thundered closer, Brown shouted, "My lords and lady, stop, please!"

Then the drawing room door burst open, and Annalise's parents stormed inside with Alex directly behind them.

Dare and Mother leapt from the sofa while Raven and Bear sprang upright with deep growls and Leaf and Sand surged into the air then turned invisible.

His fists clenched, Lord Greysnowe hurtled across the drawing room with his wife beside him. "Where is she, you treacherous cad?"

As Alex strode to stand between his parents and Dare, Lady Greysnowe fisted her hands on her hips then leaned forward with a scowl. "We want our daughter returned at once, Ravenstone. Goddess knows what lies you told Annalise to cozen her into eloping."

Dare inhaled and set his jaw while he calmed the hellhounds and draklizards with his nature magic until they sat again. If only such magic would work on Annalise's parents. Instead, he must use words to calm them enough to listen to the truth. Yet they always took umbrage no matter what he said because of the feud.

He gritted a genial smile at Lord and Lady Greysnowe. "I've never lied to Annalise." He turned to Alex, who'd speak sensibly rather than shouting accusations. "What's going on?"

Alex grimaced. "After our Longnight feast, Annalise said she was going to nap, but when Mother checked on her an hour later, her chambers were empty." He sighed. "Mother and Father began browbeating Annalise's maid to tell them where she'd gone, so to protect poor Grace, I had to reveal your love and plans to elope. I'm sorry." He arched his brows. "Is Annalise resting upstairs? She looked wretched this morning."

His breath halting, Dare stilled. Annalise had meant to spend Longnight with her family, so where was she? Perhaps she'd slipped away for time alone in the park. He reached for her, but she was much farther away than that, in the direction of the docks. But why? Perhaps Lady Kiera had invited Annalise to Longnight festivities at Lady Kiera's orphanage near the docks.

He exhaled a sigh. "Annalise isn't here. I'm not certain where she is, but I believe she's across Ormas."

Lady Greysnowe scowled harder, her pale skin mottling. "Liar! Don't you *dare* conceal Annalise from us."

Mother stepped toward Lady Greysnowe with a hand outstretched. "Dare's not lying. Since I read her aura at Lady Islaye's, I'd sense if she was here. She's bound to my son, after all."

Dare scrutinized Mother. So *that* was the spell Annalise had sensed. Doubtless 'twas when Mother had realized the truth— she'd have recognized his aura entwined with Annalise's.

As Alex eyed them askance, Lord and Lady Greysnowe exchanged frowns. Then Lord Greysnowe growled at Mother, "What do you mean by that?"

Lifting his chin, Dare gestured for Mother to remain silent. Telling the full truth was his responsibility. "Mother means that

Annalise and I are soulbound. We have been since she healed my fatal wound on Summerday."

Alex sighed. "The fatal wound *I'd* given Dare during our duel. If she'd not used her powers to save him, I'd no doubt be executed by now."

Their eyes wide, Lord and Lady Greysnowe gaped at Dare and Alex. After a moment, Lady Greysnowe whispered, "But 'twould mean Annalise is a soul healer."

Blinking, Mother stared at Annalise's parents. "You didn't know?"

Dare almost winced. Mentioning how little they knew their daughter wouldn't endear them to the Greysnowes.

Alex snorted and glared at his parents. "Of course, they didn't know Annalise was a soul healer. She concealed her powers, so no one could exploit her."

As Lord and Lady Greysnowe stiffened, Dare sighed. Although true, Alex's insinuation would only hurt them. Not conducive for peace, nor what Annalise would want. He offered her parents a warm smile. "Why Annalise concealed her powers doesn't matter. That she and I are irrevocably soulbound and love each other does. We intend to marry after the Longnight season."

His hands fisting again, Lord Greysnowe sneered at Dare. "You just want Annalise to exploit her rare powers."

Mother tsked. "Why would he? As my son, he's a powerful, Rhiannon-descendant nature witch, so he has no need for your daughter's powers." She turned to Lady Greysnowe. "Surely you recognized his powers felt like mine."

Lady Greysnowe glowered back. "After you deceived me, I never remained around treacherous Ravenstones long enough to determine their magic. Besides, not *all* of us can perform aura spells."

As Mother winced, Dare raised his palms. He must convince Annalise's parents to forgo the feud and accept their marriage. "Please, let's not argue. We'll be family soon enough. With our irrevocable soulbond, Annalise and I have no choice but to marry. And she'd much prefer having her parents at our wedding. Knowing our marriage would upset you and make you despise her has been distressing her since she healed me and formed our soulbond six months ago.

Lord Greysnowe bared his teeth at Dare. "Emmeline and I shall *never* accept our daughter marrying a Ravenstone."

Snorting, Alex raised his eyes skyward. "Father, don't be idiotic. Such declarations have been too late since Annalise healed the fatal wound *I* caused." He arched a brow. "You should be grateful Annalise found a gentleman who adores her for herself rather than wanting your wealth and influence or her beauty and rare powers. She and Dare shall build a joyous life together full of abiding love, magical pets, and boisterous children."

Lady Greysnowe pursed her lips. "If Ravenstone is *so* wonderful, why is he concealing Annalise from us? Let *her* rhapsodize about him."

Dare grimaced and rubbed his beard. Not surprising that Annalise's parents hadn't believed him earlier. Perhaps providing her location would help. "As I said, Annalise isn't here. She's across Ormas somewhere. But I can ask her where she is using our soulbond."

As he reached out to Annalise through their entwined souls, her radiant presence suddenly flickered like a dying candle. A chill bolted through him. Even during her miscarriage, her presence hadn't flickered like that. :*Annalise?*:

Her presence still flickering, Annalise didn't reply.

Ice filled his chest. :*Annalise, what's wrong?*:

Silence.

Disregarding everyone in the drawing room, Dare flew toward the door. Something terrible must have happened. Maybe she wasn't at Lady Kiera's orphanage. Had someone kidnapped her then fatally wounded her? Thank the Goddess he could use their soulbond to find her, even with her presence being so faint. Please let him reach her in time.

But before he reached the door, Lord Greysnowe seized his elbow. "Just like a treacherous Ravenstone to promise something then flee before delivering."

His pulse surging, Dare glared at Annalise's father. They didn't have time to debate this. "I can barely sense Annalise's presence. I think she might be dying. I must go to her."

After ordering the hellhounds and draklizards to stay, he wrenched his arm free then raced through the door, past Brown, and outside to the stables. Without bothering to saddle Ebony, he led the stallion from the stables and vaulted atop him. Then he kneed Ebony, but Mother, Alex, and Annalise's parents leapt before him, forcing him to halt the stallion. He glared at them. They were delaying him, and Annalise mightn't have long. "What?!"

Mother narrowed her eyes at him. "We're all going with you."

Dare almost growled. He gulped a breath then replied, "Fine. But hurry. I shan't wait for you. Annalise needs me." He jerked his chin at Alex and his parents. "Take any of my horses you like."

Mother and the three Greysnowes dashed past him into the stables. Within moments, they all returned and leapt atop their unsaddled mounts—even Lady Greysnowe.

Dare kneed Ebony again, and they thundered through the quiet streets of Ormas with the others close behind. Thankfully, since 'twas Longnight afternoon, few people were in the streets, so they needn't slow to avoid anyone. As he strained to sense Annalise's flickering presence, he and Ebony galloped with the others toward the docks. Goddess, please let him be able to save Annalise.

MEANWHILE

When the loud thump sounded behind them, Cassandra and everyone else in the orphanage's dining hall whirled to face the lady crumbled on the floor. The beauteous Lady Annalise was as white and frozen as snow—the heart-shaped, sapphire firegem flickering in the hollow of her throat appeared more alive than she did.

Wren, Queen Kiera, and several other adults surged toward Lady Annalise while Hawke and the remaining adults distracted the orphans with Longnight caroling.

Waving for Amaranth to remain with their grandparents and enjoy the caroling, Cassandra rushed across the dining hall toward Lady Annalise. Even though she'd just started her training four months ago, she was the only witch here, and perhaps her magic could help. She was a Rhiannon descendant, after all. She slipped into the circle surrounding Lady Annalise at the fallen lady's feet between Peter and Priest Melchior.

Kneeling beside Lady Annalise, Queen Kiera pulled Lady Annalise's head into her lap and shivered. "Dear Goddess, she's freezing and barely breathing. We must summon a witch healer at once."

Beside Queen Kiera, Wren hummed and rubbed her rounded stomach. "I think we should summon the veiled witch instead."

Cassandra nodded. Although no healer, her mentor—who she knew only as Tihdseare, "teacher" in the witch's tongue—was an incredibly powerful Rhiannon-descendant seer. Tihdseare would be able to see what ailed Lady Annalise and know how to cure it.

Across from Queen Kiera, Lady Moonbud flicked her midnight tail. :*Yes, the veiled witch shall see how to heal Annalise. Plus, the veiled witch is much closer than any witch healer. I'll call her.*:

As they waited for Tihdseare, Cassandra eyed Lady Annalise. No magic glowed about the unconscious lady, but she was becoming more and more pale, and her faint breathing was slowing. She mightn't last until Tihdseare arrived. So Cassandra crouched and pressed a hand on Lady Annalise's leg then said, "I'm going to send Lady Annalise some energy."

As the others around Lady Annalise nodded, Cassandra gathered her will then muttered an energy spell. She gasped and almost fell as most of her magic was devoured. Her head whirling, she wrenched her remaining magic free. Goddess, what had just happened?

Their brows creased with worried frowns, Wren and Queen Kiera leaned toward Cassandra, then Wren asked, "Well?"

Cassandra shivered and rubbed her aching forehead. She must eat to recover, but finding food would require rising. "I'm not certain if my energy spell helped or not. But even though no magic glows about Lady Annalise, whatever ails her must be magical because it devoured my magic like a manticore devours a unicorn herd."

While Mary bustled away, Wren and Queen Kiera traded a glance, then Queen Kiera murmured, "But Annalise was convinced her exhaustion was simply due to the shorter days."

Mary bustled back over with a plate bearing a massive slice of Longnight cake and handed it to Cassandra. Smiling her thanks, Cassandra began devouring the rich dessert. Once her head no longer whirled, she told Wren and Queen Kiera, "I doubt Lady Annalise's ailment is due to shorter days. Not even nature witches are this drained by that."

Wren and Queen Kiera exchanged another glance, then Wren said, "I wonder if 'tis due to—"

Suddenly, Lady Moonbud stamped her front hoof then craned toward Wren and Queen Kiera. She must be privately speaking to them.

As Wren winced, Queen Kiera sighed then replied, "True. Annalise wouldn't want that."

Swallowing her last bite of Longnight cake, Cassandra eyed Wren and Queen Kiera. What secrets were they keeping for Lady Annalise? And why did they believe her secrets were involved with her ailment?

Then Tihdseare swept into the dining hall, her concealing black veils fluttering. She halted for a moment and scrutinized Lady Annalise before taking Wren's place at the supine lady's head. "I can see why you called me, Moonbud."

Now behind the still kneeling Queen Kiera, Wren swallowed and laced her fingers atop her rounded stomach. "Should we summon Healer Althea as well?"

Tihdseare shook her head. "A witch healer would be no help here. Your friend is under a curse—a virulent one."

Cassandra and the others around Lady Annalise gasped. No wonder the white glow of magic was missing—powerful curses, typically cast by one or more Rhiannon-descendant black witches, were only visible to seers. Other witches couldn't see them, even when analyzing active magic with a probing spell or reading auras using an aura spell.

A sigh wafted Tihdseare's black veils. "I might be able to cure her, but I'll require help." She glanced at Cassandra. "Go tell your grandparents I'll need you the rest of the afternoon."

As Tihdseare began reassuring the others, Cassandra nodded then darted across the dining hall. She glanced at Amaranth to check that her little sister was still too engrossed with the caroling to overhear then whispered to Grandmother and Grandfather, "The veiled witch says she requires my help with Lady Annalise for the afternoon."

Grandmother embraced her, then Grandfather squeezed her shoulder. Her dark eyes concerned, Grandmother said, "Very well. We'll send the carriage for you before dinner. Please be careful."

Cassandra beamed at them. Although not her adored, departed parents, Grandmother and Grandfather loved her and Amaranth just as fiercely. "I promise I'll be careful. Don't eat all of dinner before I get home."

She darted back to Tihdseare just as King Devon and Priest Melchior were draping Lady Annalise atop Lady Moonbud. Then Peter tied Lady Annalise to the nightmara queen-heir.

Her bracelets and tiny bells jingling, Tihdseare beckoned Cassandra. "Come, we must hurry. Most everyone we need is already galloping toward us, and I've summoned the royal witch to help too—despite her petty grumbling. We must prepare everything before they arrive, and I need more time to study Lady Annalise's curse."

Cassandra bobbed her head then strode with Tihdseare and Lady Moonbud outside toward Tihdseare's tiny witch shop, Rhiannon's Veils.

CHAPTER 55

As Dare and Ebony neared the docks with Mother and the Greysnowes flanking him, he turned his weary stallion right onto Mermaid Street to follow Annalise's flickering presence. Was her presence weaker despite being so close? Goddess, please let him reach her before 'twas too late.

He urged Ebony faster then made a sharp left onto Mountainglass Lane and halted his damp and winded stallion at the first door on the left. A tiny sign beside it read, "Rhiannon's Veils." Annalise was somewhere behind that weathered red door. Why had she traveled across Ormas to visit such an unprepossessing shop, likely a witch shop given its name? Or was the witch here behind her sudden malady?

He leapt to the ground and strode toward the witch shop with the others hastily echoing him.

He was about to grasp the doorknob when Miss Weston burst from the alley between Rhiannon's Veils and the miscellany shop next door. "The veiled witch sent me to lead you to her garden. Follow me, and bring your horses. They'll be safer in the garden."

The girl whirled then darted back into the alley, and Dare and the others raced after her with their horses. While she waved them through the green wooden gate, she grimaced and said, "Please hurry. I doubt Lady Annalise shall last long. Lady Moonbud and I shall tend to your horses."

While Lady Greysnowe almost sobbed and Lord Greysnowe, Alex, and Mother gasped, Dare gulped a bracing breath, his heart wrenching. Oh, Goddess.

He surged through the gate then gaped at the veiled witch's magical garden. Despite it being Longnight—the shortest day of the year as well as the first—'twas summer in the veiled witch's garden. The balmy air was sweet with the heady scent of wild roses, honeysuckle, and apples, while the verdant wildflowers, herbs, and fruit trees in the garden buzzed with butterflies, faebirds, and melissae. Just how powerful was this veiled witch?

Then his gaze fell on Annalise lying inside a circle of lavender, clear quartz, and faedust. In her deep-blue gown with his faegift flickering at her throat and her chest barely moving, she was as white and frozen as an ice sculpture in an arctic elf's palace. His pulse pounding in his ears, he flew across the magical garden toward her.

Yet just before the circle, a hand seized his elbow and yanked him back.

He glared at the woman halting him, who must be the veiled witch from her potent air of magic and the black veils concealing everything but her exotically lined eyes. "Why did you stop me?"

A sigh rippled the witch's black veils. "I've stabilized Lady Annalise as best I could with a healing circle, but its power shall shatter if you breach it. And we must wait for the royal witch before attempting to break the powerful curse killing Lady Annalise."

Dare inhaled as ice burst through his veins and froze his chest. A powerful curse? Dear Goddess. Typically created by Rhiannon-descendant black witches, powerful curses were impossible for any but a seer to see, and they were often grueling to break.

Clinging to her haggard husband, Lady Greysnowe glared at

Dare with tears coursing down her cheeks. "'Tis your fault! You cursed our daughter—you're *worse* than your vile and treacherous mother!"

Before he could reply, the veiled witch tsked and shook her head. "No, the curse is killing Lord Ravenstone as well—albeit slower. Only to be expected given he's been gathering natural energy, which has offset the curse's drain. Plus, he's a Ravenstone, and she's a Greysnowe."

As Alex frowned, Dare and Mother traded a bewildered glance. Must the veiled witch be so cryptic? He swallowed then said, "I think you'd best explain everything before Lady Juliet arrives and we can break the curse."

The veiled witch nodded then released his arm. "The curse's roots are the same as the Greysnowe-Ravenstone feud. The jilted Ravenstone unearthed three Rhiannon-descendant black witches to create a curse to punish his former betrothed and his cousin then any other Greysnowes and Ravenstones who defied the feud and made love."

His stomach lurching, Dare swallowed. So Annalise's mother was right—the curse killing Annalise was his fault. Despite their irresistible soulbond, he never should have succumbed to his hunger for her.

As Lord and Lady Greysnowe bristled and scowled at Dare while Mother glared back, Alex hummed and frowned at the veiled witch. "The curse is over three hundred years old? It must be strong and shall be almost impossible to break."

Sighing, the veiled witch inclined her head. "Unfortunately. The black witches cast the curse using the jilted Ravenstone's life then made it self-sustaining using the first lives it stole—the jilted Ravenstone's former betrothed and cousin. Since then, the curse has renewed and recharged itself using the power generated from the continued hatred between the Greysnowes and Ravenstones as well as the lives the curse steals. So 'tis much stronger now than when 'twas first created—especially after feeding on such a powerful soul healer and an equally powerful nature witch."

Dare clenched his eyes shut and swallowed a bitter laugh. Wonderful, his and Annalise's powerful magic had made the curse even more impossible to break. He started at a gentle touch on his arm then opened his eyes.

Her hand on his arm, the veiled witch arched her brows. "How long since you and Lady Annalise consummated your soulbond?"

A blush burning his cheeks, he glanced at Annalise's furious parents then at an unusually sober Alex and Mother. So embarrassing. He muttered, "Two months ago."

The veiled witch's brow furrowed. "How peculiar. Although your powerful magic and soulbond protect you somewhat, the curse should have killed you both by now."

His gaze drifting to the melissae buzzing in the flowering plants, Dare stiffened and inhaled a ragged gasp. The melissae's life-giving ambrosia! "Two months ago, the melissa queen in the royal forest gifted Annalise and me some ambrosia. I believe the melissa queen said we'd be protected from illness for one moon."

Tilting her head, the veiled witch hummed. "That explains it. I'm guessing you both began feeling ill around a month ago when the ambrosia's protection ended. It would have started small—just vague tiredness and malaise at first."

He nodded and rubbed his beard. 'Twas when he and Annalise had begun sleeping later. He stiffened as his chest clenched. And when Annalise had lost their child. No doubt the malevolent curse was behind that and had gained power from it too.

Alex brightened and leaned forward. "Could we get more ambrosia from Esme the Great's melissae hive to save Annalise and Dare?"

The veiled witch sighed. "Without a soul healer to communicate with them, 'twould take too long. Besides, ambrosia would only treat the symptoms of the curse, rather than break it."

Dare hummed. But treating the symptoms would allow them more time to break the curse. His stomach fluttered. "I can communicate with the melissae, and the melissa queen may remember me as Annalise's mate. Surely, she'd gift me some for Annalise."

Her brows arching, the veiled witch blinked at him then shook her head. "Even so, I doubt 'twould help. Tell me, did you eat the ambrosia before or after consummating your soulbond?"

He glanced at Annalise's parents again, who were scowling as fiercely as ever. Blushing anew, he replied, "Before."

The veiled witch nodded. "The ambrosia protected you both then because 'twas between you and the curse, so it kept the curse from reaching you. If you or Lady Annalise ate ambrosia now, the curse would simply devour its power." She grimaced and nodded at Miss Weston approaching with the nightmara queen-heir Lady Moonbud. "Like it did for my apprentice's magic when she cast an energy spell to sustain Lady Annalise."

Dare swallowed and eyed Annalise inside the healing circle. Goddess, was her faint breathing slower? His heart stuttered. They must act soon. Why wasn't Lady Juliet here yet?

The veiled witch patted his arm. "Don't fret so. Your soulbond is keeping Lady Annalise alive right now, and you being so close strengthens your soulbond's power."

He gritted a weak smile. Hopefully, 'twould last until Lady Juliet arrived. He studied the others. Annalise's parents were still glaring, but their glares now appeared softer—worried rather than irate. Mother and Alex were frowning but didn't seem surprised that his and Annalise's soulbond was keeping her alive.

Suddenly, Lady Juliet thundered into the magical garden atop the nightmara stallion Annalise usually rode. Thank the Goddess.

Her dark eyes narrow, the veiled witch sniffed while Lady Juliet slid to the ground. She drawled, "*Finally.* What took you so long, royal witch?"

As Darkthorn joined Lady Moonbud and nuzzled her, Lady Juliet glowered at her fellow Rhiannon descendant and patted her bulging satchel. "I was enjoying Longnight with friends, so I had to return to the palace to change into a riding habit and gather spell ingredients. And although Darkthorn graciously carried me, even a nightmara takes time to cross Ormas."

The veiled witch tsked. "I've plenty of spell ingredients here, you know."

Before the two rival witches could argue further, Dare asked, "Now that everyone has arrived, how can we break the curse?"

Still clinging to her husband, Lady Greysnowe scowled at the veiled witch and Lady Juliet. "As *fascinating* as your quarrel is, you should be saving our dying daughter."

The veiled witch and Lady Juliet both winced, then the veiled witch inclined her head and replied, "Our apologies. 'Tis the first we've met, and our mutual disdain distracted us. But you're correct, we must see to breaking the curse on Lady Annalise and Lord Ravenstone."

Dare leaned toward the veiled witch and Lady Juliet. "Just tell us what we must do to save Annalise."

Annalise's parents, Alex, and Mother all nodded—possibly the first time the head of the Ravenstones and Greysnowes had agreed on anything since the feud began eleven generations ago.

Humming, the veiled witch studied Dare and the others. "To break such a powerful curse, we require the same number of Rhiannon descendants that created it—three. Myself." She nodded at Lady Juliet. "The royal witch." She turned back to him and the others. "And one of you. But breaking the curse requires a powerful Rhiannon descendant and might permanently drain your powers or kill you."

His pulse surging, Dare stepped forward. Saving Annalise was worth any price. "I'll do it."

Her black veils fluttering, the veiled witch sighed. "You can't. As Lady Annalise's soulbond and a focus of the curse, you're unable to break it. That must be done from outside the curse."

He set his jaw and glared at the veiled witch. "I must do *some-thing* to help save Annalise. *Please*."

Lady Juliet hummed. "While we're breaking the curse, you could fully mesh your soul and Lady Annalise's like when you're intimate. 'Twould strengthen her."

The veiled witch leaned toward him. "But doing so would mean if we can't save Lady Annalise, you'll die as well. If you don't, we should be able to save you even if we can't save her. The curse's hold isn't as strong on you."

His heart seizing, he shuddered. He'd rather die attempting to save Annalise than live knowing he'd failed to try. "I don't care. I'll do whatever I must to save Annalise."

As Annalise's parents gaped at him, the veiled witch nodded. "Very well." She faced the others. "Which of you shall be our third?" The veiled witch eyed Miss Weston. "Not you, Cassandra. We require an adult with fully developed powers as well as one whose power isn't drained." She glanced at Lady Moonbud and Darkthorn beside Miss Weston. "We also require a human witch rather than a magical creature."

Alex lifted his chin and stepped forward beside Dare. "I'll be your third witch."

Dare smiled at Alex. Not surprising Alex would risk so much to save his beloved sister.

The veiled witch and Lady Juliet exchanged a look, then Lady Juliet sighed and said, "Sadly, you can't, Lord Alexander. Although families that produce soul healers are technically Rhiannon descendants, only the soul healers have the full powers of a Rhiannon descendant. The rest merely have the power of ordinary witches."

The veiled witch turned to Lady Greysnowe. "And you can't help either because you're not a Rhiannon descendant."

As Alex and Annalise's parents drooped, Dare eyed Mother. She was the only witch remaining. Surely she'd help.

Flashing a vibrant grin, Mother stepped forward. "But *I* am a Rhiannon descendant. I'll be the third that you need to break the curse." She winked at Dare and Alex. "I would have volunteered sooner, but the boys are younger and faster than me."

As Lady Greysnowe gasped, Dare exhaled, and warmth eased his chest. Thank the Goddess Mother was in Ormas.

Lady Greysnowe stepped from her husband's arms and stretched a hand toward Mother. "You'd risk your powers and your life to save *our* daughter?"

Mother beamed at Lady Greysnowe. "Of course. My son adores her, and she's my best friend's daughter." As Lady Greysnowe began crying and Lord Greysnowe pulled his wife back into his arms, Mother turned to the veiled witch and Lady Juliet. "Just tell me what we must do."

Dare almost smiled. Doubtless they'd begin the spell to save Annalise soon. At last.

Before the veiled witch or Lady Juliet could answer Mother, Darkthorn stamped his front hoof then said, :*Although we can't be one of the three Rhiannon descendants to break the curse, Moonbud and I shall help to save Annalise as well.*:

Her tail flicking, Lady Moonbud nodded. :*We can channel energy into you three to sustain you while you're performing your spell.*:

The veiled witch and Lady Juliet glanced at each other, then the veiled witch replied, "That *would* improve our chances of success." She gestured for Lady Juliet, Mother, and the two nightmara to join her. "Come, let's discuss the details of our spell. We needn't bother the others."

Dare swallowed then scrutinized Mother and the others huddled together. Please let them hurry. Then he inhaled and turned to face Annalise's parents. "I'm sorry for endangering Annalise. If I'd known about the curse, I never would have so much as kissed her."

Their eyes widening, Lord and Lady Greysnowe blinked at him.

Alex snorted and punched Dare's arm. "Then Annalise would have kissed you. As I recall, she said 'twas excruciating to resist your soulbond." He shook his head. "And don't apologize for loving her, or her loving you."

Dare smiled at Alex. Annalise's brother always saw to the heart of others. "Thanks, Alex."

He was about to continue, but the veiled witch strode over and asked, "Are you ready to begin, Lord Ravenstone?"

His stomach tensing, he nodded and stepped beside the healing circle around Annalise. Time to save her.

After Mother had given him a fierce embrace, the veiled witch said, "When I tell you, break the healing circle then mesh your soul with Lady Annalise. Your mother, the royal witch, and I shall assume our positions while you do that. We'll begin the spell once you tell us your souls are meshed. Understood?" At his nod, she continued, "Good. Then go!"

Dare inhaled and strode through the healing circle. Disregarding her parents and brother as well as Mother watching, he lay beside Annalise and wrapped her in his arms. Then brushing a kiss against her frozen lips, he meshed their entwined souls, and her flickering presence steadied. He whispered against her lips, "Come back to me, my heart. Please." He drew back slightly and called, "We're ready."

Then the voices of Mother, the veiled witch, and Lady Juliet rose in a singsong chant, and the white glow of powerful magic exploded about him and Annalise.

He kissed Annalise again. Please, Goddess, please let this spell be enough to save her.

CHAPTER 56

When Dare's presence suddenly surrounded her, Annalise reached out to him with her final bit of energy. At last! Goddess knew how long she'd been shivering in the stygian and empty blackness that had consumed her. But regardless, being apart from Dare like that had been excruciating.

After their souls had meshed and his strength revived her, she asked, :*What's going on? The last I remember is being at Kiera's orphanage.*:

Dare's love and relief surged inside them. :*I'll explain later. For now, focus on meshing our souls like when we kiss or make love.*:

Annalise purred a laugh. After being apart for days, their souls couldn't help meshing. :*Gladly.*:

Then the blinding white glow of intensely powerful magic shattered the stygian blackness. She winced away. Such radiance burned after being in the dark for so long.

Reassurance from Dare filled their meshed souls. :*'Tis simply the spell to break the curse that's killing us.*:

Annalise gasped as a chill skittered through them. :*A curse?! I think you'd better explain now rather than waiting.*:

Dare sighed. :*True. Here, let me show you.*:

She gasped again as a deluge of images, thoughts, and feelings flooded her. Dear Goddess. She clung to Dare as she sorted through it all. Then she shuddered, and her heart clenched. *:The curse killed our unborn child?:*

As their anguish flared, Dare rasped, *:I think so.:*

Annalise began to sob, and soon Dare silently joined her. However, when their tears slowed, he said, *:We must remember the wisdom nature showed us.:*

Dare's memory of the sleeping plants and death's purpose washed over her. She meshed their souls tighter, and his calm seeped inside her heart. She sighed. *:We'll always grieve our loss, but without our unborn child, I might never have been strong enough to upset Mother and Father by marrying you.:*

Dare echoed her sigh, and their love warmed their meshed souls.

Then as one, they gazed at the brilliant magic glowing around them. Inside the blazing white light, colorful motes danced—bronze from Dare's mother, ivory from the royal witch Lady Juliet, and blinding silver motes from Kiera and Wren's veiled witch.

Annalise sighed again. *:The magic is so lovely once you become accustomed to its radiance.:*

Dare's awe swelled inside them. *:Very. With its dancing motes, 'tis like none I've ever seen.:*

Humming, she smiled. *:'Tis how I see magic. With our souls meshed, we sense everything together.:*

Dare inhaled. *:This is how you always see magic? 'Tis beautiful, if somewhat overwhelming.:*

Annalise couldn't help a wry chuckle. *:It can be, although I can't imagine not seeing it.:*

They exhaled together then gazed at the brilliant magic in contented silence until its radiance faded.

Dare blew a sigh. *:I think the spell might be completed. Shall we attempt to return to the conscious world?:*

Although remaining meshed with Dare was wonderful, they must return. So she sighed then replied, :*Yes.*:

Together, they rose from the velvet darkness.

Her eyes fluttering open, she smiled at Dare wrapped around her with his rugged face almost touching hers. "We're alive."

Dare's chuckle rumbled through them. "So it seems."

Annalise smiled brighter. "Good." Then she captured his mouth in a ravenous kiss. Goddess, he tasted perfect.

Their hunger flaring, Dare eagerly returned her kiss for several heartbeats. Then he wrenched free. His amber eyes dark with passion, he murmured, "We've an audience, remember?"

A blush burning her cheeks, she blinked. Right, she'd forgotten that. Sighing, she separated their meshed souls. Then she glanced up at Mother, Father, Alex, Dare's mother, Darkthorn, Moonbud, Miss Weston, Lady Juliet, and the veiled witch all standing above them in a circle. Oh my. She managed a serene smile. "Happy Longnight, everyone."

Yellow joy bursting around everyone, Mother and Lady Ravenstone smiled yet cried, the nightmara nickered, and the others grinned.

His joy and love warming her, Dare rose and pulled her to her feet but kept his arm firmly about her waist. :*Although I should release you so you can reassure your family, I can't just yet, my heart.*:

Blinking as her head swirled at suddenly standing, Annalise gulped a steadying breath. Then she sent her love through their entwined souls and cuddled against Dare. :*I don't want you to release me, my love.*:

Tears still coursing down her cheeks, Mother flung herself against Annalise and wrapped her in a fierce embrace that displaced Dare. As Lady Ravenstone embraced Dare, Mother drew back and kissed Annalise's cheek then said, "Thank the Goddess that spell succeeded. We nearly lost you."

Father wrapped both Annalise and Mother in his arms then

pressed a kiss against Annalise's brow. "Don't scare us like that again."

Annalise smiled at Mother and Father, warmth suffusing her chest at their love. "I'll attempt not to."

Beaming, Mother and Father stepped back. Then Mother said, "You'd better. I doubt we could survive another such scare." She tugged Father away. "Come, we must thank the veiled witch and Lady Juliet."

Once they'd left, Lady Ravenstone released Dare. Then despite her tired eyes and dimmer bronze motes in her aura, she briskly embraced Annalise. "Thank the Goddess you and Dare are free of that malicious curse."

Annalise returned Lady Ravenstone's embrace. Her future mother-in-law was so like Dare—kindhearted, steady, and strong. "Thank you for risking yourself to break it, Lady Ravenstone."

Dare's mother winked. "How else was I ever to get any grandchildren?" She kissed Annalise's cheek. "Welcome to the family."

As Lady Ravenstone stepped back, Alex shook his head at her. "Dare and Annalise aren't married yet."

Dare's mother simply smiled then drifted over to the nightmara.

After Lady Ravenstone left, Alex embraced Annalise with a teasing frown. "I'm glad you didn't die, but must you and Dare keep kissing in front of me? I almost lost the Longnight feast I'd gorged earlier."

Giggling, she shrugged then drawled to tease him back, "We can't help it. You'll just have to learn to look away."

Alex laughed then twirled her several times before releasing her beside Dare and waggling his brows. "Did you lose this?"

Lightheaded from Alex's twirl, Annalise swayed until Dare wrapped his arm about her.

Dare grinned at Alex. "I did lose her. Your mother plucked

her right from my arms. Thanks for returning Annalise to her proper place."

Smirking, Alex clapped Dare's shoulder. "I'm glad you didn't die too, my future brother. Who would I best with that invincible sword you gave me?" Then he winked and joined Lady Ravenstone with the nightmara.

Alone at last, Dare eyed Annalise, and his concern echoed in their entwined souls. "How are you feeling?"

She sent him reassurance and caressed his face, her palm tingling at his beard. "A bit weary, but nothing like before, thank the Goddess." Then her stomach rumbled, and she smiled and lowered her hand. "Ravenous too, despite all the food I devoured at our Longnight feast a few hours ago."

Chuckling, Dare quirked a wry grin. "Me too. Apparently, surviving a curse is almost as strenuous as breaking it. I expect I'll devour several plates of food then collapse."

Mother and Father rejoined them, still smiling even though a Ravenstone held their daughter. Then Father arched his brows and said, "Perhaps we should all return to Greysnowe House for an early dinner to celebrate."

Her heart stilling, Annalise gaped. Had Father just invited the *Ravenstones* to dinner? Then her heart leapt and began to race. Did that mean Mother and Father had *finally* learned to live in harmony with the Ravenstones and would accept her and Dare marrying? She and Dare exchanged grins. Then she beamed at Mother and Father. "We'd like that very much."

Her calm blue aura blazing with so many blinding silver motes that she almost rivaled the sun's radiance, the veiled witch glided beside Annalise and Dare. "Unfortunately, a celebratory dinner wouldn't be ideal tonight. Everyone involved in breaking the curse, including Lady Annalise and Lord Ravenstone, shall likely succumb to slumber within an hour or two."

Mother and Father grimaced, then Father sighed and said, "Understandable. How about we do dinner tomorrow evening at Greysnowe House instead?"

Mother smiled at the veiled witch then at the others in the magical garden. "All of you must join us. 'Tis the least we can do to thank you."

The veiled witch and Lady Juliet traded a glance, then the veiled witch nodded at Mother and replied, "Thank you for the kind offer, Lady Greysnowe, but your celebration tomorrow should be for just family. After all, the Greysnowes and Ravenstones have a great deal to discuss."

Dare sent to Annalise, laughter echoing in his mental voice, :*I suspect they don't wish to attend in case our dinner deteriorates into a brawl.*:

Annalise swallowed a giggle. :*Most likely.*:

While they suppressed their laughter, Miss Weston gave the veiled witch a tray with five glasses of clear yet shimmering liquid that glowed with magic.

The veiled witch handed glasses to both Annalise and Dare. "Unicorn water isn't as strong as ambrosia, but it shall ensure you last long enough to return home. Excuse me, I must give Lady Ravenstone and the royal witch glasses."

Once the veiled witch glided away, Annalise and Dare drank their unicorn water fragrant with clovers, lilies, and spring dew. Energy trickling back into her veins, Annalise straightened as they drank. Refreshing yet definitely not as potent or as heady as ambrosia. Probably good, considering she and Dare had made love hours after eating ambrosia.

After they finished, she arched a brow at Dare. "We should thank the veiled witch and Lady Juliet then return to Greysnowe and Ravenstone House."

Dare sighed but nodded. "Yes, we should." As they began across the balmy magical garden, he added, :*Although I wish we could return to one townhouse.*:

Blushing, she smiled and squeezed his hand. :*Me too, but despite their joy, none of our parents would allow that while we're unwed. And now that they seem ready to accept our marriage, we shouldn't risk provoking them into refusing.*:

Dare sighed again. :*True, and at least we'll see each other tomorrow—without slipping away to meet.*:

She beamed. Just like an ordinary courting couple, rather than one whose families were ancestral enemies. :*I know. Isn't it wonderful?*:

Then they reached the veiled witch and Lady Juliet, who were quarreling with Miss Weston goggling between them.

Annalise coughed to interrupt the quarreling witches then swept a curtsy as Dare bowed. "We're about to leave, but first, we wanted to thank you both for risking yourselves to help break the curse."

Lady Juliet smiled and nodded. "I'm glad I could help save Calatini's first soul healer in ages." She narrowed her eyes at the veiled witch. "Despite the churlish manner that I was summoned."

As the veiled witch glowered back, Annalise interjected before the rival witches could resume their quarrel, "We're grateful you both spent much of your Longnight saving two people unconnected to you."

Dare leaned forward with a genial smile. "Yes, without you both, Annalise and I would doubtless be dead by now, so thank you again." His smile tightened. "Although we must request you don't discuss today with anyone, not even King Devon or the council. 'Twould be dangerous if Annalise's rare powers became known."

The veiled witch inclined her head. "Of course. Openly being a soul healer is a heavy burden." Her gaze flicked to Lady Juliet. "Or any other class of rare witch." Her drawl implied a seer like herself could understand while a mere Rhiannon descendant like the royal witch couldn't.

Annalise almost sighed. Couldn't the veiled witch and Lady Juliet resist exchanging insults? They were almost as bad as Mother and Father had been toward the Ravenstones.

Moonbud and Darkthorn strode over, then Moonbud winked

at Annalise and said, :*Darkthorn and I shall carry you and Lord Ravenstone home now.*:

As they left, Alex promised to tend to Dare's horses, and Lady Ravenstone said she'd return Miss Weston to her grandparents. When Mother and Father frowned at Annalise and Dare riding back alone, Alex distracted them, so she and Dare could slip away. She must thank her brother later.

Annalise and Dare both shivered when they left the veiled witch's garden. Longnight's frosty air felt even more frigid after the magical garden's summer warmth.

Moonbud eyed them. :*Darkthorn can carry you both. I know you'd prefer riding together, and although I'd not mind carrying you both, he's stronger.*:

Dare nodded then climbed atop Darkthorn and helped Annalise mount behind him. Still shivering, she wrapped her arms about his waist then rested her head against his shoulder and inhaled his scent. Yes, being close right now was undeniably better.

Dare sighed as Darkthorn surged into his smooth trot. "If only I'd enough magic to cast a warming spell right now."

Darkthorn chuckled. :*Don't fret; I'll have you back home shortly.*:

Raising her voice so Moonbud could hear, Annalise said, "Thank you both for helping save us. And the ride."

As Moonbud bobbed her head, Darkthorn hummed and replied, :*Of course. We owed you a debt for healing Moonbud's melissae stings.*:

Moonbud snickered. :*Ignore his logical talk. He was desperate to help. He's grown fond of you—despite you never heeding his advice.*:

Darkthorn snorted at his mate then grumbled, :*Well, I **was** right that visiting the veiled witch would help.*:

Annalise patted the nightmara stallion's croup with a wry smile. "So you were." Although he could learn to be less smug.

Soon they reached Greysnowe House, and Dare helped Annalise down then dismounted. Glancing about the empty street, he drew her into his arms. "I should go before someone from court spots us together. Our families shan't appreciate gossip."

Her heart quickening, she smiled up at him then licked her lips. "Surely we can risk one kiss. Everyone is immersed in Longnight festivities."

Dare chuckled and arched a brow. "Why do you think I dismounted?"

Beaming, Annalise wrapped her arms about his neck and threaded her fingers in his black hair. Goddess, he was perfect. "I love you, Dare."

Dare lowered his head until his lips brushed hers. "I love you too, Annalise."

Then he kissed her, and their souls meshed as they devoured each other's mouths.

When they were both breathless, Dare released her and separated their souls. "I'll see you tomorrow at dinner, my heart."

As Dare leapt atop Darkthorn and rode toward Ravenstone House, Annalise smiled after him and twirled his flickering faegift at her throat. So she would. Then she sighed and headed inside. She must eat, write to Kiera and Wren to reassure them she was well, and then she could *finally* get some restful slumber.

CHAPTER 57

*H*aving devoured several plates of food then collapsing into a dreamless sleep, Dare woke the following morning well after dawn like he had for the past month. However, today he was bursting with energy, although his magic did need replenishing. He grinned as he leapt from bed. His returned vigor was proof the malevolent curse was gone. And tonight, he'd see Annalise—with her parents' blessing. Even though the strife of the past hadn't yet been settled, the Ravenstone-Greysnowe feud would soon be ended.

As he dressed without Thom's help since servants never worked the day after Longnight, he reached out to Annalise through their entwined souls, but he sensed she was still deep in dreams. Smiling, he withdrew. Doubtless she needed the extra sleep after all that had happened yesterday. And they'd have plenty of time to talk later.

Dare roused Raven and Bear from the hearth before the waning fire then Leaf and Sand from their brass cage. With the hellhounds bounding beside him and the draklizards swooping above him, he headed to the kitchen to feed them before he ate his own breakfast.

With the sated hellhounds and draklizards close behind, he

headed to the breakfast room carrying a heaped plate of cold remains from yesterday's Longnight feast. He grinned at Mother still eating a half-empty plate of the same. "Morning. I see you slept late as well."

Mother hummed as she poured him a cup of tea. "How could I not after yesterday's difficult spellwork? My natural energy needs replenishing from that. Shall we ride to the royal bay after eating then spend the afternoon there?"

Dare sat and accepted his tea as Raven and Bear settled at his feet while Leaf and Sand perched on the back of his chair. "Thanks." He hummed while he stirred honey into his tea. Remaining at the royal bay all afternoon *would* prevent him from visiting Greysnowe House too early. He couldn't risk provoking Annalise's parents now. Plus, he needed natural energy too. So he smiled at Mother. "Spending the afternoon at the royal bay sounds perfect."

Mother returned his smile. "Excellent. I'll pack a hearty luncheon for us. We'll need that despite our late breakfast."

After breakfast, he changed into riding clothes then headed to the stables with the hellhounds and draklizards. Since he and Mother would be out all afternoon, the magical pets would join them. In the stables, he patted Ebony when the stallion nickered and nuzzled him. Then he ran his hands along Ebony to check that the stallion had recovered from yesterday's punishing gallop. He'd been too exhausted to do so yesterday.

Mother chuckled as she strode to Willow. "Ebony should be fine. I taught Lord Alexander how to send energy to the horses after you and Lady Annalise left the veiled witch's garden. Despite it being nature magic, he learned it rather well."

Dare smiled, his chest easing. He must thank Alex tonight for tending to his horses. "Good. Thanks, Mother."

He and Mother saddled Ebony and Willow then trotted to the royal bay with the hellhounds and draklizards. Much like yesterday, the streets of Ormas were mostly empty. The second day of the year was often quiet because 'twas about charity, so most didn't need to work and remained home with their families.

Once they reached the royal bay, he and Mother gathered natural energy until their magic was overflowing and they were ravenous again. Then he laid their blanket on the sand and cast a warming spell around them.

As Mother unpacked luncheon, Raven and Bear dropped the driftwood he'd been tossing for them and flopped on the blanket with Leaf and Sand curled beside them. All the magical pets eyed him and Mother while they filled their plates, clearly hoping for some treats.

As he and Mother began eating, Mother sighed and stared out into the turbulent ocean.

Dare frowned. Why did Mother look so troubled when everything would soon be settled? "What's wrong?"

Shrugging, Mother hummed and nibbled a slice of fresh orenge. "I suppose I'm somewhat anxious about dinner tonight. Yesterday, Emmeline and Lord Greysnowe were so ecstatic their daughter was alive that they didn't care about the past. But now that they've had time to think..." She sighed again.

He stilled as a chill prickled his neck. She sounded as if she expected Annalise's parents to resume the feud. He swallowed. "Surely they'll forgive the feud since we helped save their daughter." He winced. After he'd endangered her by making love. Perhaps Mother was right.

Shaking her head, Mother grimaced. "I hope they'll forgive the feud, but so much strife has happened between us. Strife that I've never told you about."

Dare eyed Mother as he tossed the hellhounds and draklizards some venison and wild boar before devouring the rest. She'd called Annalise's mother her best friend yesterday, yet she'd avoided discussing their history. Considering that and Lady Greysnowe's excessive rancor toward Mother, whatever had happened between them must have been devastating to them both.

He leaned toward Mother with an encouraging smile. "As a child, you always told me that the first step to resolving problems with others was to be open about your needs and admit your mistakes. Shan't doing that help?"

Mother sighed. "I've attempted to, yet Emmeline always returned my letters unopened, and she's been so bitter when we've met at court events. But although I'm not certain she'll listen, I'll attempt again at dinner tonight."

Dare nodded then asked Mother about her plans with the Islayes to distract her. After luncheon, they roamed the royal bay until an hour before sunset, allowing themselves just enough time to return to Ormas, change for dinner, then head to Greysnowe House.

When he and Mother strode into the Greysnowes' drawing room, Annalise and Alex were talking on a sofa, but their parents were missing. Hopefully, not because they no longer sought to end the feud.

Once everyone exchanged greetings, Dare smiled at Alex. "Thanks for tending to Ebony and my other horses yesterday."

Alex grinned and rose. "I was glad to help. Plus, your mother showed me the most marvelous spell."

As Alex winked then joined Mother, Dare sat beside Annalise, who was radiant once again with no gray fog tarnishing her aura. She appeared recovered, but he must make sure of that. He grasped her hands and kissed her palms, and their loved flared in their entwined souls. Too bad he couldn't truly kiss her, but her parents and Mother couldn't catch them kissing. "How are you feeling?"

Her cerulean eyes bright, Annalise beamed at him and threaded her fingers through his. "Like myself again instead of drained, although I did sleep until late this afternoon. But I doubt I'll need to do that tonight."

He squeezed her hands. Thank the Goddess she'd fully recovered from the curse too. Then he arched a brow. "And how are your parents?"

Annalise hummed and tilted her head, her white-blonde hair shimmering in the candlelight. "I've not seen them today. By the time I awoke, they were at the Duke of Oakmoor's Longnight charity luncheon. Although Alex told me they checked on me before they left as well as reminded him to make sure everything was prepared for tonight." She smiled. "Hosting dinner is *much* more challenging when the servants aren't working."

Lord and Lady Greysnowe swept into the drawing room, then Lady Greysnowe chuckled and said, "So we're fortunate the others declined our invitation, and 'tis just family tonight." She smiled at Annalise and Alex. "Thanks for making sure everything was prepared. Sorry we're late—the Duke of Oakmoor's charity auction took ages because his intended hostess, Lady Blaine, never arrived."

Dare and Annalise glanced at each other. Lady Blaine was one of the few who knew about their involvement and Annalise's powers. Why had the husband-hunting countess abandoned the duke when he was no doubt close to proposing?

Eyeing their linked hands, Lord Greysnowe hummed. "You two appear familiar."

As Annalise stilled, Dare stiffened, and his pulse surged. Should he release her hand? Yet doing so would be disingenuous. He set his jaw and caressed her palm. No, they'd not conceal their love any longer.

Before either of them could reply, Alex snickered with a smirk. "This is demure for them. Usually they're kissing."

Her embarrassment scorching Dare, Annalise blushed and glared at her brother. "Alex!"

Alex blinked back then widened his eyes, although his innocent expression was spoiled by his continued smirk. "Well, 'tis true."

Lady Greysnowe pursed her lips and shook her head. "Alexander, quit tormenting your sister and Lord Ravenstone."

Lord Greysnowe arched a brow. "Shall we go eat?"

Dare and Annalise exhaled then rose. Eating should settle

everyone. He escorted her to the family dining room. There, the gentlemen served the ladies then themselves roasted root vegetables as well as cold venison and wild boar from yesterday's Longnight feast.

Once everyone had food, Mother gulped some spiced cider then turned to Lady Greysnowe with a tight smile. "Before we discuss our children's marriage, I must tender an overdue apology."

Gripping her fork, Lady Greysnowe stilled. "Very well."

As Mother inhaled, Dare and Annalise exchanged another glance. Please let Mother's apology go smoothly. Annalise's parents accepting their marriage doubtless depended on it.

Mother leaned toward Lady Greysnowe. "All those years ago when I befriended you without revealing myself as Lady Ravenstone, I wasn't attempting to hurt or deceive you—I was attempting to heal the Ravenstone-Greysnowe feud. I thought that if we were friends, we could convince our husbands to see sense, but I wasn't certain you'd even talk to me if you knew who I was." She shuddered. "But when Henry discovered our friendship, it all went dreadfully awry."

Lord Greysnowe glowered at Mother over his wild boar. "Your husband flung insults at Emmeline that no gentleman should ever say to any woman. Emmeline was devastated afterward."

Dare inhaled, his stomach lurching. No wonder Annalise's parents had been so obsessed with the feud. How could Father have been so cruel, even to an ancestral enemy's wife?

Mother winced. "When Henry told me what he'd said, I was horrified." She sighed. "All I can say to defend him is that he assumed Emmeline had deceived *me* into becoming friends in order to pursue the feud, and that he was excessively overprotective at the time. I was carrying Dare, and I was ill for most of my pregnancy, so much so that I almost died during childbirth."

Dare frowned. That did explain Father's cruelty, although it didn't excuse it. Hurting people just goaded them into hurting others.

As Annalise laid a soothing hand on his knee, Lady Greysnowe eyed Mother and hummed. "You did look wretched back then—almost as bad as Annalise under that evil curse." She paused. "Daphne, did you mean it when you called me your best friend yesterday?"

Mother managed a tremulous smile. "I never would have said that if I didn't mean it." She swallowed. "Can you ever forgive me for the hurt I caused you?"

Lady Greysnowe nodded as she rested her hand on her husband's. "You risking yourself to save our daughter more than repaid that." She sighed. "I should have opened one of your many letters over the years, instead of clinging to my bitterness and blindly pursuing the feud. Nothing good can come of either."

Dare smoothed his beard to conceal his smile when Annalise's happiness flooded his chest. Her parents should accept their marriage now.

Lord and Lady Greysnowe traded grimaces. Then Lady Greysnowe continued, "Clinging to his bitterness made the jilted Ravenstone obtain that evil curse. And blindly pursuing the feud almost got us arrested for treason." She leaned toward Mother. "Plus, I want my best friend back."

As Mother and Lady Greysnowe smiled at each other, Dare and Annalise grinned and laced their hands together beneath the table, while Lord Greysnowe smiled at his wife and Alex shook his head.

Then Mother arched her brows. "Now that the past is settled, shall we discuss our children's marriage?"

Annalise's parents nodded then turned to scrutinize Dare and Annalise.

His neck prickling, he swallowed and gripped Annalise's hand. Although not scowling like they always had in the past, her parents weren't smiling either. Without the feud, surely they'd not forbid him and Annalise from marrying. Yet he was a mere count, and her parents had always sought higher for her.

Eventually, Lord Greysnowe hummed then asked him, "Were your attempts to seek peace truly genuine and not some treacherous scheme?"

Dare sighed. Hadn't he already proved that? "Of course. Even before my soulbond with Annalise, I've always wanted peace between our families."

Rubbing the back of his hand with her thumb, Annalise frowned at her parents. "Dare is too kindhearted and sensible to ever pursue a feud."

Their brows rising, Lord and Lady Greysnowe stared at their daughter. Then Lady Greysnowe smiled and said, "You two are certainly devoted. Not only will you both do anything for the other's sake, but you're always attuned to one another." She glanced at Annalise. "And you don't hide behind Lady Snow with Lord Ravenstone like you do with other gentlemen. Because of your soulbond?"

Her love surging through Dare, Annalise smiled at him and caressed his heart-shaped firegem. "No, because Dare sees me as a person, not just the most beautiful lady in Calatini or a rare, coveted soul healer. Even before our soulbond."

Lady Greysnowe hummed as her gaze fell to his faegift. "Exactly the husband you said you wanted."

Sending Annalise his love back through their entwined souls, Dare kissed her hand, still linked with his. "And Annalise is exactly the wife I've always wanted. A kind and strong lady who loves nature, outdoor pursuits, pets, and children as much as I do."

As Mother and Annalise's parents beamed at the mention of grandchildren, Alex snickered and finished his slice of Longnight cake. "Your wife must love pets to accept the menagerie you'll soon share."

Lady Greysnowe frowned at Alex. "Two angelcats and two faebirds are hardly a menagerie."

Dare and Annalise exchanged wry smiles, then Annalise said, "Actually, one of those angelcats is Dare's. And he has two hellhounds as well. Plus, Alex gave us both draklizards for Longnight."

Mother laughed. "I should have realized Lily's mate and one of those draklizards belonged to you."

His smile almost as impish as Alex's, Lord Greysnowe glanced at Lady Greysnowe. "Two of every different kind of magical pet might be considered a menagerie—especially if you count their horses."

Lady Greysnowe smiled and shook her head. "Very boisterous, although I expect Annalise shall adore that. Keeping her from adopting every wounded creature always was trying."

Dare grinned when Annalise squeezed his hand and said, "Dare and I shall build a wonderful life together in Wildewall."

Sobering, Lady Greysnowe swallowed as tears gleamed in her eyes. "A life that wouldn't have been possible without your and Lord Ravenstone's soulbond keeping you alive or him and his mother risking their lives to help save you."

Wrapping an arm about his wife, Lord Greysnowe nodded at Dare. "So we'll gladly support you marrying our beloved Annalise. Even if you *are* a Ravenstone."

As their combined joy echoed through them, Dare and Annalise beamed at each other. Nothing could keep them apart now. His heart swelling, he pressed another kiss against her hand.

CHAPTER 58

Tingling warmth suffusing her, Annalise sighed as Dare kissed her hand again. If only they could slip away for a true kiss, but they'd likely not resist making love if they did. Then she'd conceive another child, and they weren't ready for that yet. She beamed at Mother and Father. "Thank you for supporting me marrying Dare. Knowing you'd despise me once we married was devastating."

Mother smiled and dashed away her tears. "So Lord Ravenstone mentioned." She grinned at Lady Ravenstone. "We must begin planning our children's engagement celebration at once, Daphne. Perhaps a ball at the end of the Longnight season. If we announce Annalise's engagement while keeping her future husband's identity secret, *everyone* at court shall attend despite the ball being in less than two weeks."

Annalise and Dare exchanged a wry smile. Doubtless Mother was right, and she and Father would love if their ballroom was too crowded for dancing.

Leaning back in his chair, Alex snorted. "You should celebrate Annalise and Dare's marriage instead. If you'd ever chaperoned them, you'd know that keeping them apart is impossible. They'll never last thirteen days."

As another blush burned Annalise's cheeks, Lady Ravenstone hummed while eyeing her and Dare. "From what I've heard about soulbonds, your son is right, Emmeline. We'd best get Dare and Lady Annalise married straightaway."

Although Father nodded, Mother frowned and said, "But if our ball celebrates their marriage, then they shan't have a grand wedding before court." Sighing, she turned to Annalise. "Although I suspect you don't want one anyway, do you?"

Squeezing Dare's hand, Annalise shrugged and smiled at Mother. "All I want is to marry Dare with my family and friends there. But I don't mind having a grand wedding to please you and Father."

Indigo tenderness glowing about them, Mother and Father shared a glance, then Mother replied, "No, a private wedding shall do."

Dare smiled as he returned Annalise's squeeze. "I'll visit Priest Melchior to find out when he can officiate the wedding ceremony. I'd approached him earlier, so he already knows about me and Annalise."

She blinked and almost frowned. At Kiera's orphanage on Longnight, Priest Melchior hadn't revealed that he knew about her and Dare. Although he *had* been busy marrying Kiera and King Devon then.

Mother beamed. "The middle son of the Duke and Duchess of Childes agreed to marry you? How marvelous."

Dare inclined his head. "I'll visit Priest Melchior early tomorrow. Afterward, why don't we all go on a ride together to discuss the details of the wedding?"

Annalise sighed. A family ride would be wonderful except she already had plans. "I can't. Kiera and Wren are meeting me here for luncheon tomorrow. How about the day after that instead? When I see Kiera, I could ask her for permission to ride in the royal forest. I'd enjoy seeing Esme the Great's melissae hive again, and if they're active, they'll not attack people they know are dear to me."

Everyone agreed to meet before luncheon the day after tomorrow, but outside of Ormas to avoid anyone spotting Greysnowes and Ravenstones together. Then Dare and his mother rose to leave, and Annalise escorted them to the front door.

Once Lady Ravenstone bustled outside, Dare drew Annalise against him and kissed her.

Sighing as their souls meshed, she wrapped her arms about Dare's neck and buried her fingers in his long hair then returned his ravenous kiss. Goddess, so perfect. Then she whimpered when he wrenched their mouths apart.

His amber eyes dark with hunger, Dare stepped back and separated their souls. "Until the day after tomorrow, my heart."

As Dare strode through the door, Annalise smiled after him. She could hardly wait for their family ride.

JUST BEFORE HER luncheon with Kiera and Wren the following day, Wilson showed the veiled witch into the morning room.

Annalise squinted at the seer's blinding aura—'twas even brighter than the other day, likely because the veiled witch wasn't drained from breaking the curse. "Could you dim your aura, please?"

The veiled witch chuckled. "I should have considered that, but 'tisn't a problem for most people. Sorry." She stilled, and the blinding silver motes in her aura dimmed. "Is that better?"

Exhaling, Annalise fully opened her eyes then gestured for the veiled witch to sit in the chair beside her. "Very much, thank you. Are you here to check that I've recovered from the curse?"

Her black veils fluttering, the veiled witch sat. "No, scrying 'twould be easy enough. I'm here to give you and Lord Raven-stone a gift you'll need shortly."

A prickle skittering up her neck, Annalise studied the veiled witch. "Oh?"

The veiled witch inclined her head. "A pair of contraceptive charms that can withstand a soul healer's high-energy aura. I doubt you and Lord Ravenstone are ready to conceive another child."

As her chest twisted, Annalise pressed a hand against her stomach. Not surprising the veiled witch had seen the curse had killed their unborn child. "You never mentioned our lost child the other day. Why?"

Sighing, the veiled witch lifted a shoulder. "Revealing your miscarriage wouldn't have helped break the curse, and some secrets aren't mine to share." She arched a brow. "As another who can read auras, surely you can understand that."

Annalise nodded, and the veiled witch handed her a small box. She studied the two bracelets of entwined electrum and bronze blazing with the veiled witch's magic. "How could you create contraceptive charms that work for a soul healer? I thought only another soul healer or a Rhiannon-descendant healer could."

The veiled witch flicked her fingers, jingling bracelets and tiny bells. "My powers are somewhat... unusual. But 'tis fortunate for you and Lord Ravenstone I could—the closest Rhiannon-descendant healer is in the Tsarkan Empire, and the closest soul healer is in Orandia."

Annalise swallowed. If not for the veiled witch, the only way she and Dare could prevent pregnancy would be to not make love—nearly impossible for a soulbound couple. "Truly a gift we'll need. How can we repay you for breaking the curse and creating these?"

The veiled witch's exotically lined eyes crinkled. "One day, I'll require a boon from you and your husband. But don't fret; it shan't be something you can't or won't do." She cocked her head. "Your friends are almost here." She rose. "To renew your contraceptive charms, simply perform a soul-healing on them every Longnight until their magic glows bright again."

Before Annalise could say farewell, the veiled witch swept from the morning room.

Annalise darted upstairs to leave the contraceptive charms in her chambers then back to the entrance hall to greet Kiera and Wren.

Yellow joy and indigo tenderness flaring about them, Kiera and Wren embraced her as soon as they entered. Then Kiera said, "Thank the Goddess you're better."

Wren added, "We were so worried the veiled witch hadn't arrived in time to save you."

Her friends' concern warming her, Annalise squeezed them. "I'll tell you everything over luncheon."

Once they'd settled in the family dining room and served themselves meat-tuber pie and spiced cider, she gulped a breath. Hopefully, Kiera and Wren would forgive her for keeping secrets. She glanced at Wren. "I assume Kiera told you I was a soul healer?" Once Wren nodded, she asked her friends, "Do you both know about soulbonds?"

After Kiera and Wren exchanged a glance, Wren said, "We knew you must have a soulbond because you didn't form one when you healed Kiera's melissae stings."

Kiera nodded and sipped her spiced cider. "We assumed 'twas someone your parents wouldn't accept since you never mentioned it."

Annalise hummed with a wry smile. Her friends were astute. "Yes, 'twas Dare—Lord Ravenstone."

Kiera and Wren gaped at her. Then Wren said, "We assumed 'twas a childhood servant or tenant, although Lord Ravenstone *is* another your parents wouldn't accept."

Annalise smiled. Except now they did. She told Kiera and Wren about her and Dare's soulbond and love then about the curse and ending the feud. When she finished, she said, "Dare and I are marrying in the next week or so. I hope you both can attend—if you can forgive me for keeping secrets."

Kiera and Wren glanced at each other again, then Kiera smiled and replied, "Of course we'll attend. And we understand why you didn't tell us before. Court or your parents discovering your secrets would have been disastrous."

Wren devoured the last of her meat-tuber pie. "Besides, we've not been friends long, and everyone has secrets." She grinned at Annalise. "I purchased a glamour spell to seduce Hawke. Hence the unexpected pregnancy."

Her brows rising, Annalise nodded. So *that* had been the blinding spell the veiled witch had created for Wren.

Kiera grimaced. "And Devon and I exiled the greedy woman who birthed me when she threatened to extort us, but telling you about her was too embarrassing."

As Annalise winced at Kiera needing to exile her own mother, Wren leaned forward and said, "We shan't reveal your secret powers to anyone, not even our husbands. Soul healers are often exploited, so 'tis best if fewer people know."

Annalise smiled. Her friends were always so considerate. Then she asked about Longnight evening at the orphanage, and they discussed that the rest of luncheon. After they finished dessert, she handed them a box wrapped in festive white paper. "A Longnight gift. I forgot to bring it to the orphanage."

As they accepted the box, Kiera and Wren traded a glance. Then Wren said, "But we don't have anything for you. We typically don't exchange Longnight gifts."

Annalise smiled. "'Tis fine. My gift is really for all of us." Once her friends opened their gift and revealed the smooth granite stone nestled inside a bowl of sand with a small dagger beside it, she said, "I thought we could create a friendship stone together."

Both Kiera and Wren beaming, Kiera replied as she handed Annalise the dagger, "How perfect. But who shall keep it after we create it?"

Annalise and Wren grinned at each other, then Annalise turned to Kiera and said, "You should. Without you, none of us would be friends."

Kiera beamed back, then Annalise, Kiera, and Wren

performed the ritual to create their friendship stone. They took turns cutting their left palms then anointing their friendship stone with their blood while describing how their friendship had enriched their lives. They all cried during the ritual, but not from cutting their palms.

While Kiera returned their friendship stone to its sand bowl to dry for three days, Annalise opened the honeysuckle-scented box from Dare then handed Kiera and Wren their communication mirrors. "I've these for you as well. For Long-night, Dare gave me six linked communication mirrors, so I could speak to everyone after we return home. He said we can easily have group mirror calls with these. They must be recharged in the sunlight after every call, but Dare said he can renew the spell on all of our communication mirrors from Wildewall."

Wren caressed her mirror. "An enchanted gift I'll gladly use even though I distrust magic."

Smiling, Kiera leaned forward. "These are marvelous, although I hope you and Lord Ravenstone shall remain until my coronation and public wedding ceremony on Plantfete. I'd like both of my close friends there."

Annalise nodded. Remaining in Ormas until then wouldn't be as difficult once she and Dare married. "Absolutely." As her friends rose to leave, she said to Kiera, "I almost forgot. Could I, Dare, and our families ride to the royal forest tomorrow?"

Kiera embraced her. "You and Lord Ravenstone can visit the royal lands whenever you wish. Bring any guests you like." Stepping back, she grinned at Wren. "Wren and Hawke can do the same."

After embracing Annalise, Wren chuckled. "You realize we'll likely bring the orphans several times a year."

Kiera smiled. "Why do you think I offered?"

Annalise grinned as she walked Kiera and Wren to the door. They were both so kindhearted. She really must get Mother and Father to apologize to Kiera and King Devon for their churlish behavior toward Kiera. They'd be relieved once they did, and Kiera would forgive them at once.

LATE THE FOLLOWING MORNING, Annalise and her family met Dare and his mother outside the eastern gate with all of their magical pets, except her faebirds who couldn't handle the cold. As she and Dare beamed at each other, Lily leapt from Annalise's saddle to join Dare, and Sand flew from his shoulder to curl about her neck. Then everyone urged their horses to a trot with Raven and Bear coursing beside Dare and Ebony.

The ride through the dormant fields passed swiftly amid laughter and cheer. When they reached the royal forest, Finn and Lily leapt into the bare branches with Lady Ravenstone's angelkitten close behind, while Sand and Leaf began swooping above everyone's heads. They soon reached the clearing at the heart of the royal forest, which was much quieter than the times she'd visited before because only a few melissae buzzed about their cottage due to the cold.

Once everyone tied their horses to nearby trees, Dare and Lady Ravenstone cast a warming spell on the clearing, while Annalise and her family laid their blanket then unpacked Lady Ravenstone's picnic. Begging for treats, the hellhounds, angel-cats, and draklizards were constantly underfoot as they set out the food. After finishing their spell, Dare dropped beside Annalise as Lady Ravenstone sat beside Mother, then everyone removed their heavy cloaks.

Lady Ravenstone grinned at Annalise as all of the melissae began buzzing about the clearing thanks to the now balmy air. "Esme the Great's melissae hive is extraordinary. Thanks for arranging our ride, Lady Annalise."

Warmth filling her, Annalise handed Dare a full plate and returned his mother's smile. "My pleasure. And since we'll soon be family, please call me Annalise."

Dare grinned at Mother and Father. "And please call me Dare."

Alex waved his roasted chicken leg at all three parents. "And *everyone* should call me Alex."

After they all chuckled, Mother leaned toward Dare. "So, Dare, what did you arrange with Priest Melchior about your wedding?"

Dare grinned while tossing some chicken to the hellhounds, angelcats, and draklizards. "He's available in two days, although the Great Temple's chapels are occupied. We'll meet him at the Harvest Garden after breakfast. I figured we likely shan't be spotted so early."

As their families grinned and nodded, Annalise beamed, and light bubbled in her chest. In just two short days, she'd finally be Dare's wife—with her parents' blessing.

After a merry luncheon with their families, Dare glanced at Annalise. :*Could we speak privately?*:

Her heart quickened. :*Yes, please, my love.*: She turned to their parents. "Dare and I must thank the melissa queen for gifting us ambrosia. To avoid upsetting the melissae, everyone else should remain here."

Their mothers exchanged a knowing glance, and Mother replied, "No disappearing."

Annalise and Dare nodded, then she accepted his hand to rise, and they began toward the melissae's cottage alone. Even their magical pets remained behind—probably to keep begging for treats.

Once they were out of earshot, Dare extracted a small box. "For Longnight, Mother gave me her and Father's wedding tokens, so we've their rings and our hair spirals for our wedding. She even transformed her ring to electrum for you, but I wanted to make sure it fits beforehand."

Annalise grinned at the electrum ring etched with hearts as Dare slid it on her middle finger and resized it using his nature magic, the bronze motes in his lush green aura flaring. "'Tis lovely. I've something for you as well." After returning the ring to Dare, she withdrew the box from the veiled witch. "The veiled witch made us contraceptive charms that work for soul healers."

Dare chuckled. "Trust a seer to give such a perfect gift."

They slid the electrum and bronze bracelets on their left wrists, and with a brilliant flash of magic, the contraceptive charms welded against their skin.

Humming, Dare smoothed his beard as they reached the melissae's cottage. "The veiled witch must be incredibly powerful, much more than either of us. We're fortunate she chose to help us."

Annalise nodded then swallowed. "She's the most powerful witch I've ever met or read about, other than perhaps Rhiannon herself."

Before he could reply, the melissa queen swirled around them. :*Welcome back, heart-sister daughter and heart-sister daughter's mate.*:

Annalise grinned at the melissa queen despite her head tickling at the buzz of the melissa queen's thoughts. "Thank you for the ambrosia you gave us. It protected us from a malevolent curse, and we mightn't have survived without it."

Almost purring, the melissa queen bobbed in the air before them. :*Good. Glad.*: She darted toward the cottage. :*Want more?*:

Annalise and Dare traded a wry smile. They couldn't eat ambrosia in front of their parents. Like before, they'd doubtless be unable to resist making love afterward. She smiled at the melissa queen. "Our families are here today. Once we marry, we'll visit alone."

The melissa queen buzzed with laughter. :*Humans silly. See later. Ambrosia then.*:

Once the melissa queen flew inside the cottage, Dare grinned and wrapped an arm about Annalise's shoulder. "Since we can't slip away, shall we rejoin everyone?"

She nodded, and as they walked back, she beamed at their joyous families. Their mothers were giggling together as they fed the three angelcats slivers of meat. Beside them, Father and Alex grinned while bantering and tossing sticks for the hellhounds and draklizards. The green harmony glowing about everyone was as glorious as she'd always dreamt.

Her heart overflowing, Annalise sighed as she and Dare rejoined their now united families. Today was one of the first days in their wonderful life together full of abiding love and family.

At last.

Want more?

Sign up for my newsletter for a bonus epilogue about when Annalise and Dare can finally return to their beloved Wildewall as well as other exclusive stories and book extras, new book announcements, giveaways, and more.

And order the next book The Goddess's Illusion about Kit and Mel today! Keep reading to learn more about the next book in the Calatini Tales.

Like The Secret Soulbond?

Please consider writing a review. Reviews truly help spread the word about the titles you love.

THE GODDESS'S ILLUSION

The Regency-inspired kingdom of Calatini is filled with magic and tender romance. But even in Calatini, magic comes with a cost, and sometimes a curse can become a blessing.

Kit, the young, widowed Countess of Blaine, must remarry. She's already chosen the perfect husband—except she can't stand his kisses. But on Longnight, the Goddess blesses her with a powerful illusion: Kit shall appear a hideous crone until she becomes who she was meant to be. Before anyone from court sees her, she flees to the one person she knows shall help—Mel, the gentleman she loved as a girl who is now a priest for the Goddess.

Mel, the middle son of a wealthy duke but called to serve the Goddess, has been avoiding Kit since discovering her cruel lies separated his brother from the girl he loved. But when Kit begs Mel for his help, he feels compelled to agree for the sake of the devout and tender girl he'd once loved.

But no one can break the Goddess's illusion, not even a wise elf or a powerful seer. So with Mel's support, Kit settles into life at the Goddess's temple. She and Mel continue to clash, and those clashes soon lead to passionate kisses—ones she actually enjoys. But a priest would never marry an unworthy lady like . her, and she can't live the rest of her life as a crone.

Somehow, Kit must break her unwanted illusion, forget about Mel, and return to court where she belongs. Yet the Goddess's plans are not so easy to foil, and she has other ideas for Kit and Mel.

THE GODDESS'S *Illusion* **is perfect for fans of** *The Undertaking of Hart and Mercy*, **with the outpouring of magic, fantasy, and clean romance that make the Calatini Tales beloved.**

WANT MORE? *Order* **The Goddess's Illusion** *today!*

CALATINI TALES

The enchanting Calatini Tales includes...

The Spellbinding Courtship (Book 0.5)
The Enchanted Bird (Book 1)
The Nightmara Affair (Book 2)
The Secret Soulbond (Book 3)
The Goddess's Illusion (Book 4)
The Sun-Nymph Bride (Book 5)
The Beast Curse (Book 6)
The Lethe Elixir (Book 7)

ABOUT KATHERINE

A lifelong creator of her own bedtime stories, **Katherine Dotterer** writes cozy tales of fantasy romance inspired by Regency England. Born and raised in Maryland, she still lives there in an almost cottage surrounded by trees. When not writing, she enjoys reading anything she can find, singing in local choruses, hiking in nearby parks, watching the wildlife outside her windows, and cuddling with her cats. Visit her at Katherine-Dotterer.com to learn about her book releases, read her many book extras, and sign up for her newsletter.